Praise for John Connor

'Fast-moving with plenty of exotic locations and tense action, this is a highly entertaining thriller' *Sunday Mirror*

'From the horrifying defenestration in the opening pages to the ultra-violent denouement, Leeds-based barrister John Connor drives his complex tale of secrecy and betrayal along at a cracking pace' *Irish Independent*

'A first-rate thriller with a terrific climax' *Sunday Telegraph*

'Connor's plot is enthralling, his characters sharp and vital: *Falling* is a compelling, intelligent thriller, placing everyday normality in dramatic relief against the horrific experiences of Sharpe and her colleagues' *Financial Times*

'It'll be a rare reader able to put *A Child's Game* down after a chapter or so' Barry Forshaw, *The Express*

'The action never stops in this exciting thriller about the pathological amorality of the hyper-rich and the heartbreak of their pawns' *Morning Star*

John Connor left his job as a barrister to write full time. During the fifteen years of his legal career he prosecuted numerous homicide cases in West Yorkshire and London. He advised the police in numerous proactive drugs and organised crime operations, many involving covert activity. He now lives in Brussels with his wife and two children.

By John Connor

Phoenix
The Playroom
A Child's Game
Falling
Unsafe
The Vanishing

The Ice House

John Connor

An Orion paperback

First published in Great Britain in 2015
by Orion Books
This paperback published in 2016
by Orion Books,
an imprint of The Orion Publishing Group Ltd,
Carmelite House, 50 Victoria Embankment
London EC4Y ODZ

An Hachette UK company

1 3 5 7 9 10 8 6 4 2

A CIP catalogue record for this book
is available from the British Library.

ISBN 978 1 4091 3615 6

Typeset by Deltatype Ltd, Birkenhead, Merseyside

Printed and bound in Great Britain
by Clays Ltd, St Ives, plc

MIX
Paper from
responsible sources
FSC® C104740

www.orionbooks.co.uk

For Anna, Sara and Tom

He wore hooded, black, sterile overalls, nylon galoshes and a filter face mask that covered his mouth and nose. A small, lightweight pack went under the disposable outer layer, and he carried the gun in a long, padded bag, slung over his shoulder. It was an L115A3, a British-made, bolt-action sniper rifle fitted with a suppressor, firing .338 magnum cartridges that came in five-round magazines. He'd been very careful only to handle it with gloves, whilst wearing the overalls – the intention was to discard it later. It weighed nearly seven kilos and was over 1.2 metres long. It wasn't what he had asked for, but it was good. A soldier firing one of these in 2009 had reportedly killed two Taliban machine gunners at a range of 2,475 metres. It had taken nine rounds to get the range, a luxury he wouldn't have. As a sports shooter, in an altogether past life, he had hit targets at just over half that distance. His objective now was to locate a good position, in cover, about five hundred metres from the road.

Earlier, in a parallel valley with a dirt track, he had sat in the car and attached the suppressor, set up the gun and the sights, so that he didn't have to fumble around in the dark. It was nearly 2 a.m. as he got over the ridge and into the valley. There was a moon, but enough cloud to conceal it and make progress slow. He moved without a flashlight, as slowly as necessary. There was no rush. He had about four hours before daylight. In that time he would need to dig himself in and set up the gun so that it was stable and pointing in the right direction, then get comfortable. After that he didn't intend to move until after he'd taken the shot, which, if all went to plan, would be mid-afternoon. So there was a lot of waiting ahead.

It wasn't ideal. The more he rested in one place the more DNA he would shed, despite the precautions. But the arrangements had forced him out of his normal routines. The money had transferred in the usual way, two weeks ago, but it was twice the amount he was accustomed to. With care he could live on it for two years. No objection to that. But other changes had left him exposed.

Normally the contact initiating a contract was at a distance. There were complex and laborious procedures to transmit the details, a supposedly anonymous notification system limiting the paperwork and information trail that gave him funds and a target. But this time he'd been informed there was to be a team involved and to coordinate it he would need to meet someone in person.

He knew enough about law enforcement to guess that nearly every precaution he could take was a waste of time and money if they were *already* looking at him, but on the assumption they weren't, he'd spent the better part of nine years taking meticulous care to minimise his traces. He kept up to date with forensic science developments, court cases and police techniques. The most crucial prophylactic measure, throughout the nine years, was not being on any DNA databases. But all this was farcical if he then had to meet someone face to face. If the security was that compromised then why not go cheap – hire an Albanian for five hundred quid? The whole point of his service was the guarantee of invisibility. For this reason he had wasted almost two days of his preparation time querying the arrangements, but to no effect. This was how they wanted it.

The designated contact called himself Philip Jones. The meet with him had gone down five days ago, in London, without apparent hitch. At the time he had no idea who Jones was, no way of verifying the site used was clean, no way of knowing that Jones wasn't undercover police, or, more likely, just someone earning a sideline by selling info to some agency. Jones had looked genuine enough – clean-shaven, dark hair cut neatly above his ears, blue eyes, angular face, very pale skin, dressed in the usual suit, about thirty years old, trim physique, an ex-soldier's build and bearing. No scars, twitches, odd mannerisms, nothing conspicuous. He had spoken with confidence and experience, as if the work was very familiar to him. They had met in the Chelsea Club, a private health and social facility attached to the back of the Stamford Bridge development.

But appearances were rarely reliable. So here he was in the middle of the night, determined to get in early, to wait, to watch. Jones had told him that key local police were on the payroll, bought off, and that there were six in the team, dealing with other targets in the same area. If true, that would make it the most complicated and well-funded job he had been involved in. But the more people used, the greater the risk. If there were others in this valley then he wanted to know their positions *before* he squeezed the trigger.

He had looked at maps and photographs of the terrain. He knew roughly where there were a range of suitable positions. In the past he might have used the GPS he had in the pack to locate them, but he had recently learned of a case where police in America had got a court order and gained access to records of GPS location searches, proving an interest in a key building in a murder case. Spain – where he was – might not be quite so advanced, but he wasn't certain of that, so he was feeling his way around in the darkness, GPS and phones switched off.

It took nearly an hour to get down to the level of the road. The hillside was a mix of knee-high grass, dense bushes and scattered groves of small, stunted trees, with knurled bark, all interspersed with boulders and rocks of varying sizes. He had to go very carefully. He thought it would have taken him fifteen to twenty minutes to cover the same ground in daylight.

Once at the road he crouched for a while considering the options, trying to get a clear picture of the angles. To his right was the house Jones had briefed him about, where the target lived, though from where he was he couldn't see it. The next nearest house was roughly two kilometres back down the valley. He looked in that direction but could see no lights. The night around him was still and warm, filled with the rasp of crickets and the scent of wild rosemary. He could smell it even through the mask. There were dogs barking every now and then lower down, but a long way off, maybe even as far as Marbella. That was the next big town. Between the dark, jagged shapes of the hills he could see a lighter area that he assumed was the sea, and somewhere way out in that, twinkling gently, lights that were probably over the straits, in Africa.

He moved back up the hill, looking for flatter ground, counting his paces until he was about three hundred metres back. This would be an optimal range, he thought, but yesterday, seventy kilometres further in land, in deserted scrub, he had zeroed the rifle and scope for five hundred metres, so now he worked his way a couple of hundred metres higher. The shot would be marginally harder, but it was a shorter distance back to the car after he'd fired. He found an area effectively screened with the thick bushes, a little overgrown ledge above some boulders. He crawled under and got out the spotting scope, checked the field of fire. He saw no one, heard no cars. When he was sure he'd found the best position available, he started to dig a shallow indentation with a small, lightweight trenching tool.

The soil was dry and loose, once he got the roots away, and he worked quickly. By 4.30 he was settling in with the rifle positioned, foliage pulled over him, thinking about whether he could risk dozing for an hour. He calculated he was so well hidden that you wouldn't know he was there until you tripped over him.

If everything Jones had told him was true then the shot would be relatively easy. Certainly smoother than the last time he had done this. That was only about eight weeks ago. The target then had been a man called Barsukov, a Russian. When he had finally laid the sights over him he had been on the patio of a house near a Black Sea resort, lying on a sunlounger beside a pool. There was a woman with him, on the next lounger, and a child, a little boy, running around between them and the pool. On that occasion his position had been seven hundred metres away, in woods.

He had lined up three times, but each time the little boy had come over and stood right in the cross hairs, at the side of the lounger, his head or upper body blocking the shot.

The first three times he had paused and waited. But the fourth time he had started to compute the thing, keeping the aim steady. Seven hundred metres with the bullet travelling at near enough one thousand metres per second. A clean, sunny day, no head wind, perfectly still air between his position and the target. He reckoned the bullet would enter the child's head through the back, exit through the face and still be accurate enough to take down the target, who was lying just the other side. It was even possible the round would still be supersonic as it hit. So it was a solution.

Or he could wait, and go through his set-up again.

Time had been limited. He was actually within the grounds of the house, and there was a security presence – albeit a sloppy one – to be factored in. As he went through the options his finger was on the trigger, his breathing controlled, everything ready. He had watched the child's head bobbing around, giving him an intermittent view of Barsukov. Barsukov was laughing at something the kid was saying, perfectly relaxed.

In the end he hadn't fired, because he wasn't sure about the parameters of the contract. Back in London his brother had been working to get past the anonymity. They had discovered the company behind the money, but hadn't got behind the company yet. For all they knew the woman lying next to Barsukov had placed the hit. And if the child was hers – as seemed likely – then she wouldn't be happy, which would be bad for future business.

So he had waited and taken his shot about five minutes later. Then paused whilst the child had run off screaming in fright, watching to see the security reaction.

It wasn't quite the same as this job, but nevertheless Jones had found it necessary to provide him with some specious justification: they had picked him because that way it would be more humane, he had said. They – the others in 'the team' – were not to be so clinical in their methods, it seemed, but this way, with a clean shot from a high-powered rifle, the death would be quick. A concession to humanity. Jones had thought he would need that rationalisation as he fitted her face under the cross hairs.

2

It was a nightmare – the recurrent nightmare. She was in a tightly constricted, airless space, chilled to the bone, shivering so her teeth were chattering. Where her hands were pressed against the trapdoor centimetres above her face – trying to force it open – she could feel a slippery layer of ice covering the wood, rivulets of meltwater running through her fingers, dropping down into her eyes. Beneath her was a half-frozen puddle, getting deeper by the minute.

She got her elbows against the trapdoor and heaved at it with all the strength she could summon. But the angle was restricting her. It wouldn't move. Yet she had shut it herself, it wasn't locked – she *knew* it wasn't locked. She gave in momentarily and started shouting out for him, the words swallowed dead in the pitch-black enclosure, then held her breath and listened to the noises from above. The seal was so tight she could see nothing, but the sounds came through clearly enough. Had they heard her? Her muscles twitched and shuddered as she strained to hear. The temperature below her had to be sub-zero. The living heat was being sucked out of her. She wanted to scream with panic, kept moving her hands away from the trapdoor, down to her mouth, pushing her knuckles between her teeth and biting down on them.

She had to get out. Not for herself, but because if she didn't they were going to kill him. She had to get out and get to him. She could hear shooting now, and screaming. She knew what they were doing. She could hear him gasping for breath, could see it happening as if she were up there, in the room with them – they were putting a noose around his neck, hauling him off the floor …

The image shifted without warning. The person under the boards vanished and now she *was* outside the hole, not even in the house, but on that hill where the stables were, to the west of the place. She was standing looking back at the house – the enormous, beautiful sprawl of it – up to her knees in snow, her breath puffing out in front of her, ice crystals on her eyelids and in her nostrils. And he was right beside her, standing with her, holding her hand. *Alex.* She whispered his name. She couldn't see his face, but she could feel his presence like something intoxicating, exactly as it had been back then. An enormous wave of relief flooded through her. There was no danger, no screaming or gunshots, they hadn't got to him, or strung him up, or killed him. She had been imagining it – none of that had happened. He was here, back with her, everything OK.

I thought I'd lost you, she said, and started crying quietly. *I thought I'd never see you again.* She let her head rest against his shoulder, felt him squeeze her fingers. She took a huge breath.

It was something she had only ever experienced with him – a feeling that she was *home*. Not here in this place in the snow – not anywhere that depended on a specific place. She belonged *with him*. As if it were programmed into her DNA.

She moved in the bed, opened her eyes. For a few seconds she couldn't orientate herself. She lay in confusion with the aching loss like a gap in her chest, her heart thudding uselessly, his absence blotting out the fear that had preceded it. She tried to listen to the real night around her. Then gradually her pulse slowed, the feeling of his physical presence slipped away. She put her hand on her chest, over her heart.

The transition was painful. From that intense, rich feeling, coursing through her, filling her with an overpowering, physical sense of completion – to *this*, the shabby reality of where she was, who she was. The horror, the trapdoor, the feeling of his hand – *none* of it was real. She had been dreaming.

She turned her head and looked to where her husband was, in the bed, centimetres away. She could smell him, smell his faint night odour of male sweat. Juan Martín. That was his name, and that was who she was – Julia Martín. She started to piece together the essential elements of the existence she was living – who she was, who she was with, who she loved, what she did, where she lived.

When she was relatively calm she slipped the sheet aside and slid her feet onto the floor, stood up quietly, carefully, not wanting to wake Juan, not wanting to have to explain. She looked around, noting the objects that should be familiar to her – the bed, the man, the pictures on the walls, the bathroom, her clothes on the chair, the mirror. She was here, at home, in the warm Spanish night, in the hills to the west of Marbella, windows wide open, mosquito frames in place. No danger anywhere.

She moved quickly and silently to check the room next to theirs, stared at the bed where her ten-year-old daughter lay. Rebecca. She could see her in the half-light, on her back, sheet bunched up around her, sleeping peacefully, her face beautiful, yet unlike anything else Julia might call beautiful. Something consoling kicked into her blood like a drug and brought a smile to her lips. But it couldn't get rid of the memory of him.

She disabled the alarm and walked out onto the terrace in her T-shirt and pyjama bottoms. The night was hotter out here, replete with insect noises, the dry smell of undergrowth in need of a downpour, and the ubiquitous, intermittent dogs, barking somewhere off in the distance. She sat down on one of the chairs by the little metal table and looked at the dark, jagged line of the mountains almost ringing the house, the lights from the next house twinkling down the valley, about two kilometres distant. She thought it must be about three in the morning. She could smell the sea.

The recurrent nightmare. It wasn't the same every time but the key elements were always there. The snow and ice were new this time, not even part of her memories of the place. When she had been there, a naive silly girl, out of her depth and barely out of her teens – or so it seemed now – it had never been like that, frozen in midwinter, everything frosted and glacial, clothed in shimmering ribbons and fantastic shards of ice, the thermometers showing thirty below zero. That wasn't how she knew it at all. Her imagination had supplied all that, maybe because the place had been called *The Ice House*, though not in English – she had seen the name in Russian, in indecipherable Cyrillic lettering. She had even learned how to say it in Russian.

A vast eighteenth-century mansion in a forgotten corner of Russia, hundreds of unused rooms, cupolas of gleaming glass, copper domes rearing out of nowhere in the endless forest. It belonged to a man called Michael Rugojev, the man she had gone there to work for, the man who had showed her that hole beneath the kitchen floorboards, *just in case*. But when she had been there it had been high summer, with long, bright northern nights and heat. And the place had been like a dream for her, not a nightmare.

Until that day. The fifteenth of July. Her whole life had changed that day. She was thirty-five now, but it was still with her, waking her each night. Parts of the dream were false, invented – figments of her dream consciousness – but parts of it were terribly real, indistinguishable from memories she had worked hard to lose. Because men *had* come there dispensing unspeakable brutality, and she had been under the floor, cowering in terror, in that hole with the trapdoor flat against her face, struggling to breathe. She had heard it all happening above her – just like in the dream – heard the screams and the blows. And she had come out to see him hanging on the end of a rope.

3

He hadn't always killed for money. But once it had started he hadn't looked back, and hadn't ever wanted out, something that, in any case, would have been virtually impossible. Once you were in, you were in – they made sure of that. But he was OK with it. He lay beneath the covering of dry soil and leaves, the tight bushes shading him from the midday sun, his face resting on the stockpiece, his eyes closed and his concentration relaxed, and he thought that overall he was OK with it.

He was thirty-five years old and he had killed five men – pulled the trigger and watched the consequences, but without anything tugging at him inside, telling him it was wrong. Instead, it had felt insignificant. The men he shot fell to the ground and life moved on, almost immediately. *Everyone* moved on, even the people who stood wailing above the corpses. Because they all knew they were headed there, into the vast forgetfulness of history. Time was short. *Carpe diem.*

That was one way to look at it. There were others. For example, he could see himself slotting into their lives like bacteria or fatal accidents slotted into other people's lives. What did the precise timing or method matter? And the five he had killed had been in the same game, one way or another – the money-making game. They had killed too – business rivals, witnesses, in two cases even members of their own family. They were as dirty as he was, morally indistinguishable from those who paid him. They were all pissing in the same pot. Except this one, of course.

There was no getting around the fact that this one was different. A ten-year-old girl. Rebecca Martin. Viktor had told him not to go through with it.

But he still didn't need justifications. Children were dying all over the world – in Syria, Afghanistan, Gaza, Iraq. Hundreds each day, probably. So what? Death was a natural process, however it arrived. There was nothing to make this child special. He thought his attitude probably meant that a part of him was missing, a capacity to empathise. That was why it didn't bother him much. He could date it to Liz, perhaps – to Liz Edwards disappearing, to the end of that chance and everything he had felt then – but that would be just glossing the truth, twisting a familiar story to fit himself. But real life wasn't like that. More likely he had always been this way, even when he was with her, or even before that – as a teenager and a child. The opportunities to reveal himself just hadn't yet arisen.

The name he had been living with for many years, the name on his fake passport, was Carl Bowman. The passport was Swedish, but he wasn't from there. His mother was from a sparsely populated border region that seventy years ago had changed hands more than once between Finland and Russia, so that her passport had originally been Russian. But she had moved, at some point, abandoning the house, the land, the relatives, the husband – discarding all those attachments – and had met his father, who was from Helsinki, and started again.

She had insisted always, throughout his childhood, that she was Finnish, because that part of the world she was from – Eastern Karelia – was rightfully a part of Finland. Russia was the enemy who had occupied it, and hence though she had been born there and her birth certificate said she was Russian, *he* – her second son – was one hundred per cent Finnish. That was what she told him. But he didn't feel it.

It was different for his older half-brother, Viktor, whose

father was the Russian she left behind, the man her family had insisted she marry at sixteen years old, the man whose violence, family and criminal connections she had finally fled. Viktor had been old enough to remember all that, but his memories had a warmer tint; loss of a loving father, friends and home, that was what he carried with him, and Finland hadn't filled any of it. So he had chosen to return as soon as he was old enough, leaving Carl behind.

At fifteen and sixteen Carl had missed Viktor like a part of himself. The way Carl thought about it, the way they had been, it was more like they were twins. They were that close. They looked similar too, walked the same, spoke the same – at least when they used Finnish. In their twenties it had been possible for strangers to mistake them for twins, despite the age difference.

He had joined the Finnish military at the first opportunity. At that point Viktor had been virtually untraceable, lost into the chaos that was the failed Russian state. But four years later he was back with cars and houses and money and offers too good to be turned down. So Carl had quit the army and followed him. He hadn't even considered that there might be a choice. Russia had been just opening up – ripe with opportunity. Viktor had looked out for him, protected him, passed on the chances and connections he had cultivated, introduced him to key relatives – the criminals his mother had railed against. And that had led – eventually – to here, to what he did now. To lying in the dirt in the mountains north of Marbella, waiting for a human target to walk into his kill zone.

When he thought back on it, thought about the trajectory his life had taken to this particular point, he felt like he hadn't chosen *any* of it. His life had run along rails that other people had laid out. The truth was that it was a massive struggle to change direction, to actually take the chances you were dealt

14

and *choose*, and he hadn't managed it. Neither of them had, neither Viktor nor himself. Yet they were successful. 'Successful',
in that they were alive, surviving – *biologically successful* – the
rest wasn't something he wanted to dwell on. He liked to stick
to essential facts, clean details. He didn't like his head to feel
cluttered, out of control.

Still. What he was doing right now – this particular job – it
was different. Different enough to worry him. Earlier, lying
here with nothing better to do, he had imagined bumping into
Liz in the middle of a London street, maybe as he was making
his way to Heathrow to get here. It was one of the peculiarities
of London life that that kind of thing could happen. He had
run into other people he knew, despite the odds, so why not
her? She would appear in the crowd of faces – the mindless
single face of the commuters – she would separate out from it
and be there, standing in all her shocking singularity, as amazed
as he was, speechless. *Imagine running into* you *here. What are*
you doing? She would be standing very close, with the crowd
moving around her. What are you doing these days? She would
ask something like that.

And what would he say? He couldn't tell her what he had
been doing, couldn't get near it. In fact, he wouldn't even be
able to look her in the eye.

4

I just don't want you to freeze. Rebecca remembered her mother's words right now, as the man first came into view. What else had she said? This had been one of their little 'security' conversations, about four weeks ago. *I just don't want you to freeze. When you do that you give them all the time they need. Someone comes at you, someone tries to grab you, you do not freeze, you scream and yell and run, immediately.*

She had cringed inside, listening to her mother, because this kind of conversation had been a refrain throughout her life. Her mother was paranoid; always stopping her doing normal things that everyone else did, because they were 'too dangerous'. And worse, she went on like that in front of her friends. It was embarrassing.

This was the first year her mum had let her get the school bus home, despite her being ten now, despite all the other kids having done that for years. Some of them lived out in the hills too, like they did, so that wasn't the reason.

It meant she had to walk from the bus stop to the house, along the track that led from the junction with the surfaced road, which was as far as the bus would go. It was one point nine eight kilometres from there to home, her mother had told her, a gentle slope up the side of the valley. It usually took Rebecca about thirty minutes to walk it, going slow. The weather was good right now, warm but not too hot, and the view across the other side was great, with the peaks all hazy like something out of an adventure story. If you went right up there – where it really was wild – you could sometimes see a warthog, getting out of your way, then smell it as you crossed the trail it used. Warthogs smelled like pee, she thought, all pigs did. She didn't like ham or bacon because it came from pigs and she knew what pigs smelled like. She still sometimes ate pork though, if it was cooked in a stew. Her mother cooked fantastic stews.

You couldn't see the warthogs from here, from the track, but you could sometimes see a herd of ibex – the little, wild, Spanish mountain goat – up on the ridges. And there were butterflies and birds, sometimes a snake, and many lizards. And the buzzing of the insects, flies and mosquitoes. These things interested her because her mum had always told her things about them when she was little, interesting details – like the fact that the lizards lost their tails if you grabbed them, but didn't die, or that it was only the female mosquito that made the really irritating high-pitched whine that woke you up, and that it was a mating call, the same thing birds did, only it sounded nice when birds sang – *It's just the mosquitoes' song*, her mum would say, when she couldn't sleep. *They're singing for you.* That was a nice way to put it – typical of her mum – but it didn't stop them biting her. Her dad used to come in with a can of fly spray afterwards, spray the room even though she hated the smell and didn't want to be the cause of anything dying, not even a mosquito. Her dad was generally irritating at the moment.

Right now she couldn't hear any insects or birds or anything, because she had the headphones in. She was listening to a track by Katy Perry when the man stepped onto the road ahead. He was still about three hundred metres away, too far to see properly. It looked like he had stepped out from behind the clump of olive bushes at the bend in the road, but she might be mistaken. Maybe he had just walked up from their house. Their house was the only one past that bend, the only one on this stretch of road for another two or three kilometres. After their place, over the top of the hill, there was a long, twisting track down into the next valley, the hillsides overgrown, then, at the bottom, the big villa they called 'The Italian's Place' because that was just about all they knew about the owner, despite having lived here for almost five years.

She shifted her school bag onto the other shoulder. She wasn't used to seeing people on this road. She thought her mum was mad, but it still made her pause when she saw him there. Since she had started getting the bus back, this was the first time she had seen anyone else here. She slipped the headphones out and stopped walking. What should she do? He was in her way, between her and their house.

She looked back behind as she realised that she was doing nothing – exactly what her mum had tried to teach her not to do. But he was still far away – though walking towards her, quite quickly – no danger yet. She could turn and run back down the hill to the road. The neighbours lived at the junction there – the Ramirez family. She could go in there. He wouldn't be able to catch her because she was an excellent runner. It was just about the only sport she liked. She had won competitions at school, both at sprint distances and longer. This year they were to enter her in a national athletics competition in Madrid, representing a group of clubs in the area. She usually found it easy to outsprint adults, unless they were runners too. He would have to be fit to catch her when he was starting so far back.

But that was silly. None of her friends would think like this. She shaded her eyes from the sun so she could see him better, and immediately relaxed. It was a policeman. When she put her hand up she could see his uniform and hat. She smiled to herself, wondered vaguely what he could be doing here, a long way out without his car (had she seen a car back at the junction? She didn't remember one, but she hadn't been looking specially), then started to walk towards him.

He called out to her when he was still a little away, then shouted his name, or maybe his rank, but she didn't quite get it. He stopped in front of her, looking down at her, but not too far down. She was already one metre sixty-five, very tall for her age. He had the sun right behind him when he was talking to her, so she couldn't see his face too well. He looked like a teenager, she thought, spotty, slightly unshaven. He was sweating like he'd just run from somewhere, but not out of breath. He asked her for her name, age and where she lived. She told him. Spanish was her second tongue, but not far behind English. She had gone to Spanish nursery before school. She was at an English 'international' school now, but she had Spanish friends and spoke it all the time with her dad. 'Rebecca Martin,' she said, pronouncing Martin the Spanish way – *Marteen* – though her mother said it the English way quite often, as a joke, to annoy her dad. 'I'm ten. I live just over there. The next house.'

He asked her what she was doing out on the road alone and she told him. He nodded. She did this every day after school, she said. He licked his lips and gazed off at the ridge line on the other side. 'Good,' he said. 'I'm just checking the area.' He reached a hand out and patted her head, clumsily, because she was a little tall for that. Then he stepped around her and walked on.

She would tell her mum she had seen him, because that was another of her mum's little rules – that she should always report back if a stranger spoke to her, no matter who they were. She watched him for a bit before starting off again. She would have about half an hour alone in the house before her dad got back. That was good. Later they would do pizza. Even better. She put her headphones back in, selected her favourite tune from Gaga's second album – a song called 'Born This Way'. The beat started a little after the intro, lifting her mood – then she felt like dancing her way home. She started waving her arms around, singing at the top of her voice as she went.

Carl had seen the policeman. The man had walked straight through his sights, in the direction of the house, then back again fifteen minutes later. Was he really a policeman? Hard to determine at this distance. He had looked young, but policemen were young these days; either that or he was getting older. But Jones had told him the local police were involved, so unless squad cars started to arrive in force he wasn't going to change plan.

In between the man's appearances the school bus had arrived at the bottom of the valley dirt track. Carl had heard it, then shifted position to search for it through the spotting scope. A stand of trees and a fold of land had prevented him from watching anyone get off or on. But he knew it would be her. Jones had given him the timings and they were accurate. It would take the girl about half an hour to reach the point directly below him. So it was on. Right now. It was happening.

He concentrated on his breathing, on keeping everything calm and slow. His heart wanted to pick up, of course, the adrenalin starting already. But a fast heartbeat made the shot harder. He could control it through his breathing, up to a point, the rest was mental state. A certain increase in pulse couldn't be avoided.

Aside from the policeman there had been one car, an hour and a half ago, a Nissan. The same car that had come down the road, going in the direction of Marbella at 9.30 that morning. There had been a Toyota right behind it and so far the Toyota hadn't returned. He hadn't been able to see the drivers, but he knew that the occupants of the house used these cars, which meant there was someone back there now, waiting for the girl, probably. She would come on the school bus, and walk up the valley, right into his zone. If she didn't then he would abort and seek instructions.

He moved off scope and picked up the spotting sight again, focused on the ridge across the other side of the valley. At 5.30 that morning, in the grey dawn light, he had seen movement up there and had got the sights onto a single man, moving in amongst the rocks, dressed in camo khaki. He had settled there with binoculars and started to search the valley. Carl didn't recognise him, so it wasn't Jones, but he hadn't met anyone else in 'the team'. He assumed it was someone involved, maybe even someone sent to locate his position and watch the hit, make sure it went to plan. He had seen no weapon – just the binoculars. He was sure the man wouldn't have spotted him. He looked now for him in the two places he had moved between, but the hillside was empty. That didn't mean he hadn't moved to somewhere further up the ridge, out of view. Carl had a limited range of movement in the shallow trench.

He got his eye back on the scope, moved the gun slightly, then heard someone shouting, from back in the direction of the bus. A moment later he realised it wasn't shouting, it was singing. He slipped his finger over the trigger and listened. It was her, he thought, singing very loud, slightly out of tune. He didn't know the song. She sounded breathless, happy.

Then suddenly she was there, at the edge of his area, moving fast. He hadn't expected that. She was almost running, waving her arms about, singing at the top of her voice. Rebecca Martin. Ten years old. She was tall, he thought, for a ten-year-old. The blonde hair was tied back into a ponytail. She had a small backpack on one shoulder. It took him a couple of seconds to track her because she was moving so erratically. Was she actually dancing? Either that or skipping.

He cursed silently, forced himself to stay calm. As he took deeper breaths she stopped for a moment, right in the middle of his set-up zone, catching her breath. He got the cross hairs onto her head, then he could see her properly. The scope had a twenty-five times magnification and she was just less than five hundred metres away. Her face was large and clear. He could see her eyes, her mouth, the freckles across the bridge of her nose. He thought, *Would you have shot through that little boy?* – in Russia, the hit on Barsukov – *if you had known that the woman wasn't involved, that there would be no repercussions, would you have shot through his head?*

The girl started moving again, but walking slower now. She was smiling to herself. She had earphones in, snaking away to a phone or music device. That accounted for the singing out of tune. But her voice had sounded ... *what?* He realised suddenly that he was shaking. Her voice had brought to him a tiny little piece of her personality. What she was like, what she sounded like.

The singing of children. He had no children and rarely thought about them. Viktor had no kids either. Kids were not a part of his life. But the singing. It had caught hold of something in his chest, pulled a smile onto his face. That was why he was shaking. His arms were shaking, his legs, his chest. He had to get control of it.

She was still walking, oblivious. In a few moments she would be out of the zone he could aim within, hidden by the spur of land where the road curved. He tracked her movement, slipped the sights a little ahead of her, ran through the calculations. She was moving so slowly that hardly any adjustment was needed. Suddenly she stopped singing and stood still, looking down at either her phone or the music player. He slid the cross hairs over her head again. But the gun wasn't steady now. The trembling in his limbs was getting transmitted down the stock. He thought, instantaneously, *No, I would not have shot the boy*, and something inside him paused.

This was the story they had written for her, for both of them – someone else's plot. His part was to pull the trigger and end her life.

But he had a choice.

He took a long breath.

She started moving again, no longer singing. He slipped his finger off the trigger and his eye off the scope. He couldn't do it. He didn't know why, but he couldn't do it. He didn't want this girl to die.

Looking down the barrel, he watched her walk right past the kill zone, then brought his knees up, rolled, shook the mud and branches off and thrust himself out of the dirt and bushes, like some giant grub being born. The sun blazed in his eyes. He looked down at her from his exposed position, now behind her. Standing up he was high enough to see straight over the spur of land where the road turned. He saw her approaching the bend with the house just beyond it. He could see the sun reflecting off the swimming pool, see the red roof tiles.

They would try to kill her without him, he knew, the guy on the ridge opposite was probably already reporting to Jones. No matter what he did she would probably be dead within twenty-four hours. A six-man team meant lots of back-up options. He had a useless thought – that he should shout at her, warn her. But right then he saw the flash at the house. He ducked automatically, knowing instinctively what it was. He saw the roof of the house lift at one end, then explode outwards and up, debris showering into the sky. There was a massive crack echoing off the valley sides. He dropped to one knee and watched a coiling fireball burst upwards in a cloud of black smoke. In an instant it was subsiding into a high column of swirling dust. He could hear the noise of alarms going off, tiles and bricks raining over the hillside.

5

Rebecca still had the headphones in when she saw the flash, above the rocks right in front of her. She was about seventy metres from the house, at the curve in the road, with a steep wedge of land between herself and the drop down to their plot – the house itself was out of sight. She stopped immediately, then a split second later heard the bang, even above the noise of the music. She pulled the earphones out, let her school bag slip off her shoulder to the ground. Tiny bits of stone started to drop all around her. Some pieces struck her head. She could hear alarms, see smoke rising into the air.

Without thinking, she started to run, coming round the bend to a cloud of dust, still billowing outwards. Her house was somewhere behind it. She had no idea what was happening but her first thought was that a car had come off the road and crashed down there – the Italian's car, maybe, if he had one. In town she had once seen a car crashed into the wall of a building, on fire – there had been a lot of smoke. She kept running, going towards the smoke and dust, flapping her arms in front of her to clear it.

She was about fifty metres down their driveway before she could see a corner of the house. There was a car buried in a wall that had collapsed there, it looked all white with dust, she couldn't tell what kind of car it was. It wasn't her mother's, it might be her dad's. But her dad couldn't have crashed here, because he hadn't passed her on the road, and he wouldn't be here

24

already – her mother had told her that he would come back at the normal time. The house alarm was going off, very loud, and something was on fire, crackling behind the broken front wall; she could smell the burning, really sharp in her nostrils, but she couldn't see what it was. There was glass all over the road – her feet were crunching on it. The car alarm was shrieking too, on and off.

A wind stirred the smoke and she saw more of the house, all of the roof caved in, bricks and tiles all over, and something that looked like tiny shreds of paper, floating through the air. The smoke was coming out of the hole where the roof had been. That was *her* house. She stood mouth open, staring at it.

Now she saw the damage she thought it must have been a gas leak. What else could it be? They had two big, metal gas cylinders in the kitchen. She thought, *I have to get to my bedroom, get my things out.* She wasn't running any more, just walking slowly, in a daze.

She was about thirty metres from it, past the gateposts, in the yard where the cars were normally parked, when she heard someone shouting, and thought it must be someone inside the house. She kept going, feeling frightened, then realised it was coming from behind her – someone shouting out at her, telling her to stop.

She turned to see a man coming down the hill towards her, running. He was carrying a backpack, and something long, shouting at her very loud. She had never seen him before. He was very tall, with blond hair and was wearing some kind of plastic suit or overall – a crinkly thing like she had seen the police wear at crime scenes on TV programmes, except his was black and the police suits were always white. There was a thing like a gas mask hanging around his neck. Still, she thought he must be police. He was running very fast, so he reached her before any other options could occur to her.

'Stay there,' he panted, in English, when he got beside her. 'Don't go further.' He wasn't looking at her, but over her, at the house. For a moment he was very out of breath. He bent suddenly, so that he was actually lower down than her. 'Do you understand English?' he asked. 'Can you understand me?'

She nodded. 'I speak English,' she stammered. 'My mother is English.'

He looked at her properly for the first time. She realised only then that she didn't know him, didn't know where he had jumped out from, didn't have a clue what was going on. All her mother's words came back, all the warnings. Her hand closed around the mobile in her pocket. 'I don't know what happened,' she said, her voice wavering. She should turn and run, she thought. He was speaking English to her, but the police here spoke Spanish. 'That's my house,' she said.

'It was an explosion,' he said, looking past her again, squinting towards the smoke.

'Like a gas explosion, you mean?'

He looked back at her and his eyes met hers. She was shaking now. But his eyes looked OK, she thought, his face looked OK. But her mum had said things about situations just like this, had warned her.

'A gas leak …' he said vaguely. 'Maybe.' He stood up. 'Wait here. I have to go and check.' He glanced behind them. 'Better still. Wait over there.' He pointed to the rocks up by the start of the lane down from the main road, where he had just run from, about thirty metres back, behind the gateposts. 'Get behind those rocks and don't do anything,' he said. 'Just wait there for me. Keep your head down – in case it happens again. OK? You understand that?'

Had he just been driving past, maybe? She looked down at the long thing in his hands. It was a gun. Maybe he was one of the hunters who went after the wild boars, up in the scrub.

But whatever he was, if he had wanted to hurt her he wouldn't suggest leaving her alone. She nodded again. She would walk up there, call her mum, right now.

6

Carl waited until she was behind the rocks, just past the gates. He saw her move behind and then wave to him, to signal she was there. *She speaks English*, he thought. *Her mother is English.* He thought her mother must be in the house somewhere. Suspicions aside, he hadn't known the girl's nationality, or anything else about her, just her name and age. In the normal course of things he wanted to know as little about the target as possible, consistent with getting the job done, neither the personal details, nor the reasons for the hit. That was meant to be a feature of the anonymous contract system – that it distanced and protected him, as well as the client and the cartel.

She had done well to mention the gas leak. He hadn't been thinking about that at all. He'd been thinking about another bomb, a secondary – she had been walking towards it and he had wanted to stop her. He was still thinking about that possibility, thinking very quickly. There was the guy on the ridge and the policeman too. Both within range. And the gas thing. If they had gas bottles in there, or a gas main, then that might blow now. There was fire inside the building somewhere. A fire or burglar alarm had been ringing as he came down the hillside, but it had stopped now.

He had to get in there, check for life, do it quickly. Both her parents were inside – through the spotting scope he had watched a car, a Nissan, returning earlier with two occupants – a man and a woman – one of the two cars that had left the place that morning. Jones hadn't told him who else was on the list, but her parents had been his first guess. Unless the bomb had been planted to get the girl, as a back-up, if he failed to make the shot. In which case they had fucked it up, triggered it too early. The car alarm was still sounding intermittently, coming from the Nissan. The girl hadn't realised about her parents, he assumed, hadn't worked it out yet.

He started to walk quickly forwards, then stooped and placed on the ground the gun and the backpack with his ammunition and kit. He checked back, but couldn't see her. She would be behind the rocks, out of the line of a direct blast. She had been lucky to be just around the bend in the road when the bomb had detonated. He thought the guy up on the ridge must have detonated it, or it was on a very long timer. He had been in the valley since well before dawn, and had seen no one come up the road except the policeman, and he hadn't been carrying anything, so they must have planted the thing yesterday sometime.

He kept his hand up in front of his face and skirted round the walls of the place. It was a single-floor villa, typical Spanish style, but modern, built mainly from breeze blocks, with a light brick cladding. The bricks had exploded all over the place. It was built onto the hillside, just below the main valley track, with terraced levels which were gardens, and a pool. The water there was coated so completely with a layer of floating dust that it looked like a solid surface, perfectly still now. There was a low perimeter wall about ten metres past the pool, then past that he could see the side of the valley dropping away, heavily forested with some kind of low, deciduous tree.

The blast wouldn't have needed to be huge to demolish a house like this. Parts of two of the outside walls had collapsed, one onto the car, the other, further round, next to the swimming pool. He stepped up towards the place and could smell the burning, but still couldn't see any fire. There was smoke coming through a hole in the roof, further back where it had collapsed inwards. He couldn't interpret the layout through the wreckage and the smoke, couldn't see where a front door would be, so near the pool he picked his way over the fallen masonry and went through a wide hole in the wall. He was listening for people calling out, buried, but couldn't hear anything. His heart was beating very fast now. Fear and adrenalin. If they triggered a second blast he would get it full on.

He moved quickly, searching through the mess, coming into what must have been a bedroom. There was no roof but he could make out a bed – the wooden frame upturned, broken. There were bookshelves standing against a wall, perfectly intact, books still in them, everything coated in the white dust. He called out, shouting in English, asking if there was anyone there.

The far wall was still up, a picture hanging there, not even at an angle, but the wall next to it had caved in. A door was swinging on one hinge. There was a jagged pile of bricks, tiles and wood all over the ground, mixed in with fluttering paper and torn sheets, a metal bedstead poking up through the mess. He could see some flames licking through the smoke in the room beyond the collapsed wall. There was a light haze of choking smoke all around him.

He put his sleeve over his mouth and nose, then looked down. Right at his feet there was an arm protruding from beneath a wooden panel of some sort. It was poking out, the fingers closed on the palm. He bent quickly and tried to shift the panel. It was only the back of a cupboard, and came away easily, revealing a woman lying in a twisted position, a big puddle of blood all around her. He crouched and put his fingers at her neck, feeling for a pulse, but nearly all her head and face was a horrible ragged mess. He thought something large had hit her. The body was still as warm as his own, but there was no pulse. She had a light cotton dress on, spattered all over with blood. It would be the girl's mother.

He stood, and shouted again, desperate to get out quickly. But then saw another body behind the pile of rubble: a man. He was just lying there, face up, eyes wide open, chest terribly still, the skin pale and mottled with the dust. There wasn't any blood around him. Carl stepped through the broken furniture, over a mattress with the insides bursting out, and saw the body was naked. He couldn't see a mark on it. But the eyes were wide open, the face rigid.

He had to get out. Now. He had been up close to the effects of a bomb blast once before. It also had been just like this, a random mix of devastation and safety. He had seen people dead like this too, without a mark on them, killed by compression. He started to cough as the smoke got into his lungs. He shouldn't have left the girl alone. There were houses two kilometres away and the people there would have seen the smoke, heard the explosion. But the police were bought off, so maybe that wouldn't deter Jones. There was the guy on the ridge. At least him. He could be closing in on her right now. It might even be possible to disable communications into a little valley like this – take out the GSM masts, cut the landline, giving them plenty of time. He stumbled back to the hole he had come through. He had to get back to her, quick.

7

Rebecca started a text to her mum but her fingers wouldn't work properly – they were shaking, plus she couldn't see properly, so it was really slow. She kept making mistakes and having to go back and start again. She was continually looking up as she was doing it, to see if he was coming back yet. She didn't want him to see her doing it. She had no idea why, but knew she didn't want him to know she had a mobile phone.

Normally she was really quick texting, much quicker than any adult she knew, but now it wouldn't work. She had started it because she was frightened he would hear her talking if she actually called her mum. She stopped, looked up for him, then moved further behind the rock. She would have to call her mum, speak quietly.

She spoke her mum's name almost in a whisper, so faintly the voice recognition didn't register it, so then she had to speak it louder, move again to the edge of the road, look to see if he was coming out yet. There was still some smoke coming out of the roof. Would he call the fire brigade? she wondered. She held the phone to her ear and watched the house, waiting for him to appear. After a few seconds of complete silence she looked at the screen and saw she had no signal, no bars at all.

She cut the call attempt and felt a panic fluttering in her tummy. No signal wasn't normal. There was a mast right on the hill opposite. She looked up to make sure it was still there and out of the corner of her eye she saw movement to the side of her, back along the road down the valley. She turned towards it.

There was a man there, coming quickly forwards. He was at the bend in the road, up above her – where she had been standing when the explosion had happened. When he saw her he stopped immediately. It was the policeman who had spoken to her, she thought. He looked young like that, in the same uniform. He had something in his right hand which, after a moment, she realised might be a pistol, though he wasn't pointing it at anything. She thought she would shout out to him, warn him, or ask for help, but something stopped her.

As she watched, he crouched down on the ground near to one of the bushes edging the road. He peered across to the house then, before she could decide what to do, he shouted to her: 'Come. Come to me now.' In Spanish, same voice – definitely the man she had just spoken to.

She moved out from behind the rocks, took a step towards him. He was a policeman, so it must be safe.

'Where is he?' he shouted, again in Spanish, not looking at her, but down at the house. 'Where is the man you were with?' So he had seen the tall guy. She was about to tell him he was in the house, but again something stopped her. She took another step towards him though. Why was she uncertain?

'The house is on fire,' she shouted. 'There's been an explosion.' She didn't want to walk up to him. The tall guy had told her to wait behind these rocks, in case there was another explosion. She risked a glance back. There were wisps of smoke coming from the roof still, but no longer a big black column of it. Up above them, high in the air, the cloud was still hanging there. No sign of the tall man yet. 'There was an explosion,' she shouted again, still in Spanish. The policeman was about thirty metres away from her. Not far. She didn't have to shout very loud.

'I am police, little girl,' he said, speaking bad English

suddenly, and looking irritated. 'You do what I tell you. Come over here now.' But still he didn't get up from the crouch. He was looking off towards the house, looking very nervous, like he was frightened the tall man would appear from there. That's what it looked like. He shouted again, 'Where is the man you were with? Tell me now.'

'I don't know,' she said. She was still taking slow steps forward. *Why had she lied?*

He stood up, beckoned her with his hand. 'Walk to me,' he said. 'You are safe.' The gun in his other hand was pointed forward, not at her, but in her direction. She stopped.

'Come,' he said, more urgently. 'Come now.' He looked down the hill again, then started to come towards her, warily. She saw the gun coming up. She had followed none of her mother's advice today. What would her mother say about this? *She would tell her to run.*

She spun quickly and started across the junction, heading up the road beyond, away from him.

Carl was already coming round the side of the house when he heard the first shot. He sped up, kept his head low, ran to where his pack and gun lay. As the front area came into view he could see a man up on the road, in uniform, a handgun held out at arm's length. He was about seventy metres away. The man fired the gun as Carl watched. Carl couldn't see what he was shooting at, but knew. He felt a flush of fear in his blood, then heard her scream – a short yell of fear, rather than pain. He tried to keep calm, got his hands onto the gun, dashed sideways towards some bushes.

Then he could see them both. She was about thirty metres from the man, lying on the ground. She was off to Carl's left, about forty metres distant, above him, on the road that led past the house. She was partially screened by the low bushes there.

Carl felt his scalp prickle, the kick of adrenalin high up in his chest. The policeman was further away than her, to Carl's right, but moving forward quickly, not looking towards him.

He got the rifle up and the scope to his eye as she scrambled to her feet and started to run. The policeman aimed at her again, moving towards the rock where Carl had told her to wait. He fired twice very quickly, before Carl could do anything. Both misses, because she didn't pause. The policeman started screaming something, then disappeared behind the rock, into cover. Carl had the cross hairs on the rock, but no clear shot. He could feel his heart thudding as he tried to steady his legs. The gun was difficult to shoot accurately from a standing position. He needed to go down onto one knee, brace it against his leg, but there was no time. He kept his eye against the scope, waiting for the man to emerge at the other side. He heard the girl cry out again, decided he couldn't wait. He started to move clumsily sideways, just as the guy came out.

The man was holding the gun with both hands now, pointing it towards her, completely focused on the shot. Carl had the cross hairs over his chest, but he was still moving, off balance. He squeezed anyway. The shot smacked out with a loud whipcrack. The gun was big, the round powerful – so even with the muzzle brake and the fat suppressor mounted on the end of the barrel, the recoil spun him, pulling his eye from the scope. The guy disappeared from view. There was a puff of stone and dust from the rocks behind where he had been, where the bullet struck.

Carl recovered and put one knee on the ground, eyes on the road still. He slid the bolt, felt the next round chamber, then stood and moved up the hill, moving very cautiously, holding the gun ready in front of him.

But there was no need. As soon as he got to the junction he saw the guy lying there, flat out, face in the dirt, arms spread wide, the pistol discarded in the road some distance away. There was some blood. The round must have gone straight through him before ricocheting off the rocks behind. The girl was over by some trees at the side of the track, on her backside, cowering, staring at him.

'Did he hit you?' Carl shouted over. 'Are you OK?' She didn't reply, but he couldn't go to her yet. He had to check the man, be sure.

He walked over to him with the gun still ready. But from five metres back he could see enough to lower it. It was a clean headshot, though a lucky one. He had been going for the torso. The limbs were still twitching, but not with life. He turned away from it, ran back to the girl.

'He tried to kill me,' she blurted out, indignant. 'He shot at me ...'

'Did he hit you? Are you hurt?'

She shook her head. She was trembling like she was freezing. That was mild shock. He could see her looking past him at the body, her eyes very wide, her face very white.

'You're safe,' he said. 'Don't worry about him.'

She stared at him, her expression aghast, then said, 'I was running. He fired at me. I *think* he tried to shoot me ...'

'He did try to shoot you, but those guns are inaccurate. It's almost impossible to hit a moving target, so you did well to run ...' He put the gun down and helped her stand up, checked her front, just in case. He had seen her on the ground. Her clothes were dusty. Had she been hit without realising it? Her pupils were a little dilated, like she was full of adrenalin, but there was no blood on her.

'I fell over,' she stammered. She looked confused. 'I fell over when he started firing. He was pointing it at me and shooting ...'

'He was trying to kill you. And he wasn't alone. We need to get out of here. Right now.'

8

Carl moved quickly and deliberately up the hillside, stooping low, taking a route that led from cover to cover, stopping periodically to raise the rifle and hunt the ground within small arms range, to either side and above. There were broken rocks strewn all over, easy to gash your leg on if you fell, so he couldn't move as quickly as he would like, not with the girl in tow. She was behind him a little and he had to repeatedly slow and hurry her along. She was still stunned, he thought, automatically obeying him because something frightening had happened and he was the nearest adult. She stumbled from rock to rock, less out of breath than he was, but saying nothing. It wouldn't be long before that changed though – then she would start to ask the questions he was fearing. Like what had happened to her parents? What was he going to tell her?

Mostly, he kept his eyes on this side of the valley. That was what he was most worried about. If they were over the other side of the valley – where he had seen Jones's man – then they would need to have another sniper to pose a threat, and he thought they wouldn't have hired more than one sniper. He was having difficulty understanding why they had hired *even* one. If they had gone to the trouble of planting a device then why not simply wait until all the targets were in the house? When Jones had told him they were using him as a kind of humane killer he had bought it only because he had imagined that the other targets were to be brutalised in some way, perhaps questioned before being executed, or worse. But a device didn't do that. A device was haphazard – it could kill effectively, maim people, or leave them untouched. Which meant that, by using him instead, they must have really wanted a certainty that this girl was dead, and that wasn't how Jones had explained it. And if that was the case, why detonate the device before she reached the house? That had to have been a cock-up. It was impossible to think it through clearly now, though. Right now he had to keep his concentration focused on the threat.

He paused for breath. He still had the sterile overalls and gloves on, and was sweating heavily, but didn't dare strip them off until he was in the car. His hands were especially uncomfortable. He glanced back. She was still there, ten paces further down, looking up at him. He moved a bit higher then checked his field of view using the rifle scope. He could see nothing, no one following, no cars coming up the road, no movement back at the house. No sirens. No reaction. The longer that continued, the more it bothered him.

The valley here was deeply wooded but all the trees were low, stunted things, not much higher than bushes. There was a kind of scrappy, dry grass coming out of the soil, but it was thin and looked thirsty and brown. It grew about as high as his knees. The ground was hard, cracked like in a drought, dusty, the soil a faint shade of red. Here and there were flowers, but not many. Earlier in the day he had thought he could smell wild rosemary, but now the only thing in his nostrils was the smoke he had inhaled down in the house. He saw lizards scampering away from him, heard the clicking of crickets, the whirring of cicadas. There wasn't a cloud in the sky but luckily it was far from high summer. He needed water, but he wasn't too uncomfortable.

He set off again as soon as she caught up with him. After five more minutes he got to a prominent stand of rocks he had seen from the house and climbed round them, then up onto a high ledge. They were big, broken slabs of stone, rising above the little trees, giving him a good field of fire. As she scrambled up behind him he warned her to stay below, in cover, then lay down and started searching, using his eyes first, then checking through the scope. Still he could hear no sirens, though the dissipating smoke cloud was high in the sky now. Why hadn't the neighbours driven up? He didn't understand it.

He checked the ridge opposite. There was no sign of Jones's man, so he started to scan around him, working methodically. As he concentrated, his mind kept flicking back to the girl. She looked really scared now, but the horror hadn't even started. Both her parents were dead. He felt a weight in his stomach thinking about it. He had played a part in that. The whole situation was totally fucked up, well beyond his comfort zone. Why hadn't he seen that it would be like this two weeks ago, back in London, when it had all started?

He slid back off the rocks to where she was standing, squinting up at him. 'Ten minutes more,' he said, 'then we're over the top.' She looked like she hadn't heard him. He repeated it, then wondered whether he should try to say something encouraging to her. But he didn't have a clue what. He didn't know how to deal with children.

'Where are you taking me?' she asked suddenly. 'Why are we climbing up here? Why are we running away?'

He pointed up to the ridge line. 'There's another valley over there. My car is there. We can use that to get out of here.'

'Your car? I don't want to get into your car.' She took a step back from him, a look of obvious fright on her face, her lip trembling. 'My dad will be back soon,' she said, like it was a threat. 'I want to wait for him. I don't want to go anywhere with you. I don't know who you are.'

He put the gun down and stared at her. He hadn't seen anyone else when he searched, but he was sure they were here, somewhere in this valley. They would know what route he was taking, they would be reacting right now. The time to discuss things was therefore not now. But if she went back down to the house they would kill her. He was sure of that. 'The explosion in your house wasn't gas bottles,' he said. 'It was a device, a bomb. Someone triggered it on purpose, to kill people. That's why we're running.'

She frowned at him. 'A bomb? I don't understand ... to kill who?'

He opened his mouth to tell her, then shut it. He couldn't start on that. He needed her to be in control, not screaming with grief. 'The policeman tried to kill you,' he said. 'You were there. It was you he was shooting at. You *know* that. That's why we're running.'

Her face crinkled up. 'I want to call my mum,' she said, urgently. 'I need to speak to her.'

He shook his head. 'Up there. When we get to the top so we can see this place more clearly, make sure my car is still there. Then we can call her. Not now. Right now we have to keep going because if we don't someone is going to find us and start shooting again. It's not a joke or a game ...'

'I didn't say it was.'

'OK.' He took a breath. 'It's really urgent we get out of this valley. It's like a kill zone. It's making me very nervous. I'm sorry if I'm not explaining things well. I'm not used to dealing with kids ...'

'I'm not a kid. I'm ten.'

'Whatever. If you don't do what I say you'll be a dead ten-year-old. Can you understand that?'

She flinched, then the tears really welled into her eyes. He crouched down, so that she was actually taller than him. 'It's true,' he said. 'There are men here who want to kill you ...'

40

'Why? I don't understand … Why is this happening?' She started sobbing badly, her chest heaving.

'I don't know,' he said. 'But I need you to trust me. I'm not going to hurt you. I'm trying to protect you. You have seen already that that is what I'm doing. I stopped that man from killing you. I promise you that that is all I will do – I will protect you. I promise. Now can we get going? We can talk about it when we're out of here.'

He didn't know what else to say. Was he meant to reach out a hand, touch her? How did you reassure a ten-year-old? He had no idea. He shouldered the gun, turned his back on her and set off. He was thinking: *Go. Run. Run back down the hill and wait for your dead dad.* She *wanted* to run from him. He had seen it in her eyes. He wished she would.

What was he doing here? What on earth did he think he was doing? It was absurd. He had stood beside her and watched himself doing it – *offering to protect her.* That was what he had just done. He was fucking insane. She was nothing to do with him, not his problem. He had done his bit already to save her life – he had moved the sights off her, staked his life. He had acted instinctively, without considering anything. Up to this point. But now he saw he should have left it there. She wasn't any longer his problem. If she turned now and ran he would be relieved. Then he could really speed up, get out of this situation. He widened his stride a little, hurrying over some flatter ground, not looking back. Maybe if he went fast enough she would get the idea.

He went right to the summit without looking back. When he finally paused, almost ten minutes later, she was close behind him, struggling to keep up, tears still running down her cheeks. He breathed hard. Too late, he thought. He had made the choice when she was within his sights, now he was going to have to deal with the consequences. *All the consequences.* He was just beginning to comprehend what they might be.

'Now can I call my mum?' she asked him. He pretended he hadn't heard.

He got behind a narrow ridge of rock running along the top and told her to get down beside him. Then he got out the spotting scope and crept forward.

'You promised I could call my mum,' she insisted from behind him.

He held up a hand to her, then looked down the reverse slope. No obvious movement. He put the scope to his eye and searched the hillside down to the dirt track, then the parking area beyond that. His car was still there, by itself, as he had left it, about a kilometre away. The place was marked on the map as a beauty spot. The valley over this side offered less cover, looked drier, but with more impressive cliffs and escarpments to catch the eye. His eyes followed the snaking tourist route back down to the little village about five kilometres distant and could see no traffic at all on the road. The road was a dead end below him, finishing without warning a few hundred metres after the parking space.

He moved back and turned to her. She was about five metres away, kneeling down. He saw her fumbling quickly to put something in her pocket and immediately realised that she would have a phone of her own, of course. All kids did these days, no doubt. She didn't want him to know she had it because she didn't trust him. 'Have you got a signal?' he asked her. She looked startled, then guilty. She was still quietly sobbing to herself. He sat up and got his own mobile out, switched it on, waited for it to boot, then waited for a signal. There was none. They had taken down the masts covering the area, he decided. Probably the fixed line too, if there was one. That partly accounted for the absence of response to the explosion. They must have done it while he was lying there, waiting, during the morning – planted some small timed device to do some specific damage. Perhaps that was what the guy on the opposite ridge had been up to. There was a mast up there – he could see it now, still intact across the other side of the valley. Or maybe they arranged it with the service provider, paid to have it cut on some computer system. That was possible, though more risky, unless you knew people clever enough to hack in and do it remotely.

'I have no signal,' he said to her. 'What about you?'

She shook her head, then sat back in the grass and started chewing her lip. She was getting more and more agitated. She wanted to speak to her mother. He understood that. But her mother was dead. He needed to work out a way to deal with that. He needed to tell her. But not yet. That news would slow them down, take some dealing with, and he didn't know how to do that. The first priority had to be to get out of this area, change cars, get lost in a higher density population area. Then get out of Spain.

At least, *he* had to do that. He still had to work out what to do with her. He had promised her protection. But how could he achieve that? So far he had given it no thought at all. She would have relatives here, or even in England, maybe, but they wouldn't be able to protect her without using the police, and the police here, at least, were in on it. That had just been demonstrated in the most effective way imaginable. Official assistance was out of the question. Whoever he was up against, it was just him and the girl as long as he was in Spain.

The only sure solution would be to trace the contract, find out who wanted her dead, then do something about it, and he would need to be in London for that. All his resources were there, including the connections within his brother's world. And Viktor himself – he would know what to do, maybe, or at least he would help. He could help extract him from this mess too, of course – set up a charter so they didn't need to go near a public airport. But Carl would have to consider all those options when he was capable of clearer thought. Right now things were out of control.

He switched his phone off. He would have to tell her to do the same. If Jones had resources enough to take down part of the communications network then they might have the capability to trace her mobile and pinpoint her via triangulation of the signal reception at two or more masts, once everything was switched back on, or once they passed into an unaffected area – maybe as soon as they got into the next valley. If you had money enough things like that were possible. He knew because he'd arranged it once in the past, though not in Spain.

'My dad will be coming soon,' she said again, looking back in the direction they had come. He pushed himself a little closer to her and started to pack the spotting scope away. 'Come here,' he said, trying to talk gently. 'I want to show you where we are going.' She didn't move. 'I can see my car over there,' he said. 'It's still there, about a kilometre away. I can't see anyone over there, so we will be safe. We'll run to it, get there as quick as we can, get out of here. OK?'

She shook her head. 'My dad will be coming back to the house,' she said again. 'I should go down there, wait for him.'

'So why did you follow me up here? I didn't force you. I'm not forcing you now. You can do what you want.'

She started to cry again, then wouldn't look at him. 'I'm frightened,' she said. 'Because the policeman was shooting at me ... because you say they were trying to kill me ...'

'I'm frightened too,' he said. 'But that's OK. Fear can keep you alive sometimes. Sometimes you need it.'

'I need to speak to my mum,' she said. 'I need to ask her what to do ...'

He sighed. He would have to lie to her, he decided. That was the quickest way.

'Your mum and your dad won't be coming back to that house,' he said. 'Not at the moment. Not with this all going on.'

'How do you know?'

He stood up, shouldered the pack, turned his face from her. He didn't want her to see his eyes as he spoke. 'Your parents hired me,' he said. 'They paid me to protect you.' The lie made him shudder slightly. He didn't like lying. Despite everything, he didn't like it.

She didn't respond so he had to turn to look at her. She was frowning very hard, obviously sceptical. 'My name is Carl,' he said. 'You can call me Carl.'

'They hired you?'

'Your name is Rebecca Martin, right?'

She nodded. He registered the surprise that he knew her name.

'Your parents must be in some kind of trouble, Rebecca. I don't know what. But they paid me to protect you. That's what I do. That's why I was here today. They must have known something was going to happen.'

She shook her head. 'My mum would have told me.'

He shrugged. 'Send your mum a text now. Tell her who I am, ask her if it's true. We will probably get a signal as we head to the car. As soon as it's back up your phone will send the message. Then you can wait to see what she says, or speak to her. But right now you have to decide whether you're coming with me or not. Your choice.'

9

She chose to come with him. He waited nervously, gun ready, constantly scanning the slope behind them, while she composed a text message he knew her mother would never get. They crouched within the broken rocks as she flashed her fingers over the touchscreen, very fast. If he stood up he could see right back down the valley to the house near where the school bus had dropped her, see a few cars winding along the surfaced road there. But no one seemed bothered about the slowly dispersing pall of smoke further up the valley. Beyond the hills he could see a faint strip of sea, glimmering in the heat haze. That was where they needed to get to.

They set off when she was done, he jogging as fast as he could through the grass, carrying the gun on his shoulder. They quickly had to slow as the slope got steeper. She kept up easily, either just behind or to the side of him. When they reached the road – another unsurfaced dirt track, this one heavily rutted – he pointed along it and started running in the direction of the parking area, keeping up a brisk pace as the sweat poured off him beneath the hot plastic overalls.

When she asked, he slowed to a walking pace and let her dig out and check her phone for a signal. 'It's dead,' she said. She looked like she would start crying again.

'The people who did that – to your house – may have done something to the phone transmitter masts,' he said. 'Tell me your number and I'll call you now, to test it.' He looked directly at her as he said it, expecting her to resist that, but she told him the number straight away, forgetting her previous caution. He switched on his phone and put the number in, made as if he was trying to call her, then told her his wasn't working either. 'You can try again when we get to the car,' he said. 'But switch it off now, just in case.' It would be better to get rid of her phone, and his own. Change phones, change cars, change clothes, as quickly as he could.

'In case of what?' she asked.

'You can trace where someone is by using their mobile. We don't want them to do that.'

'You mean the people trying to kill me?'

'Yes. What did your mother do? I mean, who does she work for?'

'She has an ice cream shop,' she said, reluctantly.

'Has she always done that?'

'Yes.'

'And your dad?'

'He helps her. Why?'

'So I can try and work out what's going on. Ice cream? That's it?'

'Yes.'

There would be something else, something in the past. Or was the contract a mistake? That could happen.

'If I switch my phone off the text won't send,' she said. 'You said I could—'

He held a hand up to silence her. He had heard something, up ahead. A car or a truck? He tried to focus on it, work out its position. He couldn't see it because now they were actually in the trough of the valley, with a small stream off to their left and steep slopes to either side. The parking area was over the next lip of land, on a kind of flattened escarpment.

'It's a car,' she said. 'Someone is coming up the road, ahead of us, coming this way.' She was standing very close to him. He could hear the fear in her voice.

'It's a tourist spot,' he said. 'It's no problem.'

'It might be *them* though.'

He considered it, brought the gun off his shoulder and automatically checked it. She watched him, moving rapidly from one leg to the next like she needed to pee. Maybe she did. He hadn't thought of that.

'Just keep going and don't worry,' he said. 'Nothing bad will happen to you. You have my word.'

He started off again, moving quicker. It was a car, he thought, just as she'd said. It was travelling at a normal speed, in no hurry. The sound drifted away and came back as it negotiated the bends in the valley road below. He thought it might still be over a kilometre away. All the same, he started to run properly, glancing behind every now and then to check she was with him, but there was no danger there. She looked scared enough to go twice the speed.

Within a hundred metres the land started to fall away and parts of the road far below came into view, masked in stands of pine trees. But not the car. It was closer than he thought.

They came over the lip of land behind the parking area and he saw his car waiting there – the one Jones had hired for him. They were about seventy metres from it. He had miscalculated though. As they came into view a car was already turning into the parking area – a black Audi SUV. It braked sharply. Whoever it was had seen them, or seen his car, and reacted. He glanced back, checking her position, considering ducking to the side, where there were rocks and bushes, but it was too late for that.

'Shit,' he said. He had a feeling about it. He stopped running.

'What is it?' she asked. She was almost shouting. He felt her catch hold of his arm.

48

The front doors opened. It had stopped beneath two lone, windswept pines flanking the entrance to the parking area, blocking the road out. In between there were big wooden picnic tables and a toilet block in tasteful logs. The view behind was breathtaking – a vast scenic prospect where the valley opened out in steep cliffs, leaving a view as far as the coast. The Mediterranean was a shimmering, beckoning line of washed-out blue. Beyond it, in the far distance he could see the snow-capped peaks of the mountains across the other side of the Mediterranean, in Africa. But there was no one here to take it in – the only people in the picnic area were himself, the girl and the people in the Audi. 'Let go of my arm,' he said quietly. 'I need to be able to move it. Stand a little behind me.' She moved quickly behind him.

Two men got out. That was all of them, he judged, though he couldn't see clearly into the rear. He put the distance at seventy-five metres. There was hardly any wind, though at this range, with this gun, wind was irrelevant. He watched to see what they would do. One was possibly the guy from the ridge opposite, though he couldn't be sure – he was dressed in the same light-coloured clothing, quite short, with cropped blond hair. The other – bigger, with a leather jacket on – he definitely hadn't seen before. They could be police. They looked like police. They were looking over at him, but not doing anything. The one in light-coloured clothing started stretching, like he had just got out after a long journey. He had been the driver. The other, obscured by the front of the Audi, was doing something in the open door, bent over. Tying his laces?

'Maybe they're just tourists,' Carl said to Rebecca. The one in light clothing wasn't even looking at him now. He'd gone back to the open driver's door and was leaning in. Carl could hear them talking to each other but couldn't make out the words. 'Can you hear them?' he asked her. She was ten – her hearing would be better than his. 'Can you hear what language they're speaking? Or what they're saying?'

'I can't hear anything,' she whispered, from right behind him.

'OK. Let's keep walking towards my car.' He couldn't think of what else to do. 'You keep a bit behind me.'

They walked at a normal speed, resisting the urge to make a dash, Carl keeping both hands on the gun. He had closed the distance to about sixty metres when it started to happen.

The one in leather came from behind the door and leaned across the bonnet of the Audi. The girl shrieked, really loud. There was a fraction of a second when Carl didn't get it, before he saw the guy had a pistol pointed at them. Immediately, he thought that they must be police, that they were now going to shout at him to freeze, or get on the ground – and what would he do then? But he didn't have time to work that out because the man started firing. He had a shot off before Carl was even reacting.

Carl dropped a knee to the gravel, brought the gun round. As he started fitting the stock to his shoulder the one in light clothes started firing as well. He wanted to tell the girl to get down flat, but didn't have time. A part of his head catalogued the details as the adrenalin kicked at his system – the reports and the size of the weapons – the positions of the shooters, the distance. Everything was streaming at him, very fast. They were shooting small calibre pistols, almost impossible to control at that range. The one in light clothing was actually running at them as he fired. The leather jacket was bracing his weapon on the car, but only with one hand. So no need to duck and panic, no need to hide. It was in the hands of fate. Just take it calmly, slowly, deliberately. The chances were that they would empty their little guns without hitting a thing.

He had time to tell himself that, very clearly, as he counted off the rounds. Two now from the leather jacket. As the gun

50

recoiled the third time Carl had the rifle up and the sight to his eye. Two from the other, and counting. Five bullets, all fired off in under two seconds. He wasn't aware of the rounds striking anywhere near them.

He tracked right, got the cross hairs onto the moving guy and fired. Then moved the rifle off to the side, eyeball on the guy as he went down, picked up off his feet like an invisible block had hit him. He worked the bolt smoothly, three rounds left, felt the top one shift and snap into position, gun straight back up to his eye. Two more shots from the one behind the car, then Carl had the sight on him. He was standing, turning. He was going to run. Carl squeezed without taking a breath, knew at once the shot was solid. The guy disappeared from sight.

Just like that. Silence.

It had taken about five seconds from start to finish, he thought. Maybe slightly more. He stood up, looked behind for the girl. She was flat out on her stomach, staring at the Audi. 'You hit?' he asked. But her eyes were screwed shut, her face rigid. Had she even heard him? 'Wait there,' he shouted. He would get back to her.

He ran over to the one in light clothing, looked down at him. He was still alive, though hardly moving, lying on his back, one leg bent beneath his body at a very awkward angle. The chest was going rapidly up and down. His eyes were open, blood pulsing out from between his lips. The round had gone through the chest, in one side and out the other. There was a lot of blood gathering in the dust around him. Carl wasn't sure he could see anything, or hear, but he had questions for him.

He moved more carefully behind the Audi to find the other one, chambering another round from that magazine before doing so, letting the spent casing eject onto the ground to cool. He held the gun up to his shoulder and came round the back of the car in a crouch, ready to fire, but the body was just lying

51

there. The shot had gone through the back of the head. In at the base of the skull, out through the top, just above the forehead. The exit wound was not survivable, under any circumstances.

Carl stared at it for a moment, trying to link the gentle squeezing action of his finger on the trigger to this consequence. Then he bent beside the corpse, the thin latex gloves still on, and went through the pockets of the man's trousers and jacket. Every now and then a leg would jerk. When it happened Carl paused, but didn't feel anything for the person. No thoughts about his lost past or history, or none that he couldn't just push away. The leg spasms didn't mean he was alive, but he checked anyway for a pulse. There wasn't one. There was a wallet with cash and a few credit cards. The name was Arturo Flores. Aside from that, no ID of any sort. Carl doubted it was his real name.

He went quickly back to the other, recovering the shell case on the way, noticing that Rebecca was standing now, but still where he had left her. 'Are they hurt?' she shouted out to him, her voice wavering wildly. He looked down at the one who had been alive. He was still staring up at the sky. He looked very young, almost like a little boy. Carl couldn't tell whether he was alive or not.

He bent down and spoke to him. 'I can get you help,' he said. His voice sounded unreal, high-pitched. 'You'll be OK.' A bubble formed in the blood at the man's lips. He was still breathing, just – the eyes didn't change focus though, didn't blink. One of the hands started trembling. The pool of blood was still growing. Carl decided he wasn't going to last long enough to say anything. He searched him carefully, trying to keep the blood off himself. This one didn't even have a wallet. He could search the Audi for ID, but didn't want to touch anything in there. It was bad enough what he was doing now. And time was against him.

He turned away from the man and walked over to Rebecca.

'Are they hurt?' she asked again. She sounded terrified. He nodded, scanning the ground for the first case he had ejected. He found it, picked it up. The nearest would be dead soon, he thought. He would just leave him to bleed out. 'Nothing to worry about,' he said, trying hard to keep his voice steady. He was wound tight, all his muscles bunched with stress and adrenalin, his eyes super-dilated, his heart pounding like a drum. He made an effort, took a deep breath, then reached a hand out and touched the top of her head, very gently. 'You're OK,' he said. 'You're safe.'

10

It didn't hurt to confuse things, so Carl took the right hand of the one behind the Audi, and pressed his fingers all over the rifle. Then he put the rifle carefully on the back seat of the Audi, made sure it was in neutral and released the handbrake. The car was on the edge of the slope leading into the car park, blocking the entrance, and a short push was all that was required to get it rolling backwards. The dead man was lying behind it, a little further back, so the car rolled over him with a couple of bumps, paused, then careered back down the dirt track to come to a halt about twenty metres lower, off the road, rear end in a clump of bushes with the front facing the valley below.

Rebecca was sitting in the front of his own car, shivering and shaking, barely able to speak. He worked very quickly, not only to exit the scene, but to get back to her. Way off in the distance he could hear sirens now, many of them, though it was hard to tell where the sound was coming from.

He took the gun from the other one, the one he had left still alive, though by the time he'd moved the car the position there had changed and the haemorrhaging had done its work. The gun was lying on the ground and he found two clips in a side pocket of the crumpled, bloody jacket. One of them was sticky with blood, so he left it. The weapon was a Sig Sauer 1911-22, a lightweight common handgun that Carl was familiar with. He spoke to the guy again as he went through the pockets to remove the ammunition. The eyes were still open, so it didn't seem totally mad to say things to him. Carl wondered if he had kids. He looked too young.

When he got back in the car Rebecca stared at him like she was about to start screaming. He said some reassuring things – or what he thought might fit that bill – then he drove carefully past the dead body blocking the entrance, talking to her to distract her, making sure the wheels didn't contact.

Five minutes later they were approaching the little village he had seen from higher up when he heard her phone beep. He'd forgotten it was still on. 'Did you hear that?' he asked her. She was sitting ramrod straight, glaring out of the window, her face looking blanched. He wasn't sure she had heard the beep. 'That's your phone,' he said. 'You've got a signal.' She pulled the phone out and looked at it. The text would have been sent, he assumed. She would want to call her mother now. 'Do it,' he said.

She called and, predictably, got a message that the phone wasn't operational at that moment. Her mother's phone would be somewhere near her dead mother, in the house. If it was still working, which he doubted, then it was likely it would still have no cover. They had a signal now because they had moved into the range of a different mast. 'It doesn't matter,' he said. 'You've sent her the text. She will reply if she can.'

She didn't reply. She was in a stranger's car. She had just seen him shoot three people. She would be terrified, no doubt about that, even if she knew, at some level, that those men had been trying to kill her. He had to change the situation, reassure her.

He pulled the car over when they were still half a kilometre from the village. 'I have to make a call too,' he said. 'You can try your mother again.' He got out and walked a little away, then quickly got her number up and composed a text to her. *Rebecca. I have had to change phones. I'm OK. I got your message but don't use that number any more. I will explain everything when I see you. Don't worry. You can trust Carl. He will protect you until I can get to you. Give me two days.* He looked at it, trying to work out if it was too much or too little. He wanted to sign it off 'mum' or 'mamma', or do an 'x', but wasn't sure how her mother would do that, so left it out. It couldn't be from anyone else. He thought for a moment about her crying, then added, *I love you. Everything will be fine.* He sent it.

Back in the car he asked her if she had reached her mum. She shook her head and started crying uncontrollably. She was sitting pressed up against the window, as far away from him as possible. 'You can get out if you want,' he said. 'I'm not stopping you.' She pulled at the door handle immediately but it was locked. She started to shout something at him, becoming frantic in an instant, but he quickly pressed the button to release the lock. 'It's automatic,' he said. 'It locks itself. It's open now.' She was out at once, door swinging wide. She ran to the other side of the road and stood there, panting, looking back at him as if she thought he might get out the little gun and shoot her.

He leaned across the passenger seat and closed the door, started the engine. He counted slowly to ten, then put it in gear. She was still standing there. *I will have to leave her*, he thought. *It's her choice.* But he didn't want to now. If he left her he was certain she would be dead within twenty-four hours. He didn't want her to die. She was his responsibility. Because he had done this, brought this situation about. If she died then he had killed three people for nothing.

But he couldn't force her to come either. He started the car rolling, saw she was looking down at her phone. He slowed, stopped, lowered the windows. In the wing mirror he saw her running towards the car, heard her shouting for him to wait. She got to the door and looked in through the open window.

'She had to change phones,' she said, breathless, voice really high-pitched. 'That's why I couldn't get her.'

'OK,' he said.

She opened the door and got in. 'She says I'm to stay with you.'

She had to change phones, she said, breath, voice really high-pitched. That's what so-and-so her.

He said

He opened the door and the way I think they with you

11

The shop was so busy Julia was going to have to turn people out to get away on time. It was typical – slack all morning, and now a rush. She'd forgotten about the delivery too. A new freezer unit that had been on order for weeks. There were two guys manhandling it through the rear service doors now, as she stood watching them. She'd had to leave the teenager serving out front.

The shop/ice cream parlour – selling 'speciality ice cream' made mostly by Julia herself from frozen yogurt – was right on the beachfront road, the pedestrianised lane that ran along the embankment wall from the tip of Marbella old town, as far as the marina. It was hers – or at least the long lease on the place was. She had used all of her money, none of Juan's, kept it separate, got a lawyer involved. Juan had resented that, at the time – they had been about to get married, after all – but she had just weathered that storm, waited for him to forget it. Now he worked about as much as her in the place and she assumed that gave him some rights, given their legal status. She had never checked, but maybe she should.

She was almost certain he was having an affair with a young waitress she had employed until about a month ago. If true it wouldn't be the first time in their marriage. The third, in fact, and each time she had confronted him he had reacted the same – he had been crestfallen, seized with panic that she would leave him or tell Rebecca, crippled with guilt and full of apologies and promises. He insisted, of course, that it meant nothing. Maybe she believed that the first time.

She shouted out some instructions to the delivery guys, to stop them taking half the wall away as they came through, then walked back through to the front to check. There was still a queue but it was getting smaller. The girl was doing OK. Beyond the open doors she could see the sun, bright on the sea. The weather had brightened up mid-afternoon – that was what was doing it – a little heat and it had brought them out.

She walked back to the storeroom and saw they were almost done. She looked in her pocket for her mobile, to check the time, remembered it had died on her and was by the till out front, charging. She needed to call Rebecca, check she was back safe, check Juan had got there, as they had arranged.

As one of the men stripped the protective card and styrofoam from the edges of the unit she switched the phone on. A text message came in straight away, but then the other man was in her face wanting her to sign something, saying she had received the fridge in good working order.

She argued with the men, telling them they needed to plug it in and start it up before she would sign. Whilst they were doing that she walked back through the shop. There were only two customers left. 'Well done, Ester,' she said to the girl. 'Sorry about that.' She nodded a smile at the front customer. Everyone looked happy enough. She looked at her phone, got the text up. It was Rebecca's number. She started to read the message. She frowned. Her heart skipped, the blood drained from her face: *Mum get home qckly scared dont know what to do. Some kind of explosion at the house. OK, but need u to get here phones down so cant get anyone. A policeman dead. He tried to kill me. POLICEMAN TRIED TO SHOOT ME. This man says u r also in danger. Someone trying to kill us, he says. He thinks thats wot explsn was. knows my name, says here to help me. Carl. Says u have paid him to protect me. On hill. Will try to wait. He says I need to come with in his car. He saved my life. Call me back. Quick.*

She threw the bunch of keys at the girl as she was running out. The shop suddenly didn't matter – she had to get to the car, get up the valley.

She tried desperately to call Rebecca as she ran. But her phone was off, or disconnected. She composed a quick, clumsy message telling her she was on her way, then got to the car and tried to concentrate on getting up there as fast as possible.

The fear was screaming in her skull all the way up through the town, then out onto the twisting, terrible road home. She kept the phone lying on the seat beside her whilst she kept her eyes on the road. She used the voice recognition to shout at the thing to call Rebecca without having to stop. But there was only ever the same dead voice telling her Rebecca was unreachable. She got the same message when she tried Juan. She wanted to send texts to both of them, but driving was the priority. She wanted to call the police too, but the message itself stopped her each time she started – she had to try to work out what the message meant. She couldn't get her head round it. *A policeman had tried to shoot her???* Was that a mistake? She had to get up there, see what Rebecca meant for herself.

The drive took half an hour, if there were no tractors or tourists, forty-five minutes during the rush hours, when the routes out of Marbella were blocked. She cursed again and again that she had ever bought a place out in the hills.

It had been cheap, spacious, isolated, and back then isolation was what she thought she had needed most of all to be safe. But that was a stupid idea, and she had known it was stupid for many years now. Isolation hadn't kept her hidden, it had merely left her exposed without help and witnesses. Michael Rugojev had found her here a year ago, his assistant turning up at the shop out of the blue. She should have done something then, moved house, sold the shop, moved countries, but she had trusted him, trusted the promises he had given. So here she was.

She told herself it would be OK all the way up. Rebecca was clever, she had been told how to protect herself, taught caution. She would do what she had to.

But when the phone signal went down she started to really panic inside. Cars passed her coming back the other way and she had to slow to check who was in them. Was it anyone she recognised, with Rebecca bundled into the back, out of sight? She knew no one called Carl. She remembered again the most prominent part of the message. Rebecca had written it in caps, shouting it. *A policeman had tried to kill her?* Maybe someone *dressed* as a policeman, or who looked like police. It had to be that. An error. But someone had *shot* at her. Julia went into a kind of frozen stupor thinking about it, unable to process the information in any useful way.

As she got past the Ramirez place she saw smoke hanging in the valley, in the distance, and felt the shock kick at her heart. Was that from her house? Now she had to call the police, regardless of the message – she would have to *assume* Rebecca had made a mistake. But then she saw a yellow ambulance and a red fire brigade truck crawling up the road ahead, saw a police car with lights flashing just behind them. The police were already onto it.

The road was a one lane dirt track, barely maintained by the local council. It was just under two kilometres from where it turned off at the Ramirez house to their place. She knew the ruts and potholes well and was driving furiously, so that she quickly caught up with the trailing police car, but there was no room to pass. The passenger in the police car kept waving to her out of his window – trying to signal that she should stop or turn back.

As they came to the last stretch of straight road she saw the house in the valley below and went numb with fear. It looked like the roof was completely destroyed. Both the fire truck and the ambulance had turned down the short lane to the front of the building. She could see there were already at least three cars there, on the flat parking area outside the front door, one another marked police car. She was going to drive straight down there, join them. But the police car she was following stopped abruptly in front of her, by the little olive trees at the bend, blocking her way. She braked to a halt and was already out and looking to run round it, her engine left on, door wide open, when one of them got out of the passenger side and moved to block her with hands in the air.

'I live here,' she shouted at him in Spanish, trying to push past, desperate. 'It's my home. I have to get to my daughter …' She dodged low to go round him but he dropped an arm across her chest and caught hold of her arm. 'You can't go down there,' he said firmly. 'It doesn't matter who you are. It's dangerous …'

'My daughter is down there. I have to get to her.'

'Calm down and I will call my boss to speak to you. You can't go down there.'

She stepped back. She felt like hitting him, but that wasn't going to work. She thought she might be able to twist away from him, duck under his arm, head down the valley side and run through the trees, but then the other one – the driver – appeared, shutting down the space between them and the car. She began to plead with the one holding her, telling him again and again about Rebecca, then started to shout for Rebecca at the top of her voice. The other was on his radio. She heard something about someone being killed. 'Who has been killed?'

she yelled, voice becoming hysterical. 'I live here. You need to tell me. This is my house.'

She couldn't get her eyes off it. It didn't look like the place she lived in. She had an unreal sensation of being somewhere else. Walls were caved in, smoke coming through the roof. There were firemen moving in through the holes. For some reason she didn't notice the half-buried car until they started to break its windscreen. She put her hand to her mouth. She thought it could be Juan's car. Was he in it, was he the one who had been killed? She took a huge breath, feeling a premonition of something terrible, something truly terrible, coming right at her.

12

More police cars appeared from the road behind her, then a woman officer took hold of her arm and the others walked off. The woman started asking questions in an aggressive voice but she couldn't answer any of them, could barely understand them, because all she could think about was Rebecca.

Rebecca was somewhere here and they weren't letting her get to her. She gave the woman her ID, got her phone out to check for a signal, only to have it promptly snatched from her grip. She started to protest hysterically – the phone was her last link to Rebecca. But no one was listening.

Because of the position of the police cars she couldn't see the body on the ground or the group of people around it until the woman moved her forward. It was lying in the road almost exactly in the middle of the turn-off down to the house. There were two police officers in uniform crouched beside it, someone in ordinary clothes standing a little further away. She couldn't see it properly, only that it was an adult, too large for Rebecca. It looked like a policeman – she could see the uniform. But if it was the man Rebecca had texted about then she assumed it wasn't a policeman. Because why would a policeman try to shoot her daughter?

When the guy in charge appeared she started shouting at him, angrily, repeating over and over again that she was the girl's mother so she had to be allowed to be with her and to use her mobile phone. 'It's my ten-year-old daughter Rebecca. She's down there somewhere. I know she's here.'

'There is no little girl here,' he said. He looked tired and irritated. 'Your daughter is not here.'

She forced herself to stand still in front of him, to look at him, to deal with him. 'Who are you?' she demanded. 'Do you have ID?'

'Diego Molina,' he said, but he didn't offer any ID as he turned hers over in his hand, scrutinising it as if it might be fake. He had her mobile in his other hand. 'I'm an inspector.' His face came into focus. He pocketed the phone and ID, held out his hand for her to shake. She ignored it, but he barely noticed. 'I'm in charge here,' he said. 'You are Julia Martin? This is your house?' He looked too young to be in charge of anything – thirty at most, clean-shaven, pretty features, unusually blond, wearing a pastel-blue open-necked shirt and off-white slacks, as if about to enjoy an evening in town, before this had struck. A beautiful lock of hair dangled over his forehead. He smelled strongly of aftershave.

'This is my house, yes. Are you saying my daughter isn't in the house, or *anywhere* here?'

'No. There is no little girl here. Or anywhere near. Why do you think she would be here?'

'She texted me. She told me she was here, only twenty minutes ago. She said she was on the hill, waiting.' She was on the verge of reporting other things Rebecca had texted, but simple caution stopped her. What if the dead man, lying there, really was a policeman? She had a sudden thought that she should have erased Rebecca's last text, then immediately thought the idea foolish, because surely Rebecca had made a mistake. In any case this man would need her access code before he could read the text. He hadn't asked for that. Not yet.

'OK. Then we will search again,' he said. He motioned back to a man she saw was standing just behind him, also in ordinary civilian clothes, who nodded and started speaking softly into a handheld radio. 'But not in this immediate area,' Molina added. 'We've already searched the house and grounds for survivors. We're waiting for the helicopter now. It's on its way from Malaga. It has specialist search capabilities. It will quickly cover these hills – better than we can on foot alone. Is there anywhere nearby that she would run to, if she was startled?'

'She could be hiding in the garden, or down the slopes there. I think she probably meant the slopes below the house when she said she was on the hill. She knows them, she plays there. You need to let me through, I can look and I can shout for her …'

'You already have shouted. I'm sure she would have heard. I did, very clearly. And we've already been through the property. She's not there. If she's further out we will find her soon enough. She will not come to harm.'

He didn't have a clue. He didn't know what he was up against, what had happened. But she couldn't put him right. She had to keep her mouth shut or she would end up in some cell answering questions about the past instead of free to look for Rebecca. He was meant to be in charge though, so he was the one to work on. He looked honest – the way he looked at her, spoke to her, the way he wasn't bristling with male hormones and the need to stamp his authority all over her – more intelligent than the types she was used to dealing with from the national or local police. When they came to the shop asking to see paperwork she was never sure whether she was meant to bribe them in some way.

He suggested they get into a car and he would take the details he needed, instead of standing out in the open. 'We are not sure it's safe,' he explained. 'There has been an explosion. We thought it could have been an accident – a gas leak, perhaps – but then we found the dead man. He has been shot.' He looked closely at her as he spoke. She struggled to assimilate it, her mind wanting to link it to what Rebecca had texted. She needed to know more, but he was already starting on his questions.

'Did you have anything particularly valuable in your home?'

She shook her head, then said, 'That car – the one buried there – I think it belongs to my husband…'

'Yes. We can talk about that,' he said, and she had a feeling that he was holding something back. She thought, *So Juan is in the car or the house. That must be it.* If he was, she assumed he would be dead, because if he was only injured they would be taking her to him. The thought disrupted her concentration like an awful shadow. She tried to turn away from it. 'I don't want to sit and talk to you,' she said. 'Right now I need to be looking for my child.'

He nodded sympathetically, looked like he was considering that, then said, 'In a short while they will have checked the house and made sure it's safe. But it's only firemen I have in there. They are pursuing ordinary checking procedures, on the basis that burglars set a fire, which ignited something in your home. Maybe they did that deliberately. Is there any reason that assumption might be false? Is there any reason you can think of why I should pull the firemen out, to protect them, then wait for a specialist bomb disposal team to get here?'

She looked straight at him, straight into his eyes, held his gaze and said, 'Why would someone plant a bomb in my home?'

He stared back. 'I don't know. You don't know either?'

'No. I sell ice cream. My husband too. Why would someone want to plant a bomb here?'

He considered that for a while, brows knitted, still looking at her, then looked away and moved a hand up to push the beautiful blond lock away from his forehead. 'OK,' he said, looking at his feet. 'There's something I need you to do for me. I'm sorry, but it's not pleasant and it may involve something tragic for you.' He looked up at her again. 'There are two dead bodies in your home ...' He saw her reactions starting at once. 'Not your daughter. There is no child here, as I told you. We will find your child. But two other people were killed in the blast and I will need you to come in with me and try to identify them.' He took a breath. 'I should warn you – it is possible that one of them is your husband.'

13

She hadn't loved Juan Martin, not ever, not how she understood the word. The only person she had ever loved, as she saw it, was Alex. But love like that – an overwhelming thing that dominated your existence – love like that was useless in the real world. It was like a life on heroin. You couldn't live with it, at least not a normal life.

In the beginning she had shared something different with Juan, something a little like love, a little like friendship, something that had allowed them to lead normal lives – an accommodation with the real world. The shared sentiment had trailed off, without either of them properly noticing, years ago – but they had remained bonded nevertheless, pending a resolution that would now never occur. So his death would be affecting her, she knew, beneath the surface. If it were all that was happening his death would have been a fact close to devastating.

They had taken her in to identify him. They hadn't warned her about the woman he had been with – perhaps because they had wanted to watch her reactions – and it had been an unpleasant surprise to see her body there, in their ruined house, and work out what must have been happening. Juan had come home early with the ex-waitress called Maria. The fact quickly paled into insignificance as the horror of the scene sank in, but it was an additional shock nevertheless, something more she had to absorb and control.

She told them the identity of the woman, though without seeing her face – they hadn't let her see the face – it was really a guess. It was possible it was someone else, she told them. It was possible Juan was seeing more than one woman. She had only glanced at Juan's face, from a distance, and nodded. She hadn't wanted to look at him, lying there like that, so obviously inter-rupted in something, humiliated, naked. She hadn't wanted to let any of it in. She didn't want to collapse crying. So she had flicked her eyes onto him and off, bolted down the thoughts. The desperation caused by Rebecca's absence was constant, her panic reactions so barely suppressed that she felt continually on the edge of an uncontrollable screaming fit.

She had waited now nearly three hours at the house, either in the car Molina placed her in, her own car, or standing around outside as the helicopter clattered overhead. The helicopter had quickly found something – over in the next valley – but it wasn't Rebecca. Two more dead bodies. She wasn't told who they were.

Molina had obviously briefed a couple of the uniformed of-ficers, who were now hanging around the garden and road, to watch that she didn't leave. They seemed unsure whether they should treat her as a suspect or a victim. When Molina wasn't personally occupied with asking her questions, there was always one of them near, ready to tell her to wait, or stay where she was. They had confiscated her phone and then later demanded the access code using some official, legal wording. Was it meant to scare her? She had given the code, hoping that would be it, but then they wouldn't let her leave. She hadn't been formally arrested, and they hadn't searched her, so she wasn't sure what her rights were.

Before the helicopter started she had wanted to run down into the valley, where the stream was, about five hundred metres below the garden wall. She knew Rebecca went for walks down there. There were men she could see searching down there, but she thought Rebecca might be hiding, and wouldn't come out unless she could hear her mother calling for her. But Molina wouldn't let her go near the house again.

At some point they had found Rebecca's school bag, lying at the side of the road. Molina had shown it to her – to identify it – wrapped up in a big brown paper bag with a transparent window. She had wanted to touch it, but that too was forbidden. It was 'evidence'.

They were saying now that it looked like a bomb had been planted in the guest bathroom. It meant someone had got into the house at some point without them knowing, someone who had wanted to kill Juan. Or so Molina was suggesting. Now that she had made Juan's infidelity clear she wondered how long it would be before he arrested her. She had to be a suspect, though presumably it suited him to pretend she wasn't at the moment. They were asking her lots of questions about Juan and his past, but she knew that was the wrong track.

There were three of them who spoke to her – Molina and two sidekicks, one of them the aggressive woman about her own age. Usually they did it in the back of a car, whilst other cars and vans arrived and left all around them, emergency lights flashing interminably. Molina had told her she would have to come to the station in Marbella and answer formal questions, put to her by an investigating judge. They were still waiting for the judge to arrive.

In between questions, she sat in her car, angry and scared, fretting and crying, digging her nails into her palms so much that they bled. The panic was like something alive twisting inside her. She kept telling herself that she was being unreasonable, because by five o'clock there must have been nearly a hundred police officers searching the valley, plus the helicopter. They were doing their best. They were professionals. But she couldn't stand not being a part of it. She wanted to drive out of the valley and try calling Rebecca from somewhere where there was a signal. There was no signal throughout the valley and they were trying to work out why – they thought it was part of the 'attack'. But leaving the scene was out of the question. So all she could do was wait, uselessly, answering their misguided questions while the fear ate at her insides, the constant adrenalin making her shiver like she had a fever.

It was almost six now. Soon the light would be fading. Molina was walking up to the car again, signalling her to get out. She got out and stood in front of him, then listened as he told her that the helicopter was leaving, that her daughter wasn't in the valley or on any of the adjoining hills. 'It has infrared search devices,' he explained. 'It's very easy to find people. She's not here.'

She felt an acid emptiness opening inside her, a different feeling to anything she had ever experienced before, even back in Russia – it was something physical, real, like a heart attack. She had to crouch down and gasp for air. He bent beside her and put a hand on her shoulder, said half-comforting things about finding Rebecca, about the resources available.

'Where is she, then?' she stuttered. 'Where is she, if she's not here?'

'We have to work on the assumption that she's been kidnapped,' he told her. 'By this person she called "Carl".' There was tremendous sympathy in his eyes, but she didn't want it. She wanted to wake up, she wanted this all to go away. She wanted to be sick. She could see a group of plain-clothes officers back down by the body of the shot man. The body was still lying there in front of her driveway. They were taking photos of it now.

'Do you know anyone called Carl?' he asked quietly. 'We have to identify him.'

She shook her head. *Her daughter had been kidnapped.* She

72

felt like she would fall over, black out. She didn't want to believe it.

'You read her text?' she said, then forced herself to look up at him. Her legs were shaking and the bile rising in her throat. He nodded.

'She's confused,' she said. 'She might have got it wrong. She said there was a policeman shooting at her ...'

Molina nodded again. 'I'm assuming the officer was trying to shoot the man she was with, trying to stop him. She made a mistake.'

She frowned, then pointed towards the dead man. 'You mean that man *is* police?' she asked. 'He's a police officer? Rebecca was right?'

'She was right he is a police officer, yes. But he won't have shot at her. He's from the municipal police here. Ricardo Perez. He was only twenty-two years old. We think he tried to save your daughter and was shot. Again, we assume this "Carl" person has killed him.'

She glanced towards the body, in disbelief, then looked back to Molina. He was staring at her, questioningly. Her eyes shifted focus to the house behind him, all the movement and activity, the policemen going in and out. The images moved and rearranged themselves. What she had seen before – all these policemen working to find her daughter – was suddenly in doubt. She knew her daughter, knew how she had brought her up. If Rebecca said that the policeman lying there, on her drive, had tried to shoot her, tried to kill her, and had been stopped by this stranger called Carl, then she had no doubt that that was exactly what had happened.

Now there was a new tension in her muscles, a different kind of fear. *I have to get out of here*, she thought. *I have to get away.* She leaned in a crouch against the ground and tried to make sense of all the options and interpretations. But she couldn't do it. There were too many open questions. *A policeman had tried to kill her?* Until this moment she had thought it could not be true. She started to retch, but there was nothing in her stomach.

'I need to leave,' she muttered. She stood up and faced him. 'I need to go right now.'

He shook his head.

'Am I *under arrest*?' In confusion she used the English phrase.

'It's not like that,' he said. 'If you wanted to leave I would have to detain you – you can be detained as a suspect or witness. But if you don't try to leave then we don't get into all that. I need you to stay because I need your help. It's the quickest way to get Rebecca back.'

Could she trust him? She didn't think so. Now she didn't know *what* was happening. She needed time to think it through. She turned abruptly away from him and got into her car, closed the door with a bang. The car was empty. She pressed the button to wind up the passenger window, shutting herself off from him. He watched her for a moment, looking concerned, then another officer came up to him, said something in his ear. They both walked off quickly.

Up the hill she saw one of the green military vehicles belonging to the guardia civil arriving. It stopped because it couldn't get down any further – there was a queue of vehicles all the way back up the track. A man in military uniform got out and started walking down towards Molina. She had the impression someone of higher rank had arrived. Molina looked bothered as he went up to greet him. They exchanged salutes. The man was tall, older – at least fifty years old. He stood in a way that suggested he was in charge, that Molina was nobody. He leaned over Molina, jabbed a finger into his chest. She half considered opening the door and making a run for it while they were distracted. But at that moment the female officer opened the

74

driver's door and got in. She leaned back and demanded the keys. 'I will drive you to the station,' she said. 'That's where they want you now.'

14

Eight-thirty in the evening. Darkness, finally. Carl stood at the balcony doors of a hotel room reeking of cigarette butts, the dirty net curtains half pulled so he could keep behind them, the twin doors open onto a narrow concrete platform with a metal guardrail. They were on the tenth floor, just off La Plaza de la Constitucion, in La Linea, the last Spanish town before the British colony of Gibraltar. The balcony faced south, giving him a good view across the run-down apartments, parks and roads between there and the border, less than two kilometres away.

To the left the night sky was dominated by the Rock, a four-hundred-metre peak rising sheer out of the flat landscape at the southern tip of Spain. A dense clutter of brightly lit buildings – houses, apartments, hotels – hugged the lower slopes, spreading south and west on the narrow strip of land that skirted the high ground, out to the promontory called Europa Point. Above the buildings the black unlit hump rose steeply to its pointed summit, the slopes forested, the peak crowned with radio masts and warning beacons for any aeroplanes that might somehow mistake the lie of the land. The east side of the thing – the sheer face – was lit with very powerful floodlights, so you could see the cliffs from many kilometres away. The lights cast a diffuse glow against the sky all around, blotting out any real darkness, obscuring stars and cloud alike. To the west, where the town ended, lay the dark waters of a horseshoe bay with the lights and dock cranes of Algeciras at the other side, about ten kilometres away. Beyond the bay was the Strait of Gibraltar, a mere four-teen kilometres of the Med, separating Europe and Africa.

There was a British airstrip just over the flat strip of land that constituted the international border between La Linea and Gibraltar. The single runway, running west–east, cut straight across the only road into the town from Spain. They had to stop the traffic across the border whenever a plane took off or landed. He was hoping to be on one of those planes in just over three hours.

Viktor had arranged – or promised to – a charter flight from a tiny outpost of the UK to a private airstrip somewhere in Kent. Carl had spoken to him about an hour ago and listened to the astounded silence as he had recounted his decision not to shoot the girl. The conversation had been in Finnish, with Rebecca right beside him. It was true to say that thereafter Viktor's main worry hadn't been the girl but what the consequences would be for Carl. He was sure the cartel would want to save face with the contract owner, the person or persons who wanted the girl dead. He still didn't know who that was, but would be working on it full speed.

Discussing the arrangements with Viktor had been his stand-ard practice each and every time over the last ten years, and this job was no different. If something happened, if something went wrong, then at least Viktor knew where he was and what he had been doing. And just in case there were complications, Viktor had always been able to trace the funds and identify the people behind the job. The cartel was meant to guarantee anonymity, but nothing was anonymous these days, not if it was set up through a computer system of some kind. Usually they were people Viktor knew well, people Carl had even met, very wealthy people who had got to where they were via these kinds of techniques; Russians, one and all – no surprise there.

But unravelling the electronic trail hadn't proved so easy with this one, and now everything was urgent.

There wasn't much Viktor could do to smooth things at the border between Spain and Gibraltar, which meant Carl was still going to have to show a passport, still work out some way to get the girl across either just with her ID card, or without showing anything at all. His preferred option would be to put her in the boot of the car, but she would have to consent to that. She had relaxed a little since the fake message from her mother, but maybe she would draw the line there. He was thinking about alternatives.

The car Jones had hired was in a side road off Plaza de la Constitucion and that was the actual reason they were in this shabby room. Besides keeping an eye on the crossing point itself, he wanted to watch the car while the clock ticked over. He had no intention of taking that car across the line – he would find another from somewhere when they went out – but he wanted to see if it attracted any attention. He needed to gauge how much the local police knew about him. Did they know he had that car, for example? If they did it would reveal something about how Jones was working, how deep his support in the ranks of local law enforcement.

But in the two hours he had been watching no one had come near it. There were police down on the streets, but it didn't seem as if there were more than might be usual. La Linea – aside from a few half-built condos near the waterfront – had the feel of a town that had thrived for too long on drug, cigarette, alcohol and petrol smuggling, then had to do without even that, because of the economic crisis – so the police presence was constantly visible, mostly patrol cars. But over at the roads leading to the crossing point Carl could see no unusual activity. He had used the spotting scope to check.

He had got rid of the overalls and anything surplus to

requirements in woods off one of the back roads on the way here – not an ideal solution, but it would do. He still had the backpack with the pistol and ammo, his spotting scope, the GPS satnav he had brought with him from the UK, a hunting knife, the phone and the basic rations he had put together the day before, most of which had now been eaten by Rebecca. He was keen to get rid of the phone, but needed a replacement and hadn't found a suitable shop yet. He had her phone in the pack too, the SIM card removed. She had agreed to give it to him 'temporarily', to make sure nobody traced her.

Right now she was sitting on a chair about two metres behind him, watching him watch the street. Earlier she had talked a lot, but now it was more of a shocked silence. She had cried too, though less than he would have expected. He had tried to ask her questions about herself, her family, her mother, their past, trying to tease away at any information that might help solve the big question – why someone wanted her dead – but also to keep her mind from fretting about things, to stop her asking questions about the dead people.

She had told him the policeman at the house was the first dead person she had ever seen. She had those images in her head now: bullets striking bodies, dead people, head wounds. Whilst she was in danger the images weren't important – he knew exactly how it worked – but now the adrenalin was wearing off, the images would get a life of their own, along with the thoughts surrounding them. They would grow quickly into little mental malignancies if she didn't keep her mind off it until everything was more secure. He had no idea when that was going to be.

There was a TV in the room but she hadn't wanted to watch it – too nervous, she said. He had wanted to scan the news channels to see if there was any kind of big search for her going on, complete with photos, but he didn't want to do that with her in the room. And there was no way he could let her out alone, though at one point she had asked if she could go out and buy a Coca-Cola.

'Did you always do this?' she asked him now. 'Protect people?'

He felt the hairs on his neck prickle. There was a hint of sarcasm in her question, he suspected, because she had already made a remark about him being so good at 'this', meaning shooting people. To which he had curtly pointed out that there hadn't been much choice – he had killed to protect her.

He picked up the spotting scope and braced it against the door frame, used the integral low magnification finderscope to find the car and then scanned very slowly along the cars parked facing it on the same street, checking through the windscreens to see if there were people watching it.

She had asked almost as many questions about him as he had about her. He didn't mind answering, for the same reason – it kept her thoughts occupied. He lied where necessary, but that wasn't easy. He didn't like lying. 'I used to be in the army,' he said.

'Is that what you always wanted to do,' she asked, 'go in the army?'

'No.' He started on the square below them, checking each car in turn. 'My father was in the army. He was an army nurse. So I wanted to be a doctor when I was your age.'

'Because your dad was a doctor?'

'Because he was a nurse.'

'I thought only women were nurses.'

He could see nothing on the square. He switched to the border area, again just using the finderscope, to see if there was any increased activity. 'It used to be like that,' he said. 'But not any more.'

'So why aren't you a doctor?'

'Because I'm stupid.' He took the scope off his eye and

winked at her. 'Too stupid for that, anyway. I didn't study hard enough. Take note.'

'My mum is always telling me to study more.'

'She's right. What about your dad? What does he say?' He'd noted that all her contact worries so far had been centred on her mother.

'Yeah,' she said. 'He says the same.' It sounded like she didn't want to talk about him.

There was a steady queue of cars on both sides of the border post, plus a line of pedestrians nearer the buildings where they were doing passport checks. That was an option too – to simply walk over. 'And what will you do – when you're older?' he asked. He was running out of harmless things to ask her.

'I don't know,' she said.

'Too soon to choose. You're right.'

'I wanted to be a vet for a long time. Nearly all my life, in fact.' She said it like she was three times her age. 'We had a few ponies and I used to look after them. But they all died. Then I wanted to be an artist.'

'You good at drawing?'

She didn't answer, so he had to look back at her, check she was OK. She was frowning hard. 'My dad isn't really my dad,' she said, out of the blue.

He raised an eyebrow, considered why she might say that, now, to him. Nothing sprang to mind. But it might be important information. 'You just find that out?' he asked.

'No. I've always known. My mum married him after I was born. He's always been my dad. But not my real dad.'

Well, he's dead now, he thought, with that heavy feeling in his gut again. 'You like him?' he asked. He *wanted* to ask who her real dad was – that too might be important information – but maybe that would upset her too much.

She shrugged. 'Not much. Not at the moment.'

'What does he do?'

'I told you already. He helps my mum.'

'Did he always do that?'

She sat in silence, her lip stuck out a bit, her legs folded under her on the chair. He asked her again: 'Did your dad always do that – help your mum?'

'He plays guitar as well. He was in a band. But he's not my dad. I told you that. I don't know who my real dad is.'

That was that, then. He went back to the scope, counted the police up near the crossing. There seemed to be uniformed police in the post itself – a building with a flat concrete awning spanning the roads, with booths for cars to pull up to and hand their passports through the usual windows. That was on the Spanish side. There were similar structures a little further on, on the British side. Then a short stretch of road before the airport runway cut across, with barriers and lights for when they needed to close it. That had happened once in the last two hours.

He looked back at her and saw she was beginning to brood again. 'Look,' he said. 'You're going to be OK.' He wished it were true. But sooner or later the truth about today was going to sink her. She shrugged her shoulders, didn't look at him.

'It doesn't matter if he isn't your real dad,' he tried. 'My dad died when I was your age. I hardly remember him. You're tougher than you think. You can do without parents.' Maybe that wasn't the right thing to say.

'I don't want to,' she said. 'I want to see my mum.'

'I know. But life throws all sorts at you, and you can live through it all. Whatever happens you always get a choice. You can choose.'

'Choose what?' She didn't look convinced.

'Sorry,' he said. 'I don't really know what to say to you. I'm not used to talking to ten-year-olds. I told you that. I mean you can choose between right or wrong. That's all that counts. The rest – whether you're happy or sad, a vet or an artist or a doctor, with no dad, a fake dad, a dad and mum, whatever – none of that matters.' It sounded too harsh, he thought. Where had the speech come from? From his mother, he assumed – straight out of her mouth into his. So much for free choice. Did he even believe those things? He hadn't followed his own advice, that was for sure. Except for today, perhaps.

'If I ever see my mum again,' she said, 'I'm going to try harder to do what she says.'

He put the scope down on the empty chair next to him. He was about to say 'You will see her again, you have my word', but then couldn't tell that lie. He felt his insides twisting with the responsibility.

15

about her personal life. All the people she knew, all the details

The guardia civil were now involved, and the older man who had
jabbed his finger at Molina, a colonel called Arroyo, insisted on
questioning her personally. Or so Molina told her. He seemed
unhappy about it. Molina was with the national police, the
guardia civil were a quasi-military organisation. She had heard
bad things about them, but she'd heard bad things about the
national police too.

The female officer had driven her down the valley to Marbella,
to the police station there. She was still there now, two hours
later. She was in what they called an interview room, a three-
metre-square, airless space, without windows, cork tiles on the
walls, scribbled with lewd graffiti, two microphones hanging
from the ceiling above the single table they had fitted in there.
One table, four chairs, all fixed to the floor, but only two of
them occupied. She was at one side – the side furthest from
the door – Arroyo was at the other. He was 'interviewing' her,
recording everything through the microphones.

They had been at it for over an hour – endless questions
about her personal life. All the people she knew, all the details
about the shop, her daily schedule, the school Rebecca went
to, her routine, her likes and dislikes. Most of it seemed like
background probing to her, but some questions came out of the
blue. Did Rebecca have a boyfriend, did she use drugs? Did Juan
go to any political meetings? She answered in a kind of daze,
automatically, wary only that he would start on her past – the

real past, ten years before. But that hadn't happened so far. He would get there, she supposed, then she would have to lie.

So far, there had been no attempt at anything but a kind of formal sympathy. She had lost her husband, her daughter was kidnapped, yet it felt like she was being forced to be here, forced to talk to them, though she was repeatedly told that wasn't the case, that her status was of someone assisting them, not a suspect.

As Arroyo spoke to her he sat with his elbows on the table, one hand continually straying up to the side of his face to finger a nasty burn scar. When he took his military cap off and placed it on the table she saw that some hair had been scorched away too. Whatever had caused it had just missed his eye. The skin at the right temple looked glossy, plastic. It was impossible not to focus on it, despite her best efforts. His touching it didn't help. She kept thinking of Juan, poor Juan, who had been killed by a bomb blast. Had he been burned too? She hadn't looked at his body long enough to know. Where was he now? Where had they taken him? She got that thought mixed up with Rebecca and sat there quietly crying, completely powerless. But Arroyo didn't seem to notice the tears. Molina had been warm, by comparison.

'Terrorists,' he said to her now. His voice had a kind of rasp, like he had laryngitis. 'You understand me? Terrorists.'

She shook her head, not sure what to say. In the beginning she had tried to look him in the eyes, but he was too intent on doing the same, no doubt to intimidate. So now she mostly looked at the table, deliberately seeking to avoid eye contact. His eyes were unpleasant – brown, with black pouches of skin beneath, as if he hadn't slept in months.

'A device.' He opened his big hands, palm upwards. 'It was undoubtedly an explosive device – it killed two people, and an officer was then shot. So we have to assume the worst. That is why I need to ask you these questions. This is obviously the work of terrorists.'

'Why?' she asked, feebly. 'Why would terrorists target my family?'

'That's what we need to work out. Right here, right now.'

'I understand that, but—'

'I have requested a unit come from Madrid,' he interrupted. 'A specialist anti-terror unit.'

'OK. Good. But what about my daughter?'

'She is our number one priority.'

He sat staring at her in silence. Waiting for some response? She wanted to ask him *how* Rebecca was the number one priority, what they were *actually* doing, but when she opened her mouth to say something he put a hand up to silence her. 'You have to help me,' he said. 'There has to be a political connection. If not you, then your husband, or even the woman he was with.'

The woman he was with. Stated like it meant nothing at all.

'You think a political group kidnapped my daughter?' she asked. 'Like ETA, you mean?'

ETA was the Basque terrorist group he had probably spent his entire career fighting. He smirked at that though. 'Not a Spanish political group. But there are others. Many others. They come over from Africa. Jihadists. There is a war on terror, an international war, and we are part of it. No one is exempt.'

'So you think *fundamentalists* kidnapped her?' She could barely believe he was suggesting it.

'It can happen.' He reached in his pocket and pulled out a phone. He placed it on the table. 'I have the impression that you are reluctant to help me,' he said.

'I don't know what you mean. I'm doing everything I can.'

He nodded, staring at her. 'Your phone,' he said. 'We have copied the card, read your messages. Your daughter said a policeman tried to shoot her. Did you read that message?'

86

'Yes.'

'But you didn't tell us about it,' he said. 'Why not?'

'I gave the access code when asked. Molina read the text.'

'Why did you not tell Molina immediately? Surely it was important?'

'Because I trust my daughter.'

He frowned. 'What does that mean?'

'She's not stupid.'

'But she was mistaken, surely?'

'Was she? I wasn't there. She texted me that a policeman tried to kill her.'

'And you believed that?'

'Like I said, she's not stupid. She wrote that he shot at her. Hard to make mistakes about that. Even if you're ten.'

'He might have been shooting at the man she was with.'

'OK. Yes. You're right. But will talking about it help find her?'

'Is that why you did not trust Molina? Because your daughter wrote that? Because you think his men are involved?'

'Involved? Again I don't know what you mean. Involved in what?'

'In the explosion, the kidnap. What else?'

'You're suggesting Molina is involved?' She was confused now. Was he being serious, or was this some ruse?

'I'm not suggesting that. Only that you don't trust him. You withheld information from him.'

'I trust my daughter.'

'Of course. But you should trust me too. I am not Molina. I am nothing to do with the national police. You can say things to me, give me information, and it will not go back to them. The guardia civil is separate. You understand?'

'I don't understand. No.' She dragged her sleeve across her eyes, wiping them.

'She wrote the man was called Carl,' he said. 'Do you know anyone called Carl?'

'No. I already told your colleagues that.'

'It's important that you strive to assist *me*. Forget what you told Molina. I am different.'

'I *am* assisting you. She's my fucking daughter, remember? My husband was killed.'

That just bounced off him. 'Why would this "Carl" say you had hired him to protect your daughter?'

'I have no idea.'

'Is it true? Did you hire a man to protect her?'

'I told you already – it's not true. Maybe he said it to get her trust.'

'But you think he did actually protect her from one of the local police? You believe that?'

'That's what she wrote. If you find her we can ask her what she meant. We shouldn't be sitting in here, we should be out looking for her.'

'That is all being dealt with—'

'What is it you want to know? I don't understand this. Am I being questioned as some kind of suspect? That's what this feels like.'

'I've already made your status clear.'

'Do I get a lawyer? Do I have rights?'

'You're not a suspect. You're helping us to try and locate your daughter – remember?'

'Are you doing *anything* to locate her? Are you actually doing *anything*?'

'Talking to you, now, is part of what I'm doing. Be reassured that *she* is my priority, *you* are not.' He smirked again. She could feel her stomach tightening, the emotion coming to the surface.

The door opened. Molina put his head into the gap and said something very quickly to Arroyo. He needed to speak to him.

'Can I have my phone back?' she asked. 'You've copied the chip. I need it in case Rebecca calls me.'

Arroyo put a hand up, to silence either her or Molina, she wasn't sure which. Molina paused a moment, looking at her, then withdrew, the door left open a little. Arroyo pushed himself out of the fixed metal chair, standing so that his head almost touched the ceiling. He straightened the belt at the waist of his tunic and she saw large patches of sweat under his arms, a gun on the belt, hands with bony knuckles. 'I think not,' he said. 'This whole inquiry has been handled badly before my arrival. You should not have been permitted near the scene. Nobody should have. It should have been treated from the outset as a terrorist attack. There could have been a second device.' He stepped sideways, opened the door and walked out without looking back at her or offering anything else. She heard the door snap shut, but not the lock, which meant it was open. She stepped quickly round the table, determined to simply open it and walk out. She wasn't detained – he had made that clear. But she could hear them talking just behind the door – Molina and Arroyo. She moved closer, tried to make out individual words, but then the door opened, almost hitting her in the face.

Molina stepped in. 'They are in La Linea,' he said. She felt her heart kick in her chest. La Linea was the town on the border with Gibraltar, only about forty-five minutes away.

'How do you know?' she asked. 'Have you spoken to her?'

'No. But we triangulated her phone signal – it's no longer transmitting, but it was on about an hour ago, briefly. We can plot locations to within about half a kilometre ...'

'Half a kilometre from La Linea?'

'The phone was actually in La Linea somewhere, in the zone near the border. We've already taken steps to seal off the area. We think they might be headed for Gibraltar. It's an easy way to avoid our systems. We need to go there right now and you must come with us. We have only photos of Rebecca – from her national ID fiche. But you will recognise her immediately.'

16

They were walking in the dark, somewhere in the backstreets of La Linea, looking for a suitable car. They had come about a kilometre and a half from the hotel, heading away from the border area, sticking to side roads, many of which were unlit, skirting the edges of the town. Beyond the centre, the town seemed to be slowly crumbling, everything dusty and dry and faded, cracks in the buildings, paint flaking off, an atmosphere of abandonment hanging in the air. All the people they saw were standing around – outside houses or shuttered shops or bars, at the entrance to overgrown playgrounds with screaming kids in pushchairs. No one looked like they had anywhere to go or anything to do. Everyone was either smoking or drinking from cans of beer.

There was a large group of maybe a hundred and fifty young men gathered outside some public building with placards and banners, arguing vociferously, using gestures like it might spill into violence. He gave them a wide berth. He saw a few bars and restaurants open – and virtually empty – but many more boarded up. Boarded up shops too. Houses with ragged washing hanging from balconies. Piles of uncollected refuse in a few streets. It was very far from the Costa del Sol image.

Rebecca said very little as they moved, kept very close to him, told him she didn't like the place, that she was frightened. She was getting more upset as the hours wore on. He could see her struggling with what was happening, trying to fit it into some normal pattern which didn't exist any longer. She kept asking if she could call her mother and he kept asking her not to. Once it got as far as her demanding her phone, him giving it to her. She had switched it on, he thought, but only for a few seconds, before fear got the better of her. The images from back at her house were still there, the primeval sense of overriding danger.

In a dirty, badly lit, all-night store he bought her a Coke, some nuts and crisps. For a while then she walked along beside him eating and drinking, and then began to look less forlorn, even began to talk a bit about her friends. She wanted to call them too. And some cousin, in London. He told her there would be time soon for all that. Her mood picked up enough for him to think there must have been a blood sugar thing going on. 'You need to tell me when you're hungry,' he told her. 'I haven't a clue about these things.'

A few young men stared at them like they might be an opportunity for gain. But no one tried it on. And no one shouted at them, or pointed, or got on their phones as they passed. If the Spanish police were looking for a man and a young girl then that news hadn't penetrated to here. He saw glimpses of TV sets in the bars, but no images of Rebecca on the screens. Where they had bought the Coke, the guy behind the counter had been occupied with a magazine and had barely looked at them. Carl thought most people would guess they were father and daughter.

He was no expert at breaking into cars and starting them without keys. He'd learned how to do it as a teenager, in the years between his brother leaving and him joining the army. He'd been trouble for his mother then, a teenager in a rural town with nothing much to push against. There had been some bad incidents in those years, including many stolen cars. He was lucky none of it had ended in a criminal conviction.

The army had saved him. The military had discovered he

could shoot, put him in a special unit. After that he'd shot as part of the national team for two years, while still in the army, getting as far as the 1998 Winter Olympics in Japan – but there had been no future in it. So he'd turned to Viktor, started doing security work for the wealthy Russian relatives he was working for. Then met Liz, maybe the only bit of his life that had been worth it. But he'd fucked that up, somehow, then drifted into using the only skill he had left – because the cartel had made him an offer. He hadn't stolen a car in nearly twenty years.

He assumed the technique was much the same now as it had been then, except more models were impossible to take, due to electronics, computers, et cetera. There were plenty of clapped-out fifteen-year-old rust heaps in La Linea though, too old to have immobilisers and alarms. Finding one he could actually get into wasn't the issue. He had to find one that wouldn't be missed for a while. With people lounging at every street corner that wasn't so easy.

They didn't have an abundance of time either. He thought they would need to start towards the border just after ten. It was ten past nine now. He had thought about crossing over immediately they had arrived here, before there was any chance of the Spanish police getting organised enough to stop them, but then they would have been stuck in Gibraltar until half eleven – the time Viktor had given him for the charter flight he was arranging – and he didn't like the sound of that. Gibraltar was tiny. If there was any kind of cross-border cooperation then the place would be like a net, with limited exit possibilities. If things were going to heat up then he preferred to be able to find a car and drive across the border into France or Portugal. From the position they were in now they had all of Europe to get lost in. Once they were in Gibraltar they were stuck.

At nearly 9.30 he left Rebecca at a corner, within sight, and walked down a back alley full of rubbish skips – the service alley for a dilapidated row of shops – to a Ford Escort he thought might be a mid-nineties model. The doors were all open – with rusted locks that looked like they wouldn't work – so he paused, listening in the dark for anyone approaching, then got in and tried to get it going. It looked like someone had already had the same idea. The steering column casing was missing, the wiring exposed. He looked at it and tried to remember what he should do, then started experimenting. Nothing happened. It was possible the battery was flat.

He kept at it, trying different combinations. Then he realised he was guessing, making it up. He'd forgotten what you were meant to do, which wires you were supposed to touch together. But there were a limited number of them hanging out and it was only a matter of logic to try them all, in sequence. All the key did – if you had it – was make the connection between two wires. He just had to find those two wires.

He had more or less done that – gone through every combination – when someone spoke from right beside him. 'Will it not work?' she asked. He jerked his head up in surprise, banging it on the steering wheel. It was Rebecca, standing at the open passenger door. He rubbed his head. He was getting very careless. 'I've forgotten what to do,' he said. He got out. 'Maybe we'll just use the other car.' He looked at his mobile and started to worry. They had a brisk walk to get back.

'I thought you said the other car was dangerous?'

He opened his mouth to argue with her, but then heard sirens, close.

'Are they coming for us?' she asked, but the sound was already drawing into the distance. He thought they were headed towards the centre of town. More followed close behind, one or two at first, intermittent, but building up. Within a few seconds he could make out maybe nine different sources. Something was going on. 'Time to get back,' he said.

They walked quickly, taking a different route to the one he'd used previously. As they got back towards the centre the sirens were still there, coming from behind him, moving past along parallel streets. He slowed, started to check junctions before they got to them. He thought they could only be about a kilometre from the hotel and car.

A police car turned into the street behind them. Lights and sirens off, it sped past them before he could even push Rebecca off to the side. Another followed. They were headed in the same direction he had intended to use. People started to come out of the houses, onto the streets, started shouting to each other. There was enough noise up ahead to suggest something big. Not just the sirens. He could hear shouting too, he thought.

'Change of plan,' he said. 'We'll head towards the beach.'

They took a route through the streets which he estimated moved around the square where the hotel was, but kept moving a little closer to it, so he could try to see what was happening. The town was built on the land falling away from a spine of hills marching out of the interior and down the Mediterranean coast of Spain. The heights stopped fifteen kilometres from Gibraltar, falling quickly into a thin isthmus of flat land that stretched out to the sudden mass of the rock. From the bay on one side of the isthmus to the Mediterranean on the other, it was only about a kilometre across; right at the point they had the border posts. That was where they were, at the tip of the town, the tip of Spain.

The hotel was less than a kilometre from the border. As they came within sight of the sea he could also see back towards the hotel, looking in the other direction along one of the streets leading towards the town centre – a straight road running about half a kilometre inland to where he could see the top floors of the hotel. But he couldn't see the actual square. About halfway along there were police cars blocking his view, stopping the traffic. There were officers out with riot shields and automatic weapons. They wouldn't be able to get anywhere near the car using that route.

They kept going towards the shore instead, passing other streets into the town centre, but it was the same at every turn. Police cars, riot gear, all eyes focused away from them. They must be setting up a ring round the central zone. If they hadn't left to find another car they would be trapped inside it, right now.

They had everything with them – they didn't need to go back to the hotel – but the car was there, inside the security perimeter. That was a problem.

'What's happening?' she asked him again, as they came out onto the wide promenade that ran along the beach. The sea was over there, the night bright with artificial light, everything visible. He could hear waves rolling along the shore, smell the fresher air. Groups of people were moving away from the thin strip of sand, heading towards the police cordon. Locals, not tourists. There were no tourists here, as far as he could see.

Off to the right, in the town, there was a continual noise of sirens now. He could hear chanting behind them, shouts, anger. It sounded like there was a sizeable crowd somewhere, back near the hotel. He stood still and watched the people moving quickly across the road, trying to assess the information. There were hardly any cars. 'We can't get back to the car,' he decided.

There was a sudden surge of noise, a huge massed shout, then a sound like gunshots. She said something to him about people shooting, but he told her it was only firecrackers. He felt her take hold of his arm and hold it, near the wrist. 'Don't worry,' he said. 'You're OK.' Then they saw some rockets bursting in the air above the bay. Was it a party?

Ahead of them there were wide areas of vacant land, the beach widened out and there was a ruin – a broken fortress sticking up from the sand. The road ran past it, to the side of a local football stadium, with four floodlight towers, but it looked deserted, dark. Past it was the border area – behind the stadium, so they couldn't see it yet – and, beyond that, always there, dominating every view, the Rock, a towering white floodlit cliff, beckoning.

He shouted out to a woman walking past them, her eyes on the back streets they had just left. He asked her in English what was going on. She shouted back at him in Spanish, but he didn't understand Spanish.

'She says it's a *huelga*,' Rebecca said. She let go of his arm. 'That means a strike,' she explained. 'There's a strike, a demonstration.'

'A strike?' He felt a little twinge of hope. Maybe it was nothing to do with them at all. He asked Rebecca to go over to a woman who was closing up a tobacco kiosk, on the promenade, overlooking the dirty strip of beach. 'Ask her what's going on,' he said.

He waited on his side of the road whilst she did it, then came back and told him. There was a strike going on – public service workers. Because they weren't getting paid by the local government. Because of 'the crisis'. Because of the border checks. It was the same every week. They set fire to things, smashed some cars, the police came and arrested them all.

'OK,' he said. 'Maybe we're OK.' He guessed, from the noise, that the confrontation was going on in the square near the hotel. Maybe it was the group of men they had seen earlier.

He still didn't want to risk walking through the police lines, however. 'Maybe we can just walk over the border,' he said to her, thinking aloud. 'We'll walk to the end of this promenade and look. If we get past that football stadium we should be able to see the border post.'

Maybe there was nothing to worry about after all. Get in

97

the short queue he had seen from the hotel, walk through the customs post whilst the authorities were concentrating on the strike.

17

'This is organised crime,' Molina told her during the car journey, on the toll motorway south to Gibraltar, siren wailing, blue lights flashing, all traffic moving over to let them pass. 'There is no need for the guardia civil to be involved, no need for anti-terror units. The national police will handle it. You should have confidence in that. You should trust me.'

It was the same speech Arroyo had given her. She nodded dumbly, watching the hills streaming past in the darkness, thought how only hours ago these hills had meant something to her, something beautiful, something she might point out to her daughter. But right now they were just lumps of rock, part of the distance to be covered to get to where Rebecca might be.

Organised crime. He was right about that, she supposed, though he wouldn't get near working it out.

'I'm sorry you had to deal with Colonel Arroyo,' he said. 'It won't happen again. I have resolved the jurisdictional issues. This is my case now. And I want you to be clear – for me you are a victim here. You are assisting me. I am assisting you. You are not detained.'

He had even added a smile. But she hadn't believed a word. The other one – Arroyo – had been fixated on terrorists, but he had taken seriously Rebecca's statements – he had been weighing whether it could be true that a policeman had shot at her. Molina wasn't even considering that. He wouldn't return her phone either. It was in a lab somewhere.

99

She didn't trust any of them. She needed to get away from them all. He had told her she was free to do that, but now she couldn't because he was the best chance of getting nearer to Rebecca, because he was telling her they knew where she was. For now she had to stick with him, follow this through.

That conversation had been half an hour ago. Now they were in a part of the customs post, on the Spanish side of the border with Gibraltar – a long, low building, with tinted, one-way windows facing onto the line of cars slowly moving through the passport check lanes, not ten metres in front of the building. There were lights all over, so they could see the front of the queue quite easily, see inside the cars, see the faces. It was like daylight.

Just to the other side of the cars there was a shorter queue of pedestrians walking along the pavement to get in. The queue of cars was nothing compared to the last time she had travelled to visit Gibraltar, with Rebecca, about a year ago. Back then she had waited in the mid-afternoon heat for nearly three hours to filter through the customs checks, due to some dispute with the UK. But the cars and trucks stretched only to the first round-about now, about two hundred metres away. It was nearly ten in the evening.

The route out of the colony was at the other side of the building they were in and she couldn't see it at all. Molina had left other officers watching that. He had asked her to check every face she could see. He was standing next to her, looking over the shoulder of a woman who had a bank of CCTV monitors ranged on a set of desks in front of her, scrutinising the images on the screens. There were twelve cameras covering various parts of the border, Molina said, but mostly the entry side, for those coming into Spain. That was the direction contraband goods passed – alcohol and cigarettes, mainly – out of the colony and into Spain, to be resold at higher prices.

'There was a riot here last week,' Molina said. 'You must have heard about it.'

She had. La Linea was threatened with bankruptcy, the local government unable to pay the wages of its workforce – so they had set fire to the mayor's car, or the town hall, or something like that. The week before there had been something else, an attack on the border crossing in protest against the checks Spain had put in to prevent contraband.

'That's what the noise is?' she asked.

'That's the noise,' Molina said. 'The strike, the demonstration. It's been going on every week for nearly a year.'

She could hear the continual wail of sirens, shouting and chanting, coming from the other side of the dividing road that ran across the neck of the isthmus, from the bay in the west to the sea in the east. Whatever was happening was somewhere over there, in the town of La Linea itself. She could see the lights of police cars speeding along the roads into the town centre.

'So all these police cars,' she said. 'They're not looking for my daughter?'

'Of course not. These are Arroyo's men. The guardia civil has responsibility for disorder. *We* sent in plain cars, no lights, no noise. The man will bring her nowhere near the border if we barricade it off. We don't want him to know we're here.'

Fat chance of that, she thought. Was this Carl likely to think that as all those police weren't there for him he could just walk through them? She doubted it. 'But are you sure something isn't happening over there?' she asked. 'You *sure* it's not connected?'

'Something is happening, yes. As I said: it's a riot.' He was angry about it. 'The same as last week. Just concentrate on the faces out there.'

'What if they've already gone through?'

'I told you. We'll find them. If they're already in Gibraltar then they can't get out. They know about them at the airport and the harbour. They have your daughter's photo. They know she's English, so they will be interested. They'll find her if she's over there.'

'Can't we go across the border, to check?'

'Not yet, no. There's a process. It's not Spain. We are awaiting the diplomatic clearance for cooperation. But they can't fly out without—'

'They could just get a boat out.'

'They can't. The coastguard knows – the Spanish coastguard. All boats out of Gibraltar have been queried for over three hours now.'

Queried? What did that mean? 'It would be safer if I could go over and look around the airport and the harbour.'

'I need you here to look.'

'They're not going to come here. Not now. There are police all over. You said it yourself.'

She heard a series of small explosions from beyond the road, a loud shout of many voices raised together.

'They're fireworks,' Molina explained. 'They shoot fireworks at the emergency services.'

From where she was to the road was only a hundred metres. Further to the west, traffic coming into Gibraltar took this same road into La Linea, then edged around the actual town, following the curve of the bay before turning off, right in front of her, to use the short single road into the colony. The road continued down to the other side of the isthmus, to the football ground she could see there, then the Mediterranean, a little beyond that. From the bay to the sea was about one kilometre of flat sandy land, much of it given over to lorry parking on the Med side. Across the far side of the dividing road was an apartment development and a series of dusty public parks that stretched down to the football ground and the sea. Inland from the apartments and parks was the central part of La Linea. That was where all the noise was coming from, that was where all the police cars were headed.

But even as she watched she saw a crowd start to emerge from the street directly opposite. They were coming straight towards her, though still about two hundred metres distant, and not moving with any obvious purpose or direction – just spilling out of the town, chanting, shouting, fists in the air. They looked more like a football crowd, like they were celebrating. Molina picked up a handheld radio and spoke to someone brusquely.

She watched the initial group of people quickly swell into a crowd large enough to be threatening. They stopped just the other side of the road, roughly a hundred and fifty metres away. The police hadn't closed the road yet – or the border – so the line of cars and trucks waiting to turn towards the border post was still there, an obvious target. A bottle sailed through the air and smashed against the windscreen of one of the cars. From the corner of her eye she saw the occupants starting to get out, cars turning in the road, trying to get away.

They were between her and where she needed to be. Rebecca's phone was over there somewhere, in the town itself. There was no obvious reason to be here instead of there, and Molina had given no sound explanation. It was his *assumption* that if they had come to La Linea then they would be trying to get to Gibraltar. But she didn't understand that, didn't understand any of what they were doing.

'Do you have any men over there?' she asked him. Her heart was continually racing now, so that when she spoke the words came out slightly breathless. 'Do you have any men actually covering the area where you think the phone is?'

'I already told you that,' he said. 'You should trust me more. Calm down. I'm trying to help you. We put in place a discreet cordon, over an hour ago. But then the demonstration kicked off and they worked out we were there. That's why things are getting heated. They think we're trying to move in on them – the demonstrators, I mean. They don't realise it has nothing to do with them.'

'And are they still there now – the people you put in?'

'It's more complicated now. The guardia have priority now – they are just trying to manage the crowd, to prevent a repeat of last week.'

'He could just walk away from the town then, or drive away.'

'You have to be patient—' He stopped as the radio crackled into life again. He held it to his face and listened as someone said something quickly, something about a girl. She held her breath. He asked for clarification and coordinates, then raised his eyebrows at her and pointed through the window, towards the crowd. The voice at the other end said something about a man and a girl. Molina gave an instruction. What had he said? She didn't quite understand it – some police jargon. He lowered the radio. 'A possible sighting,' he said, quietly. 'A man and a girl, behind the crowd there, about twenty metres further up the street.' He picked up the pair of binoculars lying on the desk. The woman at the desk started to say something into a microphone, something unconnected, speaking to someone else about one of the cars coming through.

Molina stood for what seemed like minutes, staring through the binoculars. She kept her mouth shut, watched the crowd growing larger at the other side of the road. She could see no little girl over there. All she could see was angry males, most of them with bandanas covering their heads.

'I can't see anything,' he said, finally. 'You look.' He handed her the binoculars.

'What did your man say?' she asked, her voice almost strangled off in her throat.

'A possible sighting at the back of the crowd. It's not confirmed. There was a sighting like this an hour ago ...'

'You didn't tell me.'

'It was a false alarm. Look up that street straight opposite, the one the crowd are coming down – look at the faces about halfway up.'

She got the binoculars focused and started to scan the chaotic jumble of faces, everyone moving, the image too dark to be useful. 'I can't see anything,' she said, desperately. 'Did your man say anything about her – did he say what she was doing?'

'No. Just try to scan the crowd methodically ...'

'Is he sure it's her? Did he mention her height? She's very tall for her age – it's distinctive.'

'No. He's not sure. That's why you're looking. He didn't mention her height, just the possible age. He thought a teenager.'

'But she's tall for her age, so it could be her.'

But still she could see nothing, partly because the trees and street lights in the space between blocked the view, partly because the crowd was now very large and flowing right out of the street. She lowered the binoculars and watched as police cars sped along the road from both directions, to head them off, to stop them getting anywhere near the border post. From where she was there was a one-hundred-metre stretch of bare concrete – the customs area – then the dividing road – a wide, four-lane avenue with a large central island. Then the apartments and the town. From inside here it was impossible to see behind the ringleaders.

'I will step out a moment,' Molina said. 'I have to call my sergeant out there.' He was brandishing his mobile. 'Stay here. Keep trying. It's important.' He turned from her and walked to the other side of the room, pushed through a door there and let it close behind him.

That left her and the desk woman, who wasn't looking at her at all. She was still speaking quietly to someone on the microphone. Julia put the binoculars down and stepped over to the door they had come through. Beyond it, she knew, was a fire escape that opened right onto the concrete area in front of the customs post. She couldn't see Rebecca from here, so she had to get out there.

Carl was about four hundred metres away from the customs post, on the dividing road that led along the edge of the distant bay then came down past him and the football ground, as far as the coast. There was a turn-off about four hundred metres in front of him – a short road to the customs post and the border. He couldn't see the border itself, just the queue of cars moving through. But ahead, spilling across the road he was on, opposite the turn-off, there was a miniature riot going on. Rebecca stood beside him, watching it also.

He estimated there were around three hundred and fifty people in the vanguard. They were coming out of the street that he guessed would lead back to the hotel and the car, so there would be no going that way. There was a turn-off towards the centre only twenty metres from where they were that would cut behind the crowd, but there was a guardia civil car across it, blocking it, officers crouched by the car as if someone was going to start shooting at them. Their caution wasn't shared by the townspeople – there were groups of them all over the road, standing around, watching, laughing like it was a carnival. No sense of fear, or danger. People were hanging out of the windows of the apartments near the commotion, jeering.

There were at least five police cars up near the border post, positioning themselves between the queue of traffic that had been caught up in it all – the cars and trucks waiting to get over to Gibraltar – and the ringleaders in the crowd. Most of those involved were doing nothing, just standing there on the town side of the road, or on the central reservation; a few were chanting political slogans, some waving banners. At the front were ten to twenty with masks and stones, taunting the police, or running forward to throw missiles at the line of cars. It wouldn't have taken much to go in and arrest the vanguard, he thought, before things really heated up, but the police were hanging back, sheltering behind their cars, guns drawn, riot shields up. The queue to get over the border was vanishing rapidly as cars reversed out of it and drove off in the opposite direction.

'Is it dangerous?' Rebecca asked him, nervously. She was still eating a hamburger they had just picked up at a kiosk near the boarded-up football stadium.

'I wouldn't want to try to get through it,' he said. He was tempted to get the spotting scope out and have a proper look at the border area, but that would be pushing it. He didn't like standing around here with her in the open. It wasn't the police that worried him, it was the possibility that Jones had anticipated they would make for here. Jones was still alive, out there somewhere.

'We could walk up the side there, by the police,' she suggested. 'I've been to Gibraltar before, last year with my mum – that's the way you go.'

'I don't like it,' he said, turning away. 'We'll find another way.'

18

Julia whacked her palms into the fire exit bar, springing the set of double doors open and running into the lights outside. Behind her the fire alarm started to ring – or was it an alarm Molina had triggered? Straight ahead there was a stretch of bare concrete between herself and where the front line of protestors were lined up on the dividing road, fists in the air, shouting furiously, some of them already throwing bricks at the police vehicles parked to block access to the border post. She cut right, slightly towards the football stadium, away from them, then started to really run.

She could hear Molina shouting behind her but it was unclear what he was saying, the blood pumping too loud in her ears. As she got to the road she glanced back and saw him stopped, a good twenty metres behind her, speaking into his radio. She dodged between two police cars that were coming to a stop. Uniformed men got out, night sticks waving, but they weren't looking for her. Only ten metres away people were hurling bottles and stones with all their strength, trying to hit the police. A bottle came over her and smashed against the side of one of the abandoned trucks that had been waiting in the queue to go through the border. The queue was down to a handful of empty vehicles now – everyone else had turned and driven off. She could see a ragged line of men across the other side of the road, near the apartments there, the leaders of a much larger crowd trailing into the streets beyond. Nearly all of them were masked. She had to get over there and behind them. Behind her other policemen were shouting, possibly at her.

There was an island of grass in the middle of the road, with a bronze of a statue figure standing with a bicycle on a plinth – she ran straight past it and onto the road on the town side. She was halfway across before she realised exactly what she was doing, and by then it was too late. To get into the customs buildings they had given her a big plastic, laminated ID badge, hanging round her neck. And she had run straight out of the police buildings, in full view, run straight for the protestors.

The men in the front started to react. They started yelling abuse at her whilst she was still thirty metres away. Then the stones started and she got it – they thought she was police. She looked back, but no one was chasing her any more. She was between the two sides, stuck in the middle. She skidded to a halt, turning away from the men shouting at her, then started to run back towards the police, stumbling slightly. She would have to get back to safety then find a way round them.

A car was speeding up from the side. It swerved to a halt in front of her. The doors opened and four men piled out, sticks in hand. There were stones and bottles flying, bouncing off the ground, shattering. She started shouting in Spanish that she wasn't police, yanking off the ID. She aimed for the space between the car and the crowd of men with bandanas and started to sprint. She saw them coming at her from the left, sticks up. Beyond them there was a line of police with shields and batons, but they were easily thirty metres off, further down the road. She couldn't see Molina at all. She ducked, felt something graze her shoulder, swerved to the right, saw four or five men all screaming at her from over there, saw missiles curving lazily through the air towards her. She dodged, swerved, kept going.

There was a small guy in jeans, face uncovered, mouth twisted in anger. His arm flicked forward and he skimmed something at her, something small. Her eyes tracked it as she was running, saw it scything through the air at leg height. She broke her step, tried to stop to avoid it, then felt it strike her knee and bounce off. A stone. For a few seconds she kept going, her legs still carrying her forward, then the knee just collapsed on her, the whole leg folding so that she went head over heels, rolling across the tarmac.

She came up into a sitting position, looking around, trying to get her bearings. Her hands were automatically clutching the injured knee. There was no blood but she couldn't feel a thing, couldn't get the leg to work. A second later an intense pain shot up the leg as she tried to scramble backwards and get to her feet again. She dropped down. There was nothing she could do but crawl. A bottle smashed just to the side of her, showering her with glass fragments.

The men with sticks were running back to the car now. Something was happening from the police line. She tried to turn towards it, to see, but a man appeared from nowhere, stooped and grabbed her by the arm, started pulling her back towards the crowd. She yelled that her daughter was missing, tried to pull away from him, but another ran up to help him. It was like they were trying to rescue her, pull her to safety, but the guy was screaming at her, telling her she was a filthy police bitch, that she deserved everything coming to her. The other let go of her arm long enough to start hitting her head with his fist. She felt her head jerking sideways, shouted again that she wasn't police, tasted blood in her mouth.

Their faces loomed in and out of her field of vision as she was dragged forwards, numbed by the blows. She could see the street stretching behind them towards the town, the buildings white and tall on either side, hundreds of individual doors and windows, see a huge crowd there watching them doing it, but no one moving to help her.

They were trying to get her away from the police so they could hurt her. She started to violently shake them off, fighting to wrench herself away, but the leg still wouldn't work and she kept falling back down. She crouched in the road, staring towards the crowd. Suddenly the two who had dragged her were also fleeing. She could hear movement from behind, whistles blowing, men shouting orders.

Her eyes scanned the crowd, watching to see if anything else was thrown, passed over a man right at the front, came back to him. He was moving against the flow, in the front row of the crowd, his eyes fixed on her. He was dressed like the rest but she knew instinctively that he wasn't with them. He was focused on her. Short, dark hair, a normal face, a backpack off his shoulder and held in one hand. As her eyes met his he was lowering his right arm to his side, bringing it back, out of sight. He had a pistol there, held as if he had been about to fire it. Or had already fired. She was certain. She saw the black metal, the barrel. He slipped back a row and was instantly gone, lost in the sea of movement and noise.

Then legs were running past her, uniformed men all around, charging towards the crowd. She saw at least twenty thunder past her, shields up, batons held ready over their heads, roaring like animals. The crowd panicked in front of them, splitting up and fleeing in all directions.

There was a small stand of taxis near the stadium, three cars in line when Carl had passed it on the way up, all looking very 'local'. He guessed they were a smuggling asset, rather than taxis for tourists. But they would do.

The noise continued behind them as they put their backs to it. Rebecca kept up with him, walking by his side, mostly passing people hurrying in the opposite direction to watch the show. He could see there were only two taxis parked up now, both drivers out on the pavement, talking, pointing towards the demo. He crossed the road with her and said, 'We'll try to get one of these cars. I'm going to say we need to get to Malaga, to reach your brother in hospital ...'

'I don't have a brother.'

'It's a lie. I need them to sell me one of those cars, or agree to take us out of here. Back me up if they don't understand. OK?'

'OK.'

The two drivers separated as they drew near, one going for the nearest car, pointing at it and shouting something in Spanish. Carl kept going, walked past the first car, shook his head, pointed to the car behind. The one in front was a SEAT, fairly decent and clean. The one behind was a Vauxhall Astra that hadn't been washed in years, much older. There was some objection to him choosing the second in line – from the first driver – but he ignored it, walked straight past him, keeping Rebecca close. Both drivers had cigarettes in their mouths, lank black hair. They were about Carl's size. They could have been brothers.

He apologised in English as the first one got close to him, coming from behind, then started speaking to the second one. But the second one was shaking his head too. They might be nothing but contraband cigarette shuttles, but there was a system – the clean car was first. Carl took his wallet out, handed ten euros to the first guy, apologised again. The man took the money but kept arguing. Carl got Rebecca's hand and turned his back to him, looked past the second driver at the Astra, tried to guess what it might sell for. Certainly not more than a thousand euros. It was a car from the early nineties. 'My car,' he said to the driver, 'my car is over there.' He pointed back towards town. 'It's inside the police cordon. I can't get to it.'

'I can't take you through there,' the guy said, immediately. 'The roads are closed.' His English seemed good enough. Carl tried to look disappointed. Behind him the first driver was still muttering on, but starting to move away. 'I have to get to Malaga,' Carl said, as if the guy hadn't understood properly. 'Right now.' He pointed at Rebecca. 'Her brother is sick, in hospital there.'

'Very expensive,' the guy said. He pulled a face, like a wince. 'I take you Malaga for two hundred.' From behind them there was a huge shout from the crowd. Carl turned to look – everyone did. But all he could see was people running across the road, police chasing them. They weren't coming towards him. He turned back to the guy. He was babbling something in Spanish to the first driver now. The first driver had lost interest – he was watching the distant unrest, leaning on his car. It was like a riot was a form of entertainment.

'I want to borrow your car,' Carl said to the second guy.

The man turned his head from the noise, frowned. 'I don't understand,' he said.

'Borrow it. I want to drive to Malaga in it, come back tomorrow.'

Beside him, Rebecca said something quickly in Spanish, a translation.

The guy started shaking his head, laughing.

'It's very urgent,' Carl said. 'Her brother is in hospital.' He looked down at Rebecca. 'Tell him that as well,' he said. 'Just in case.' She spoke again but the driver was hardly listening. He started shouting something to the other driver.

'I'll give you one thousand five hundred euros if you let me borrow the car,' Carl said. That shut him up. Now Carl had his full attention. 'I'll give you one thousand five hundred now, you give me one thousand back when I return the car tomorrow. That's five hundred euros, plus a one thousand deposit, to have the car for twenty-four hours.'

He watched the guy computing it in his head, working out,

most likely, how he could keep the other one thousand. 'Show me,' he said, finally. 'Show me the money.' He grinned, showing a mouthful of dirty teeth, then took a drag on the cigarette, stepped back, sceptical.

Carl counted one thousand five hundred from the wallet and handed it over. The notes were one-hundreds, which he thought might be a problem, but the guy took them, counted, dropped the cigarette on the ground. 'One thousand for the car,' he said. 'Five hundred deposit.'

'No problem,' Carl said.

'OK,' the guy said, grinning again. 'The car is yours.'

It was over as suddenly as it had started – the crowd dispersing like a miracle, scurrying back into the streets behind with the police in pursuit. One or two men tripped and were set upon by the police. Julia watched the brutality in horror. Two police vans followed the line of riot police and a second serial of men ran to arrest those the first wave had caught. She watched it all from the same spot in the road, blood streaming from her nose, her knee pulsating with pain.

Molina arrived within minutes, helped her to stand, let her lean against him. He had ordered an attack, he said, to try to save her. She started to cry, trying to talk and sob at the same time. 'I've lost her,' she kept saying. 'She was there and I lost her.'

Carl took the car back along the road by the coast, away from the border, driving steadily, carefully. Police cars came past going in the opposite direction, lights and sirens on. Then an ambulance.

'We're not going to the border?' Rebecca asked, from the passenger seat.

'Too dangerous,' he said. 'We'll get out of this area in this rust heap, find another car then head west, towards Portugal. I'll call my brother and he can arrange something else.'

19

Carl had been working for Viktor's people for nearly a year when he met her. Initially, he'd been attached to Viktor's New York office, because Viktor had thought that would be the best place to get his English up to speed. He had lived in an apartment belonging to Viktor (in as much as anything belonged to Viktor at that point) on Roosevelt Island, in the middle of the East River, directly under the Queensboro Bridge, and travelled every day to the downtown offices to do various security tasks, mainly involving computer work. Viktor hadn't been there and he had known no one. The job had been very easy, but mostly he had hated his time there. He had been only twenty-three years old.

He came to London in the summer of that year, for a four-week period, when Viktor had just started on a Polish project that meant he was never in the London house but still kept some staff there. When Carl arrived there was only one person in the house, a chef de partie called Liz Edwards – the assistant to Viktor's boss's personal chef, who usually followed the boss. Viktor had told him nothing about Liz, except that his job was to provide her with 'general low-level protection'. Carl had suspected an interest on Viktor's part, but since Viktor hadn't spoken about her he assumed it wasn't significant. There were always women on the fringes of Viktor's life, they were always attractive, but they never lasted long, and it was seldom the case that there was only one at a time. It wasn't unusual for Viktor to want to protect his belongings – whether they were people or objects – so Carl worked on the basis that if there was a more specific threat he would have been briefed.

Because he thought of her in this stock, degrading way, the first meeting was destined to be awkward. He could remember it with painful clarity. It was the first time he had been to the house, he had just arrived from Heathrow, but Viktor had given him the keys and the alarm codes, so he had let himself in without ringing. The house was part of a terrace about seven storeys high on a square surrounding a little public park in the Bloomsbury area of London. There was a garden to the rear, but it was about the size of a bedroom, and enclosed by very high walls. Someone had tried to plant herbs there but the rest of it was overgrown. Viktor didn't bother with gardens and, aside from his place in Helsinki (maybe the only place that was really his back then), not much with houses either. Whoever actually owned the London house clearly had it as an investment, and there was nearly always some improvement programme under way, with builders hammering and drilling and trailing in and out.

When Carl got there that day there was a skip full of building rubble on the street outside, but no builders. It was a hot Saturday in July. There was a big stairwell with mahogany rails rising the full height of the house from the entrance hall. He had stood at the bottom listening to the cool silence above him, decided there was no one in, then started to take a look around.

He got as far as the third-floor landing when she appeared, coming down the stairs from above. She was just out of a shower, it seemed, with wet hair, a long towel bathrobe wrapped around her, not expecting to see him standing there, blocking her way. He started to apologise even before she saw him, clumsily introducing himself, saying he would have shouted but hadn't heard her. She stopped, holding the bathrobe in place, frowning at him, then stepped quickly forward, blushing terribly. She held out a hand for him to shake. 'Viktor told me to expect you,' she said. 'His little brother.'

He shook her hand quickly and for a moment they stood staring at each other. 'We're only half-brothers,' he said.

She was almost exactly his height (almost exactly his age, he discovered later – they had birthdays one day apart), with red hair and masses of freckles. He could see the freckles where they spread out from her nose, across her face, down her neck and onwards. Her shoulders were covered with them. The hair wasn't so obvious – a light red ('strawberry blonde' she told him later, joking) – not bright ginger, or dark red. When, out of embarrassment, he looked down at the floor, he saw there were even freckles spread over her shins and feet. He could remember staring at them, as if mesmerised, feeling something odd starting. There were pleasant, floral fragrances hanging in the air around her and drips of water falling to the parquet floor from her wet hair. 'I'm sorry,' she said. 'I'm just out of the shower.'

'No. My fault. I should have rung the bell.'

'Your English is good. Better than your brother.' She smiled. 'Sorry. Half-brother.'

He nodded and began to feel very awkward. Partly, obviously, it was that she was only in a bathrobe. But there was something else too. At the time he had no idea what, because it definitely didn't feel like he fancied her. He wasn't even sure she was attractive, if he thought about it – at least not in the way that usually appealed to him. In terms of meeting Viktor's various women, that was unusual – normally they were tall, blonde and conventionally stunning. This one was none of that. But *something* was going on.

He cleared his throat, let his eyes come back to her face and fix again on the freckles. They were incredible. The concentration on her shoulders peculiarly and immediately reminded him of the pattern he had seen on very dark nights, far to the north, when you could see so many stars the sky looked almost white. He couldn't recall ever seeing anybody with so many freckles. He had an urge to tell her that they were beautiful, that he'd never seen anything like that before, except in a black night sky full of stars, but didn't have a clue how to put that sentence together so it didn't sound rude and idiotic. He wanted to reach out his fingers and touch them.

He got his eyes off them with difficulty and met her gaze. She was still frowning, watching him. Could she tell what he was thinking? He cleared his throat again, shifted from one foot to the other, couldn't think of anything to say. He could feel himself colouring, feel the heat rising up his neck.

'I'll get dressed,' she said. 'Show you round.' She turned and walked back up the stairs.

After that it had only got worse for him. Crippling, childish embarrassment when he was near her. He hadn't even been like that as a teenager, and until now had no problems speaking to women, even women he was attracted to. It caused him enough discomfort for him to think a lot about it, when by himself, because he couldn't work out why he would be struck so stupidly dumb when he was certain that he didn't want anything more to do with her than the contact that Viktor had required of him. If he had wanted more he supposed it would have been simply a matter of asking Viktor for it. That was what usually happened. Problems wouldn't arise because neither of them were ever *that* interested in the women, and Viktor had never been averse to sharing with him. Paying women for 'favours' was the order of the day. Indeed, the provision of protection was already a kind of favour. So Carl assumed, in those first few days, that if he wanted to sleep with Liz a call to Viktor would bring that about, one way or another. But he didn't want that. The thought of it seemed demeaning. As did, increasingly, the idea that Liz might fit into that pattern, might just be another one of Viktor's temporary, kept amusements – a cook he could also screw.

But at that time she wasn't doing any cooking – she was on leave – so the contact with her required by his work mostly consisted in accompanying her when she went shopping. In the first week he drove her – in Viktor's Merc – to wherever she wanted to be then just stayed in the car and watched from afar. If she went inside somewhere big he followed at a discreet distance, trying to do it so she wouldn't know he was there, keeping his eyes on her, but also scanning around her. It wasn't work he'd ever done before, so he was making it up as he went along.

He found himself doing it badly, because it became hard not to just watch her as she moved around, often unaware, for the first week at least, that he was there. He got to know the way she moved very well, got to recognise various facial expressions as she was thinking – the tight frown as she listened to someone saying something to her, a habit of chewing at her lip as she walked along, the way she frequently moved hair out of her eyes. She had something against clips and hairbands. She had a selection of them – he saw her take them out of her bag, fix her hair back, put up with it for a few moments, then pull them out as if they were an irritation.

Moving so often behind her, he had plenty of time to scrutinise the freckles running up the backs of her calves when she wore short dresses – which, in that heat, had been often – noted that they stopped at the place behind her knee, then started again on the lower thigh. He began to feel like a sad, twisted voyeur. It got so uncomfortable he decided to tell her what he was doing. He waited until she was back in the car one day, then told her Viktor had asked him to watch her.

'Watch me?' she had asked, clearly surprised. 'What does

that mean?' She sat in the front seat when he drove her, so it wasn't quite like he was her lackey, but so far she had rarely said anything to him on their trips. Quite often she had earphones in and he could hear music. She hadn't seemed to notice his unease with her, hadn't seemed to notice him much at all.

'I mean watch over you,' he said. 'Protect you.'

'From what?' She started to laugh, like it was absurd.

He shrugged. 'I don't know.'

'There's nothing to protect me from.' She laughed again, then her look soured and she stared out of the window. 'Unless it's from your half-brother himself,' she added, more quietly.

The steady, percussive clatter of a helicopter engine got his thoughts off her. He opened his eyes and looked around. He was in a small room with easy chairs, low tables strewn with magazines about mining and copper, a soft drinks and snacks machine – a waiting room. They were at a private helipad in hills near a place called Nerva, on the edge of a mining area his brother must have had some connection with, because it had taken him less than an hour and a half to get back to Carl with this alternative. By then Carl had been on the motorway to Seville, still in the rusting Astra.

Until Viktor called back and gave him the details about Nerva he had been considering dumping the car in Seville – if it got them that far – and hiring a decent vehicle to get up to France the following day. The car had something wrong with the differential – Carl could hear it grinding as he decelerated – plus a transmission problem that made it jump out of gear as he shifted down. However, it ran fine at about ninety, on the motorway, so in the end he had driven it all the way here. It was the safest option because he couldn't imagine the owner reporting it missing.

He had driven for nearly three and a half hours without a

break, except to fill the tank near Jerez, without being stopped once at a road block, without even seeing a police car, once they were clear of La Linea. That had brought them nearly two hundred and fifty kilometres, according to the satnav, across Cadiz and into Huelva, the last province before Portugal. They had driven in darkness, in the end along a twisting single lane road, into low hills which were only visible as darker shadows above them. They had found this place, left the car outside and walked through the chill air to be met by a Spanish man who introduced himself as a friend of Viktor's – Raul Nuñoz.

Aside from the cover story Viktor had suggested, Carl had tried to say very little to Nuñoz, and after a while he had given up with small talk, got someone out of bed to open up this place, lit the pad like a beacon and left them to it, in this room, with inadequate heating and travel blankets. By then it was 2.30 in the morning and Rebecca was walking with her eyelids drooped, stumbling up steps, silent. Now it was past three and she was in the chair next to Carl's, her head resting on his arm, very asleep.

He listened to the helicopter approaching and when he was sure it was coming for them put a hand down to shake her gently.

Caught in a cross between a dream and a nightmare, Rebecca could feel something biting her leg. When she sat up she could see a mosquito sitting there on her skin, but as she raised her hand to swat it, her mother was right there, talking gently to her, telling her it was only a fly, to let it live. But she wanted it to stop biting her, so squashed it anyway, whacking the palm of her hand onto it. There was a bright trickle of blood running from under her hand, spattering down onto the bed. She sat staring at the mess.

Her mum was sitting beside her on the bed, holding her hand, so she turned to ask how there could be so much blood running out of her, but saw then that her mum was crying, tears running down her face. 'What's up, Mum?' she asked, and immediately felt awful about killing the mosquito because her mum had told her that you shouldn't kill anything, unless you absolutely had to, or there was a very good reason.

She lay her head on her mother's arm and started to go back to sleep, with her mum still crying quietly and the tears dropping down onto her face. Then she woke up again, and it all started afresh, with the mosquito back where it had been, the sharp pricking in her leg. And each time she couldn't stop her mum crying, couldn't even work out if she was to blame.

Then she woke properly, into reality, a man's face right above her, his hand on her shoulder, shaking her. 'Rebecca,' he was saying. 'Wake up.' There was a deafening clattering noise coming from behind him somewhere. She got up immediately, startled, pushing herself off a seat and standing in front of him. She could feel a pain in her leg where the edge of the chair had been sticking into it. She had no idea where she was.

The man stood as well. He was saying something to her but she couldn't hear because the noise was so loud. He pointed over to a window and said something about a helicopter. 'Where's my mum?' she yelled, at the top of her voice. 'I want my mum.' She started crying.

Then it all came back to her. It was worse than a nightmare because this place she was in – waiting for a helicopter – this place was real, and her mum wasn't here. No one she knew was here. Just this stranger who was walking towards her, saying things. She turned to run from him but the room was too small, with nowhere to hide. There were big glass windows right down to the floor on one side. She saw lights blazing in the night beyond, saw a man moving out there, doing something with a thick cable. She screamed at the man in front of her to tell her where she was, what was happening. But she had already remembered, already knew it all.

He crouched down in front of her and tried to take one of her hands, but she wouldn't let him. 'You're going to hurt me,' she shouted at him. 'You're going to kill me.' She could hardly breathe. She was backed up against one of the walls, with him right in front of her. He was boxing her in. She could hear herself shouting without any control. She could see herself doing it but couldn't stop it. Her head felt fuzzy, confused, like she'd had a bang and couldn't hear properly.

'I'm not going to hurt you,' he said. He had to speak loud because behind him she could see a helicopter hovering in the air above the blazing lights, getting lower and lower. The noise it made was beating at her ears like when you left a car window open and you were going really fast on the motorway, only worse. She put her hands over her ears and sobbed. She felt confused and frightened. What was happening? Why was she with this man? She wanted it all to stop, everything to go back to normal.

'I'm not going to hurt you,' he said again.

The rhythmic beating began to slow down. The helicopter was out there now, on the ground. She was meant to get in it, she knew that. They had spoken about it. She took her hands from her ears. 'I'm not doing it,' she shouted at him. 'I'm not coming with you.'

'Look at me,' he said. He was frowning at her, but not like he was angry. 'Look at my eyes.' He pointed at them with two fingers. 'You know I'm not going to hurt you. I will never hurt you. Look at me when I tell you and you'll know it's true. I'm not lying. I'm here to protect you. That's all I'm doing.' He was staring at her so hard she had to look.

She remembered what he had done. He had killed men who had shot at her. She had seen them dead, on the ground, the blood running horribly out of their heads. But he had stopped them doing *that* to her. She felt sick suddenly, like she wanted to throw up. He was still saying things to her, still talking.

Then he smiled. It was the first time he had smiled at her, the first time since he had appeared yesterday afternoon, running down the hill behind her house. A man appeared in the doorway behind him and shouted something, but he just ignored him and kept his eyes on her, with the smile changing his whole face. It was a stupid smile, like a little kid, completely different to the way he had looked before – it broke up the way he frowned, turned his face into something friendly and nice, because something about it made him look clumsy and normal, like he couldn't be serious, like all he could do was tell jokes or take the piss. It made her want to laugh, despite everything. She brought a hand up and wiped her eyes. 'I don't have to go?' she asked him. 'You won't force me?'

'I will never force you to do anything,' he said. 'The helicopter is here to take us to a plane which will get us to London. I think we should do it. But you can choose. If you don't want to then I'll think of something else. You have my word. It's entirely up to you.'

20

Julia sat in the front passenger seat of Molina's car, wiped her eyes on her sleeve and suppressed a sob. Her arms, her legs, the muscles in her face – everything was trembling. She had read about people who lost their kids, read about a kind of numbness that fell over you, paralysing your capacity for fear, but she wasn't getting any of that. What she was experiencing was continual, sustained terror – a fear so powerful that it was flooding her bloodstream with adrenalin, stretching her senses to a kind of hallucinogenic awareness of every single detail around her as her brain ploughed the million horrific things that Rebecca might be suffering. Her need to hold her daughter, to have her right there, in her arms, was like a hole in her heart, a physical absence that radiated a pounding pain up into the back of her skull and down her limbs with every beat of her pulse. She was past the point of exhaustion, past worrying that the irregular thumping meant her heart was about to stop, past being able to process anything clearly. Her life had become an inflamed concentration of anxiety. It had been going on since the moment she realised Rebecca was missing, growing in strength with each minute that passed without news or progress. What she had thought of as reality was not that at all. What she was living *now* was reality – a terrifying exposure to the worst thing that human life could throw at her.

Molina was outside the car, in the darkness, talking on his mobile in a whisper. They were on some minor road between

Gibraltar and Marbella, on the way to Malaga, supposedly. He had taken this route without telling her why. There was a huge, empty motorway that at this time of night could get them to Malaga in half an hour. But he had turned off it, climbed into the hills, used back roads, stopped repeatedly to speak to people on his mobile. The only explanation he would give was that it was part of the investigation. There was no police radio in the car, so he had to use the mobile.

He had used it in La Linea too, almost constantly, whilst she had sat impatiently in a first aid van, in amongst a handful of riot police with blood streaming from injuries, waiting for the single doctor to look at her knee and bleeding nose. The result had been predictable – bandages and painkillers – then back out with Molina whilst he tried to coordinate a four-hour search of a certain section of the town.

But he was competing for resources by then. The riot had not ended with her injury, and Rebecca had slipped from focus as flaming bottles shattered on riot shields and the town began to resemble a minor war zone, with broken glass carpeting the streets and upturned cars on fire. By the time it was dying out and Molina's men could get on with what Molina thought was the priority, it was well past midnight and all Julia could think was that it was too late. They were gone, if they had ever been there. She could feel it in her bones – her daughter was gone.

But she had sat through it all despite that, answering his questions until nearly four in the morning, when he had decided to end the fruitless search and told her that Malaga was the priority. In Malaga they had set up an incident room with all the right equipment, including phone lines and dedicated staff. His theory was that a criminal gang had burgled her house, set the fire, caused the gas bottles to explode, killed Juan and Maria. Rebecca had stumbled into it and been kidnapped. A ransom demand would follow, but not soon. They would wait weeks before making contact. He hoped to find her before that. His plan was to go to the media at daylight, have her sit in front of cameras and beg for help from the public.

But first they had come here. She had no idea why. She looked out of the open window she was leaning on and could see vague, dark shapes in the night. Hills and trees – in the distance a line that could be the sea, at least forty kilometres away. They were high in the hills somewhere. There was a smell of wild rosemary and pine resin, the clicking of crickets and, more faintly, the sound of a stream or waterfall, from higher up, ahead of her. They were a long way from any houses, even further from the nearest town. That had been Casares – from the sign she had read – a tiny *pueblo blanco* with a narrow road winding up through its deserted, sleeping streets.

The driver's door opened and Molina leaned his head in. 'We walk from here,' he said, in Spanish.

'Walk where? Where are we? Why aren't we on the motorway, headed for Malaga?'

He sighed and got in beside her. 'OK,' he said. 'This is what's happening.' He was looking right at her with those same worried eyes. 'I've been trying to set up a meeting with the informant . . .'

She shook her head, not getting it. 'What informant?'

'The one who gave the info that they were in La Linea. The same guy—'

'You told me you traced her phone. You never mentioned an informant . . .' She saw something flick through his eyes, a small mental adjustment.

'I thought then that was what had happened,' he said. 'Arroyo told me that. But it wasn't accurate. You can't trace phones that quickly. It was an informant who gave us the information. A reliable informant.'

She frowned. He was lying, she thought – the first time she had suspected him directly. He didn't lick his lips or change expression, but she picked it up somehow. 'Arroyo was in with me when you came and told him you had located her,' she said. ' So it can't have been Arroyo.'

He shrugged, looking vexed. 'His people, I mean. Does it matter who exactly told me?'

She stared at him. Where was the lie? Which bit of what he was saying? She couldn't work it out. Was he trying to conceal the phone trace, or was there never one? She was going to ask him but he started to get out again. 'We're in a hurry,' he said. 'I've arranged a meet with this guy. I'll meet him here, in the car. The guy will drive here in his own car, then meet me right here. It's arranged. But you can't be here, so I have to move you into the woods there. There's an old hunting hut that belongs to my family. You can wait there, I'll meet him, see what he has to say, then I'll come back for you. We need to be in Malaga in fifty minutes so I can brief the whole team.' He paused to check she had got it all. She had, but she said nothing. 'Get out,' he said. 'We have to be quick.'

He closed his own door, walked round the car and opened hers, then stood there, waiting for her to get out. But she had an alarm bell ringing. 'I don't like it,' she said. 'Just take me to Malaga, then meet with him—'

'The meeting is in fifteen minutes. We can't get to Malaga before it happens.'

'Who is he? Why do you need to speak to him?'

'I can't tell you who he is. He's a top-level informant, well-connected to organised crime networks here. He's the man who told us your daughter was in La Linea. He's helping you. He has more information. It could be crucial. He might be able to tell us where she is right now. Get out. Come on.'

Still she didn't move. 'Why can't he give you the information by phone?'

He sighed again. 'It doesn't work like that. Phones aren't safe ...'

'And where's my phone? Do you have it?'

'I already told you I don't have it. It's at the lab. You won't be getting it back until we find Rebecca. Now please get out and follow me. If he arrives early and sees someone else he will simply drive away. This is important. You understand?'

She looked up at him. 'Where are you wanting to take me? Tell me again.'

'A hunting refuge. Just over there a few hundred metres.' He pointed. 'Some of this land belongs to my family. That's why I came here, why I arranged it for here. The place is comfortable enough. You will only need to wait twenty minutes probably.'

She got out carefully, trying not to put too much weight on her bandaged knee – though there was much less pain now, she could feel that there was swelling. She stood in the open door facing him and looked into his eyes, from very close. 'Are you telling me the truth?' she asked. She remembered again Rebecca's message about the policeman shooting at her.

He frowned at her. 'Why would I not tell you the truth? I'm trying to find your daughter. That's my job. I know what you're going through.' He spoke quietly, his eyes on hers, his voice inflected with a wounded tone.

She felt a tightening in the back of her throat. There was nothing to tell her he was lying, except that tightness, something operating below a conscious level. But was she being stupid? She was exhausted, living on adrenalin. Could she trust reactions based on some kind of instinct? If anything, he had seemed relatively sympathetic to her, had seemed committed and honest.

She decided quickly. She would go with him, look at the place, but that didn't imply she trusted him. She didn't trust him, no matter how decent he seemed. She would need to make

him think the opposite though. Because that was the safest way.
'Sorry,' she said. 'I don't know what's real and what's not. Not
any more. You lead, I'll follow.'

21

'Her mother is alive. The dead woman was a *friend* of the husband. The dead woman was not her mother.' Viktor's voice, speaking to Carl through a headset given to him on the plane. 'I saw it on the news and checked separately. The dead woman was Maria Jimenez. The girl's mother is Julia Martin.'

'Christ above,' Carl whispered, in English. They had been speaking Russian.

'Your call, brother,' Viktor said. He didn't sound amused. 'What now?'

Carl looked up to where Rebecca was stretched out in a wide leather-upholstered reclined seat, at the back of the cabin, blanket over her, eyes closed. He assumed she was asleep, assumed she wasn't listening, assumed she didn't understand Russian.

They had been airborne for only twenty minutes, en route to London, having taken off from a municipal airstrip just inside Portugal. It had taken the helicopter just over half an hour to get them there. There had been no going through customs, no passport checks, no questions at all. The helicopter had landed about fifty metres from the jet and they had simply walked over to it. Carl was used to that from previous travels with Viktor, but the efficiency and speed with which Viktor's people had cleared and set up the whole itinerary had certainly surprised him. Previously, he had no idea that Viktor had any interests inside Spain or Portugal.

The plane was small – a Learjet converted to carry six passengers, though right now they were the only two. There were four luxury seats, facing each other in banks of two, with a table between, then another row of two seats further back, to sleep in. The cabin was quiet – less noisy than a commercial airliner – but the ride was bumpy by comparison and the space very constricted. He had thought Rebecca would find it difficult to sleep, had expected her to need more reassurance. But she was past that, it seemed – she had been asleep within ten minutes, at the end of her reserves. Carl had got the blanket out and spread it over her. He had then walked to the cockpit and asked the co-pilot to set up a call to Viktor, via the satellite link.

'We need to get her out of Spain,' Carl said to Viktor now.

'The mother, you mean?'

'Yes. They will come for her again. Can you get her out? Get her to London – then we can give her back her daughter. Can you handle that?'

'You could turn back and get her yourself. You're already there.'

'I can't go back. Not with the girl. I need the girl someplace safe before I can do anything.'

'I'll try,' Viktor said. 'It will take longer than this has taken though. I had someone there I could trust, but I can't use him again.'

'Thanks. When we get to London I'll make a decision. If necessary I can go back for the mother.'

'Not London. I diverted the flight to Helsinki.'

Carl frowned. He had promised Rebecca that they were going to London. 'Why?'

'It's always safer to change the flight plan. You don't know who has had access to the original. But anyway, you're coming to me, and I'm not in London, I'm in Helsinki. I found out who is behind it.'

Carl stood up and walked towards the cockpit end of the cabin, a little further from Rebecca. 'Tell me,' he said, quietly.

'Sergei Zaikov paid for it.'

That led to a long silence. Carl chewed his lip, tried to organise his thoughts. 'You sure?' he asked.

'No. But pretty sure. I'll know more later today. But that's what I'm being told right now.'

'Zaikov.' He cursed under his breath. 'Why would Zaikov hire me? I don't get it.'

'I'm certain he never knew it was you,' Viktor said.

'He would surely know who he was hiring.'

'Why? You never knew who was hiring you. That's the way it works, isn't it? Guaranteed anonymity. On both sides.'

That was how it was supposed to function – an anonymous cartel of businessmen hiring anonymous contractors, but the screening arrangements had never prevented Viktor from getting behind the façade, as he had now – so why couldn't Zaikov do the same? 'Why does he want her dead?' Carl asked. 'You get anything on that?'

'Nothing but rumour. It's possible the husband had a debt.'

'The guy I found in the house?'

'I assume so.'

'So Zaikov wants the whole family put down? How much was the debt?'

'I don't know. I don't even know if that's good information. It's the middle of the night in Europe – difficult to get as much as I would want. I'll have more later. You'll be in Helsinki in three hours, so we can talk face to face. Zaikov will arrive here either today or tomorrow, on one of his boats. He has a conference. That's why I'm here.'

Carl was impressed. 'You can find out where Zaikov is going to be? Your people gave you all this in the middle of the night?'

'No. I already knew that. Zaikov is important to me.'

That puzzled Carl. There was an obvious way that Zaikov had been important to both of them during the last ten years, but Viktor hadn't meant that.

'Does it change anything?' Viktor asked.

'That it's Zaikov? No. I don't have an alternative. I need the girl safe, I need her mother out of Spain, then I need to see him. I need it cancelling.'

Viktor grunted. 'I'm ahead of you, little brother. I've already considered that. I think it might be possible but I can't say more now. Not on this link. We'll discuss it when we meet.'

The conversation over, Carl walked back through the cabin, pondering the new information. He stood near Rebecca, watching her, trying to work out the meaning. She was asleep, no doubt about it. He thought about waking her, to give her the good news that her mother was safe and well, that his brother would get her out of Spain and they would meet again, soon. He could tell her all of that without lying, but then realised he would have to tell her the destination was no longer London. She might not like that. It could wait until she had rested more, he thought. He didn't want a repeat of the screaming fit in the waiting room at the helipad.

22

The hut really was a hut – a one-room log cabin buried in the woods about one hundred metres from the road. But the door had a lock, and Molina had a key for it. Inside there were bunk beds for four, a table, two chairs and a corner with a sink and a cooker that ran on a gas bottle. Above the sink there were shelves with pans and cups and plates. There was a single drawer beneath the sink. There was no electricity, so holding a torch in one hand he had to fiddle around for a few minutes with an oil lamp, striking matches to light it before placing it on the table. 'This place is hardly ever used these days,' he said. 'But you won't be here long.'

'You're going to leave me in here?'

'Only while I meet him. Twenty minutes most.'

'You won't lock me in?' She smiled at him as she said it, like she was making a joke. He frowned back, like he hadn't understood the joke.

'When will you meet him?' she asked.

'I have to ring him. I'll step outside now and ring him. There's no signal in here. I have to walk back towards the road a little. Sit down. Relax.'

She sat down on the edge of one of the lower bunk beds. There were mattresses, smelling of dust, but no blankets she could see, no pillows. 'I might sleep,' she said.

'That would be good, if you could manage it.'

'I might not be able to stay awake ...' She lay carefully on the mattress, closed her eyes.

'Can I make this call?' he asked. 'You OK?'

She waved a hand at him, like she was already almost asleep. His voice had a different tone, she thought.

She heard him open the door, step out, close it, heard his footsteps on the pine needles. He hadn't locked the door. She sat up. There were two windows in the hut but both were shuttered fast. She stood, walked to the door and listened, with her ear to the hinges. After a few moments she could hear him talking, but it was indistinct. She placed her hand on the door handle, eased it down, pulled the door open a fraction and put her ear in the crack. Now she could hear him. He could only be about ten metres away. There was a danger he would see the light from the oil lamp but she couldn't control that and she had to know what he was up to. He was talking quickly, saying something about speed. 'Yes, yes, yes,' she heard, in Spanish. 'She's here, exactly as I said. But you have to be quick.' A silence. She could hear her heart speeding up. She held her breath. 'No, I will not leave her. I will keep her here. I will wait.' He had said that in English.

She closed the door quickly, looked desperately around the hut. He had lied to her. He had brought her here so people could come for her. That was the only way she could interpret it.

She walked quickly to the drawer under the sink, pulled it out and quickly surveyed a collection of rusting knives and forks, spoons and spatulas – she moved her fingers through them, found a bigger blade, for chopping. She took it out. It was a normal carving knife, about thirty centimetres long. She ran her finger over the edge – it was blunt, but pointed. She heard herself struggling to breathe. *Not again*, she thought, *please God, not again*. She shut the drawer and went back to the bed, slid the knife between the mattress and the boards, with the handle facing out, sat on top of it, took long, deep breaths.

The door opened and he stepped in. He looked at her, his face unchanged from when he had walked out. 'You OK?' he asked. He could see she wasn't. She couldn't control her breathing, couldn't conceal it.

'I had a panic attack,' she said quickly. 'Have you heard anything?'

'He's coming. It will be—'

'Not about that. About Rebecca.'

He shook his head. 'He will tell me when we meet.' He pulled the door shut and turned the key from the inside, left the key in the lock.

'Why did you lock it?' she asked.

He shrugged. 'Force of habit.' But he didn't unlock it. He walked over to the table and sat down. The oil lamp was flickering, casting unfortunate shadows over his face.

'You're not going out to meet him?' she asked. She was trying very hard to get her breath even.

'In ten minutes.' He looked at her, but then looked away again.

'You're telling me the truth?'

'Why wouldn't I be? What do you mean?'

'There's no informant, is there?'

His eyes flashed with anger. 'I wish you would just trust me,' he said sharply. 'I'm getting tired of having to ...' He stopped and cursed.

'Tired of having to lie to me?'

'Christ above! Don't be stupid. I'm a police officer. Remember?'

'I remember. One of your men tried to kill my daughter.'

'Not that again.' He ran a hand across his face, looked like he was sick of all this stupidity. 'You don't know what she meant,'

138

he said. 'We've been over it. We don't know what the dead officer was doing, what he was shooting at – but it can't have been at Rebecca, can it? It must have been at this other guy, the guy who has taken her.'

'I should have walked away from you when I had the chance. I almost trusted you. I really thought you were trying to find her.'

'I *am* trying to find her.'

'Maybe. But not to help her. I know what's happening here.' She kept her eyes on him. 'We both know.'

'What do you mean?' He looked genuinely puzzled. 'Is that a question?'

'A statement. I know. You know. Stop pretending.'

He stood up suddenly and paced back and forth, once, twice, then stood by the door, back to her.

'Someone tried to kill my family,' she said. Her voice sounded stretched. 'They tried to kill me and my family. It wasn't burglars, it wasn't kidnappers, it wasn't terrorists.'

'So who does that leave?' He turned and stepped in front of her, a facetious smile on his lips.

'Don't smirk,' she said. 'Not when you already know the truth.'

He sighed. 'You're very stressed, Señora Martin. I can understand that.' He took out his mobile, glanced at it. 'Only five more minutes.'

'Until what?' She was sitting on the edge of the bed, rigidly. He was about two metres in front of her. He didn't think she would do anything, was confident about it. He wasn't relaxed, far from it, but he wasn't bothered that she might jump up and go for his throat. He thought he knew her, thought she wasn't that type. Or if she was, no doubt he thought he could brush her off. She was a woman, and not a particularly big or strong one. He was a fit, well-built male, younger than her.

'This is about something I've done in the past,' she said. 'What happened was a "hit" – that's the English word. A botched hit, because they didn't get me or Rebecca. But they had police help to do it, and they have police help now to try to get a second chance. You know all this already.'

He changed stance, spreading his legs a little, but was still staring down at her with that frown.

'"They"?' he asked. 'Who are "they"?'

'You know who.'

'I wouldn't ask you if I knew.'

'Sergei Zaikov. There is a man called Sergei Zaikov ...'

'Zaikov? I've never heard of this man. This is the first time you've mentioned him. You cannot withhold information that—'

'He's Russian. Very wealthy. I understand why he's doing this, understand the reasons. But that doesn't make it right – killing a child and her family. That can never be right. You're a police officer, you must agree with me?'

'Of course I agree with you. But let's step back a bit, go over what you just said ...' He checked his mobile again. 'You say that a man called Sergei Zaikov—'

'They're coming here, right? That's who you're waiting for.'

He stopped speaking, looked straight at her. Colour flooded into his cheeks.

'Don't deny it,' she said, almost whispering. 'They're coming here. Coming for me. That's what you've arranged. I heard you talking on the phone.'

His confidence vanished. His eyes darted around the cabin, looking anywhere but at her. She could see his brain working feverishly, assessing what she might have heard, how much he had given away, what he could do now. He licked his lips, put the phone in the pocket of his jacket, moved his arms to his sides, said nothing.

'I heard what you said,' she repeated. 'I *know* what's happening. There's no point in lying now.'

He let out a long breath, ran his hand over his face again, pushed that lovely lock of hair out of the way.

'You know what they will do to me?' she asked. She started to cry as she said it.

He shook his head. 'No one is coming here—'

'You don't have to do this, Señor Molina. You have a choice. We all have choices. I chose in the past, and that choice is catching up with me. But you can choose *now*. You know what they will do to me?'

'I don't know what you're talking about.'

'They will kill me.'

He was silent. He started working his jaw muscles.

'I don't know what they told you – maybe they told you that they would kill me, or maybe they told you something else, to make it easier – like they would only kidnap me, or something like that, hold me to ransom. But that's not Zaikov. I know Zaikov and I know why he's doing this. He will send men here to kill me. Here, in this place. If you let it happen then these are the last few minutes of my life.'

'You have to be calm, Señora Martin,' he tried, his voice softening.

'You don't want to do this,' she said, persisting. 'I can see you don't want to do it. Have you ever done anything like this before? Arranged for someone to be killed? You don't seem like an evil man to me. I've met evil men, close up. I know what they're like. You're not that. You can walk out now, leave the door open, get in your car and go. It's as simple as that. Leave me. I will look after myself.'

'I can't do that.' He licked his lips again. 'I can't do that.' He couldn't look at her now.

'You *have* to do that. It doesn't matter what happened before, what you said to them, what you promised. You have to look at me now and decide. Decide whether you will let men come here to kill me, then kill my daughter.'

He was sweating, quite suddenly. His face started to twitch. She watched him in silence, letting him grapple with it, hoping he was the person she had judged him to be. Her heart was whacking against her chest, she had to use short sentences, get herself to breathe properly, but she felt a sudden clarity. She knew what was happening, what had been happening all along. Rebecca had been right.

'I don't know ...' he said. He was wavering.

'Help me,' she said, sobbing a little. 'Don't let them kill me. Not for me, but for my daughter. She has done nothing. Please. Help me.'

He gulped at the air. 'What did *you* do?' he asked, his voice strangled, harsh. He swallowed hard. 'What did you do that they have done all this?'

'I didn't do anything,' she lied. 'They thought I did something. That's all. And Rebecca is only a child. She *cannot* have done anything. She doesn't deserve any of this.'

He shook his head again. 'I can't. It's gone too far. I'm sorry. It's not personal. It's nothing to do with you. I made mistakes and they have me. I can't walk away. If I walk away they will kill me and my family.'

'You have a child?'

He shook his head. 'No, but they will kill my parents, my girlfriend.'

Not the fucking same, she thought. Not the same at all.

'I have already taken their money,' he said. 'There's nothing I can do. I'm sorry.' He put his face in his hands, standing there, like he was going to cry, then shook his head sharply, looked at her. As his hands came down, fists clenched, there was a different look in his eyes. She thought, what if they weren't coming, what if *he* was meant to do it?

'Will you let me go?' she begged. Her right hand was by her leg, she was touching the knife handle. 'Will you just let me go?'

'No.' He shook his head. 'You stay here. And shut up. Shut up now.'

She was moving immediately. He expected it, expected her to do something. He took a step sideways, towards the door, barring her route, thinking she would make a run for it. But she turned the other way, half in a crouch, hand slipping over the knife handle, pulling it out. She registered a flash of pain from her damaged knee, then felt one of his hands on her back trying to push her down, into the bunk beds. She turned into him, fast, the knife held back, the arm flexed. He shouted something as she spun. She saw him moving to block her, still not realising what she was doing, unaware of the blade. He was leaning forward with his arms outstretched, the jacket open. Probably he thought she was trying to push him out of the way. She could see the pastel blue shirt he was wearing beneath the flapping jacket, see the gap between the lapels, the triangle of flesh at his throat. She snapped the blade up at him with a yell, using all the force she could get into it.

Her fist hit his chest. At that moment she was so close to him that he was only a blur of movement coming towards her. She pulled her arm back at once, stepped sideways two steps, saw with amazement that she still had the knife in her hand. She screamed at him. 'Let me go! Don't come near me.'

His face was contorted in a grimace of shock. He stumbled slightly, got both hands onto the frame of the top bunk and stood there, leaning on it, his face turned sideways, looking at her. The blood drained from his features and he muttered something. But still she couldn't absorb the information. Her hand had hit his chest, she had felt that, but she had felt nothing else, no resistance to the blade. It was like she had struck him with the side of her hand. Had she *only* done that, somehow? Had she botched it and simply punched him clumsily, the knife held sideways? She took another step away from him, frantically thinking about what to do next, then looked down at the knife and saw the blood on it.

He collapsed to his knees. 'What have you done?' he hissed. 'What have you done to me?' His eyes were already rolling in his head, his hands still hanging onto the bedframe. He slipped backwards, letting go, and his head smashed off the chair he had been sitting on, overturning it. His shirt was dark with blood. The oil lamp flickered like it would go out.

She dropped the knife in horror, took a step towards him, thinking she would try to do something, to help him. He was flat out on his back, his chest heaving. It looked like he was trying to get his hands up to his shirt, but couldn't move them. She went down onto one knee, a little away from him. Did he have a gun? She couldn't remember. She started to sob out loud. 'I'm sorry,' she cried. 'God, I'm so sorry.' His eyes were on her, but it looked like he was dizzy, didn't know what was happening. He started making a kind of choking noise. She put her hand in her mouth and bit into her knuckles. 'Oh God, I'm so sorry.'

'Help me,' he gasped. 'Please help me …'

She moved forward and opened his jacket a bit wider. All she could see was blood. What could she do? There had to be something she could do. She didn't want him to kill her, but she didn't want him to die either. His legs kicked out suddenly, banging into the bunk beds, his back arching. She tried to pull the shirt away, feeling the blood on her hands. She couldn't find the buttons, so pulled it up from his trousers. She got it up above his stomach and still couldn't find the wound. The blood was all over, running across his skin. She said something to him about calling an ambulance but he just lay there, the breath rasping in his throat, his eyes unfocused. His hands were trembling on the floor. She scrambled backwards, overcome with disgust and horror. She couldn't believe it. There was a loud hissing in her ears, in time with her pulse. Behind it she heard his phone.

She took deep breaths, deliberately didn't look at his face. Then went forward and searched through his jacket pockets, very quickly and clumsily, her hands shaking all over. He hardly reacted as she did it. Just his chest moving up and down. His eyes were fixed on the ceiling, blinking rapidly.

She found two phones. One was hers. He had lied about that. She put it aside and looked at his. It was still ringing. She looked at the screen but there was no information about the number. She couldn't answer it. It would be the people he had sold her to, coming here, telling him they were coming.

She stood up, pocketed both phones, his still ringing. She looked at the door, stepped over to it, turned the key, glanced back at him. Would he die? His friends would be here soon. It would be up to them. She couldn't wait. He had brought her here so they could kill her. She had to get out.

23

The mobile phone he had given her told Rebecca it was 9.30 – in the morning, she assumed. She sat on the wooden jetty in an exhausted trance, staring at the sun, low over the line of pine trees at the other side of the bay, or sea, or river – or whatever it was the jetty stuck out into. The water was still and dark all the way over to the other side, everything very quiet. She could hear only a very gentle rustling in the banks of tall grey-green reeds growing either side, fringing the water. How far was it to the other side? Too far to swim, and too cold, probably.

But why would she want to do that? He hadn't hurt her, he had told her that her mother was safe and that his brother – who was rich – was sending people right now to bring her here, to be with her. He had *promised* her that her mother would be brought here. He had given her this phone – it was safer than her own, he said – and said she could try her mum as much as she wanted, and to shout for him if she got her, so that he could speak to her too.

But her mum wasn't answering. Her phone wasn't even switched on, it seemed. She had tried her dad's as well, same result. She didn't know her cousin's number – in London – and didn't even have it in her phone. She knew her best friend Louisa's mobile and had left her two messages now, asking her to call her back straight away. But maybe this phone didn't auto-matically send its number with a message, so she would need to ask Carl for the number of the phone, then leave another message, and she wasn't sure he would let her call Louisa. She would ask him later.

He had told her it was OK to use her mother's normal number now that they knew her mum was safe, and she had called it almost every minute for the time she had been out here. How long was that? She couldn't remember. They had come here in a helicopter – another one – and a car, and he had given her something to eat and drink in the kitchen of the house, then told her she could go wherever she wanted, but to be careful at the water's edge. So she had come down the pathway through the garden to here. The trees in the garden were birch trees, already bare, with leaves all over the grass. She knew how to identify birch, pine, oak, sycamore, chestnut and a few other kinds of tree, because her mother had taught her all that while they were out walking. Birch was easy, because of the white bark.

She was wondering if it was possible that it was 9.30 at night, that the low sun was actually sinking, not rising. How long had the plane journey taken? She had been asleep the whole way, then felt sick during the bumpy helicopter ride.

They were in Finland, he had told her, near a city called Helsinki. Finland was north of Spain, she knew, and could tell, because it was freezing. He had given her his jacket on the trip, then a fleece that was too big for her, once they got here. She had it wrapped around herself, but was still shivering a bit. Soon she would have to get up and go back into the house.

The house was huge, built of wood and painted pale blue and white. All the rooms she had passed through looked like something from one of her mum's magazines – with posh-looking furniture, everything glass and wood and silver. There were only a few pictures on the walls, very big things, mostly abstract, so she didn't understand what they were meant to be. Everything was very neat and tidy, not like her house at all. 'I'm guessing no kids live here,' she had said to him.

'Viktor lives here,' he had said. 'As much as he can. It's the first house he built, when he first made some money.' Viktor was his brother. When they had arrived he had been out. There was meant to be someone here to 'look after the place', but they couldn't find him either. 'You'll be safe here,' Carl said. 'Until your mum arrives.'

She pressed redial on the phone again and listened to the same message in Spanish, telling her the number was unavailable. She frowned and felt her chin twitch, tears pricking at her eyes. She had cried so much she was sick of it, but couldn't do anything to stop it. She cried even when there was nothing immediately upsetting her.

What was happening to her was so odd she felt like she was suspended, floating through something that was all stretched out and weird and gave her a headache. She didn't understand any of it. Not really. It was like her life had stopped – everything that she knew and was familiar with – but not like it had vanished completely. She thought her old life must still somehow be going on somewhere else, over there where she was from, in Spain, continuing like it always did, but without her. Like there might be another girl called Rebecca who was right now on her way to school, with nothing unusual happening at all, her house still standing, no dead people with blood running out of their heads, her mother kissing her forehead as she left to get the bus. Probably that Rebecca had eaten pizza the night before, made with her mum, in the kitchen there – because Monday night was always pizza night.

She had been split off from that person, had slipped into this place where nothing at all was real, where a man kept telling her that people were trying to kill her. It was like a computer game, and she was trapped inside it. She'd read a book like that once. Maybe seen a film about it too.

She heard someone shouting to her, in English. 'Has he left

148

you out here? Come in. It's too cold. Come in.' She turned and looked. There was a large man at the end of the jetty, waving to her. For a moment she thought it was Carl, but the voice wasn't the same. It would be his brother, she guessed. But maybe not. Maybe it was the man who looked after this place. She stood and walked towards him.

'You're Rebecca?' he said, when she was nearer. 'You should come in. It's not so warm out here.' He was smiling at her, looking very intently into her face. He looked very like Carl, though was wearing different clothes. She had to look twice, as it were, to be sure it wasn't him. The voice was different and the face older, rounder. He had on a thick grey overcoat, unbuttoned, beneath it a dark suit, with a white shirt and polished black shoes. He looked like a politician or a businessman, because of the suit. He had one of those earpieces in his ear, and was as tall as Carl, with the same wide shoulders and big hands. Same short blond hair. He had a nice smile. He smiled with his eyes – more with his eyes than his mouth, different from Carl. The skin around his eyes wrinkled up and the eyes were a beautiful blue – quite startling.

All her friends said that she either liked someone or disliked them immediately – she made her mind up before they spoke to her, before they even looked at her. It was like a joke about her, and not true, she thought. But she smiled back at this guy. He looked OK. He held out a hand for her to shake. She took it and he barely touched her fingers. 'I'm Viktor,' he said. 'It's nice to meet you, finally.'

She walked back up to the house with him. He asked her if she was OK, if she wanted anything to eat, or wanted to sleep. She said, 'Have you found my mother yet?'

'They might have found her,' he said. 'I don't know. I've arranged for someone over in Spain – a good friend of mine – to find her and get her to you. They'll bring her here. Don't worry.' A pause as he glanced at her. 'I'll let you know when I find out things. I'm sure it will be OK.' He sounded like he was telling the truth. 'You shouldn't worry about it,' he added. 'Try to relax and rest. My brother tells me some pretty bad things have been happening.'

She nodded.

'He's a good man, my brother. He'll make sure you're OK.'

They reached the house and he held a door open for her. They went into a room with black sofas and a glass coffee table. It was warm and smelled faintly of pine smoke. The walls were all wooden panels. There was a big fireplace, but it wasn't lit.

'My chef's not here,' he said, taking off his coat. 'Usually I have some people who help me out, cook for me. I don't know how to do much by myself. They'll get here by Thursday, I think. Meanwhile, we have to look after ourselves a bit. You know how to cook things? I bet you know how to cook already.'

She knew how to cook a few things, but shook her head.

He laughed. 'That's OK,' he said. 'I can't even fry an egg. Maybe my brother can cook us some breakfast. He's good at that kind of thing.'

'Or we could order in pizza,' she suggested.

He smiled. 'We could do that, yes. What do you want?'

'What is there?'

'I've no idea. I don't even know where the nearest pizza place is, or if it's open. If it's back in town then the pizzas might be cold when they get here. They might not even deliver this far out. We're quite a way from any other houses and shops and things. But I can try.' He threw his overcoat onto a sofa and took a smartphone from the jacket pocket. 'Pizza for breakfast. Why didn't I think of that?'

24

Carl was in the room they had once used to watch TV when he had been here. It was on the first floor with windows facing onto the inlet and the boat jetty. There was a flat screen that covered a whole wall – the biggest Carl had ever seen – plus a bar enclosing a corner of the room. He had watched an ice-hockey match with his brother here, maybe three years ago, and hadn't been back since. The flat screen was new.

Carl didn't like this place. Too many uncomfortable memories. They had been here when Liz had vanished, ten years ago.

From the window alcove he had watched Rebecca talking to his brother down by the jetty, watched them walk up towards the house. He had set up a laptop on the interior window sill, got online and started searching for news stories from Spain. He found nothing about Rebecca or the explosion at her house. There was coverage of the unrest in La Linea, but not much. There was no mention of the three men he had killed, one of whom had been police. There was something about a stabbed policeman in intensive care, but that had nothing to do with him. The silence was odd but due to a lack of Spanish he was only getting the English language hits, so maybe there was more. He couldn't find the coverage Viktor had referred to.

Before trawling the news he had made several calls, to people here, or in Russia, people who might be described as part of his network. He was waiting for them to get back to him, waiting for answers.

He closed the laptop and decided to go down, to make sure Rebecca wasn't in tears again, but then Viktor came through the door.

'I met her,' he said.

'Is she OK?'

Viktor nodded. 'I think so. She's handling it.'

'Do I need to check on her?'

'She's fine. I've left her with my phone, looking for pizza places. She wants pizza for breakfast.'

'She doesn't speak Finnish. How will she find a pizza place?'

Viktor frowned. 'Right. I didn't think of that. But she'll be all right. I gave her a credit card, told her to order what she wants. If she speaks English they'll understand. She's ten, she seems smart – she can handle it. Anyway, nowhere will be open.'

'Where's the staff?'

'They'll be here later. I think I'll be safe for a few hours without them. Things are not so dangerous as they used to be.' He winked at Carl. 'You'll understand when I explain what's happening. Be patient. We can go to the gym. We need to talk.'

The basement gym was screened constantly for surveillance devices. As they walked there Viktor removed the cellphone earpiece and switched the phone off, leaving it upstairs and reminding Carl to do the same. A side effect of the automatic detection and screening system built into the gym structure was that the phones wouldn't work down there in any case.

The room was full of the usual machines, plus a boxing ring. Carl had never seen anyone actually get in the ring, but Viktor wanted him to now – 'We can spar as we talk,' he suggested, but Carl refused. Getting his head thumped for fun wasn't his idea of an effective way to unwind.

'I think better when I'm moving,' Viktor said. 'I'll hit the bag a bit, blow off some tension.' Carl shrugged. He was about to get a lecture from Viktor, he assumed, a brotherly reprimand. That was OK, as long as they could get to a solution afterwards.

Viktor stripped to the waist and pulled on a pair of practice gloves, then walked over to one of the bags hanging from the ceiling. He started to punch, rights and lefts, quick combinations, short jabs mainly. Carl leaned against the counter at the opposite wall, reached over the other side of it, found a bottle of mineral water and took a long drink. He felt very tired.

After a few minutes Viktor paused, then started to speak at the same time as he punched. His face was already red, his brow damp with sweat. He spoke in short sentences, taking frequent breaths, punctuating the words with big, heavy punches.

Carl listened, though it didn't seem to have much to do with his problem. It was a ramble about families and power, honour and greed. It moved on to politics and business, and all the while Viktor kept punching away, slow, methodical blows, never looking at him.

Mostly the speech was in a language Carl didn't understand – the language Viktor had learned on the way to making all this money. But when the Zaikov family started to feature, Carl paid more attention. There followed a lot of stuff about the Zaikov clan being *men of honour*, men to be trusted, and so on. They were men who could forgive and forget, men Viktor could do business with – because there was no real *black history* between their two families. That was the crucial thing – they were not *natural enemies*. All of this was surprising to Carl, though he could see where it was leading.

'We are all from the same part of the world,' Viktor concluded. 'We are Karelians first, Russians or Finns second. We have learned the same ways to survive, in the same schools of necessity and poverty. We are here because events forced us here.' He stopped punching and turned to face Carl.

'You're doing business with Zaikov,' Carl asked. 'Is that it?'

Viktor nodded, a light in his eyes. 'There has been contact. Yes. And there will be a deal, a big deal. The past will be forgotten.' He unveiled it like it was something triumphant, of historical significance.

But Carl couldn't see it. 'Just like that?' he asked.

'No. Not *just like that*.' Viktor started walking towards him, a different expression on his face. 'It has taken time and investment to build trust. But what I want you to understand is that Zaikov's fight isn't with us. It isn't with *our* family. The bad blood is between *Mikhael Ivanovich* and Zaikov.' He spoke his uncle's first name and patronym as if the words were something filthy, yet Carl could only remember Viktor being treated like an adopted son by Mikhael. Mikhael was Viktor's father's brother. If it weren't for Mikhael taking him in as a spotty eighteen-year-old, then Viktor would have nothing today. Mikhael was the Russian relative who had welcomed him back with open arms, passed on all his connections, promoted Viktor's rise to wealth and status, treated him as his own. And as for their immediate family, he and Viktor were the sole survivors. There was no dynasty, no tribe, no organisation that he wanted to be part of. They had grown up in Finland, with a Russian mother. They were from nowhere, belonged nowhere. In London Carl lived with a girlfriend – a Swede called Annika – but he felt little for her and tolerated her mainly to boost his cover. And the nearest Viktor had to an extended family were the people he paid.

'The past was only a barrier because Zaikov never knew what happened,' Viktor continued. 'That had to be dealt with.'

Carl felt suddenly very uneasy. 'So how did you deal with it?'

Viktor smiled. 'He needed to know who killed his son. I told him.'

Carl stood straight, took a breath. 'What did you tell him?'

Viktor laughed, put a gloved hand out and shadow boxed

towards Carl's chest. 'Not the truth, little brother. Don't worry. I gave him the two dead bodyguards. I gave him the whole story, with proof. And the names of the bodyguards.'

'And he took that?'

'Of course. He needed closure. We all did. It was ten years ago. Time to move on.'

Carl couldn't believe any of it. Zaikov was the type who never forgot, never moved on. 'Are you sure Zaikov was behind this contract?' he asked.

'I'm sure. Federov will be here later and you can get the details off him. But he traced the funds. The money you've been paid originated with one of Zaikov's companies.' He stepped back towards the bag. 'You're lucky it's Zaikov,' he said. 'Because right now we are on the brink of something. There is goodwill between our families. A year ago and things would have been very different. I don't think I would have been able to help.'

'So you can talk to him, get him to cancel it?'

Viktor smiled. 'I've started already. Your problems won't get in the way of what we have planned. We'll find a price to cover it. We'll pay. That will be that.'

25

Julia crouched soaking wet in the rain, shivering. Below her – beyond the road and over the edge of a short cliff – an expanse of still water, the western rim of the Guadalteba reservoir, vanished into the curtain of rain. Across the other side, she knew, there were houses and people, holiday homes, resorts for water sports – but the rain had come suddenly half an hour ago and was thick in front of her, reducing visibility to a matter of a hundred metres or so. She couldn't see the other side and hoped no one over there could see her.

She had brought Rebecca here on a drive, during the summer, two years ago. From Malaga, over the sierra, it was a little over an hour to reach this place. It had taken her a lot longer just now, using whatever back roads she could find, coming via the pass that took you to Ronda, further to the north-west.

She was learning on her feet, she thought. There was an urgent need to learn quickly. That was what she was trying to focus on. Not on Molina, or his body, or his family. She couldn't let her thoughts go near Molina. She was here again, right back where she had been ten years ago. And it had happened again, *exactly the same*. She had thought she could disappear, escape the past. But it had hunted her out, the consequences dragged around behind her like a secret trace of entrails.

Only now she had a daughter they were trying to kill. So it wasn't going to be like last time, because it couldn't be. Ten years ago she had collapsed, mentally and physically. But this time she had to keep going, find Rebecca. She had to keep the causation clear in her head. She had chosen none of this – not now, not ten years ago. It had come to her and she had reacted, without any real choice or freedom. This time Molina had made the choices, despite her repeatedly trying to give him a way out.

His car was down in the reservoir waters now, submerged. From where she was she couldn't see it at all, but still had doubts about whether it would be visible from a police helicopter. The reservoir – made by damming and flooding a vast shallow valley system – could not be that deep. But it would have to do. About three kilometres back, on the main road, she had passed a bus stop, which meant there were people living round here somewhere, but she hadn't seen them. The land all around was sandy scrub, desolate, throughout most of the year more like a desert. There were trees and bushes nearer to the reservoir but out beyond that you were beginning to get into the immense, parched, flat interior of Spain.

The bus stop was a back-up, but things would be desperate if it came to having to catch a public bus. She had killed a policeman. She assumed the body would be discovered sometime today, maybe already had been. It depended who knew what Molina had been up to. She assumed there would be some kind of major hunt for her. So the window for being able to get on a public bus without being detected was pretty small.

She would have preferred to have stuck to the coast, to the heavily populated areas. More police there, but more places to hide also, harder to find people. But she hadn't been thinking clearly five hours ago, fleeing from Molina's hut. Her main fear had been that Zaikov's people were on their way there to kill her. She had to put distance between herself and that place. So she had driven inland without planning anything, intent only on getting away.

Her phone wouldn't work, because the chip had been

removed. Maybe the chip had been somewhere else on Molina's body, maybe she could have found it if she'd forced herself to be calmer, but by the time she had pulled over – still in darkness – and got out her phone to try Rebecca again, there had been no possibility of going back to the hut to check. Which had only left Molina's phone. She had called Rebecca using that, got a message, in Spanish, saying the number could not be reached. That was enough to convince her. She needed help, needed it very badly – and there was only one way she could think to achieve that.

She called the emergency number she had memorised two years ago, at the meeting with Michael Rugojev. It wasn't in any phone memory, it wasn't written anywhere. It was in her head only, as he had requested. She had learned it carefully but still feared a digit might be wrong, or he might have changed it. But it had been answered immediately. Not by Michael, but by someone speaking Russian. She had told them who she was and what was happening. In poor English, they had said they would call back.

Within ten minutes the phone had rung and she was giving the details again – again, not to Michael himself. Whoever it was this time had told her to drive here, get rid of the car and phone and wait. They would send someone. They had given her a car registration plate to watch out for.

That was over four hours ago now. She had found this place using the car satnav, then rolled the car off the bluff and found a thick growth of bushes near the road, pushed her way into them to wait. She could see the cliff edge – the drop was only about ten metres at this point, straight into the water – see the road as it twisted along the edge of the reservoir before disappearing into the rain.

She had kept the phones and, whilst waiting, taken a closer look at Molina's. It had to be a phone he had got just to contact

Zaikov, she decided. There were no numbers in the memory and he had – according to the call log – called only one number over the last two days. No calls had come into the phone. The number he had been calling – the number he had called when he had stepped outside the hut to get them to come for her – was there in the log. So she could call it.

She had tried hard to think that idea through, rationally, working out what could go wrong, what she might achieve or give away. She couldn't see any additional danger that would come of it. They wanted her – to kill her, no doubt about that – but they wanted her, so why wouldn't they speak directly to her?

But it hadn't worked out so easy. Crouching in the bushes before the rain started, she had keyed the number – it looked like an ordinary Spanish mobile number – and for a long time it had just rung. But the second time someone picked up, or she thought they did. The sky turning grey above her, she had listened intently to the silence at the other end, holding her breath. She wanted them to speak first, to hear the voice, in case she recognised it. But no one said anything. She cut the connection and waited ten minutes, to see if they would try her, but nothing happened.

So she tried again. This time they picked up at once. She waited again, ear pressed tight to the speaker hole. She imagined she could hear him breathing. She assumed it would be a man, because the chances of a woman being involved in this kind of thing seemed slim. The man called Carl, maybe. She wanted to scream something at him. She managed to control the urge for what seemed like minutes, then finally, she could stand it no longer. She spoke. But the voice that came out of her mouth was surprisingly cold: 'You have my daughter. What do you want?' she said. She listened for a response, repeated the question, but could hear no reaction at all. There was someone there though, she knew there was someone there, because moments later the connection was cut.

She had rung back again, immediately, again speaking the question quite calmly, or at least hoping it sounded that way. This time he spoke back. 'Where is Molina?' he asked, in Spanish. It was good Spanish, no foreign accent.

'Not here,' she said. 'Where's my daughter?'

'Let me speak to Señor Molina.'

Did that mean they didn't know he was dead yet?

'Molina isn't here,' she said. 'I'm here. Deal with me direct. Where's my daughter?'

'I don't know what you're talking about,' the voice said, then the line was cut again.

She had let her breath out, felt it turn into a protracted high-pitched scream, saw herself banging her forehead off the branch nearest to her. 'Give me my fucking daughter!' she screamed. 'Give me my daughter back!' She broke into sobs. Then started howling. She had actually spoken to them, to him, to whoever it was Zaikov had hired. Had Rebecca been right there, with the fucker, as she was speaking? Had her daughter been able to hear her? Was it this Carl person? Was *he* working for Zaikov?

But if so, why kill the policeman? It was too much to bear thinking about. She was more desperate than she had ever been. If Rugojev didn't do what he had promised then she had no options at all that she could see, except to give herself in to the police and tell them everything. But how could she do that now? It wasn't just that she had killed one of them. It was not knowing who Zaikov had bought off. The police couldn't be trusted. She banged her fist off her head, wanting to feel the pain. Her nose started to bleed again.

She was trying to find a tissue to wipe it when his phone buzzed with a message. She had let it fall onto the ground. She picked it up with shaking hands, got blood all over it, found some tissue in her pocket, wiped it, read a text written in English: *She is alive. Seville at 8 p.m., or she's dead. Come alone, or she's dead. Tell no one, or she's dead. No excuses. No more contact. She will live longer if you comply.*

She gasped. Read it again, and again. She had no thought of not complying. She wiped her eyes, stuffed a roll of tissue up her nose to stop the blood, and wished bitterly that she had not just slid the car into the water. Now she was going to have to persuade whoever Rugojev sent to get her to Seville.

She heard a car decelerating, out in the rain somewhere, coming towards her. She had been waiting a long time and not a single vehicle had passed along the road. She shifted position so that she could see straight down the short slope in front of her. They had told her it would be a silver Audi RS5, that it would drive the entire perimeter road, going round the reservoir as many times as it took for her to spot it. She had no idea what an Audi RS5 looked like, but she had the car's registration plate. She was running that through her mind now, as it came into view. It was travelling fast and was almost on a level with her before she could read the plate and recognise it.

She pushed herself forwards at once, starting to run down the slope, shouting out. The car was past her and she thought the driver could not have noticed her, but saw the brake lights, suddenly glaring in the rain, then – as she got down to the road – heard the car reversing quickly, swerving around her, stopping. She ran to the passenger side and pulled open the door, leaned in. There was a young guy in the driver's seat, in jeans and a light sweater, dark skin, dark eyes. 'Julia?' he asked, with a sort of smile. 'I'm Drake. Get in.'

He drove for half an hour without saying much to her, going very fast in the rain, headlights on full. She slumped in the passenger seat, waves of exhaustion making her head swim. She watched the signs appearing, tried to stay alert, to make sure he was doing what he had promised. He had told her that Michael Rugojev had instructed him to assist her, that he knew a great deal already. She had said she needed to get to Seville, that that was all she wanted him to do. The signs they passed seemed to suggest they were heading that way.

'Did you do what they asked, with the car?' he asked, at one point.

'It's in the reservoir.'

'And the phone?'

She looked at him. They had told her to leave the phone – Molina's phone – in the car. 'I need the phone,' she said.

He nodded, like that didn't seem very significant, but she felt the car slowing immediately. He eased it into the side of the road, where there was some space. They were in the middle of some kind of irrigated farming zone, inland from the reservoir – everywhere there were low hills with low bushes growing in ordered rows, maybe olives. The rain had stopped, or they had left it behind. There were other cars on the road now, streaking past them. He stopped the car, engaged the handbrake, leaned back in the seat. 'So they contacted you?' he asked. He looked over at her.

'I don't know what you mean.'

'Otherwise why would you need the phone? I'm here to help you, Julia. I'm being paid to do that. I know how these things work. You have to ditch the phone – or at least take the chip out – because they will trace you using the phone. You understand?' He spoke English with an accent, she thought. No doubt Drake wasn't his real name. She had a sudden doubt about trusting him. Had she thought properly about it? Everything was a kind of blur in her head. She hadn't slept, hadn't eaten, her system had been repeatedly swamped with adrenalin. She wondered whether she was even capable of perceiving things clearly. This right now – this thing going on in this car with him – this seemed *very* unreal, like something she was watching, not something she was involved with.

'I need to eat something, and to rest,' she said.

'Before the meet?'

How was he guessing that? And why did he want to know about it? 'Michael told you to help me?' she asked.

'That's what I'm doing.'

'Are you Spanish?'

He frowned at her. 'Why?'

'Speak Spanish if you're Spanish. I will understand. Your English has an accent.'

'I'm from Croatia. My Spanish is poor, my English is better. We can speak Croatian if you like. I'm paid to help you. Do you want the help or not?'

'I want to get to Seville.'

'Why?'

She shook her head. 'Will you take me there?'

'Yes. But your daughter isn't there. She's on her way to London.'

She felt her stomach twist. 'How would you know that?'

'I don't. Not personally. That's what Mr Rugojev has told me to tell you. He has access to a network of information – people who work for other people, people who have access to computer systems, flight control information, telephone companies, bank accounts. The best information he can get at this time suggests she is on her way to London.'

'How? On a plane?'

'A private charter. He knows where it took off from, knows it is scheduled to land at Heathrow. He wants me to take you to London – or make sure you get there. Someone else will take over then.'

'Can he stop it? Can he have people waiting for it?'

'Not in the airport itself, I wouldn't think. But he will handle it. He will want to make sure your daughter is above all safe, whatever course of action they choose.'

She couldn't handle it. She started to breathe quickly, felt the panic starting.

'The people you spoke to – they told you to tell nobody the arrangements, right?' he said. 'That's standard. But they're not here, in this car, so they have no idea what you're saying, what you're telling me. So I suggest you tell me it all, everything that's happened. Then after that I suggest we ignore whatever shit they fed you, because all it will lead to is you flat on the ground with a bullet in the back of the head. And meanwhile your daughter will be in London, with a man called Carl Bowman. That's what Mr Rugojev is working on right now. This is a solvable situation. You understand? Almost anything is solvable if you throw enough money at it, and Mr Rugojev has no shortage of funds. So take deep breaths, think it over and stay calm. You're on the run, you're desperate, sure – but you're not alone, not any more. And I can get you to London within five hours.'

26

He had only ten days left in London when it started. Afterwards, telling it to themselves, Liz would always say that it started the very first time she saw him, that something had passed between them in that moment, with her standing in her bathrobe in the stairwell, that the subsequent days were a nightmare of deception for her as she struggled to keep it from him, to give him no clue. But Carl could never bring himself to believe that, because he had seen nothing in her eyes but disdain.

What *he* remembered as the start was the hours before they went out to the club, ten days before he was to leave, when she was getting ready to go out. She had told him during the afternoon that she was going to go to a club and had asked if he would insist on dragging along behind her. She hadn't seemed too irritated by the prospect, so he had thought that perhaps by then she was getting used to him being there, though she still talked to him only infrequently, beyond the necessities.

He had replied that that was what he'd been asked to do by Viktor – stick with her – so, yes, he would be coming. If she didn't want that then she would have to contact Viktor. Then she had said, 'Well you might as well enjoy it, then. You can come up to my room while I'm getting ready, keep me company – instead of being a freaky shadow lurking round the corner. Pretend you're my girlfriend.' He had frowned at that, not being sure what she meant. 'And bring some wine,' she'd added. 'You look like you would never enjoy anything without a drink.'

Was that true, he wondered? It was not how he imagined himself.

He had been asked to shadow her, to watch out for her, so the dynamic between them was peculiar. She occupied a tiny suite of two attic rooms on the top floor of the house, and as far as he knew then she was officially a minor member of Viktor's staff – he had not asked her what else she might be. Whereas he had the use of Viktor's rooms – the whole of the third floor – and he was family, clearly above her in some respect. He had access to Viktor's funds too – a practically unlimited resource, relative to the things he needed – whilst she had only the wage Viktor gave her, he assumed, which might or might not include some extra remuneration for additional services. That was how he thought of it, and it shamed him afterwards to recall that, though certainly her spending habits were frugal enough; in two weeks she hadn't gone out during the evenings at all. But his having to follow her around, dutifully alert to some non-specific threat, as if *he* were the hired hand, the mere employee, skewed things and made it seem like she was the one in control.

It was the first time he had been inside her room, that night, though he had thought about it often enough, wondered what it was like, what she had done with it in terms of furniture and decorations, what she did inside it when alone. It had become a bit of a habit during the long afternoon hours, when she was mostly up in the room, for him to sit down in the kitchen thinking about her. He sat in the kitchen instead of his own rooms because then he would see her if she emerged to go out, or get something to eat. There were 'work' reasons to do that, of course, and when he thought about her up there above him, moving around, listening to music, reading – whatever it was she did – it never strayed further than that. There was nothing obviously sexual about it. In fact, there was nothing sexual about the way he was reacting to her at all, at least nothing that he would recognise as sexual from the way these things had progressed with other women in his life. There was no thinking about getting into bed with her, or touching her, or kissing – thoughts of that type seemed like some kind of dirty betrayal of whatever it was he felt about her. But what exactly was that?

It was obsessive, he knew that. It wasn't normal for him to sit for hours on end wondering what she might be wearing as she read her book – throughout those three weeks, he remembered, she was reading the same book, something by a writer she had told him was South African. Or guessing whether she did little dances for herself when she had her music on. He couldn't hear her music unless he went up to the landing below the room, but every time he had tried that there had been music and some-times a noise of footsteps on the boards, rhythmically, as if she might very well be dancing with herself. She had told him she was into jazz but he had never heard any jazz coming out of the room. It was always pop or dance when he heard it. There was a current hit by Scooter that he heard often, though didn't know its name – he hated Scooter.

He went up at about nine, as she had instructed, with a bottle of champagne, a single fluted glass, and a couple of cans of beer, not sure what was expected of him but definitely nervous. She was on the bed in a pair of ragged jeans and a T-shirt, the book in her hands, leaning back against the headboard. 'I thought you were never coming,' she said, sliding off the bed. She had already showered, it seemed, and her hair was almost dry, hanging in thick, tangled red locks. He wanted to put his hands into it, but – incredibly – *still* didn't think that was something sexual.

'You said nine,' he said. He knew it was exactly nine without looking because he had waited on the landing below for it to be exactly nine.

'You brought champagne?' She stood in front of him, duck-ing slightly because the roof of the room sloped at an angle above

167

her bed. 'But only one glass? Are you mad? I'm not drinking alone. You'll have to go and get yourself a glass.'

'I brought beer. I thought I would drive you ...'

'We'll catch a cab. Beer is for real men. You're my girlfriend, remember?' She winked at him and he suspected she might have been drinking already, though there was nothing to suggest that other than her changed manner. He was confused but did what she said, went back downstairs and got another glass. He was halfway back up when he heard the champagne cork pop and the music start. This time a song he knew well, Flip and Fill's 'Shooting Star', with Karen Parry vocals, a dance hit that had been big the winter before, even over in the States.

He had sat on the bed. There was only one chair in the room, at a table in the dormer window on which sat an open laptop – the source of the music, he was to discover, which was being played from a program he had then only heard of – iTunes – and fed through an amp and speakers. These had been a gift from Viktor and might have given away a lot about what was going on had he known anything about the price of such things, because while Viktor happily spent money on his women, he didn't usually spend *that* much. It would have been a surprise to him back then to learn that you even *could* spend that kind of money on a music system.

The speakers were mounted on the wall, the amp set on top of a set of bookshelves filled with paperback books – he looked through the titles, but had read none of them. He had expected there might be pictures on the walls, posters, even, things from her past – but there was nothing. The room itself was a bit shabby, the paint old, discoloured and flaking off around the window frame. The window had been open, the night warm.

The single chair was unavailable because she sat on it, facing him, and explained what was going to happen as she poured him a glass of the champagne. What was going to happen was that she was going to get ready and he was going to advise her as to what to wear, what to do with her hair, what jewellery to put on, what shoes, et cetera – and while doing all that they were going to chill, listen to music and drink, get to know each other a little. At around eleven they would catch a cab into town and he would pretend to be a friend of hers, and gay – so as not to put off any men she might be interested in.

And so it had happened, almost. He sat in the bedroom, on the bed she slept in, he thought, and she disappeared into the other room and put clothes on, came out, showed him. She stood in the centre of the room, no more than a metre in front of him, turned, held her hands up, showed him what she had chosen, her eyes always on his, a teasing half-smile on her lips, knowing exactly what she was doing. He sat rapt, bewildered by her attentions, puzzled by her intentions, sipping the drink very carefully, trying not to stare too obviously at those freckles, trying instead to think of something to say about a long series of dresses, skirts and tops, as he slowly revised his view about her relationship with his brother.

All of them were designer labels, she told him, all of them the height of what was presently fashionable. Most of them were outrageously revealing, either very see-through, or slipped off her shoulders, or split up to her waist. And all the time there was a heady mix of scents in the air, not just the perfume she sprayed quickly on her wrists and neck, but also the soaps and shampoo from the shower. Every woman's room he had ever been in had smelled like this – clean, scented, intoxicatingly alien – but it hadn't meant what it did now.

The first chance he had he picked up the perfume bottle she had used and sniffed carefully at the top. She came out as he was doing it. She was wearing a very light, silver, ankle-length dress that was so thin he could clearly see her breasts and nipples. He got his eyes quickly off them as she said the name of the perfume. 'But in the bottle it doesn't smell like it does on my skin,' she said. She held a wrist under his nose. 'See?'

Red with embarrassment he quickly took a sniff, caught the warmth from her body mingled with the perfume.

'What do you think?' she asked. She turned in the dress and he heard it moving against her skin.

'You have a lot of dresses,' he said, awkwardly. 'They're all beautiful. I like them all.'

'You don't think I look like a slut in this thing?' She frowned at him. 'Be honest, please.' She took a drink from her glass and stayed there, daring him to look.

He shrugged, very uncomfortable. 'I thought you said they were all designer clothes?'

'And rich people can't look like sluts?'

He didn't know what to say. He had nothing against sluts, after all – one or two of the most attractive women he had been with had been prostitutes, or 'friends' of Viktor, which until this moment had more or less amounted to the same thing. 'They can, obviously,' he offered. 'But that kind of woman can look great too. I think you look incredible in everything you have put on.'

'I hate them all.' She moved her hair out of her eyes. 'I fucking hate them.' The frown was very intense. 'They were gifts,' she said, with a sigh. 'You must have guessed that.'

He had. He didn't know what to say.

'You don't have to like them,' she said. 'I didn't choose any of the things you've seen so far.'

'So show me something you chose.'

She went back into the other room like she was offended, closed the door. He was to find out later that it was in fact her bedroom – with a large double bed and a little more space – the bed he sat on was only used as a couch or guest bed.

The music stopped and she shouted through for him to change the playlist. He didn't know how to do that but turned the chair round and sat in front of the laptop. He expected to see a list of songs, but instead saw at once that what was on top was her email program. What he was looking at was a list of messages. They were all from the same person though – he read the name before he could get the mouse up and close it down – it was impossible for him not to see the name, though he wasn't trying to do that at all. The list he could see was about forty mails, all sent over a two-day period, all from Viktor.

She stepped back into the room and he looked round guiltily, feeling like he'd been caught snooping. She was wearing the same jeans and T-shirt she'd had on when he'd first got there. 'You look best like that,' he said, too quickly.

She smiled. 'These are my clothes. This is me.' But she had seen what he was looking at. She stepped over and focused on the screen. 'You saw that?' she asked.

'Yes. Sorry. It was on top.'

'They're mails from your brother.'

'I saw that too. Sorry.'

'I get about twenty a day, at least. It's been like that for the whole time he's been away.' She leaned forward and used the mouse, scrolling down through the list, showing him. Everything there was from Viktor.

'The dresses are from him too.'

He nodded. 'I realised that.'

'The mails are all love letters. Or at least he thinks they are. He thinks he loves me, but he doesn't really know how to write a love letter.'

He looked up at her. 'He tells you he *loves* you?' He felt an awful weight in his stomach. He had badly miscalculated Viktor's position.

She nodded. 'That's why he wants you to watch me. To make

sure I don't meet anyone else. He told me that if he catches me
with anyone else he'll kill me.'

27

The sky was bruised black and grey, the ground colours dreary shades of the same, the trees brown bare lines poking broken fingers at a washed-out suffusion of light lost behind the cloud-bank. Carl sat in the wicker window seat and watched a slow, desultory rain streaming across the panes. This was why he had left Finland, he thought, or one of the reasons: there was a short and glorious summer, usually no more than a month of good weather; a winter consisting of four months of unremitting darkness and cold; then this – greyness, everything grey and chill. The light had a fuzzy, diluted quality, like they were living under the sea. It wasn't surprising the suicide rate was so high.

He turned from it and looked at Rebecca, standing at the next window along, leaning an elbow on the long, wooden, curved sill, smiling at him. He smiled back. She looked like she wanted to jump up and down with excitement. 'That's great,' he said. She had just told him that Viktor had informed her that her mother had been found safe and measures were in place to get her here.

'I can't wait,' she said. 'I can't wait to see her. I tried calling her but her phone's still not working. Your brother says she's probably already on a plane.' The face creased up again in a grin which for a moment eclipsed the grey view across the water behind her, the lowering day. He let his eyes stay on the freckles across the bridge of her nose, then put a hand out and touched the top of her head. 'I'm very glad,' he said. 'It will all work out.

I told you it would.' She bent her head slightly and laughed, said something like 'thank you'. He saw the clean parting of blonde hair running away from her scalp and for the first time realised that the hair must have been dyed, not originally blonde. He could see the roots, about a centimetre of her natural colour. He turned in the chair. 'You have red hair? I didn't notice before.'

She nodded. 'You mean ginger. I hate it. It's dyed. I need to redo it.'

He stared at her, stared at the freckles and the hair, tried to see her with hair completely red, but couldn't.

'I like this house,' she said. 'It's massive. My mum will like it too.'

I hate it, he thought, but said nothing. Ten years ago, when he had finally returned from the States to Europe, around Christmas of the same year he had first met Liz in Viktor's London home, it had been in this house that they had met again. There had been, by agreement, no contact at all between them in the four months he was away, but that hadn't been any use. It had all just started again the moment they saw each other, behind his brother's back, under his nose, in *this* house. And when she had left without warning, that too had been from here. He could remember all too well the miserable, tense time that had followed. Viktor had set people looking for her – though it had quickly become apparent that she had left of her own accord – and they had waited here for news. Just the two of them. It had been a weird period, Carl's relationship with Liz a desperate secret. His brother's reactions to her departure had been public and extreme. He had been sobbing and crying about it, telling Carl that he had planned to live here with her, have children with her, that this was 'their' place, the place they had agreed would be their family home. It was the only time he had ever seen Viktor like that. It had been like watching someone he didn't recognise.

174

'I'm sorry I woke you,' Rebecca said, 'but I just had to tell you.'

He nodded. 'It's great news. And I wasn't asleep.'

They were in the wooden tower at the western end of the house, on the top floor in a circular room with 360-degree windows and views across the inlet and the forest. Once he had slept with Liz in here, whilst Viktor was out on a boat. The whole house was full of snapshots like that, bristling with electric richness, laced with guilt. There – behind him – was the actual pine lounger they had used, the same one. The cushions and blankets would be different. The table, the new fireplace, the bookcase with a selection of reading material someone on Viktor's staff had doubtless been paid to pick – none of that he recalled.

He had been sprawled on the lounger for most of the morning, in a fresh set of clothes which were now as crumpled and creased as those he had taken off. He looked at his mobile again. It was just before two in the afternoon. He had slept for nearly four hours, without disturbance, without dreams that he could recall. That would have to do.

'I'm glad this is almost over,' he said. 'You've done well.' He grinned at her and held a hand out in the air for her to high-five. She slapped it then grabbed his palm and held on, smiling at him. He nodded, half to her, half to himself, acknowledging the feelings. A short time ago she had meant nothing to him, but something had changed that. They had been through things together. They had a history. 'I was in the army,' he said. 'Did I tell you that?'

'You told me.' She was still smiling, still holding his hand, looking right into his eyes.

'Me and you – we have a bond now,' he said. 'A bond that doesn't go away.' He pointed at her heart, then at his. 'I only ever got that feeling before when I was in the army, with people in my team. It's unique. It only happens when you've been through that kind of thing – the stuff we've just survived. What you've seen now has been terrible. Like combat. No different.' He tapped his temple, held eye contact with her. 'It's in your head now. When it pops up in future – as it will, all these scary images – you can choose what you think about it. You can choose to remember what it gave us, this positive thing. It gave us this permanent bond.' He put his free hand on his chest, over his heart. 'We went through it and we survived. We *know* each other.' He laughed awkwardly. She laughed back. Her face was more serious now – she was listening – but she was still holding his hand. 'It's hard to explain …' he said. 'I'm not too good at this.'

'No. I get it,' she said. She smiled again, then winked at him.

He let go of her hand. 'Good.' He took a deep breath, then stood up. 'I might have to go out later,' he said. 'I have to talk to Viktor now to find out.' Viktor had been 'communicating' with Zaikov. Things weren't working out quite as smoothly as anticipated.

She frowned. 'When will you be back?'

'I don't know. As soon as possible.'

The smiles were gone. She was frowning.

'Until then,' he said. 'Until I get back, or until he gets your mother over here – you're with Viktor. OK?'

He found Viktor in one of the lounge rooms downstairs, finishing a mobile call, the earpiece in, pacing around the room, in another suit now, the jacket thrown across a chair. He ended the call as Carl came in.

'You found the mother,' Carl said, but immediately Viktor pulled a face, looked behind Carl to see if Rebecca was following.

'She's in the round room, in the tower,' Carl said. '*Did* you find her mother?'

Viktor shook his head. 'I just told her that,' he said. 'Sorry. She seemed really worried. I couldn't get anything done because she kept asking me about her mother. You were asleep and the fucking staff still haven't got here. I had to play kids' games with her, or try to.' He shrugged. 'So I told her we found her mother. It worked. She cheered up, left me alone.'

'She's really excited.'

'What else could I do?'

'You shouldn't lie to her.'

'Like you haven't?'

Carl frowned, but let it go. 'Have you spoken to Zaikov?'

'Yes. He wants to see you.'

Carl sighed, sat down on one of the chairs. 'What for?'

'It's the right way to do things. *A question of pride and honour.*'

'Fucking bullshit.'

'I agree. But that's the way he thinks – he's old, it's the world he's come from. Will you do it?'

'What's the point?'

'To show respect. To apologise. Because you took four hundred thousand euros of his money and fucked up.'

Carl looked up at him. 'Because I didn't kill an innocent kid?'

Viktor sat down opposite him, shrugged. 'I'm not judging you. I would have done the same. But these are the consequences. He comes from a long-disappeared age when there was nothing but promises between crooks. No law, no state. I'm talking about the nineties, when the Soviet state collapsed.' He smiled wryly. 'So he thinks that way, maybe? Or maybe he just wants to sound you out? I have no idea, really. But I thought it was a small concession to make, something we can easily do. So I've arranged a meet at three. Will you do it?'

'I say sorry? That's it?'

'Go and meet him, show respect, say sorry. Like in a movie.

177

Imagine he's Sicilian....' He laughed, but Carl didn't find it funny.

'Do you come with me?'

Viktor shook his head. 'I have other things to deal with. I've spoken to him, set it up. Your safety is guaranteed. You're my brother.'

'Do I take *anyone* with me?'

'You seem worried, but there's no need. This is being done on trust, as a favour to me. You can go in alone, as my brother – that's all the protection you'll need.'

'So I go in alone and I apologise. Then what? He gives us a price?'

'No. And then we move on. The apology is the price. We repay the fee, of course – all four hundred thousand. Compared to the amounts we're set to gain from this alliance it's a drop in the ocean.'

'And this is not about his son? You're sure of that?'

'He has never suspected you of involvement in that—'

'I wasn't involved—'

'—because I protected you from suspicion. You know I did. As far as that goes the danger was always to *me*. But no longer.'

'Because you told him it was the bodyguards that killed him?'

'Because of the money involved. It will make both of us as strong as Mikhael Ivanovich. That's a powerful incentive for Zaikov. And for me.' He smiled. 'I know what I'm doing.'

Carl sighed. The money. It was nothing to do with honour or connections, he thought, everything to do with the money. It always was. 'Did you find out the reason he wanted Rebecca's family dead?' he asked.

'That's his business. I didn't ask.' He stood up. 'Obviously, I would never wholly trust Zaikov. But I trust what's at stake here. Believe me, the money will mean more to him than the life of a little girl.'

28

Julia stood in the steadily moving queue of people waiting to go through UK passport control in Heathrow, with Drake just behind her. She had in her hand the passport he had given her. It had got her onto a plane in Seville without any problems, but now she was more worried. She turned back to Drake and whispered quietly into his ear, 'They will have some electronic checking device – they will check it against my face.'

He put a hand on her elbow and smiled, 'They don't.'

The passport, he had told her, was valid and real, not stolen. She didn't know how that worked, but the picture in the back bore only a very superficial resemblance to her. 'It was issued ten years ago,' Drake said, when she pointed that out. 'You are bound to look a bit different now. They take that into account. If they notice at all.' He seemed unworried.

He had been a model of calm, controlled efficiency since she had got into his car, nearly five hours ago. Places had already been booked on a flight out of Seville and to get through the gate in time he had driven far in excess of the speed limit once they got onto the motorway. When she had asked him what might happen if the police stopped them he had simply said, 'I'll get a ticket,' and shrugged.

'You don't think they'll recognise me?'

'You clearly don't know how useless they are. Besides, the information I have is that they're not even looking for you.'

She had told him what had happened with Molina in a kind

of desperate confessional rush which she had later regretted, because when he had it all he had simply commented, 'OK, that's way more information than I expected. More than you ever need to say again, to anyone. For future reference don't ever tell anyone the knifing bit. Not ever. If you have to give an account of it, say he went out to make a call and you ran, stole his car. That's a safer version.'

There had been a long silence between them then, and she had sat fretting about it and the possible consequences until a few minutes later he had said, 'But I'm impressed. You handled it well.' She had started to cry. He had passed her some tissues but hadn't slowed down.

After that he had showed her the documents they had prepared for her. She had no idea how he had arranged everything in the time available but imagined they must have a pre-prepared stock of false documents they could choose from as need arose. 'They' being people who worked for Michael Rugojev, people back in Spain, she supposed, but wasn't clear about that. Things Drake said seemed to suggest he was usually based in Germany.

The papers were all in the name of Alice Rogers, someone five years older than her, British. She wondered what had happened to the real Alice Rogers. In a brown envelope he had given her Rogers' passport, a selection of visas, three of her credit cards, a London tube pass, an AA membership card, a driving licence, and other paperwork, all in Rogers' name.

'The credit cards draw on Mr Rugojev's funds,' he said.

'This woman doesn't exist?'

'She exists. But she doesn't know she exists in two places.' He smiled again, then added, 'It's harmless. Don't worry.'

The woman checking their queue looked Somalian, very tall and thin, in a blue uniform. She scanned the passport as Julia held her breath, wondering frantically if Drake had any idea what to do if they started questioning her. But the woman only looked at her as she handed the passport back, without any interest at all, saying nothing. Julia walked through, sighed, turned and waited for Drake. They then both walked past the one-way customs windows without any problems, out into the circle of people holding signs, or watching out for relatives. 'Told you,' he said.

He steered her through the small crowd by gently holding her elbow. She was wearing clothing he had given her in Seville: pale blue slacks and matching jacket, a white shirt, her own boots, a little shoulder bag. In the car at the airport he had even produced a hairbrush and carefully brushed out her hair while she sat in the passenger seat, turned away from him. There had been blood matted into it, he said. Then he had produced the clothing and she had changed into it sitting in the car, with him helping, because her knee was still stiff and there wasn't much space to pull clothes off and on. The clothes fitted quite well. He gave her a pair of his own black socks from a briefcase. It would have to do, he said, for now. 'How did you know my size?' she had asked. 'I didn't,' he replied. 'These all belong to my girlfriend. We were lucky.'

She imagined she looked like she was on a business trip, and had asked him about that, whether there was a story to stick to. 'We're in business together,' he said. 'We buy cheap property in Spain. We're coming back from a trip. But no one will ask.'

Outside the terminal it was a normal, grey, London day. There was a car waiting for them in the drop-off zone. The driver got out as they walked over, handed Drake the keys, nodded and walked off. He opened the driver's door.

'Who was he?' she asked.

'No idea.'

'You do this all the time? This kind of thing?'

'This and other things.' He smiled at her again. 'Get in.

We're on a pretty tight schedule now. I have to hand you over to someone else. They're waiting.'

29

Viktor's place was on an inlet in Gumbacka, to the west of Helsinki and south of Espoo, so Carl took a bike from the garage – a scruffy twelve-year-old Honda CB500 with a big top box mounted on the end of the saddle. Viktor thought it might belong to the guy he retained to maintain the house, who still hadn't appeared, but the keys were there, so Carl took it anyway. He got into central Helsinki in just under thirty minutes. Compared to London, Helsinki was a village – on a bike you could get from one end to the other in about forty minutes.

He drove straight through the downtown area, over the Pitkasilta Bridge and up into the area to the north of the city known as Kallio. There was a square there with a large, ugly stone church at one end and high stone apartment blocks enclosing the remaining sides. He squeezed the bike between two parked cars, clipped the helmet to the top box and walked slowly over to a grill kiosk at the eastern edge of the square. Behind it drunks were sleeping on nearly every bench in the square.

The kiosk had a short queue and he waited in line, taking his time to methodically check around the square and the area of park the drunks had taken over. He didn't really know what he was looking for, what his fears were. How would anyone know that two hours ago he had made an arrangement to meet someone in one of these blocks? To know they would have to have access to the phone he had used, a brand-new, unused model given to him by Viktor. Or the guy he was going to meet might be either dirty or compromised. He had got the guy's details from someone he knew well enough to trust a little, but didn't know the guy himself – and anyway, all these face-to-face arrangements were filled with gaps you couldn't cover. Would he be able to spot undercover police vehicles parked in this square? He doubted it. But he searched anyway.

When his turn came he ordered a takeaway mess of industrial chips and chopped sausage, dosed with mustard, ketchup and relishes, something of a Finnish 'speciality' – it was a long time since he had ever tried it though. It came in a polystyrene container with a plastic fork. He thought the sausage had probably never been near an animal. He sat on one of the few unoccupied benches and picked at it, letting his eyes scan around the square.

The buildings were of a depressing dark stone, rust-coloured, cut in huge blocks, the sky above still grey and low, the trees round the outside of the park area long bare of foliage. Winter came early here. He had on a leather jacket he had selected from Viktor's wardrobe. It was new – he had to cut off the labels. With a fleece beneath he was warm enough, but the air was freezing, like it wouldn't be long before the real winter started. He had read that there was already deep snow further north and east, at least a month earlier than usual – it was being put down to climate change.

The block he was going to meet the guy in was directly opposite him. It looked like something Soviet, he thought. So much of Helsinki looked eastern, though the impression was less dramatic than in the small town where he had grown up, less than thirty kilometres from the actual Russian border. There all the churches had Orthodox domes and spires, all the houses were wooden. There were no garden walls or hedges, and chickens and livestock wandered through their patch of land to the rear of his mother's house. There was a lake where the men went every winter to fish through holes carved in half-metre thick ice.

That place, that village, that was his home, where he was meant to *belong*. It had looked exactly like the peasant villages across the other side of the border, like all of rural Russia, in fact. The way of life was the same too. He had spent enough time there to know. He had plenty of family on the Russian side. The occupation of Eastern Karelia during the Second World War meant families had been forced to choose sides. Not many Finnish speakers had remained in Russia, but part of his mother's family had weathered it and survived – the part that had subsequently flourished with the breakdown of the Soviet state. His mother always said they had a petty, dirt-poor, village mentality, a belief in grudges and vendettas. If they couldn't be farmers then they had to be criminals – there was nothing else they were mentally equipped for. Carl had taken that message in, from an early age. It was in his head now – because Zaikov was from that background too.

He stood after a few minutes and walked to a rubbish bin, full to the brim with polystyrene detritus from the kiosk, buzzing with flies. He placed his own rubbish on top and wiped his hands on his trousers, then crossed the square, past the snoring drunks, huddled together for warmth on the benches.

He searched the list of names next to the buzzers at the entrance to the flats. Lassi Kinnunen – that was the name he had been given. He pressed the buzzer for a third-floor flat, spoke his name, then pushed the heavy plate-glass door open and went in to a vestibule smelling of boiled cabbage and bleach. He took a creaky, tiny lift up to the third floor and in a dingy, poorly lit corridor knocked on the door with Kinnunen's name on it. He thought he could hear an accordion playing from the other side. The noise got louder, then stopped, the door was pulled open and he was greeted curtly in Finnish by a thin man with a massive box accordion slung across his chest. No explanation for that was offered.

Carl followed him into a flat that smelled of dust. The man pulled the accordion off, placed it on the floor and said, 'Wait here.' He disappeared into another room.

Carl stood in the middle of the floor and looked at some empty bookshelves, then gazed out of the window, back down onto the square he had just come from.

Kinnunen reappeared carrying a small holdall. He put it on the floor in front of Carl then walked over to a desk with a laptop. He used a mouse, typed something, looked at the screen. One hand stroked a beard, cut in the 'Lemmy' style, with the chin shaved clean, except this one was short-clipped and very neat. He wore a thin-rimmed pair of glasses. 'Your money is in,' he said. 'You can take it.'

Carl nodded, bent down, unzipped the bag. 'I'll check it first,' he said.

The man turned and watched as he delved into the holdall, but said nothing. Carl took out various pieces of gun and set them on the floor beside the bag. Viktor had decided they could deal with Sergei Zaikov, but Carl wanted an insurance plan. He would try Viktor's way, he would trust his assurances, go to Zaikov, make his apologies. Because at the end of the day Viktor was right – this was Viktor's world and he knew what he was doing. If he said it was all about money then it probably was. But if Viktor was wrong – if Zaikov refused to cancel the contract – Carl still had to get what he wanted.

There was a magazine, slightly curved, the gun itself, a silencer, a buttstock. It was a retractable stock but he didn't want the weight. 'I don't need the stock,' he said. The man nodded.

Carl checked the magazine, slid out all thirty rounds and inspected them, then slotted them back in. He screwed on the suppressor, took it off, fixed the magazine in place. He glanced up at Kinnunen, who was leaning back against the desk now, watching. He didn't look wary.

Carl took the magazine off, worked the bolt twice, checked the breech, slid the bolt again, pulled the trigger, heard the pin snap forward. He squinted down the barrel, looking for obvious obstructions. One crude way to render guns useless was to plug the barrel with a molten alloy. This one looked good. It looked almost new, in fact. There was no obvious signs of packing grease, but Carl could still smell the traces of it.

The gun was an MP5, a type of sub-machine gun made by Heckler and Koch, this one a special forces variant used by the Finnish army. He assumed that was where it had come from, but didn't ask. He didn't even ask if it was clean, since that had already been done in the exchange that had led him here, led to his transferring funds to this man. He would have liked to have tested it with live rounds, of course, but that was out of the question.

He dismantled it and put it in the holdall, except the stock, stood up, picked up the bag, nodded at Kinnunen.

'Let yourself out,' Kinnunen said.

Carl walked back to the door and went out, closed it and headed back to the lift. As he pulled open the lift door he heard the accordion starting up again, a haunting Finnish love song his mother had sung – 'Romanci' – but played in a peculiar way, with a German-type oompah rhythm, as if the guy were mocking his memories.

30

Drake looked worried – the first time she had seen him not totally assured. They were on the Uxbridge Road, in Ealing, afternoon traffic behind them and beyond the road a wide area of open grass and trees – Ealing Common.

She had never been to Ealing before. Her part of London, Woodford, was an hour and a half away on the Tube, a different world. At least, that's how she would have thought of it as a kid, though now she realised these outlying areas of the capital all looked much the same. For such a huge place, London's suburbs were disappointingly uniform. Rows of identical semis or terraces.

She had grown up in a house like that. The houses here, by comparison, bordering the road on one side with the common across the other, beautiful plane and chestnut trees lining the pavement, were all Victorian detached mansions. They even had a bit of garden in front. The tube station for Ealing Common – they had passed it driving in – was only a couple of hundred metres away, along with a stretch of road with decent-looking shops and bars. She could see one or two people sauntering around the common, dogs on leashes. Everything looked very neat and comfortable. 'Good place to have a safe house,' Drake had said. But she was sure Ealing would have its estates, tucked away behind the posh bits.

They were standing where the garden had once been – it was converted to a concrete parking stand – at the door. Drake had pulled his own car up alongside another already parked there. Then he had rung the bell and waited, tried again, knocked, been round the side, down a service alley, come back, rung the bell again, decided there was no one in, got on the phone. From his face, she assumed there should have been someone in – the person he was meant to hand her over to. He spoke quickly into the phone and waited. She didn't recognise the language.

Julia hung a few steps back and felt bewildered. This was London. It was meant to be home. It was the place where she had been born, went to school, where she had met Alex and started out on the life that had shunted her into a kind of exile for nearly ten years. Her brother still lived here, in Uxbridge. There was even a cousin that Rebecca had struck up a kind of friendship with. Yet Julia had never wanted to return here, and felt nothing returning now, no sense of familiarity or relief.

Her mother had died a year before she met Alex, her father six years before that. She had never liked her brother and suffered Rebecca's contact with his children only because Rebecca was keen. The contact – it had only started two years ago, when she had felt sufficiently relaxed about the dangers – hadn't led to any closer feelings between her brother and herself. So there was nothing here she really cared about. Yet Spain wasn't home either, very definitely not. The truth was there was nowhere that was home for her. That had been a significant point in common with Alex, something they had talked about.

After a few moments Drake put the phone in his pocket and looked at her. 'You're shivering,' he said, frowning.

She looked down at herself and saw her hands trembling. It was in her face too; she was keeping her jaw clamped shut but could still feel her facial muscles twitching. 'I feel mad,' she said. 'Fucking insane. I'm not calm. You understand? My husband was killed yesterday. A policeman tried to kill me. But all of that' – she waved a hand at it – 'all of that is manageable if I

have Rebecca. I need to see my daughter. I need to get her back.'
A tear ran out of one eye, but she felt no emotion she recognised. She had tried calling Rebecca four or five times between the airport and here but the number was always 'unavailable'. Something had happened to her phone, or it was switched off. But she couldn't give up trying. It was the only strand of hope she had. It might be lying in a ditch somewhere, but she couldn't let herself think that. 'I need Michael to fucking tell me what's going on,' she said. 'You said she was flying here. So what's happened? Is she here? Has she landed?'

He looked unsure. 'I need an update as much as you,' he said. The door behind him had an ordinary lock, but a keypad too. He keyed in a number, the door clicked and he pushed it open. 'There's been a slight hitch,' he said. 'A man called Rudy was meant to be here, to take care of you until Mr Rugojev arrives. He would have all the information you need. This is where he lives – Rudy, I mean – but he's not here and we can't locate him.'

'What does that mean?'

'I have to go out and find him. It won't take long.'

'You know where he is?'

'I know his other address. They just gave me it.' He turned to her and his smile was back. 'Come in. You will have to wait in here for a while. You will have to try to relax a little.'

They walked through a hallway, Drake looking in two rooms coming off it, then came into a kitchen. He left her there and searched the rest of the house 'just in case', then spent ten minutes talking on his mobile. After that he came back into the kitchen and opened a briefcase on the kitchen counter, not the one he had brought with him. 'He's definitely not here,' he said. 'But everything is cool. I've spoken to them. I just have to give you this before I go.' She stood by the sinks while he got something out of the briefcase.

The kitchen smelled of glue and paint, as if it had just been put in. There was no trace of mess or food, no signs that any meal had ever been prepared there. She opened a cupboard at random and saw neat stacks of crockery. The fridge was standing with the door half open, the light off. She saw Drake take out a handgun and place it on the counter he was leaning on.

'That's for me?' she asked. 'Why?'

'Just in case. Always best to be sure. I'm following Mr Rugojev's instructions.' He didn't smile. 'You know how to use a gun?'

She told him she hadn't a clue and didn't intend to learn. Nevertheless, he brought it over to her, showed her the safety catch, the magazine in the handle, how to hold it, aim, pull the trigger. He spoke quietly, hefted it easily. She nodded, not wanting to even look at the thing. It looked heavy, brutal, dangerous, though she knew it was probably only a compact model, one suitable for a silly little girl with tears running out of her eyes. 'Where's Rebecca?' she interrupted. 'Was she on the plane, like you said? Has she landed? Is she with Bowman? Why aren't we looking for Bowman? Why are we here?'

'Mr Rugojev is handling it all,' he said, putting the gun on the counter and facing her. 'You mentioned a man called Sergei Zaikov. Well, Mr Rugojev's people are talking to Zaikov's people. It's delicate. But Mr Rugojev is confident of success.'

'So Bowman works for Zaikov?'

'That's not certain – but probably.'

'You couldn't stop her when the plane landed? What happened?'

'The plane didn't land in London. It was diverted. We don't know the new destination. Not yet.'

'Jesus Christ. She could be anywhere, then.' She put her head in her hands, felt a kind of vertigo starting. 'You told me she was coming here,' she muttered. 'Do you have any idea where she is?' She stared at him. What if she *was* in Seville? What if they had totally fucked it up?

He shrugged, like the question was hard to answer. 'Probably the plane landed at a regional airport,' he said. He sounded too calm. None of it meant enough to him. 'There are various possibilities.'

'So tell me about them,' she demanded. 'You're meant to help me, so help me. I have to know what's happening. I'm her mother. Michael is doing this *for me* – remember? So you either tell me exactly where she might be or get Michael on the phone, or I'm out of here right now. I need to know what's going on.'

He smiled tolerantly at her. 'That's no problem,' he said. 'No one is keeping anything from you, believe me. I can pass on what I know. But it's not everything.'

From his own briefcase he took out a tablet and messed around on the screen for a few moments, then handed it over to her. It was a page from Google maps. She read the address he had highlighted, on the Hammersmith Road, near Brook Green. She knew that area because there had been a couple of clubs there she'd frequented when she was a teenager. 'That's Bowman's house?'

'It's an apartment, in a block.'

'And she's being held there?'

'It's possible, though she hasn't been seen there. There are other possibilities too.' He got up four more addresses in succession, all belonging to people connected to Zaikov. One was in Docklands, one in Highgate, two outside London, in Surrey. She tried to memorise the addresses.

'They're still looking for her,' Drake said. 'Still trying to locate Bowman. It's probable they're in the UK, but not certain. But finding them isn't crucial. They don't need to know where she is to get a resolution. So there is no need to panic. Certainly no need to involve the police or contemplate the use of force to enter these places. That would only lead to errors. It's not the way to handle it. At the end of the day all these Russian matters come down to business.' He smiled wryly. 'They will find a suitable price. They will agree it between themselves. Everything has a price for them, and that's a good thing, because that way problems can be resolved peacefully. Without deaths.' He closed the laptop. 'Now you know what I know. Now you just need to be patient and trust Mr Rugojev. Whatever the price, be assured that he can pay it.' He took out his phone, checked the time. There was a clock on the kitchen wall, but it was stopped. 'I have to go,' he said. He rummaged in the briefcase again and took out a smart phone, handed it to her. 'This has one number in the memory – mine. Call me if anything happens.'

'Like what?'

'Anything you think I should know about. I should be back in an hour, with Rudy. He will know more about what's happening – the detail.' He pointed to the car keys, on the draining board by the sink. 'I'll leave you that car, also just in case, but don't go out without telling me. Mr Rugojev strongly advises you wait here. OK?'

She nodded. 'OK.'

'We are doing everything we can to resolve things as quickly as possible, to get Rebecca back to you.'

She watched him leave, walking through to the front room and parting the net curtains there. He got into the car that had already been there when they arrived, drove off in the direction they had come from.

He had told her Rebecca was on a plane bound for here, but that had been wrong. She felt a wave of terrifying desperation sweep through her. For a moment it all seemed utterly hopeless. The world was vast, swamped with people. Billions of hectares, billions of people. Cities with too many buildings to count, to many places to hide a child.

She turned away from the window and took deep breaths. She couldn't wait here. She would go crazy. She scrutinised the room. He hadn't told her the code for the front door, she realised, so if she left she wouldn't be able to get back in without him. She was meant to stay, of course, he had made that clear. But she couldn't just trust others to handle it and sit back doing nothing. She had tried that already – let them bring her here, instead of going to Seville. At the very least she would need to check the addresses he had showed her, know for sure that Rebecca wasn't there. Then she could decide what to do next.

She held the mobile he'd given her and checked the time, then walked through to the kitchen, picked up the car keys, tried Rebecca again, using his phone. She resisted the temptation to fling it at the wall when she got the same useless service message in her ear. Instead, she walked through to the hallway and up to the front door. She didn't even consider bringing the gun. She opened the door and looked at the road outside. No sign of him. She stepped out, closed the door and walked over to the car.

31

Zaikov's boat was a twenty-one-metre conversion, built in Finland in the seventies, sold to the Russian state for marine research, then converted to a luxury yacht on the back of the collapse of the communist regime. Zaikov had paid for the conversion, but he would have got the yacht itself for a fraction of its value because that was the way it worked in the days of Yeltsin – everything the state had once held was sold off cheap to those in favour.

Creeping into the heart of Helsinki south harbour, into a berth often reserved for the boats of visiting monarchs or heads of state, it drew a small crowd of onlookers. Carl stood in the market square, amongst the dwindling tourists, watching the slow docking procedure. As it went on, the big boat manoeuvring very cautiously into position, the crowd began to get bored and thinned out. They wouldn't know whose boat it was. It was flagged to the Isle of Man and called *Bravo Delta Two*.

In any case, Zaikov wasn't a celebrity oligarch like those the world could read about in magazines or dedicated online sites. He kept a low profile. Even the boat wasn't slapping new wealth in your face – it was old, elegant, slightly faded, and lacking the sleek sci-fi lines that were the current fashion. Viktor leased a modern ten-metre model which looked like a spaceship. But Zaikov's yacht still bore traces of the working vessel it had been, complete with ice-breaker hull. You could see the luxury – the three-tiered sun decks at the stern, one with a pool, the helipad, the cluster of jet skis and smaller boats stowed under awnings – but it wasn't screamed at you. It was a statement of some sort to bring the thing here, to arrive in Finland like this, to take this particular berth in the heart of the capital, in full view of the cathedral, the parliament, the president's offices. But not a statement about Russia – hence the absence of a Russian flag.

Zaikov had extensive interests in Finland. He was here for an AGM for one of his largest holdings – a multinational logging company. Probably that was what Viktor was buying into. The ceremonies had already started in the Kalasjatorppa Hotel, in the west of the city, twenty minutes away, and Zaikov would speak and meet there within a couple of hours. From there, Viktor had been told, he would use a house on the small island of Kaskisaari, in Helsinki south harbour, not returning to the boat at all.

Carl had parked the motorbike in a side street a little further back, the gun left in the locked top box, the helmet clipped there too, the keys pushed under the seat. He could have left the helmet dangling from the handlebars, the top box on the pavement beside the bike, and been more or less guaranteed that no one would interfere. There were parts of Helsinki where people still left their doors unlocked.

Before they had even got the mooring ropes secured, a column of four shiny black Mercedes pulled onto the dock alongside the boat. The drivers got out and lit cigarettes, chatted, waited. Carl wondered if they were hired locally. They looked local. There would be no guns, he thought – Zaikov couldn't risk that sort of thing here. But would they have guns on the boat? He didn't think so.

He walked closer – past the old indoor market building – and watched the crew moving around on deck, organising the arrival. He tried to count them and thought he could see around ten, all in smart white uniforms. The online details for the boat – all publicly available – stated there were crew quarters for twenty-six, five luxuriously appointed staterooms and guest cabins for ten. He watched them lowering a steel gangway to the quay and securing it, then checked his phone again. He had tried calling Viktor many times, to check on Rebecca, but he wasn't picking up. That was irritating, but not unusual. Since there were no last-minute messages calling it off, the plan stood. He would meet Zaikov, apologise. Viktor would take care of the rest.

He waited another five minutes, then walked over to the cars and the gangway. There were no police vehicles, no security presence that he could see, the drivers barely looked at him, the people up on deck were all busy, so he just walked up the gangway and waited for a response.

A man in a suit – definitely not boat crew – stepped from somewhere and blocked the entrance before he was halfway up the ramp. He was about Carl's age, though shorter and slighter. Carl stopped about two metres down from him. 'I'm here to see Zaikov,' he said, in English. 'I'm here about Rebecca Martin. My name is Carl Bowman.' It was what Viktor had instructed him to say.

The man repeated back the details and Carl waited whilst he spoke into a concealed microphone. There was a visible earpiece. The man spoke very quietly, in Russian. He didn't seem to have recognised either name.

'Please wait,' he said, after a moment. Carl watched his eyes scanning the dock behind him, quick professional eyes, looking for others who might be with him, for his transport, for anyone who might be watching. After about a minute his eyes came back to Carl and he stared at him, no expression in the gaze. 'OK. Follow me.'

Carl stepped past him onto the deck and raised his arms a

little, in case a search was coming. The guy didn't touch him though. He pointed to a set of steps leading off the deck, down below, then led the way.

What he *felt* – going down the companionway into the boat, turning the corner at the bottom, walking to the open set of double doors guarded by another much bigger guy in a suit, arms akimbo, waiting to close the doors after him, shutting him in – what he *felt* was that he had missed something, somewhere along the line, missed a detail.

The risk was clear – that Viktor was totally wrong about Zaikov, that Zaikov would ignore anything he had agreed with Viktor, regardless of the business price. Zaikov was a wealthy man – maybe he didn't need an alliance with Viktor to the extent that Viktor thought he did. Maybe his 'principles' came first.

That risk had been twisting in Carl's stomach for the last three hours. But he had felt fear before and he knew how to slide his attention away from it. If he didn't then nothing would be achieved. The fear wasn't the detail he was missing.

It was something about the very idea that Zaikov was behind the contract on Rebecca. Federov, the man who had the proof on that, had not showed up on time. Instead, Viktor had showed him documentation which *might* prove that the money sent to Carl's account had come from a company which traced back to the Zaikovs. Not proof such as a court would need, but enough to suggest that Viktor was *probably* right about Zaikov placing the contract. Yet he wished now that he had taken photos of those documents with his phone, so he could check them again. Because something about them was tugging at his mind. What if Viktor had made a mistake?

The doors shut behind him with a heavy click. He didn't look behind but knew that only one of the security people had come in with him and was standing there now about three metres back, doors blocked. He kept his eyes on the man standing at the opposite end of the room. Sergei Zaikov. No doubt about it. He'd studied the photos.

The room was like a lounge in a plush bar, with low easy chairs and tables, at the moment stacked around the edges. A crimson carpet, gold fittings. Carl imagined it would be the reception room. The lights were all off and there were blinds pulled over all the windows, so it wasn't well lit. When they met people here, did corporate entertainment, there would be waiters taking your coats and orders. But there was no one now – just Zaikov and the guy behind Carl.

Zaikov was leaning against the back of one of the chairs, staring at him, his arms hanging at his sides. Carl could hear him breathing in short, quick breaths, his fingers clenching and unclenching like he was doing some arthritis exercise. He was eighty-three, Carl had read, and it was undeniably an old man standing there – an old man dressed in a smart suit, with a shirt and open collar. Short and stooped, very thin, drawn features. The eyes – at this distance – looked black, slightly recessed under a heavy forehead.

'I'm known as Carl Bowman,' Carl said, again sticking to the formula Viktor had agreed, using English. 'That's how you will have heard of me. Carl Bowman. I'm here about Rebecca Martin.'

Zaikov didn't move, didn't speak. Carl stepped forward a couple of paces, trying to better see the face, but all he could see were lips set tight, an unflinching gaze. He couldn't work out what it meant – that Zaikov hadn't heard him, or that he was seriously pissed off with him? He took a breath. 'She's a ten-year-old girl,' he said into the silence, thinking more explanation was needed. His voice sounded very shaky. 'You put a contract on her and her family. I was meant to execute it. I didn't. I've come to apologise.'

One of Zaikov's hands came across to his stomach and he clutched it, like he was in pain. The breathing was louder but still the eyes didn't move.

'I think you know what I'm talking about,' Carl said, uncertainly. 'My brother Viktor has spoken about it with you. It's because of that I'm here. I come with the greatest respect, to apologise. I come because you have arranged this with Viktor.'

No reaction. Had the man heard at all? Maybe he *was* deaf. Carl glanced back at the security guy but he was staring at the floor.

'Could you hear what I said, sir?' he asked, gently. He tried to sound polite. 'I don't want to waste your time. I'm here to apologise. I've come to assure you that your money will be repaid, and to ask you to cancel this contract.' Did he also need to say that he had taken precautions before walking in – to lie about that? Surely Zaikov would know he couldn't just kill him, here, in the middle of Helsinki harbour? His walk up the gangway must have been recorded on countless security cameras, observed by many.

He started to repeat himself but then Zaikov stepped away from the chair, taking his eyes off him for the first time. The hand went up to his mouth and he leaned sideways. He made a noise in his throat. It took Carl a moment to realise he was retching. It went on for a few seconds without him actually being sick. Then he took deep breaths through his mouth, produced a white handkerchief, dabbed at his lips, straightened up. 'I feel sick when I look at you,' he said, in quick Russian.

Carl frowned. 'I'm sorry,' he said, replying in Russian. 'I don't understand. I want to …' He stopped. He wasn't sure how to respond, or what Zaikov's words had meant. But he could read the expression on the old man's face all too clearly now – the downward twist to the lips, the bitterness in the pulled back cheeks. 'I'm not sure—' he started again, but then another door opened behind Zaikov and a younger man strode in.

Tall, fit, in his forties. 'Is this the fucker?' he demanded loudly, in Russian. 'Is this him?' There was a baseball bat in his hands. He started to cross the room, headed for Carl. Carl shifted stance, his hands coming up, his brain starting to reassess everything he had thought about the meet. There was some confusion, clearly, and he had to dispel it quickly. He tried to get the one behind him into the periphery of his vision, and started to say something at the same time – again mentioning Viktor's name. But Zaikov spoke sharply, raising a hand. 'Not here,' he said feebly. 'Not now.'

The man with the bat stopped immediately. He was halfway between Zaikov and Carl. Carl thought he might be the oldest surviving son – Andrei. Carl started to speak quickly to him, trying to get an explanation out: 'I don't know what you think I'm here for, or who I am, but you should have known I was coming—'

'Is it really him?' the guy asked, ignoring him and glancing across at Zaikov. 'Why is he here? Is he totally fucking stupid?'

Zaikov snapped something back, too quick for Carl to get because his attention was behind him now. He had heard movement there. He spun to see the security guy pointing something at him – something plastic, brightly coloured. It was like a playground toy, a joke gun. The thing went off with a silly popping noise and two little darts leaped towards him, so slowly he could see them come out of the gun, see the thin trail of wire spooling out behind them.

It was a taser. The darts hooked into his jacket. No time to dodge or duck.

There was a split second of lucidity, then his whole body tightened, snapped straight, his mouth open and yelling. A massive contraction shot through him, turning him into a rigid knot. He was aware of it, conscious, but every muscle frozen.

He saw the guy staring at him, pulling the trigger, saw the little wires in the air, connecting him to the gun, saw the ceiling spinning off as he went down. Then his head smashed off the floor, he rolled into a fetal ball.

There was a gap long enough to feel his body buzzing like a fused machine, his head spinning with dizziness, then it started again. But this time the pain was like a vice around his chest, real pain that made him scream, made him think that if they kept doing it his heart would stop.

32

Julia had driven badly at first, so badly she almost crashed reversing out from the concrete space. Wrong side of the road. She had pulled out automatically as if driving in Spain, a car had braked, hooted her. So she had pulled to the side of the road, tried to calm herself. She couldn't do something stupid that would attract police attention. When she started again she was more careful, easing herself back into it.

Traffic was lighter than she remembered in London. There was a satnav built into the car. She had to stop again coming up to Ealing Broadway and work out how to program it. She put in the first address she had seen on the laptop, on the Hammersmith Road. The device had told her it would take her twenty minutes to get there, but it had taken over half an hour.

She was behind the place now, in a side street near Brook Green. A posh bit of Hammersmith. She had been sitting in the car for a few minutes thinking about what she was doing. But nothing was clear. She couldn't see how thinking was going to help. She needed to know if Rebecca was here. Here or in one of the other addresses – she thought she could remember them all. She would go through them one by one.

She got out and walked down to Hammersmith Road, a wide, two-lane artery running towards town from Hammersmith Broadway, busy with cars, trucks, buses, courier bikes. The block Bowman's flat was in was on the north side, off to her left a little – a seven-floor structure that had scaffolding around one end. There were barriers narrowing the road in front of it, skips and building trucks. They were renovating it, a sign said. To get to the main entrance you had to walk under a section of scaffolding.

She walked as normally as she could, got to the big glass double doors and noted they were wedged open, despite the security lock and number pad. She pushed one of them open, stepped into a vestibule. It was quieter, but she could hear banging noises from inside the place, punctuated by the whine of a drill.

Straight ahead – beyond another set of doors, also wedged open – there were two lifts, to the right a large panel with individual buzzers for each flat. There was plastic sheeting, stained with boot marks, leading through the doors towards the lifts. To her left the wall was a rack of locked letterboxes. She stepped up to the buzzers and looked for his name, found it at once. Top floor, flat 75. *Bowman*. She swallowed, turned, walked out, suddenly overcome with fear.

She crossed the road at a run and walked towards the Broadway a bit, glancing back all the time. There was a coffee shop a little further on and she went in, sat at a bar in the window, from where she could see the entrance. A man took her order for a tea but she didn't look at him. She kept her eyes on the building.

She tried to work out which set of windows would be Bowman's flat but had no idea which end it would be. The furthest end was wrapped in scaffolding and protective boarding, so you couldn't even see the windows of the rooms. She couldn't get her head to compute the possibility that Rebecca might be being held inside the place she was looking at. There were builders, everything was public, life going on as normal. How would it be possible to get her daughter into the place? She couldn't believe it.

Her eyes dropped to street level, looked at the entrance again. Someone walked in, a woman with two kids – younger than Rebecca – came out. Her eyes moved sideways. A man standing near to the start of the scaffolding, on the pavement, was facing her. Her eyes switched to him because she suddenly realised he was staring in her direction. She focused on his face. He was looking right at her. She heard her breath slip out in a gasp. Was it the man she had seen in the crowd at La Linea, the man with the pistol? He had the same backpack, the same clothes. He turned away immediately and walked quite casually under the section of scaffolding. It went around the corner of the building into the next street, so she couldn't see if he had emerged at the other end or not. But he didn't walk back onto Hammersmith Road, and he didn't go into the building.

She was stunned. Was *that* Bowman? There couldn't be another explanation. But if that was him, where had Rebecca been when she had seen him in La Linea in the middle of the riot? She started to shake because the desperate, horrible facts seemed suddenly bitterly clear – she had been that close to Rebecca in La Linea, *that* close – she had looked at Bowman and he had looked at her, then he had got away. If she had followed him, shouted out to him, anything, then maybe she could have changed things. Why hadn't she run to the nearest police, told them, begged them to go after him?

She got out the phone Drake had given her and called him. He answered at once. 'He's here,' she whispered. 'I've seen him.'

'Where are you?' His voice was calm. 'And who do you mean?'

'Bowman. I saw him in Spain, and I've seen him here. I'm in Hammersmith, outside the address …'

'Why did you go there?'

'Don't worry about that. You're looking for Bowman – well, I'm telling you I've seen him. I've found him. You need to get here now.'

'You've seen someone outside the place, or inside?'

'Outside. He was standing around, watching me …'

'How did you know it was Bowman? It could be our man. There will be at least one of our people there. Where exactly are you now?'

'In a coffee shop, opposite.'

'Can you get back to the car? Did you use the car?'

'I used the car, yes. But you need to get here—'

'You should go back to the car. Now.'

'No. I can't just sit by and wait. I want to go over there. I want to check. I let him get away once, but not this time. Will you come here? Will you help?'

'Listen. There are problems you don't know about. What you're suggesting is fucking dangerous – for you, for Rebecca …' Abruptly, he sounded different – not calm at all – anxious enough to make her pause.

There was silence for a few moments. 'You should come here, then,' she said. 'We can work out what to do.'

'Listen to me!' He almost shouted it. 'You remember the man Rudy? I'm at his place now and someone has been here, there's been a fight, there's blood. Do you understand? Rudy is not here.'

'Rudy?'

'The guy who was meant to meet you in London. The guy whose house you were meant to wait in.'

That Rudy. But she had no idea who he was. So he'd been in a fight – what did that mean? And why did Drake assume there was a connection? In the front of her head there was only one thing – that Rebecca might be up there, right opposite her, metres away. 'When is Michael coming?' she asked. 'He needs to know about this. You need to tell him I've found Bowman.'

'OK.' She heard his impatient sigh. 'We'll do it this way. Stay where you are. Don't move from where you are. You understand? I will come to you. Do you hear?'

'I hear.' She cut the connection, irritated that he was giving orders suddenly. Besides, why would he think the man she had seen was one of Michael's men? She had said she saw the same man in Spain, told him that.

A blur of confusing connections formed in her head, ending with a sudden doubt about Michael Rugojev. With nothing concrete to back it up, no clear reason. But still ...

She got off the stool and walked out, without waiting for the tea. She crossed the road and looked down along the line of the building, under the scaffolding. No sign of the man. She took a deep breath and spoke aloud, without realising it. 'I might be mistaken. Maybe it wasn't him.' How clearly had she seen him? She had a good view now, but not back in Spain. Her nerves were overwrought, she was exhausted, living on adrenalin. It was likely she was being really stupid, that it wasn't the same man at all.

33

The more she thought about it, the more she was sure Drake was right and the man she had seen was someone else entirely. Because she couldn't see Bowman bringing Rebecca here. Anyone could get into the building – there were builders trekking in and out, all the doors jammed open. The pavement running under the scaffolding was relatively busy too – how would you get a little girl in, unnoticed? But Rebecca wasn't little – she just thought of her like that. In reality, she looked like a teenager. She had seen teenagers walking in and out alone whilst she'd been watching the place. And she remembered Rebecca's messages – Rebecca thought this Carl Bowman was helping her.

She got out Drake's phone and saw that he had been trying to call her. But she didn't need to argue with him right now, so she switched it off, started up Molina's instead, called Rebecca's number, heard the miserable out-of-service message for the five hundredth time. The fear started rising inside her again, the obsessive, hopeless thoughts. Rebecca might be in Spain, or here, or any other European country – or much further afield. There was no way to search effectively, no way to even start. She had heard nothing from her for over twenty-four hours. This was what it was going to be like, for the rest of her life. Never knowing, never seeing her child again.

She got her mind out of it with difficulty. The panic was misplaced, because it wasn't like that, wasn't quite so hopeless. She had one card in her hand – they wanted her too, they wanted to kill her. They had engaged with her once already to try to achieve that. So it could happen again.

And the culprits were known. And she had powerful men on her side. That limited things, brought the scope of it in. It wasn't as if Rebecca could be *anywhere*. Michael Rugojev would know roughly where she was. She had to rely on that. Rugojev would put the resources into it. He would know what to do.

But if that was true, she couldn't see Michael's resources – unless, as Drake suggested, the man she had just seen was one of them. It was possible. But why wasn't Michael himself here – why hadn't he come to explain? She stood on the pavement, feeling her body heating up with agitation, trying desperately to think things through clearly. But her brain had stopped. She was too exhausted and stressed to think about anything clearly. She just had to *do* it, go up there, find out. If Rebecca and Bowman weren't here then it was possible she could still get back to Seville in time.

She took the stairs at the side of the lifts, running up them so that when she came through the doors at the top and stepped into the seventh-floor corridor, she was out of breath. She paused to recover, taking in the layout. A long corridor that turned off at both ends. There was a plush beige carpet underfoot, to the left covered with plastic. Doors for two flats in sight. She walked to the first, right opposite the stairway. Number 73. Bowman was 75.

She went past the lifts. In the other direction there was a clatter of building works, hammers and drills, the long scrape and bang as stuff was pushed down a waste chute into a skip below. The air down there was hazy with dust. She thought the builders must actually be in the flat furthest down there, so it couldn't be that end. She went past flat 74 and got to the corner.

There it was, down a dog-leg. Flat 75. No name on the door.

She took a breath, stepped closer, heard the lift start up behind her and stepped back to watch for it, automatically. It didn't stop at her floor though. She heard it come to a halt, heard the doors open, voices on the floor below, most probably. She got her eyes back on the flat door. What was she going to do?

She crept up to it, stood very still, holding her breath, listening. She could hear nothing. Nothing at all. She took Molina's phone out again and called Rebecca's number. Same message. She got up the number she had called in Spain – the one the message had come from telling her to go to Seville. She held it to her ear, listening to it ringing, hearing nothing from inside the flat. She heard the ring tone pause, then change, as if the number had automatically diverted to another number, but that just rang also. Whoever they were, they weren't at the other side of this door.

She cut the connection but had only got as far as putting the phone back into her pocket before it started to buzz. She got it out at once, holding it to her ear without saying anything.

Silence. But someone was there. They were at the other end now, listening to her breath. She could sense it. 'Hello?' she said, to check. She thought she heard an intake of breath, very faint. She put her hand against the door, still listening, then felt it give immediately. It was open. Her eyes flicked down to the lock, saw marks, scrapings around the keyhole, some wood splintered away. It had been forced open. In her ear a voice said, very quietly, 'I wish it didn't have to be like this.'

She cut the connection quickly, suddenly very frightened. Had she recognised the voice from somewhere?

She called Rebecca's name. Not very loud, but loud enough. If she was inside she would hear. She pressed against the door cautiously. It swung open. She swallowed, stepped forwards, pushed it right back on its hinges.

She was looking at a short corridor, pictures on the walls,

doorways off only a few metres ahead. Her mind noted the details – the open doors, the complete and utter silence, the marks on the carpet. She walked slowly in, leaving the door open behind her.

There was a stale smell in the air, as if no one had been here for a few days and all the windows were closed. And something else. It made her pause before she looked around the first door but didn't manage to prepare her, so that when she saw the room beyond the breath was sucked out of her, like someone had punched her in the chest. She had to lean against the wall to stop herself collapsing.

It was a bedroom. There was a double bed, behind it curtains pulled away from the window. Lying on the floor, in the gap between the bed and the window, was a body. Long, very blonde hair covering a face. Hands clenched tight. Blood. Blood on the walls in long streaks, blood on the bed. The smell of it in her nose. She put her hand in her mouth, bit on it, said 'Christ above. Christ.' She stepped back.

It was a dead woman. Not Rebecca. She couldn't see her face, couldn't see what had killed her, but the room was in total disorder, things toppled onto the floor, items smashed. There had been a struggle. The woman was in her nightclothes, she thought, in pyjamas.

She backed out of the room, almost tripping up, then stood panting, pressed against the wall outside, her brain racing, her limbs cold.

In a daze she moved quickly through the other rooms, praying Rebecca wasn't going to be there. There was a kitchen, a lounge, another bedroom, a toilet and bathroom, all ordered and neat. Nothing had happened anywhere else, just back in the first room. There was no one else here, not Rebecca, not Bowman.

She forced herself back to it, the breath strangled in her

throat. She should go over to the body, check it, check if the woman was alive. But she couldn't. She stood in the space outside the room, planted her feet firmly, then looked round the corner and saw the legs and arms in exactly the same frozen pose. She had the urge to run, to turn and flee.

She felt a vibration in the floor, coming up through her feet, and thought it must be the lift again. She spun and hurried out.

There was no plan now except to get out and call Drake. He had been right – she shouldn't have done this. She came round the corner and heard a soft ringing sound as the lift reached her floor. She slowed, tried to compose her features as she moved, tried to look normal. She was about a metre from the stairwell doors, her face down, when the lift doors opened and someone stepped out.

She looked up expecting a builder, saw the feet – clean black shoes, not dirty boots – saw the hand hanging there, the gun, a blunt black extension of his fist. For an instant her mind didn't register what it was. She looked up at him, the white face, the ordinary hair and appearance, the clean-shaven chin, the eyes on her. The guy from La Linea.

She was right by the door, her hand starting to reach out to push it open. He took a step towards her and brought the gun up. She saw his finger on the trigger, saw his other hand moving towards the gun, a long black metal tube held in his fingers.

She thought there would be a shot, she would scream, she would try to run. She thought if she moved quickly enough the bullet might miss altogether. She had to go for it. If she didn't she was dead.

But nothing happened. No movement. Her legs were like lead, her chest so heavy she had to heave the air in. Her mind was lucid, she knew what had to be done, but her body wouldn't do it. Wouldn't do anything.

'Move back,' he said quietly. 'Go back to the end of the corridor.'

It was fear holding her in place, fixing her in front of him. If he fired it would hit her stomach. She wanted to say 'I saw you in Spain, I know you,' but instead heard her voice coming out of her mouth in a weak rasp: 'Who are you? What have you done with my daughter?'

'Go back,' he said again. 'Move back now.'

Her brain took her eyes to the metal tube in his left hand. His eyes were on hers, trying to hold her gaze, but he moved his body slightly, awkwardly, trying to shield the gun from anyone who might be behind him. Something slotted into place and she recognised, from somewhere, that the metal tube was a silencer. She imagined him getting it out in the lift, wanting to screw it onto the pistol before he got anywhere near her. If he fired at her now the builders at the end would hear. *At least* the builders – the noise would be loud. Everyone in the block might hear. So he wanted her round the corner, out of sight. He wasn't just going to let her walk through the doors and get away, but he needed time to fit the thing onto the gun. So she had time too, maybe only moments before he decided on the risk.

'Where's my daughter?' she asked again. 'Where have you taken her?'

'I'll only ask you once more,' he said, but the gun was lowered now, at his side. 'Turn around and go back.'

'So you can kill me like that woman through there?'

His eyes changed expression, but he said nothing. He knew about the dead woman. He had been in there already. 'I don't care,' she said. 'I don't care what you do to me. I just want to know my daughter will be safe.'

'So go back. Go back and we can talk about it.' He had the temerity to smile slightly, as if she were utterly stupid and feckless, as if he could fake something like that and she would go for it. 'All I want to do is talk to you,' he repeated.

'I know you work for Zaikov,' she said.

He frowned. 'Zaikov?'

'You're Carl Bowman. I know who you are.'

'I'm Philip Jones. I'm police,' he said. He had a standard kind of London accent. He sounded convincing. But she was certain he wasn't police. 'I don't know who Zaikov is,' he said. 'But I do know Bowman. I can help you there.'

'Who is the dead woman?' she asked. 'Did you kill her?'

'Of course not.' He said it almost flippantly, the little smile still there. 'I'm police. I don't kill people. She's Bowman's girlfriend. Bowman killed her, we think. He's dangerous, and he has your daughter. Go back to the flat and I'll tell you what I know. We can pool what we know. You help us and we help you.'

He raised the gun again and she could see the thoughts moving across his face – the decision, the risk. Shoot her now and run, or delay, try to get her back there where it was safer.

'I'll move if you tell me where she is,' she said. Her last gamble. If he refused she had to yell, run.

'She's safe,' he said. 'But she's not here. She's in Helsinki, with Bowman. If you help me she will be—'

Helsinki.

But there was no time to think about that, no time to work out whether it was a lie or truth. He stopped speaking because behind him a door slammed shut and a man appeared at the other end of the corridor, walking towards them. She switched her gaze over his shoulder, saw a yellow hard hat, a man with some kind of power tool held in both hands, looking straight at her.

Jones had a warning glare with his eyes. He was trying to appear relaxed, moving the gun down to the line of his leg, shifting stance so he could turn quickly. She got immediately what would happen if she shouted – he would turn and shoot the man. She waited until Jones was sideways on, his head moving to look back, then put her shoulder against the stairwell door and dived through.

34

He was coming after her. All the way down the stairs she thought she could hear him coming after her. She couldn't look, couldn't get her eyes up, because she was taking the steps three and four at a time, leaping down, gathering speed, getting more and more out of control. Hand on the rail to pull herself round the bend on each floor, banging into the walls, tripping, catching herself, ducking, breath and heart hammering in her ears, the pain bad in her injured knee.

She tried to count the floors but couldn't concentrate on anything but her footing, on keeping her eyes on what was coming. She glimpsed a sign painted on the wall next to a door she almost went straight through – '3'. The third floor. By now her legs were shaking and she was in real danger of falling head first. The swollen knee wasn't going to hold up. She made herself slow enough to keep her balance.

Then, as she plunged down the next flight, she glanced up momentarily. Saw nothing. She realised she couldn't hear anything either – just the din she was generating, echoing through the spaces – no footfall in pursuit.

She grabbed the rail to stop herself, slammed into the wall and held her breath. Silence. He wasn't following.

She heard the lift mechanism and let herself gulp in the air. He was using the lift. She set off again, slightly more carefully, her ears on the sound, trying to place it. The builder had been going for the lift too. Would Jones get in the same lift as him? Not with a gun. So maybe he was waiting for the other lift.

She heard it start up, an additional vibration, just as she came in sight of the ground level. She paused long enough to not be gasping for air, then walked the last few paces and pushed open the door very slowly, staring through the little pane of glass first. An empty foyer, the street outside.

She ran for it. Turned sharp left under the scaffolding, dodged some people – a woman and a child – put her head down, went full speed in a jerky limp, ignoring the pain. She had to get to the car.

She saw people staring at her then reached the turn towards Brook Green. She went straight over the road, not looking behind to see if any car was turning after her, relying on her ears. Someone braked with a screech, but she didn't look. She dodged a bicycle, made the opposite pavement, got her head down again.

She counted the turn-offs, didn't pause to look back once. The car was on a street three back from the main road. The turns passed her quickly. Nice little streets with trees and expensive little Victorian semis. She found the one she thought she had put the car in but couldn't see it. She stopped and concentrated. There were rows of parked cars down both sides, all the way down the street. A drop of rain picked at her face. Wrong street, she decided. She had passed only two, turned too soon. She felt panic leaping in her gut. She would have to turn back.

She walked back to the junction, looked down towards Hammersmith Road and immediately saw him, about two hundred metres back on the opposite side. He had just come round the corner. Maybe he hadn't even known where she had gone. But he knew now. She saw him pause then start to walk quicker, coming up the road towards her. She bit her lip, wanted to cry at her own stupidity, turned on her heels and limped off again. Would he try to shoot her in broad daylight, in the middle of London?

As soon as she got to the next turn she saw the car. She kept running, digging in her jeans pocket for the keycard, got it out when she was still twenty metres away, clicked it to open the doors, saw the lights flash. How long did she have?

She opened the driver's door, threw herself in, fumbled to start the engine, looked to the end of the road. He hadn't appeared yet. Maybe he wouldn't. Maybe he would change his mind.

The engine wouldn't start. She was pressing the wrong button. She made herself think it through. She was being exceptionally stupid. She had been staring at the end of the road, frantically pressing the button that operated the air conditioning. She put her thumb on the right button and the car started at once.

She slipped the stick into reverse, tried to edge back, eyes always on the end of the road. She felt it bump the car behind, gently, put the wheel on full lock, jerked into the road, almost stalling. A car pipped, but she couldn't even see it. She kept going, straightening up. But she was on the wrong side of the road again. She veered to the left, pressed the accelerator a little. Maybe only fifteen metres to the junction. What then? Turn right, away from him, pick up speed.

Then he was there, sprinting towards her, his eyes right on her. She couldn't believe it. The gun was in his hand, in full view. He was coming across the pavement at the end of the junction, running like he would come right out in front of her. She heard herself scream with fright, swerved slightly away from him, saw his arm come up and realised he was actually going to shoot. He was in the road now, almost blocking her. She would have to go round him, but then he would shoot as she passed, straight into the windscreen, point-blank.

She flicked the wheel towards him instinctively, a tiny

movement, her foot flat on the accelerator, the car still in second gear, engine roaring. She saw the shock flash across his face, saw him try to stop in his tracks. The gun was pointed at the front of the car. She thought it fired, but the noise was drowned out. There was a bang as she struck his hips and legs. Then he was a blur of movement in the air, a black shape filling her view, his head arching up and over, then down with a crack, straight into the top part of the windscreen. The glass shattered, blood spattering over the cracks. He was catapulted up and over, across the roof and back. She hauled the wheel over, foot on the brake, saw a car swerving through a tiny patch of clear glass. She braked to an emergency stop, screeching to the other side of the junction, pointed back down towards Hammersmith Road. A moment later she was knocked viciously forward by a rear impact, her head smashing off the steering wheel.

She sat dazed, foot pressed against the brake, engine revving really hard. Then pressed the button and stopped it, tried to see behind in her mirrors. There was no one in the road. No one running at her. She couldn't see anything clearly though. She started the engine again, heard someone shout something, tried to move forward and heard a violent scraping noise. She put it into neutral, opened the door and got out.

He was about six metres back, in the middle of the junction, half underneath another car, the one that had been behind her. His head and chest were out of sight, beneath it. It had clearly gone over him. He wasn't moving. There were people running towards him, converging on the scene, cars stopped across the road she had come onto. Two people were already there beside him, crouching down, shouting. Someone else, off to the side, was pointing at something near a storm drain – the gun. The driver from the car that had rear-ended her – a man, middle-aged – was sitting at the wheel staring ahead, not looking at her, not looking at anything, running a hand over his face.

No one was looking at her. No one.

But that would change soon.

She started to walk away from it. She moved around her own car, over to the kerb. She expected shouts, people trying to stop her. Her head was throbbing badly. She put a hand up and felt a bump above her left eye, angry and sore. No blood, but her nose was trickling again. She pulled some tissue from the jacket pocket, wiped it, quickened her pace, then thought better of it. She slowed, tried to move normally. Still no one shouted. She kept going, didn't look back. People were walking past her, looking behind, going towards it all, paying no attention to her. She went round them, got down to Hammersmith Road, waited for a space, crossed it, then started running towards the Broadway and the tube station.

35

He was in a pitch-black suffocating enclosure, in the bilge, beneath the lowest deck of the boat, in a curved space intersected with the thick iron ribs that braced the outer, reinforced hull structure. It was some kind of watertight compartment, turning the hull into a double-skinned structure, between sealed bulkheads, a safety feature.

At its lowest level, if he let himself slide down there, towards where the keelson would be, he sank up to his knees in bilge water. The distance across, from outer skin to inner hull, was a little further than the length of his arm at head height, narrowing to about fifteen centimetres where it curved under the hull towards the keel. The hatch they had pushed him through was about a metre above his head, just within reach. He would be able to get up to it by bracing his legs against the inner and outer walls – if his legs would stop shaking.

There was no light at all, not even a crack of it coming through the seal on the hatch, so he could see absolutely nothing. He had figured out where he was by feeling his way around, very slowly. He had worked a big boat like this once, as engine room crew, in his teens. A summer job. Sometimes they'd sent him down to clean the bilge pump, so he knew the rough structure.

The air stank of engine oil and stale sea water. He had to breathe deeply to get enough of it into his lungs but he wasn't sure if that was an effect of the repeated tasering, or because there wasn't much air down here. He had read about people sent to clean huge metal storage tanks dying because there was no oxygen in the bottom level. He tried to wedge himself against the outer hull and stay as high up as possible.

'Make a noise and we'll give you more,' they had told him as they pushed him in. Meaning more tasering. By that point everything had been a blurred daze, his brain not working properly at all, his heart labouring, his breath so constricted he had felt as if he were asphyxiating. He had dropped the two and a half metres from the hatch without really knowing what was happening, smashing his head and knee off the bulkhead on the way down. He could feel blood trickling from a cut behind his ear. But at least – as far as he could recall – the son hadn't used the baseball bat on him. Not yet.

They hadn't wanted a mess up there, hadn't wanted a mess on their clothes – they were headed for the shareholders' meeting, had no time to deal with him, and didn't want to do it there, in Helsinki harbour. But they were going to do it, sometime later, out to sea. They were going to 'question' him, then kill him. He knew all this because he had heard them talking about it all as he lay there being repeatedly shocked, his body like a quivering rigid board, but his mind – at least at first – startlingly unaffected.

He had been tasered before, as part of the military training programme, but not like this. He had no idea how long it had gone on, or what the charge was. It seemed more powerful than what he had been through before. And they hadn't stopped until he had repeatedly blacked out. How long had that taken, and how long had he been out? He didn't know that either. But they must have dragged him to the hatch leading here whilst he was unconscious, then waited for him to come round to put him in. The son and Zaikov had disappeared by then, presumably into the sleek Mercs back on shore, and it was the big man who had used the taser who had manhandled him into here.

He didn't know how long he had before they came back from their meetings, because he didn't know what time it was now, didn't know how long had elapsed since he had been put in this place. They were due to finish at seven, he knew, because that also had been discussed in front of his prone form. And it had been mid-afternoon when all this had started. But time had slipped and slid away from him as he waited for his heart and brain to recover. There had been a persistent mental confusion which was only now dissipating. When he had full control of his muscles he would need to work out what he was going to do. Or they were going to set sail, pull him out and kill him. He had no doubt about that.

He eased himself back against the freezing outer hull, throbbing with engine vibrations, and tried to get his breathing regular. He tried to relax, but still the buzzing was there, in his legs and arms, across his chest, the feeling you got when you banged the nerve in your elbow, but magnified many times over and through many sets of muscles.

What had gone wrong? Zaikov had looked down at him, writhing on the deck – looked down at him with eyes filled only with hatred – and said something like, 'He is too small, too stupid. How could he have killed Uri?' Uri. The dead son. They were blaming him for that, for the events of ten years ago. But why?

He forced his mind back there, into the past. It had been a crystal-clear memory for so long but now he couldn't get it to focus properly, not with his brain struggling to rewire itself. That was an effect of the tasering that he'd read about – the mental sluggishness, the loss of memory. It would pass, sooner or later. Maybe. Or he'd have a reaction – the name of which he'd forgotten – and pass out, stop breathing, die.

Uri Zaikov. Ten years ago. He couldn't recall the date or even the season now. But he could remember Uri Zaikov collapsing in front of him, blood pouring out of a stab wound to his back. Had *he* done that? He struggled to fill in the gaps, before and after, but trying didn't do it. Like when you had some forgotten word or detail on the tip of your tongue.

He closed his eyes, tried to empty his mind, make space for it. He could see Uri Zaikov's shocked white face, the eyes staring up at him, the voice pleading softly, in Russian. He had gone down on one knee right beside the man, pulled his clothing away and turned him on his side, found the wound. He had a clear image of it, the tiny slit with all that dark blood running out of it. The Russian's clothing had been soaked with it. He had staggered through the doors just behind Carl – big, wooden, ornate doors – then collapsed at his feet. Where was it? What place?

He couldn't get there, couldn't build the rest of the picture. Just the wound and the pleading voice. The wound was near the heart, between the ribs. Had it actually pierced his heart? There had been blood bubbling through his lips too. Flecks of it had spattered Carl's face as he leaned over to hear him speaking. So the lung must have been punctured, or the throat.

What had happened next?

He had taken his own jacket off – a light, canvas summer jacket, so the season must have been summer, the weather hot – and had started to tear it to pieces, intending to bind the wound, to try to stop the bleeding.

He had been trying to save the guy, not kill him. He had even said that to him, tried to reassure him. Then Viktor had got there, out of breath, blood all over him. Because there had been two others with Uri Zaikov, and Viktor had chased and caught them outside somewhere, shot them. Carl hadn't seen it, but had seen the bodies, later. Viktor had the pistol he had used in one hand.

He had walked up and pushed Carl out of the way. Then

bent over and cursed Zaikov, put the gun against his face and pulled the trigger.

Carl saw it all, right now, saw it happening. Viktor had shot Uri Zaikov when he was already down, already mortally wounded. Then stepped back and spat on the body.

36

He thought it was maybe twenty minutes more before he could be sure of his legs. Then he started to properly feel his way around the compartment. He found a potential weapon quite quickly, clipped to the bulkhead below the hatch – a kind of wrench, heavy, with a handle about two metres long. He tried to remember whether he had seen one before in this area of a boat, and what it would be for. Obviously there was something that you could loosen with it.

He considered banging on the outer hull with it but guessed that would only make them lean through the hatch to tase him again. Besides, from the position of the engine noises he was on the port side of the boat, and it was moored to starboard. And in any case, who would care about a banging noise from a boat? Passers-by would assume someone was doing repairs. The crew might respond, but they wouldn't be able to help if the big guy was standing guard above the hatch.

He eased himself lower down, breathing carefully. The engines were turning over continuously, either in readiness to leave or because they needed them to turn a generator or power some other system. He moved over three sets of the iron ribs, towards the stern of the boat. He decided – from the noise – that he was in a compartment right at the stern, alongside the engine room. He lay back against the outer hull with his feet submerged in the bilge water and thought about it.

There would be a bilge pump somewhere down there, in the

water. He tried to listen for it and decided it was switched off, if there was one. The water level wasn't going down. Where had the water come from?

The raw water intake vents. The engines on almost every boat were water-cooled. They needed to take in cold sea water constantly from an intake below the waterline, then pump it out through a vent above the waterline. The intakes needed a fair bit of maintenance. Usually there would be a filter of some sort, a pump in the engine room to suck the water in, tubes to bring the water from the intakes to the engine system. He started looking for them.

It didn't take long. There were five of them, thick PVC material, at waist height if he stood as near the bottom as he could, all about the diameter of his wrist. There were big nuts fixing the piping to metal intake fittings that would protrude through the hull, allowing in the sea water. One of them was leaking slightly – a broad, steady trickle of water – confirming that this compartment was below the waterline.

The wrench would be to undo the nuts, to get the pipes off for maintenance. He guessed they might be using only one intake right now, while the engines were just ticking over, and felt to see if there were any temperature differences or vibrations to give a clue as to which.

He thought he could detect movement inside two of them, including the one with the leak. If he used the wrench on them then sea water would flood into the compartment, quite quickly. It would fill to the level of the sea outside. Would that be enough to unbalance the boat, set off some warning system? Maybe not, but if the compartment was wholly below the waterline there was a danger it would fill entirely. He might drown if they didn't work out what was happening and respond. He judged they would – not because of the extra ballast but because the engine would very quickly start to overheat if he took away

227

its coolant supply. That might prompt a response. What else was there he could do? It was a risk. But if they didn't respond he could always close the vent again, when the water got too high.

He set to work on the nuts, trying to get the wrench in place, without worrying about what the second part of the plan would be, if they did respond. He saw now why the wrench had such a long handle. It was easy to lever the nuts loose. After a few turns water started to flow in. He could hear it running down the hull, splashing into the bilge below. He kept going and got the first one off. A thick jet of water started to pour in, instantly soaking him. He had to fight a moment of panic, force himself to get to work on the second intake.

By the time he got it off and there were two jets of water flooding the compartment, the level was up to his knees. He stripped off the fleece beneath his jacket and struggled for a few seconds to tear it into strips, then gave up and simply twisted the sleeves and forced one into the first gurgling intake pipe, the other into the second, at least partially blocking them. He tried to wedge them pointing upwards, so that the open ends weren't in the steadily deepening water. Then he recovered the wrench and started to clumsily climb back to the furthest bulkhead, under the hatch. It was only then he found a ladder bolted to the inner wall, coming away from below the hatch. He got onto the bottom rung and waited.

Within five minutes the water was around his thighs. Now, if he let himself off the ladder, he would sink up to chest height. He tried to listen for signs that the engine was struggling but could no longer hear anything except the gush of sea water flooding in. In the enclosed space, the noise was deafening.

After a bit he had to climb further up the ladder. He thought the speed it was coming in must start to slow now. But instead he felt a slight movement of the boat. There was a drawn-out creaking sound. Had it listed slightly? Maybe the compartment below his feet continued under the bulkheads, letting more water in than he had planned for.

Even as he was considering it he felt his centre of balance again shift a little. That would be enough to get them looking, he thought. A heavy boat like this would snap the moorings before long. He listened for signs of them opening the hatch, started to wonder – for the first time – what he planned to do then.

But they didn't open it, and the water kept rising. He had either miscalculated the height of this compartment or the depth of the boat below the waterline, because roughly ten minutes later he was right at the top of the ladder, his head pressed against the hatch, the water above his waist.

He managed to wedge the wrench behind the ladder, so he had both hands free. There was a definite list now. He wasn't imagining it. He started to worry the boat would capsize, with him trapped in there. It seemed unlikely, but nevertheless it was hard not to panic about it. He told himself the reason this compartment existed was to stop the boat capsizing by limiting the quantity of water that could enter through a punctured hull. It was a safety feature, so he was OK.

He pushed himself off the top of the ladder, keeping his feet on the rungs below the water but letting himself float back to the outer hull. He braced one hand there, fixing himself away from the area immediately below the hatch. The water crept up to his chest. The temperature had to be less than twelve degrees. The cold started to take effect, gripping his muscles. He started to shiver. If they didn't come soon he was either going to drown or freeze to death.

Time to close the vents again.

37

He got the wrench from behind the ladder and started to take deep breaths. He would have to dive down to find the ends of the pipes. Now that there was less difference between outer and inner water pressure it should be easily possible to get them back on. But just then he heard something. The background noise was less now, because the water was above the intake pipes. He could hear voices from the other side of the hatch.

He pushed himself off the ladder – his head going under for a moment – and over to the bulkhead. Beneath the water his feet scrabbled to find the iron rib curving down below him. He managed to stand on it, pushing himself back into the furthest corner, so that he was braced against the outer hull, with a firm enough footing, the water up to his chest. He was about three metres along from the hatch, a metre back, and could hear them turning the release levers. He leaned back and tried to steady himself, held the wrench with both hands just under the water.

The light flooding through as the hatch was raised blinded him momentarily. If they had come through immediately, stepping onto the ladder, he would have been helpless. But instead he had a few seconds to recover before he saw hands on the rim, heard someone shouting in. A moment later a head peered through, at an angle, trying to look for him. It was the big security guy, looking in the opposite direction. Behind him Carl could sense movement in the play of light and shade. He heard someone saying in English that the compartment was almost flooded.

The head disappeared, then a foot appeared, feeling for the ladder, one trousered leg followed by the other. The man cursed in Russian, telling those above that the water was freezing. One of them told him that he should get out, that they had to get in and shut off the intakes. But the man kept coming down. He was in up to his chest, descending quickly. As his head got below the level of the hatch he stopped to look around and behind. But it was too dark – Carl could see him squinting into the gloom, no more than three metres away, cursing the water and the darkness, but knew he couldn't see a thing. He shouted up for something – a flashlight. Carl changed his grip on the wrench, holding it like a pole-vaulter, both hands on it, to his side. The water was reaching his upper chest now. He held his breath.

There was a delay while they found a torch and passed it down. As the man switched it on Carl brought the long wrench out from under the water, holding it at head height, pointed right at the guy. The guy heard something and swung the torch towards Carl, blinding him, but by then Carl was already thrusting forward, pushing off with his feet and getting as much force into it as he could.

He rammed the wrench against the side of the man's head. The man gave a strangled grunt, the torch dropping into the water, plunging them back into darkness. Carl sank beneath the surface. He heard a frantic splashing noise around his ears, then scrambled backwards, kicking against the inner hull with his booted feet. He couldn't see anything now. But he knew he had hit the man's head very hard.

He came up again, breathed, then had to drop the wrench to find a handhold on the bulkhead. He expected to see the man coming for him but instead saw only the ladder and the light through the hatch. For a second he was confused. Could the guy have got back out so quickly?

Something heavy rolled on the surface a couple of metres to his right, a hand raised and thrashing at the surface. The guy was over there, beneath the surface. The blow must have stunned him, dropped him into the water. There was room to get past him, if he was quick, so he kicked off the outer hull, got his hands on the rungs and heaved.

He expected to see a gun pointed in his face as his head came up through the hatch, or feel the guy's hands tugging at him from below. Instead he saw two startled, uniformed crew members backing off. No weapons. He got his feet clear without being pulled back and risked a glance back down. He could hear frantic splashing, but couldn't see anything.

He stood with some pain in the stiff knee – the one he'd banged falling into the compartment – and heard the water pouring off him. He wasn't sure if the guy down there was fully conscious or not. He wanted to do something else, to take him out of the picture, stop him giving chase, or at least shut the hatch on him, but there was no time. The crew members were both silent and frightened, watching him like he might be armed, backing away as he came towards them. He pushed past them without saying anything and started to run as best he could along the corridor.

He took the companionway at the end two steps at a time, almost slipping in the water coming off his trousers, feeling the knee loosening up. He could hear a loud bellowing back by the hatch now. He didn't know what deck he was on, or how many decks there were, but saw another companionway directly ahead and went straight up.

He came out onto a floodlit deck, open to the sky, at the stern, a round swimming pool in front of him, no one using it. He went round it to the starboard side and saw he was a deck higher than where the gangway would be. He ran past crew struggling to loosen one of the mooring lines and leaped a small rail to drop two metres to the deck below. As he landed, a pain shot up from his knee and for a few seconds he was stuck. Ahead he saw two suited men running towards him. He realised that the gangway had been hauled in.

He climbed awkwardly onto the guardrail right next to him and leaped across the metre gap, landing badly on the concrete dock, rolling, jarring his shoulder. As he stood, his left leg gave way, the knee refusing to take any more weight. He started to limp away, people shouting at him from the boat. He risked a look and saw the suits standing at the guardrail, one of them speaking into a radio, the other pointing at him. The line of Mercs was gone but there was still a small group of bystanders. He elbowed his way through them and kept going, headed for where he'd left the bike. The sky was dark already.

38

The flight to Helsinki was full aside from business class. She got a ticket using the credit card Drake had given her, in the name of Alice Rogers. It was very expensive. The girl at the counter said her nose was bleeding, and pointed at it – not out of human concern, but because they had rules about it. Julia asked for some tissue and poked it up the nostril, telling the girl it would stop in seconds. A couple of days before, she realised, she would have felt terrified that the girl would suspect something. She had killed two men, was travelling on false papers, paying with a credit card that wasn't hers. But she felt no fear at all. Not any more.

She felt a new kind of cold-bloodedness. She didn't think anyone was going to stop her, or even look for her. How would they know she was here? There wouldn't be adequate enough descriptions of her, because everyone had been looking at the crash. There might be images of her on CCTV systems, but that would take more time to process, and she would be airborne in thirty minutes, on the last flight to Helsinki for that day.

In the coffee bar nearest the gate she drank three coffees in fifteen minutes, sitting by herself at one of the tables, trying to put together everything that had happened. She placed both phones on the table in front of her and watched as the one Drake had given her flashed every five minutes with a message from him. But she didn't trust Drake now, didn't trust Michael Rugojev either. They had brought her to London and Rebecca wasn't here. They had brought her to the wrong place.

Rebecca was in Helsinki. She knew she was in Helsinki not just because Jones had told her that but because she had searched through Molina's phone and found the number she had been called from while standing outside Bowman's apartment. Whoever it was had been careless, because the number had been communicated with the call, like it was recognised by the device. Maybe it was in the phone's memory already, in some bit of it she hadn't managed to find. It was a mobile number with a country code: 00358. That was the country code for Finland. She had been almost certain of it as soon as she saw it, but to be sure she had sat at an Internet terminal here and checked, so there was no doubt now – she had been speaking to someone in Finland. Someone who had said, *I wish it didn't have to be like this.*

She drained the last dregs of the last cup of coffee as she thought about that voice. She could hear it in her head now, clear as day. It brought a foul taste to her mouth, made her feel like she would start shivering again. In front of her, across from the coffee bar, they had just announced boarding for her flight.

She stood up, pulling the jacket around her and fastening it.

I wish it didn't have to be like this. The line had been clear – like he was speaking into her ear, right there beside her, an intimate kind of threat. He had spoken quietly, calmly. Why hadn't she recognised him immediately?

Because she hadn't expected to hear that voice. She had expected Zaikov's voice, a voice she would never recognise because she had never met or spoken to Zaikov. But it wasn't Zaikov who had taken Rebecca and tried to kill her. She knew that now. Because she had recognised the voice – she knew exactly who it was.

235

39

The bike was in sight when it happened. He was walking, quickly but carefully, on the twisted knee, just over the Esplanadi at the other side of the market. There were no stalls there now, the space was empty, the wind whipping litter across the cobbles, but the road he had crossed was full of the night-time, rush-hour traffic, a glare of headlights. He had asked someone the time and been told it was quarter past six, so he was in a hurry. He had less than an hour to get up to the conference centre, maybe not even that if someone told Zaikov he had escaped. It was feasible Zaikov would react to that, feel a need to take precautions.

He turned the corner past the City Hall, saw the bike about one hundred metres ahead, still there, then felt it in his chest: a quick flutter, followed by a pain that lanced into his left arm. It was severe enough to stop him. He put a hand up and could feel his heart doing something, beating too hard, too fast, too uneven. An effect of the electricity, he thought, willing himself to dismiss it.

He stepped forward to continue, sure it would wear off, but right then he felt it stop – felt his heart actually stop. He could feel the pulse, hear the beat in his ears, then it just stopped. In the split second between it happening and the rush of wrenching fear that followed, he took a deep breath and collapsed gently to the ground. He was on his knees before a wave of blackness swept over him, like he was fainting. Then he was gone.

A fraction of a second later he was conscious again. That was his impression – but it can't have been accurate, because he was on his back now, with a circle of anxious faces looking down at him, someone saying something to him with quiet concern, another person pressing down on his chest, starting the CPR routine.

His eyes cleared and he sat up. He heard gasps of relief from someone.

'We thought you were dead,' a man said.

Carl focused on him, saw a police uniform. 'I'm OK,' he said, confused, unable to even place where he was. He took deep breaths, put his hand up to his chest. The heartbeat was there, beating normally, a little fast, but regular.

He muttered thank you to the group, or something like that. His head felt fuzzy again, disorientated, like it had been right after they had tasered him. He could remember that immediately, the tasering, then most of the rest – where he was, where he had been going – but other things were lost: the wider situation. In view were a couple of men, a woman, the policeman. Behind the policeman a police bike, stopped at the kerb, blue light flashing.

'You cut your head as you fell,' the policeman said, in broken English. 'I called an ambulance. Just in case.'

Carl brought his hand up, put it on the gash behind his ear, felt the wet, warm blood. But that was from before, from falling into the bilge of the boat. He remembered that now as well.

'I'm OK,' he said, in Finnish. 'I think I just tripped up. I don't need an ambulance.'

'You weren't breathing,' the woman said. 'For about ten seconds you weren't breathing.'

He tried to stand up, got to his knees, paused to make sure he wasn't going to collapse, then stood. He looked around, saw his bike, further up the road. He laughed, trying to make light of things, thanked them again. He could recall he was in a hurry, but not why. Get to the bike, get going. Get away from the policeman. Work it out later.

But would the policeman stop him getting on the bike? He was already losing interest, Carl thought. He had turned away, started speaking into a shoulder-clipped radio, talking about some traffic situation somewhere. Carl thanked them again and started to walk off. This was Finland. People didn't speak much, not even to people they knew. No need to hang around discussing it. He said something curt, more in keeping with the national character. Thirty metres further on he looked back and saw them walking off, two of them speaking to each other. The policeman was still on his radio. Somewhere in the distance he could hear an ambulance siren. How long had he been lying there?

At the bike he turned the corner, not going anywhere near the machine. He leaned against a wall, out of sight, sank down on his haunches, listened to his heart. Was it going to happen again – that it would just stop like that? If it happened when he was on the bike he was fucked.

He tried to remember where he was going but for a minute or so nothing came into his head. Then he recalled the gun, in the box of the bike. He had to get to the conference centre where Zaikov was. That was what he had been trying to do.

He walked over to the bike, looked left. The police bike was already gone. He unclipped the helmet and put it on, got on the bike and tried to look for the keys in his jacket. The jacket was soaking. Had they asked him about that – the policeman, those people? He couldn't remember. He was shivering now. He no longer had the fleece beneath the jacket. He found the keys under the seat, where he had left them.

He started the bike, pushed off. If he felt the flutter again he would stop, immediately, call emergency services. He paused, slowed, put his foot down, searched for his phone. But they had taken his phone. He couldn't contact anyone. He wanted to contact Viktor, to ask him something. Something important. But what? That was gone. He had to try to remember it. And something else – something teasing at the back of his mind, something they had said on the boat.

He rode all the way to the Kalasjatorppa conference centre with the feeling persisting that his brain wasn't working properly. But not the part of it that coordinated his driving. He drove fast, weaved between cars, used the throttle, had no problems staying on the bike and reacting to traffic. That wasn't it. The sensation was of a gap behind all that. He could do everything on the surface as if he had already recovered from what they had done to him, but behind it all he wasn't placing thoughts where they should be, or in the right order. It was an abstract feeling of unease.

So he drove with urgency, but when he got to the hotel and saw the rows of Mercs parked up in the big turning circle, with chauffeurs holding doors open and men coming out, he just sat there, in the road, astride the bike, the engine ticking over, not knowing what he was meant to do now.

Get the contract cancelled before they send someone new to kill her. He remembered the contract. But how? Was he meant to shoot Zaikov – would that do it? There had to be a reason why he had the gun.

He felt confused, unclear about what was required. He put his hand on his heart again, under the jacket. It seemed OK, but he was breathing in short gasps. He looked around, squinting into the headlights on the road behind him, then remembered a whole chunk of details – what had happened on the boat. They hadn't given him a chance to speak about Rebecca, but they weren't going to cancel anything, clearly. So he needed to put them in a situation where they were *forced* to consider that. Zaikov was going to travel to the house on the island of Kaskisaari – Viktor had told him that – so if he was going to do something he would need to get there ahead of him. Or find somewhere on the way there, somewhere where he could force things. He needed time with Zaikov, in safety. Time to convince him. Viktor's way had failed, now he would fall back on something more traditional.

He didn't wait to see if Zaikov was in the group getting into the cars. Viktor had told him Zaikov would go to Kaskisaari, so that was that. He turned the bike round and took it down to the coast road, driving more carefully, looking for a police presence but finding none. He crossed the bridge to Kuusisaari, the first of a small chain of islands that extended out into the bay – Kaskisaari was the last. The bridge was only a couple of minutes from the conference centre. The traffic was still heavy here because you could use this route to get across the bay to Espoo, a large residential area. There was nowhere anything could be attempted in seclusion.

The second bridge took him over to a larger island – Lehtisaari. Here there were more trees, but still too much traffic. At a junction he took the turn signposted for Kaskisaari and very quickly the traffic was thinning out. Now there was nowhere to go except Kaskisaari. You could get cars over there, but not off the other end, where there was only a footbridge. But even before he got near the bridge over to Kaskisaari, he was driving through light forest, no houses around. He slowed down, pulled over. They would come this way, driving through the trees. If Viktor was right, they would travel by this route.

He followed a footpath and eased the bike across the sparse forest floor, then cut the engine and got off. He propped it behind a stand of bushes and opened the box. He kept his ears on the road as he got the pieces of gun out and put them together, blind almost, in the light of the moon coming through the branches above. He snapped the magazine in and pulled the bolt. He could hear cars behind him.

He went down low and got back to within five metres of the road. He found a spur of land crested with big old birch trees and lay down flat amongst the leaf litter. There were streetlights on the road but the nearest was thirty metres away. He steadied the gun on the ground and took aim. He saw a headlight poking through the trees, coming from the direction of Kaskisaari. It was a van, travelling slow. He watched it pass, could clearly see the driver concentrating on the road. As it disappeared he was left in silence. In the distance he could hear traffic on the big Lautasaari bridge, about two kilometres away. He waited.

He tried to estimate the minutes. Five minutes. Then ten. The cold was seeping into his wet clothing, coming up from the ground. He was shivering. What was he doing here? He asked himself the question and started to think it through. They would come down the road in a cavalcade of cars. There would be at least three cars. Zaikov wouldn't be taking chances. The first and last would contain security people. But they wouldn't be armed, not here in Finland. Or maybe they would. It was possible. It was also possible the cars were armoured. But even without those issues, how would he stop them? Shoot out the tyres? That wouldn't do it, not if the drivers were professional – they would keep going on the hubs. Kill the engine? He doubted that was certain, even at this range, not with this gun, not if the cars were armoured. They would just keep going, once again, get across the bridge to Kaskisaari, inside their compound there.

He rested his head on the ground. He didn't know what he was doing. This wasn't his thing. It wasn't even a gun he knew how to fire properly. And anyway, were they even going to come here?

The thought freed something up. Viktor had said they would come here. Viktor had set up the meeting with Zaikov. He started to shake and knew suddenly that he had already made a terrible connection, seconds before he had it laid out in his head.

On the boat, they had said something that he thought he hadn't understood, but his brain gave it to him now, crystal clear. The younger one – Andrei Zaikov – had come in with the bat and demanded of the father if it was some kind of joke, otherwise what had brought him, Carl, there, to them, into their power? And the father had snapped something back at him, very quick. Carl had heard it but hadn't understood. But he could understand it now, understand it perfectly. Zaikov had said, 'He has been given some stupid story about a girl and a contract.'

A stupid story about a girl and a contract. That was what Carl had just told Zaikov that he was there about. A stupid story? The truth was right there in the way he had said it, not to Carl, but to his son – so no need for lying or pretence. The story Carl had told him, about the contract on Rebecca, had sounded stupid to him. As if it weren't true.

There was no need to remember more, but he did. He remembered the son looking down at him, the baseball bat perched on his shoulder, then turning back to the father and saying, 'His brother says we are village idiots, shit-kickers, but we would never do this to our own.'

They had known he was coming, and they had known who he was, just as Viktor had said they would. But someone had convinced them that *he* had killed Uri Zaikov.

He stood quickly. The road was very silent and he knew at once that Zaikov was coming nowhere near this island. He was waiting in vain. It was possible Zaikov didn't even own a house here. Zaikov had never heard of the Spanish contract, never heard of the girl he was meant to have contracted Carl to kill.

We would never do this to our own.

He started to run back to the bike.

40

He drove back to Gumbacka in a panic, passing the road back to the hotel without seeing the Mercs, wondering how much of it had been there for him to see before he had even set foot on Zaikov's boat.

There were lights on in the house that he could see from two kilometres back, on the forest road. Viktor's was the only house on that part of the inlet in Gumbacka. The lights gave him a brief hope that they would both still be there, that somehow he was wrong.

He screeched the bike to a halt in front of the twin garages and ran panting to the front door. He shouted for Rebecca at the top of his voice and pushed on the door. It was shut, but not locked – he had only to turn the big handle to swing it back on the huge, deserted hallway, ablaze with light.

He knew the moment he put a foot inside that the entire place was empty. It was like something you could smell. He shouted again, shouted her name, shouted for Viktor. And all the time could feel his heart racing, skipping, pausing, feel the anger welling inside.

There was a huge nineteenth-century factory clock mounted on the wall directly opposite the doorway. According to that, it was just after eight o'clock. He had been gone over six hours.

He ran through the whole house, then down to the dock. The boats were all there. They had not left by boat.

Back in the garages both cars were there, so he took the steps up through the wooded darkness behind the house, to the big concrete helipad, illuminated by powerful floodlights. He had seen it from the circular tower earlier in the day, seen it covered in a carpet of fallen birch leaves. But now he stood in the middle of it and saw the big white H clearly. The leaves had been blown aside, not just off the helipad, but from the skirting and the lawns surrounding it. Viktor had left in a helicopter and had taken Rebecca with him. But how long ago?

He staggered back to the house, his heart doing something again. He had to know where they had gone.

He went through all the drawers in the room Viktor called his office, flinging the contents on the floor, searching for a phone that might have Viktor's numbers in it. He had none of them in his head, having relied for too long on his phone's memory. There was a blinking light on the answerphone for the landline and he pressed it and listened to a message from a cleaning company, trying to get through to the caretaker.

He went up the stairs to Viktor's room and started turning out all his clothes, his drawers of papers, not even sure now what he was looking for or trying to do. He felt a terrible tightness pressing into his ribs, sweat on his forehead.

There were computers lying all over – laptops, desktops, tablets – but they all needed passwords he didn't have. He leaned against the window, staring out into the darkness, and tried frantically to clarify what he *did* know.

Zaikov had never heard of Rebecca.

Viktor must have told them he had killed Uri.

He gasped as he thought about it. But there was no other way to interpret it. Viktor had set him up, betrayed him, got him onto that boat *knowing* that they would try to kill him. It made him flinch, curl up inside and cry out with shock. He couldn't grasp it properly, couldn't understand why. That it might *just* be about money, that Viktor would try to kill his own brother, kill *him*, for money, as part of a massive deal with the Zaikov clan ... That he *couldn't* believe.

But there was no other explanation. *We would never do this to our own.*

There *must* be something else, something that had forced Viktor into it, that gave him no choice. Because Viktor was his brother, the one person who had always looked out for him, looked after him, cared for him. Was it something to do with the girl, with Rebecca? Viktor had left *with* her. Neither of them were here. That meant he was running with her. But Zaikov had never heard of Rebecca so he couldn't be running from Zaikov on account of her. Was Rebecca just an untimely coincidence? Did she have nothing to do with it at all?

But if Viktor was running now then he *must* be running from Zaikov. There was no one else who could pose a big enough threat. Which meant Zaikov was trying to kill them both, and in desperation Viktor had tried to buy him off with Carl's life. But it hadn't worked, so Viktor had fled, taking Rebecca with him.

But why take Rebecca with him? He screwed his eyes shut and tried to weigh it, put the bare facts together, work out what they meant. But his brain was still too sluggish, his thoughts sifting slowly like a grey mud, everything knocked out of line by the voltage. He couldn't hack his way through the questions. There was too much that didn't make sense. Especially Rebecca. What did she have to do with it all?

He stumbled coming back down the stairs and fell into the hallway, skidding onto his back. He was breathing like he had run a marathon. He sat up and tried to control the things he was feeling, the fear gripping at him. It was going to happen again, he thought – the heart thing. He should do something about it or he would never find out where they had gone.

He pushed himself to his feet and walked very slowly towards the kitchen, thinking that at least a glass of water would help. But he didn't get as far as the door before he felt the waves of dizziness again. This time he was breathing so noisily he couldn't hear his heart. This time he didn't manage to get down to ground level before the blackout hit and the floor rushed up to meet him.

the further, reflecting that the I-beam right or water would help
him he didn't get close to the door before inside the edge
of her breasts again. This time he was breathing so only he
could reach his near. On his inside hide against a wave in a
to ground itself before the J-beam lit, and the doors moved
to close itself.

41

Almost one in the morning. Julia stood in the darkness and tried to control the flood of emotion. She had seen him from the edge of the forest, through cheap, low-powered binoculars bought in a petrol station. She had rested them on a stone, lay down, made sure her hands were steady, focused them carefully, forced herself to take her time, to make sure it really was him.

He was in what looked like a kitchen, standing over a sink, splashing water onto his face. She wasn't sure until he straightened up and turned from the sinks, walked over to the window and leaned against the sill – then she could see his face quite clearly. It was him. No doubt about it. Not who she had been expecting at all.

When she got past the initial shock she started to scan the place again, trying to hold down the feelings, keep her breath under control. It was almost impossible.

This was the only house for miles around, a blaze of light against the surrounding woods. From where she had lain – at the edge of the forest on the slightly higher land above the inlet – she could see straight over what she thought might be the helicopter pad, across the lawns and down to the water. The surface was alive with reflected light, a shifting pattern of flickering orange and yellow against the black forested land beyond.

Despite that, at first she had thought no one was home. She had searched every window she could see, very carefully. There were no curtains or blinds, no attempt at privacy. There was a three-metre-high security fence that she remembered well, with cameras and floodlights every twenty metres, razor wire coiled along the top, the trees cleared either side of it so it looked like a prison camp boundary, but the gates were wide open, with no one on guard. No dogs, no security personnel patrolling the perimeter. All these things had been standard when she had been here ten years before. Now it looked like you could just walk straight through the gates.

Which was exactly what she had done. She was standing about fifty metres past the gateposts now, watching his figure move from room to room. From where she was to the door was less than thirty metres. If he looked out he would see her.

The car she had hired was back in the trees, at a bend in the road. She had left it to walk through the forest and get near enough undetected to be able to work out what she should do. She had hoped that she would actually see them – see Viktor, see Rebecca. There had been a strong feeling in her heart that Rebecca *would* be here, that she would find her. But her premonitions and precautions had been off target. There was no security. No sign of Viktor. No Rebecca. Instead, *he* was here.

At the airport, she had not been able to remember the exact address – the car she had hired had a satnav though. She had paid for it – and the binoculars – using one of the cards Drake had given her, even though she knew that meant Michael Rugojev would be able to trace the usage. Some credit cards were set up to send a text message to a nominated phone number, notifying each transaction as it happened, to prevent fraud. If it was like that then he would know already that she was in Helsinki, but she had no other source of funds and so no option.

She had put 'Gumbacka' into the satnav – that was as much as she could recall – but had easily found her way once she got near.

A year ago, when Michael Rugojev had tracked her down, she

249

had sat in a restaurant with him and asked where his nephew was. Viktor Rugojev's wealth had apparently grown since she had last met him: he now had properties in America, London, Dubai, Moscow, Brazil. There was some kind of rift between Michael and he, though, a source of pain to the uncle. He had sat with his hands open at the table and said, 'Like all of us, he moves around a lot. I'm never really sure where he is based these days.' Then he'd smiled, and added, 'He still has the place in Helsinki.' He remembered their visit there, wanted to talk about it, as though the memory were happy. 'I think it's the only place he still has in Finland,' he said. 'They tell me he keeps it because he remembers you, remembers your plans together.'

His plans, not hers. But that was why she was here, because Michael had said that.

They had been here only once, all three of them – Michael, Viktor and herself. Plus the staff and security, of course. Nearly thirty security guys at that point, because it was all still fresh – the attempt on Michael's life – the fallout still with them. But that hadn't stopped Viktor. He had proposed to her here, on that night. He had done it in front of Michael, as if Michael was some kind of king or high priest who would bless the whole thing. *Mikhael Ivanovich.* That was what they called Michael, in Russian. It was like a scene out of a movie. The Godfather – Michael as family and gang boss, giving his permission to bring her into the fold. In the beginning she had thought they were all just businessmen, legitimate – she had been very young, of course – but by then she had known better.

Michael had been smiling that smile, watching Viktor's clumsiness as he asked her. Michael still had the collar on his neck, the bruising all over his chest. But he was alive. Sixty-two and alive to tell the tale. Death torn from around his neck, thanks to her. She had saved his life on that nightmare day – the fifteenth of July. Hence his new-found belief in her. She could do nothing wrong now. Four weeks before he would not have permitted his nephew to even consider marrying her – she had been a mere kitchen assistant. But now he was excited about it, wanted to give money away to do it properly, spoke about feeling like a father to them both.

That night Viktor had talked about getting some celebrity artist to create a 'celebration' of her, as an engagement gift. It was to be a huge sculpture that they would put in the garden – a statue of her, nine metres high. She would have to pose for it. He had costed it already. Michael was in on it, nodding with approval, a stupid twinkle in his grey eyes. A sculpture in honour of her. She had never heard of anything so crass, so kitsch. She had tried to keep a straight face, tried to give nothing away.

She was expected to say yes to the proposal, and had, because by then she was already too terrified of Viktor Rugojev to risk crossing him. At that point – when he proposed – her escape plans were almost complete. A week later she was gone.

That had been in August, the first week of August, just three weeks after they had all been up at The Ice House and men had come to kill Michael. She had known Michael only as Mr Rugojev then, and had barely spoken to him. Everything had been different. But that day had opened her eyes.

It had just been announced that Mikhael Ivanovich had bought a 'palace'. That was what Viktor had called it. The Ice House – that was a rough translation of the Russian name. An enormous, sprawling, Czarist mansion in northern Karelia. When she had first set eyes on it she had thought it looked like the palace in the sixties film *Dr Zhivago*. But without the snow. It had been warm then, a beautiful summer. Viktor told her the name was a reference to the decorative, arched windows, the thousands of panes of glass, which shone like ice in the sun. Most of them were smashed at the time Michael acquired it. The place needed a lot of work, a complete restoration. There was only one inhabitable wing where someone had been living previously.

They had travelled from this house, in Gumbacka, to visit it – Michael, Viktor, Alex and her, plus two security guys. A small contingent, for those days. Alex was meant to be security too. That was why he was there. Viktor was Michael's favourite. That was why he was there. Michael had no sons of his own. The occasion was to show Viktor the new place, talk about family succession plans. She went along because Viktor brought her, though Viktor had said nothing to Michael about them being 'together'. And Viktor had known nothing of Alex and her – she was sure of that. She was there to do the cooking. Officially, that was why she was there.

The thing with Alex had been huge at that point, all she could think of. They had made a decision that Viktor would have to be told, that they would have to take the consequences. If they didn't break the thing Viktor thought he had going with her then they weren't going to be able to stay together. But so far they had done nothing about that decision.

They travelled by helicopter and cars. It took half a day to get there from Gumbacka. They crossed the border at a checkpoint deep in the northern forests. The house was on the Russian side, though only just. It was in the middle of nowhere. Forests and low hills all around. No towns, no people. Hardly any of Michael's staff informed where he was. For those reasons, perhaps, he had thought it safe to go with limited security. But he'd been wrong.

They were there a week before it happened. One of the most memorable weeks of her life. Viktor had been with Michael the whole time, talking business. She had been left with Alex. The weather had been hot, the skies clear, the wild, forest landscapes breathtaking. They had wandered far and wide through the woods, finding lakes, viewpoints, rivers, never seeing another person, utterly absorbed in the intensity of the connection that had grown between them. She had never had anything like it before, nor since.

Then, on the seventh day, Uri Zaikov and his men had come.

Michael had shown her the hole under the floor, not because he had been concerned about her but because she happened to have been there when he came looking for it. It was in the kitchen, under the boards. She had walked over it many times without thinking.

He had stooped and pulled on the edge of a board that looked chipped – a gap just wide enough to get your fingers in – and it had sprung open on some kind of mechanism. She had paused from what she was doing and watched. He had been laughing, pointing at it. He started saying something about it in Russian, then remembered that she didn't speak it. Was it the first time he had actually said anything to her? Probably not. There must have been other, practical things, but she couldn't remember them. 'Just in case,' he had joked, in English, standing staring into it. She had come round from behind the big work surface and looked. It was like a coffin under the floor. She had asked him what it was. 'Somewhere to hide,' he'd said. 'It's from the Revolution, when the red guards came hunting, you would get under there.' He laughed again, then shut it and walked out. It hadn't been his intention, but the exchange was to save her life. And his.

42

The fifteenth of July. She had been in the kitchen, making omelettes for their lunch. What time would that make it? Near midday. She had the windows wide open because it was hot, exceptionally hot for the area, they had told her, though the thermometer attached to the outside of one of the kitchen windows had read only twenty-eight degrees, which she thought a nice heat – you could still function in it, it didn't drain you.

Alex had told her that this far north they were lucky to get even a few days like this, without wind or rain to ruin it. Usually, there was no difference between Finland and here – both were predominantly grey, cold, depressing. But these days were far from dull. Everything was feverish, tinged with guilt and fear, clandestine meetings with Alex that always ended in sex, everything intensified by the danger involved; the risk that Viktor would walk in on them or begin to suspect something. She performed a shadow play of the exact same deception with Viktor, vis-à-vis Michael, and in the evenings had to invent absurd excuses to keep Viktor off her.

During her break periods, lying in the forest, she plotted a future free of all the secrecy and tension, something that in her heart she knew they would never have. Because the thing between them was like something on fire. They talked about what it might be like years down the line, but only to assuage the constant fear of it ending at any moment. To get there – to pass into some kind of future *together* – what they had would have to cool into something very different, and neither could truly contemplate that. They were living in a world saturated with the colours, tastes, smells and sensations of the charge between them. Everything was a kind of constant astonishment. And always the background fugue of aching longing, crashing release. She was only dimly aware of any moral dimension. Reality was lost beneath layers of lies, but there was never a question of free choice – the emotions swept everything before them.

Why did she go to the window? She must have heard something, though could not now remember what. Or seen something out of the corner of her eye. She was hoping it was Alex, of course. She had put the whisk down, stepped over to the open window and saw instead the man who had been seated in the small courtyard area just in front of the garden. She saw him stand up and shout something. The garden right there was only a fraction of the area that had once been landscaped, though most of it now was overgrown, returned to nature, which this far north meant mainly pine trees and scrub. The part right outside the window would have been the kitchen garden once, over a century ago, with herbs and vegetables growing in a sheltered spot, screened by a low wall and an orchard full of fruit trees.

The orchard had long gone to ruin and the kitchen garden was like a jungle, the wall dividing it from the courtyard collapsed to knee height. The man had been sitting on a foldaway chair at the corner there, just behind the broken wall. He was one of the security guys, his job to watch the rear areas. The other was out front somewhere.

She had been vaguely aware of him all morning she had been in the kitchen, thinking he had an easy job; he either had his head tilted back, face up to the sun, or was smoking, every time she looked. There was a gun – she was just beginning to get used to there always being guns around, mainly because they were never actually used – propped against the wall beside him.

She thought at first he might be shouting at Viktor or Alex. They had gone up to the stable block, on a hill about a kilometre away. There was a route hacked through the overgrown gardens that led to a broken perimeter fence, then the forest started and you could take the track through the woods up to the stables, which were elevated enough for you to be able to see back to the house if you were there, across the tops of the trees. She couldn't see the building from her position at the kitchen window, because the wild fruit trees were in the way, but the security guy would be able to see up there, so maybe he had seen Alex or Viktor and shouted to them. As far as she knew, the brothers had gone up there to talk business, and Michael was in the house somewhere, somewhere in this wing they were all using, though she had neither seen nor heard him all morning.

She was going to go back to her eggs – because there was nothing in the way the man had shouted to make her worry – when she saw him turn quickly and reach a hand out towards the gun. He didn't get that far though.

The order of things was confused in her mind now. She could recall the brickwork behind him spinning off in tiny fragments, then a gout of blood coming out of his back. He fell against the wall, so hard she heard the breath knocked out of his lungs. Then, after that, there was a noise from far off like a whip crack, not particularly loud, and a moment later he was on the ground, on his knees, groaning.

Frozen to the spot, she watched blood run out of his mouth in a long stream. He fell flat onto his face, his arms limp, his legs kicking. But still she couldn't assemble the distinct parts of what she had seen into something that made sense. What had happened to him?

She saw a puff of dust and fragments again, on the bricks lower down, nearer his head this time, then a split second later heard again the cracking noise. Then, off to the left, movement through the garden, someone coming through the overgrown vegetation.

All of this took only a few seconds, with her just standing there looking at it, looking at the man on the ground, the pool of blood spreading out around him, then the other man running through the bushes towards them.

She swallowed and opened her mouth to shout something – she had no idea what – then saw that the one coming through the trees also had a gun, but it wasn't Alex, or Viktor, or the other security guy. She didn't know this man but he was coming right at her, heading for the open kitchen door, off to her right.

It clicked that what she had seen and heard was two gunshots. She had seen bullets go through the security guard, then a fraction of a second later heard the reports, seen him slump to the ground. He was dying now, in front of her eyes, his limbs moving strangely, his face pressed into the stone flags.

Her mouth was open to scream but her brain was spinning into gear, alive with the danger, her heart racing in her chest. She closed her mouth, stepped back from the open window.

She had only seconds to react. But in that time many things went through her brain, were considered, rejected. Her first impulse was to rush through the kitchen, find Michael, alert him, but she had no idea where he was and in less than a minute the man she had seen was going to be at the kitchen door. He had killed the security guard, or so she thought – afterwards she was to find out that it had been another one of them who had shot him, from a position further away – so why not her?

They were coming for Michael, she assumed. They were moving down from the direction of the stables, where Viktor and Alex had been. Did that mean that they had already found Viktor and Alex? The thought had no time to take root. She heard a noise out in the courtyard and started to cross the kitchen. By chance her eyes passed over the tiny missing piece of floorboard that was the release mechanism for the hole Michael had showed her only two days previously. Without thinking further she stooped and curled her fingers into the gap, found a trigger, pulled it, watched the boards lever themselves up. She went straight into the hole, not pausing, reached up, pulled at the leather handle hanging down and brought the cover back down onto herself as she lay down. It shut with a soft, terrifying click and suddenly she was in total darkness, her breath very loud. She struggled to control it, and the fear behind it. She could hear nothing but herself. She held her breath, but then could only hear her heart.

She felt a slight movement in her position. Had someone stepped on the boards above her? She listened intently but still could hear nothing but the blood pulsing in her ears. She expected at any moment that the boards would swing up and someone point a gun at her face.

But it didn't happen. She held her breath as long as she could, twisting her head and pressing an ear against the cold surface above her. There was muffled shouting, she thought, but nothing clear. She started to breathe again.

The space was only just big enough to fit her. The sides seemed to be of wood, the cover lined with some metal, maybe to dampen sound. The seal – whatever it was – was very tight. She could see absolutely nothing, not even a crack of light. She thought there was an odour of fish. Already she wondered how long she had been in there. She started to count off the seconds in her head, then heard voices more clearly, more movement, a sound like a bang, then a scuffle. She held her breath again and felt the panic rising in her throat. She had an urge to scream. She put her knuckles in her mouth, started to suck in air like she was having an asthma attack.

She was just getting the better of it when she heard the gunshots. Very loud, near her. She jumped so much her head banged off the metallic surface above her. Then she could hear a man shouting, and for the first time her thoughts came back to Alex. Was it him? She couldn't tell. But where was he? The thought made her forget her own predicament. If the man in the room above hadn't already been to the stables then he might go there now. Or Alex might hear the shots and run down. She should get out, try to warn him. She couldn't just skulk here and let the man surprise him. He would kill Alex as he had killed the guard. She felt a sudden leaping fear thinking about it, quite different to the emotion that had gripped her when she was thinking only of running. Because now she had to do something, she had to get out there, face it.

She pushed gently on the cover, trying to get it to move, but it felt solid. She pushed harder, putting her knees against it, but that was useless too. She started to shout, involuntarily, but shut herself up quickly and made herself think about it. She felt her way around the parts of the lid she could reach. There had to be a switch or release mechanism. She couldn't be trapped here. But what if she had got in the wrong end? What if the switch was nearer her feet? There was no room to sit up and reach down there. The man might kill everyone and she would be left here, in the middle of nowhere. Would anyone come before her air ran out?

She found it. A small metal catch. She pushed it one way, then another, heard another shot from up above. The catch clicked when she pulled it towards her and the lid moved slightly – light poked in, dazzling her. She lay still, listening intently, found the leather strap she had used to pull the lid down on her and held it from opening any further.

Now she could hear properly. Noises from the rooms above. Loud blows, grunts, furniture moving, someone fighting. She eased on the strap and the false boards swung up enough for her to raise her head and look across the kitchen floor. She couldn't see any feet. She let go of the strap and as the cover sprang back pushed herself out of the hole. She could hear a muffled cry for help, from the next room, the dining room.

What happened next became very scrambled in her memory. She thought it sounded like someone was struggling through there, shouting for help, and could remember thinking definitely that the voice sounded like Alex's. She could not remember picking up a knife as she passed the work surface, but as she pushed open the doors into the dining room she was certainly holding a long, thin filleting knife from the rack.

What she saw was not what she had been expecting. Above the long, mahogany dining room table a man was hanging by his neck, kicking wildly with his feet, a strangled, terrible scream coming from beneath a black hood that covered his head. His hands were tied behind his back and he was spinning and turning through the air as he scrabbled desperately to get one foot then the other down onto the table. The rope holding him was looped through a fixture in the high ceiling above the dining room table and another man was hauling on the end of it, trying to get the hooded man off the table, trying to hang him.

As she came in the man hauling at the rope was struggling back towards her, his body straining at a sixty-degree angle, both hands tangled in the rope and heaving at it. She couldn't see his face, couldn't see anything of him. It might have been the man she had seen earlier with the gun. He was grunting and cursing at the struggling man. He didn't turn round as she came in, didn't even notice her. All his attention and strength was on getting the man off the table.

She knew the hanging man was Alex, knew with absolute certainty, without checking the clothing or trying to interpret the cries. But she could not remember crossing the floor towards the one trying to kill him. The distance was no more than five metres. She didn't know whether she walked it or ran, had no memory of any thoughts going through her head between coming through the doors and then being there behind the man. Except that it was Alex on the end of the rope. And she had to do something.

She stabbed the man three times in quick succession, using one hand to jab the knife into his exposed back, the other to push at his shoulder, forcing him sideways and away from the rope. When he fell to the ground, releasing the rope with an exclamation of surprise, she slashed towards him again, missing this time as he stumbled across the floor, blood coming out of him, his eyes wide with surprise. Alex came down onto the table with a heavy bang, the table splitting and collapsing beneath him. She turned her attention only briefly towards it, but as she did the one she had stabbed continued to crawl away from her.

She was torn between the need to get to Alex, to get the noose off his neck and check him, and the need to make sure the stabbed man wouldn't come back at her. She glanced round for a weapon he might have ready but could see nothing. When he was about five metres across the room he pushed himself to his feet, screaming now at the top of his voice, then crashed in a half fall, half run, through the doors at the opposite side.

She dropped the knife, stepped over to the broken table. Alex was on the floor beneath a part of it, struggling and yelling, still hooded. She got her hands around the rope and pulled frantically, trying to loosen it. It gave and she got it off, then pulled the hood over his head and opened her mouth to say something.

But it wasn't Alex. It was Michael.

43

Carl had been out for hours. He had a red swelling across his left cheek, where he'd hit his face on the floor when he went down. The knee was still stiff, from the boat, but he could walk. He could not have been unconscious that long, he thought, or his memory would be scrambled worse than it had been before. Instead he could remember everything with clarity. He must have passed out for only a few seconds. But unlike the first time he hadn't returned to wakefulness when it was over. Instead, it seemed, he had remained there, flat out on the floor, for nearly five hours.

Doing what? Sleeping? Semi-conscious? It must have been something like that, his body giving him no choice over it. He had come round five hours later and started panicking about the time lost. How far away could Rebecca be now? The thought made his heart race, and he didn't need that. He forced himself to be methodical, to pick up with what he had been doing when he had blacked out – searching for a method of locating Viktor. There was no other way of finding her.

He was looking at a phone he had found in a room off the kitchen when he glanced out of the window and saw the figure. Whoever it was, they were about thirty metres away, on the drive leading down from the security gates: a figure about his own height standing off to the side of the track, just outside the halo of light cast by the tungsten lamps lining the driveway at ten metre intervals. Just standing there.

The only reason he noticed was because the light in that room was dim, a single weak bulb in the ceiling behind him, so there was less glare across the glass than in other rooms. He reached back and switched the light off, cancelling the remaining reflections across the window pane. But that far off from the house it was impossible to make out details. A man, he decided, watching the front of the house, not obviously armed, but standing so that he wasn't illuminated very clearly. He would be able to see Carl clear as day. If there were others then Carl might be in their sights already. He stepped back, went through the kitchen door, dropped to the floor. His head spun a little with the movement, but not too badly. His heart was steady.

The figure would be merely covering the gate, he thought. There would be more than one. So he would have to deal with it, get away from here altogether. It would be people sent by Zaikov – that was his best guess – either for him or Viktor or both of them. He had been careless, leaving the gates open, all the security systems off, as he had found them on his return.

He crawled across the floor quickly, trying to listen at the same time. The gun he had was in the top box of the bike, which he had left outside the house, so that was out of the question. But in the past Viktor had kept guns in the cellar – shotguns he used for hunting trips. He went to the cellar door on his knees, the damaged one very sore, opened it, stood and went quickly down.

Concentrating on noises from the level above, he switched the lights on and found the bolted metal gun case. It hadn't moved since he had last looked at it. It was secured with a chain, no sign of a key, so he took a discarded section of piping and used it like a crowbar. The chain held but not the hoop it was fed through. It came away with a bang, the pipe clattering across the floor. He paused for any sign of a reaction upstairs, then opened the doors to a selection of shotguns and ammunition.

He picked an expensive Purdey double-barrelled model and stuffed a box of cartridges into his pocket, feeding two into the barrels and snapping them shut.

There was a door and steps that led directly to the rear gardens from the cellar. He opened the door quietly, crept up, then slid quietly into the chill night and crouched low, letting his eyes adjust, scanning for movement. There was plenty of light coming from the house to assist. He would move carefully to the front, he thought, clear the area there so he could get on the bike, then get out.

The ground from the corner of the house to the front drive was clear of foliage, so before he got anywhere near it he cut into a section of garden where there were trees and bushes, a little further off from the house. Then he went low and picked a route through the cover, sometimes on his belly, pine needles pricking into his hands. He could smell the pine resin, feel the cold air on the back of his head.

Up until now he had been thinking he would get a visual on the one at the front and shoot, from as far away as would guarantee accuracy, then get to the bike. But now he thought it might be better to get a closer look at the man, take him down without firing the gun if possible. He could then try to identify who he worked for, find out for sure if it was Zaikov.

So he went a bit deeper into the ornamental trees and came back towards the drive from a position a little behind where he guessed the man would be standing. But when he parted the grasses obscuring his view he saw nothing. He dragged himself forwards and saw the guy had moved closer to the house.

He stood carefully, brought the Purdey up to his shoulder, holding it ready, pointed at the man's back. Then he stepped onto the drive, paying attention to any movement in his peripheral vision, and slowly moved forwards.

The man was facing towards the house, right in the light

from one of the lamp-posts now. Then he went down onto his haunches and something about the movement made Carl think, immediately, that it wasn't a man at all. He kept going forwards, then decided. It was a woman. That made him pause.

He was behind her. She had short hair and was squatting on the ground, one knee down, the shoulders shaking. Like she was laughing. Or crying. Or maybe just shivering badly with the cold. He could see no weapon at all. He waited until he was only five metres behind her, the gun still aimed directly at her head, then spoke quietly: 'Get up. Turn slowly.'

She sprang up so quickly he had to move the gun to keep it aimed. He kept his eyes on her hands, looking for weapons, but there were none. As she spun to face him the light from the nearest floodlight, off to the left, came directly across her face.

His jaw dropped. He moved the gun off to the side and heard himself cry out. 'Liz,' he said. 'Christ. Liz.'

She was looking at him with something like horror. 'Alex,' she said, almost shouting it. 'Where's your fucking brother? What have you done with my daughter?'

44

In the back of the Range Rover Rebecca stared through smarting, bloodshot eyes at the narrow band of road visible in the powerful headlights. She was so tired her eyes kept rolling up into her head. Then she would be gone for a few minutes before another jolt in the motion woke her, head lolling, neck sore, and she was back in the car, the same, featureless, narrow road lit by the beams, the same wall of jagged shadow towering either side.

They were passing between dense ranks of briefly illuminated pine trees, so high it sometimes felt they were driving through an endless tunnel. The road surface was buried beneath compacted snow and ice which made a weird rumbling noise as the chained wheels went over it. If she looked out of the window by her seat she could see nothing but vague, looming shadows sliding by; only very occasionally was there a gap allowing a glimpse of brilliant white stars in a clear sky.

They had stopped twice for her to go to the toilet and she had tramped through knee-deep snow and squatted shivering in the intense cold, frightened she would freeze to death before she could get back to the safety of the vehicle.

There were two men she didn't know in the front – men who worked for Viktor, one of them his driver. They spoke only Russian, and not very often. Viktor mostly acted as if they weren't there, and to help him there was a glass screen between the front and back of the car which he could close, like in a taxi in London. When it was shut, even if they were speaking to each other, you couldn't hear them in the back.

Viktor sat in the back with her. They had travelled in a small, four-seater helicopter first, then another helicopter that had been larger, with two people who looked like soldiers flying it – at least, they had on some kind of uniform and helmets. After that, in darkness, in some freezing place Viktor had told her the name of, they had got into this car. How long ago was that? She had no idea. The entire journey had been the same whenever she opened her eyes. She hadn't been able to sleep for the first part of it – up to the second toilet stop – but after that it had been hard to stay awake.

Viktor had said hardly anything to her throughout the helicopter trips – just a few words every now and then to convince her everything was OK. Then for the first hour in the car he had been working on a laptop on a shelf that came out of the partition in front, typing on the keyboard, speaking into an earpiece with a mic in some language she didn't understand.

She had asked him if he had spoken to her mother, or Carl, many times, and always he had replied politely, gently, with a smile. But he hadn't spoken to them. They were moving from Finland, he had said, because they were going to where her mum was. The people that had got her mother out of Spain had brought her to Russia, because they were connected to Viktor, and because that had been easiest. It was just a 'slight change of plan'.

After the last toilet stop he had looked tired. He had put the laptop away and started talking to her, just at the point she most needed to sleep. 'Did you ever love anyone?' he had asked her. She told him she loved her mother, frowning, but too tired to wonder why he was asking that. Then he started to tell her about someone he had loved and whom he would have given his life for but she had betrayed him in the worst possible way, and now he couldn't do anything properly, he said, it was like she had broken something in him, something that had made him able to appreciate the world and other people. 'Now I hate everything,' he said. 'The truth is I hate everyone. All these people around me ...' He waved his hands as if there were hundreds of people standing around him. 'I couldn't care less whether they live or die.' Then he laughed, as if she wasn't there. 'I need to rewind the clock. Go back. Undo what she did to me. You understand?'

She didn't. 'You don't mean that,' she said. 'About hating everyone. You can't mean that. What about your brother?'

He had looked quickly at her then, the laughter all vanished from his face, his mouth so miserable and hard that she had started to get frightened. She must have reacted in some way that gave that away because he took a breath and smiled again. 'Nah. You're right,' he said. He reached a hand across and patted the back of her hand on the seat between them. 'How could you hate your own family, your own flesh and blood?' Then he stared at her for a very long time, so hard she had to look away.

'We should all sleep,' he said. But she couldn't close her eyes then, and kept her head facing the other way, so she was looking out of the window, away from him.

'I envy you,' she heard him mutter. 'You have been with your mother all your life.'

She didn't ask him what he meant because she didn't like the way he was talking, and just wanted him to stop, but she guessed that he meant that his own mother had died.

'Some people are one of a kind,' he went on, a bit louder.

Was he talking to himself? She closed her eyes, trying to pretend she was asleep, hoping he would stop.

'They light you up,' he continued. 'So that you really live, really see things. Nothing else means anything. The money is all worthless. But then if the light goes out, what do you do?'

She kept her eyes closed but he said her name, three times, to get her to look at him, and when she did, finally, he just shrugged. 'I'm sorry,' he said. 'This is down to them. *Their* fault.'

She had no idea what he was talking about. 'When will we be there?' she asked.

He smirked. 'In fifteen minutes. Then no more travelling for you. I promise.'

'And my mum will be there already?'

'I doubt it. But you can call her. Tell her where you are. I think she will want to know. And once she knows, I'm sure she'll get there as quick as she can.'

'You said she would be there already.'

'I made a mistake. But she will come. You can call her, and she will come to you.'

'When?'

He picked a mobile up from the seat beside him. 'When we get a signal. There's a mast nearer the house. You can do it when I get a signal. I need you to do it.'

45

'Rebecca is your daughter.' He said it again, head still reeling with confusion. 'She's *your* daughter ...'

'And you're this guy Carl Bowman?' She looked like she couldn't believe it. She was calling him 'Alex', which was what she had always called him, the Anglicised version of the name on his birth certificate, which was Aleksi, the name his mother had given him. No one had called him either Alex or Aleksi for many years.

He had told her he was Carl Bowman, told her several other things to calm her. This was when they'd still been outside, because she had been flailing at him, trying to hit his face as he staggered backwards, too astonished and dismayed to defend himself. Because he couldn't take it in – Liz Edwards right there in front of him, telling him her daughter was the child he had been trying to help, the child he had been paid to kill.

Eventually, he'd had to grab her arms, hold her and almost shout it at her, telling her that he had tried to protect Rebecca, had tried to save her. He told her that over and over again until she got it. Then she collapsed onto the ground in tears. When he could catch his breath he told her more things, talking quickly, keeping his eyes on the gateposts and the road beyond, watching for headlights or movement. He told her almost everything that had happened, the rapid version, starting with how someone had hired him to kill a ten-year-old. He could see her struggling with disgust as she half knelt, half sat on the gravel outside the front entrance, head in her hands. Some of the details flew straight past her but enough connected to ensure she came inside when he asked.

He needed to get her quiet enough so he could ask her questions. He had another piece of the jigsaw now, but he needed more. Viktor had sold him to Zaikov, tried to get him killed, then he had fled with Rebecca. So there *was* a connection. There had to be. Liz could explain, then they could work out what to do.

He got her into the room nearest the entrance hall and he switched all the lights off so he could see outside, just in case. They were almost in darkness – the lights were still on in the hall but he'd closed the door so there was only a crack of light coming through. He stood at the window, facing away from her, eyes on the floodlit spaces outside. He thought it would be better to go up to the little room beneath the tower that was full of security equipment – from there he could monitor the entire perimeter using the CCTV cameras. There were alarm systems that he could reactivate. It would be better if he had the MP5 from the bike top box too. A shotgun wasn't the right weapon for this, if people came. But he didn't dare suggest any of that to her. And anyway, he was beginning to think that that wasn't going to happen. No one was going to come here looking for him, or Viktor, or Rebecca. Because something else was going on.

She was on one of the couches, in the darkness, hunched forward, asking him question after question. He answered quickly, repeating answers until she was satisfied, waiting for his turn. And all the time his head was worrying at it, trying to properly grasp the possibilities. He turned now and said, 'She's with Viktor. I'm sure of it.'

'So where is he?'

'I don't know where he is or what he's doing. I don't know

why he has done this. He told me Zaikov wanted your family dead, and I believed him. He had proof – bank transfer documents, things like that – I looked at them. But they must have been forged, because Zaikov had never heard of you, or Rebecca. So there must be something else, some other reason to have sent me to Zaikov's boat. And not just money. I don't think that could be it. Not now. He would not have sent me there unless he was desperate, unless I was the only price he could pay. But for what? I'm thinking now I was the price he had to pay to keep Rebecca safe, to protect *her* from Zaikov. Which means there has to be something that would make Rebecca that important to Viktor, something he never told me about. I think there's only one thing that can be.' He turned to face her. 'Is she his child, Liz? Is that what it is? Is Rebecca Viktor's child?'

She started to laugh bitterly, shaking her head. He went over to the couch and sat beside her. 'She is the right age,' he said. 'You were in a relationship with him. Is Viktor her father?'

She turned suddenly, straightening up. 'So who sent you to kill her? Who did that? Who killed my husband? Who tried to kill me? Who?' She was shouting it at him. 'You're being stupid, Alex, fucking stupid. Her own father wanted her dead? That's what you want to believe?'

'So he's not her father?'

'No. He is not her fucking father. And Zaikov has never heard of us – you just said that yourself. So where's the reason to send you to Zaikov?'

She was right – it didn't work. He knew it didn't work. He shook his head. Even if he accepted that his own brother had sold him to seal a deal, there were still things he couldn't understand. Why wasn't Viktor here, why had he fled? And why had he taken Rebecca if the contract on her was a complete coincidence, nothing to do with the deal with Zaikov at all?

He sat forward and put his face in his hands. 'He gave me to

Zaikov,' he said heavily. 'He sent me there knowing they would kill me; he told them I had killed his son to make that happen.' He took a breath. 'I don't understand why.' The fact of it was a physical pain in his skull. 'But if that's what happened then why does he have Rebecca with him now? Why is he still protecting her?'

She stood up suddenly and walked over to the window. He saw her lean against the pane and start to shake. He went after her, put a hand out and carefully touched her shoulder. She started to cry out loud, really sobbing. He didn't know what he was permitted to do. If he put an arm round her he thought she might start hitting him again. The lights on the driveway lit her up now. He could see her head, the beautiful, thick, red hair, see her face, twisted into a baby grimace of anguish. He opened his mouth to tell her they would find Rebecca, that she had his word on that, but she spoke first, stuttering the words through strangled sobs: 'He is not protecting her,' she said. 'He is going to kill her, Alex. He wants to kill her and kill me. *He* hired you to kill her. Don't you see it? *He* paid you, *he* sent you to Spain.'

He shook his head, frowning hard, keeping his hand there, uselessly, on her shoulder. 'Why would he do that?'

She took a massive breath. 'Because *you're* her father, Alex. Because you're her father and he has found out.'

46

Even without this, Rebecca was so tired the world seemed unreal. She dozed, woke up, was unsure where she was, what was happening... but then this; a palace, suddenly there in the thick black night, the trees falling away from the road to reveal it, the lights behind hundreds of windows painting the sky above, like something out of a Disney fairy tale. She squinted at it, too cold to want to look for long, more confused than impressed. She was just outside the car, with Viktor beside her. They were both shivering. 'The Ice House,' he said. 'That's what it's called. Your mother knows it well. She's been here before.' She looked up at him with heavy eyes and, weirdly, thought he might be crying, but she couldn't be sure and hardly cared any more. 'I'm really cold,' she said. 'I need to get back into the car. I need to sleep.'

'You can sleep all you want soon. First, we call her.'

'Can I call her from the car?'

'No. Call her from here. Tell her how cold it is. She'll hear you shivering and come quicker.' He winked at her.

'I don't want to do that ...'

'I was joking.' He handed her a phone. 'The signal is weak. That's why we're out here. Quick!' He pointed to the phone. 'It's ringing already. Tell her where we are.'

When it started to ring, Julia was watching Carl for a reaction. He was standing there staring at her, his face stricken with shock. She searched in her pockets and found the phone

– Molina's phone. The number was 'unknown'. 'This is him,' she said tensely. 'He's calling.' But Carl didn't move. 'This is your brother,' she said again, louder. This was the phone Viktor was using, the phone on which she had recognised his voice. She pressed answer and put the phone to her ear, looked away from Carl to concentrate, then heard a child's voice speaking to her. Her legs almost gave way.

'Mum? Is that you, Mum?'

'Rebecca …' The word came out in a hoarse rasp, her breath pushed past an unbearable tightness in her chest. *She was alive.* Out of the corner of her eye she saw Carl move closer to her. 'Rebecca. It's you. Thank God it's you.' She started to cry immediately, put her hand up to her mouth. She felt a relief so strong she had to sit down in case she fell.

But reality returned quickly. There was no cause for relief. She had to think, calculate, and with desperate speed. She had to guess what might be happening, what she had to say.

'Mum. Yes, it's me. Are you OK, Mum?' She could hear Rebecca breathing sharply, big breaths.

'Rebecca, I've missed you so much …'

'Me too, Mum.' There was a pause. She could hear Rebecca sniffling. Was she crying? 'But you're coming here now, right?' Rebecca asked. 'I need you to come here, Mum …'

Julia swallowed, screwed her eyes shut, pressed the fear away. Everything was urgent. *He would take the phone away from Rebecca in moments.* 'You're with Viktor?' she asked rapidly. 'Where are you? Tell me *where* you are …'

'Yes. I'm with Viktor. We're at a place called The Ice House. I don't know where it is. He says you know though …'

The Ice House. 'Where is he?' she asked quickly. 'Where's Viktor *right now*?'

Carl moved beside her and started to whisper something, but she put a hand out, telling him to keep his distance. 'Where is

Viktor?' she asked again. The tears were running down her face but she tried to keep her voice steady. 'Can he hear you?'

'No. He's over by the car. I'm freezing. It's freezing here. Are you coming, Mum? I miss you really badly. I don't know what's been happening...'

'I'm coming. I'm coming right now. But it will take me a few hours. Now listen carefully. Listen to this – are you listening?'

'Yes.'

'You can't let on that I'm saying this. You have to try to understand me. We might not have long before this call is over. So listen carefully. You are *not* to trust him. No matter what he says or does, you are not to trust him ...' She heard a gasp of breath, then another noise, like a sob. 'Are you still there, Rebecca? Are you there?'

'Yes, Mum, I'm here.'

'Be strong. Don't cry. Do as I tell you. Do not let him hear. Can he hear?'

A pause. 'No.'

'Act as normally as you can, but the first opportunity you get then get away from him and hide. You understand? Do not trust him. Do not trust anybody. Get away and hide and I will find you. I'll be there in five hours. You have to wait—'

'But, Mum—'

'You have to hold out that long ... Do you understand?'

'He's coming over.' She spoke in an urgent whisper.

'I love you,' Julia said quickly. Then heard a scratching noise, like wind across the microphone, followed by voices she couldn't make out. 'Hello?' she said, helplessly. 'Rebecca? Are you there still?' She felt the lump in her throat, the fierce, terrible longing.

'Hello, Liz.' A different voice. 'Is that you, Liz?'

'Is my daughter there?' Her voice started to rise hysterically. 'What are you doing to my daughter? I want to speak to my daughter ...'

'She's fine. She's cold. That's all. She's gone back to the car.' He sounded far away but not like he was laughing at her. More like he was talking to an old friend, like everything was normal. It was obscene. 'You have to come here,' he said, quite calmly.

'Don't hurt her, Viktor,' she pleaded, lowering her voice with difficulty, her jaw trembling. 'Please don't hurt her ...'

'Don't be stupid, Liz. I'm not that kind of man. She's only a child. She's innocent.'

But he had already tried to kill her. He had tried to get her own father to shoot her. He was a fucking psychopath. 'I'm begging you,' she said. 'Please don't hurt her. She has nothing to do with anything. She is—'

'Can you get here? Or I can send someone for you ... We need to talk, Liz. That's all I want – just to talk to you again. This is where it all started. Right here. I need to know why. I thought you loved me. But you were with him, with my brother ...'

'We can talk about all that. But don't hurt her. Please don't hurt her. I will get there. Promise me you won't hurt her.'

'Of course.'

'I will drive there. I'll come right now.'

'Of course you'll come. I'll text you the coordinates. Ring me when you're near. You understand?'

'I understand. Please don't hurt her, Viktor.'

'Come alone. It would be a bad error to call the police.'

'I won't tell anyone. You have my word.' Her voice was choking. She fought the tears back, struggling to sound intelligible, to get him to believe her.

'There's nothing here,' he said. 'Just us. Waiting for you. She told you where we are?'

'The Ice House.' She said the words in Russian, as she remembered them.

'No more discussion, then,' he said. 'Just come.'

'This isn't her fault, Viktor. Please don't harm her. I will—'
But the line was dead already.

278

47

Julia was halfway up the drive on her way to the gates before he could get her to stop. He caught hold of her arm and pulled her round. A hand came up to slap his face and she screamed something at him. Something about his family. He took the blow.

'Tell me what he said,' he demanded. 'Tell me.'

She hit him again and started to walk away, still facing him. 'Keep away from me,' she yelled.

He stepped forward and grabbed her arm again. 'You've just told me she's my daughter,' he shouted. 'I can't keep away from you.'

She sank to the ground, sobbing, then started to tell him in a rush, sometimes so incoherently he couldn't make out the details. Rebecca was alive. Viktor was in Russia, with Rebecca, he had told her to come there, to The Ice House.

'Did he say anything about me?' he asked, crouching beside her. 'Did he ask if I was with you?'

She shook her head.

'He doesn't know I'm with you, then.'

'You're *not* with me. I left to get away from you, from you and him and all of it. I don't want you near my daughter.'

He stood up, emotions churning. He had all the pieces now. He knew it all, or enough to fill the gaps. What she had said had to be true: *Viktor had contracted him.* He had got behind the cartel, or faked that it was the cartel. *He* had paid the money, not Zaikov. Zaikov had nothing to do with it. There might still be a deal between Zaikov and Viktor, there might be money between them, an extra incentive, but that wasn't what was going on. What was going on was *personal*. Because Viktor *knew*. He knew what had happened ten years ago – he knew about Carl and Liz. Somehow he had found out where Liz was and that she had a child. *He had tried to get Carl to kill his own daughter.* Deliberately. It was devastating, like a hammer blow to his head. It felt like the sudden, violent death of someone close – he couldn't begin to assimilate it. He was just completely and utterly stunned.

But he couldn't let it cripple him. Because Rebecca was his daughter. 'I saw it in her eyes,' he said, ignoring Julia's words. 'I saw it the first time I saw her eyes.' Something had passed between them on the hillside, with his finger on the trigger. That was why he had done it all, why he had tried to save her. 'That's why she trusted me,' he said. She *had* trusted him. At some level, he thought, in her heart, she had known too. He wanted to believe that. He bent down and took Liz's hand. 'Stand up, Liz. Stop crying.'

He got her to her feet, holding both her hands, speaking carefully. He told her they would go together to get Rebecca. He was looking at her face, standing so close that even in this poor light he could see the freckles again, see the colour of her eyes, see that it was, somehow, the same Liz as ten years ago – older, distraught, yes, but beyond those details still *her* nonetheless, still recognisably everything she had been to him. 'Do you have a Russian visa?' he asked.

'Maybe.' She wiped a hand across her eyes and started searching through the pockets of the jacket she had on. Her whole body was shaking. It was shock, brought on by the adrenalin. She pulled out a handful of papers and started looking clumsily through them, wiping her eyes again, breathing hard, trying to see, to organise the documents.

When he took them off her she didn't object. There was a passport, not in her name, not with her picture either, credit cards in the name on the passport, various other bits of paper. He flicked through the passport. There were six or seven valid visas in it, including a Russian business visa. 'There's a car in the garage,' he said. 'We'll take that.'

'I have a car.'

'We'll take Viktor's,' he said. 'I read there was already snow up there, and it's his winter car. It has winter tyres and four wheel drive.'

He started to walk towards the garage block, and heard her hurrying after him. 'How long will it take?' she asked. 'How long till we get there?'

The last time he had been to the place was ten years ago, but he doubted much had changed. The roads were poor once you got to the eastern part of Finland, worse over the border. 'We can get to the border in four hours,' he said. 'After that it depends…'

'I told her I would be there in five hours.'

'It will be more like seven.' He strode back through the house, through the kitchen and down the passageway that led to the garage. He pulled the door open and switched on the lights. She was still with him. 'Don't worry. We will get there. We will get her.' He could hear the confidence in his voice. He wasn't faking it. He was absolutely certain he would get to Rebecca and she would be alive. There was no other way he could think about it. *She was his daughter.* He felt his heart leaping with a kind of absurd exultation, despite everything. But Liz started to cry again and he stopped in front of her, not knowing what to say to help.

'I'm so frightened,' she said. 'I'm scared he will kill her before we get there…'

'He couldn't. He couldn't do that.' He said it without thinking and saw the look she gave him. 'I know him,' he said. 'He could hire someone to do it, but he couldn't do it himself. Not to a little girl. I saw him with her. He couldn't do it.'

Her face twisted into a grimace. 'Don't be fucking stupid,' she said. 'He could easily do it. He's fucking insane. He's a psychopath. The only reason he hasn't already done it is because he can use her to get me too.'

He turned away from her. She was right, but he didn't want her to see that he knew that. He didn't have a clue what Viktor was capable of, not any more. There were a massive questions in his head, each one a malignancy threatening to rewrite the entire history of his last ten years. He would need to get to them, work them out, try to get some sense back. But right now, he just needed to get them out of there, get started.

He found car keys hanging on a rack. There were three cars in the garage but the BMW X5 was Viktor's winter car, so he took the keys for that. There were covers on it. He started pulling them off, while she stood a little away from him, her face in her hands.

48

Rebecca stood alone in the room, staring at the door. She felt dizzy, like she might fall over. She leaned against the wall and tried to think. Viktor had brought her up here himself, left her here, walked off. She had heard his footsteps in the passageway beyond. She could come or go as she wished, he had said. He had promised the door would never be locked.

When she had come off the phone she had been very confused, not sure why her mum had said the things she had, or why she had sounded so frightened. But she had already been too tired to speak properly by then. She hoped she hadn't upset her. Freezing, she had got back in the car when Viktor had taken the phone, so hadn't heard anything he said after that.

When he had returned she had looked him in the face and told him her mum had sounded worried. It had felt scary, keeping what her mum had said from him. He hadn't done anything bad to her since she had met him. Not really. He had talked a little weirdly in the car, kept her awake, but that was it. Yet she was definitely frightened he might guess what her mum had said.

She thought he might start asking about it. But he didn't. He wasn't even watching her closely. She had concentrated carefully on his eyes when she spoke to him, because her mum had taught her you could tell if a person was lying by watching their eyes. But he had only looked down at her with a slight smile and said, 'Your mum's probably missing you. That's all. She'll be here tomorrow. Not long to wait.'

There was nothing in his eyes that would scare her. He was acting the same as before, the same as he always had. As they walked back to the house he even held her hand, to guide her across the ice on the driveway. So what was the problem? Why had her mum said those things?

Her problem right now was that she could barely keep her eyes open. Every now and then she felt them close and then woke suddenly – immediately, it seemed – with a start, frightened again, wondering where she was. She tried hard to think clearly, to remember her mum's instructions. What had she told her to do? *Hide from Viktor*? But where? And *why*?

Viktor had said one of them would bring her up a hot chocolate in a few minutes, but she didn't know whether she could wait for that. She went over to the huge bed and sat on it.

The room – like the whole house – resembled something out of a film, something for a princess. She had said that to Viktor, on the way in, and he had laughed. 'You *are* a princess,' he had said. The ceiling was very high, with patterns painted across it that she couldn't quite decipher. There was a huge double bed, with a massive quilt, as if the room might get cold. But the house was very warm – radiators along the walls, three of them, and though she couldn't now be bothered to get up and feel them, she was sure they would be hot. There was a window, but there were heavy curtains in front of it, with some kind of dark, floral pattern embroidered into the fabric. On the walls many pictures, hunting scenes, one that looked like a prince or king – someone on a horse with a crown – visiting this place, or a place that looked very similar. Crowds of people bowing in front of him.

In the ceiling there was a small chandelier, but with candles that would need to be lit, real candles. She had never seen that before. They weren't lit now – the light instead came from two tall standard lamps with very ornate stands. Black metal with bronze vines growing up to cup the hidden light bulbs. The carpet on the floor was like a tapestry – another hunting scene, she thought. There was a big flat-screen mounted on the wall in front of the bed – modern and out of place – but she couldn't see a remote.

Not that she wanted to switch it on. All she wanted to do was sleep. She sank back into the soft quilt, then tried to shift herself up the bed a little, to reach the massive, plump pillows. She should take her clothes off, she thought, or she would be too warm. But she didn't have the strength. When had she started to feel like this?

She tried to keep her eyes open by focusing on one of the pictures on the wall, but couldn't even see it clearly now. Moments before it had been OK. She didn't feel uncomfortable, far from it. Or rather, only if she tried to fight it, to keep her eyes open, then things would start to spin a bit and she felt slightly sick.

It had started after Viktor had given her the drink of water, just as they got in here. Or had it? Hadn't she been like this since they had been in the helicopter? She needed sleep, that was all.

But her mum hadn't wanted her to sleep. What was it her mum had wanted her to do? It was important she remember.

It had got worse after the water, she decided. Definitely. She closed her eyes. She couldn't beat it, couldn't think any more. Her head was heavy, her eyes rolling up. She tried to turn onto her side, but couldn't even do that.

49

It was nearly six in the morning and pitch black when Julia woke up. The car was still, silent, freezing. Beside her, in the driving seat, Alex had his head against the window, eyes closed. She had a moment of confusion before she could place herself, then another to work out that the reason it was so dark was that the windscreen was covered in snow. She started to shiver.

'Alex,' she said. He woke at once, turned his head towards her, squinted. 'Where are we?' she asked.

'I had to rest,' he said. 'I was driving with my eyes closed.' He reached forward and switched the engine on, looked at the time on the dash. 'So I slept. For twenty minutes. Not long enough.'

'Where are we?'

He put the heating on full, then turned the windscreen wipers on. They swept away a light covering of snow, revealing a long, unlit road through trees, curving towards glittering lights in the distance. The air was thick with falling snow. 'That's the Niirala crossing up ahead,' he said. 'The border with Russia.'

'You said you would wake me.'

'We both needed to sleep. If we drive with our eyes closed, we'll end up in a ditch.'

She felt annoyed with him. She pushed herself up in the seat. 'Let's go,' she said. She wanted to add, *don't do it again*, but stopped herself. She had a headache, and nausea in the top of her gut. He was right that she needed sleep, and she didn't want to snap at him.

She found the water bottle as he eased the car back onto the road. The road – presumably it was gritted and ploughed – was still clear of snow. She took a drink, then offered it to him. He shook his head. 'What do we do at the border?' she asked.

'Drive through.'

'What about the guns?' Before they had left Gumbacka he had taken a gun from the motorbike outside the house. It was in a long holdall now, stuffed under her seat, along with the shotgun he had been holding when he had appeared behind her. She hadn't said anything about them, but she would get to it. When they got there, she didn't want guns near her daughter.

'Don't worry about them,' he said. 'They won't search.'

'How do you know?'

'Because I'll pay them. That's the way it works.'

As they went forward she looked behind and saw they had been stopped in a lay-by with a small petrol station and store. There were other cars there, and trucks, a movement of head-lights through the swirls of snow.

He took the car back onto the main road, a surfaced two-lane highway that led downhill towards the lights. She might have felt nervous about it but the acid gnawing in her stomach had been a constant thing for days now. Her default state was some-thing she wouldn't have recognised a few days ago – the intense fears for Rebecca constantly dominating everything. If she had suffered anything like this before, it was ten years ago, at the place they were driving to now, where Viktor had said all this had started. He was right about that – though not in the way he must have meant – because as far as she could calculate it, it had to have been there that Rebecca was conceived. She hadn't said that to Alex. She had said hardly anything significant about the past.

Since leaving Helsinki she had done what he had told her to do, which was either sleep or drive, but mostly sleep. She had driven for about an hour in total. He had done the rest. She had not wanted to sleep but her body had overridden her. And meanwhile, he had kept them going, bringing them closer and closer to where Rebecca was. She reminded herself that, however else she was with him, she didn't need to be sharp with him, or take it out on him. He was doing exactly what he'd said he would do, he was helping her.

She hoped her intuitions about him were sound. When she had first seen him she had gasped with shock but, in the gap before reason could get in, there had been relief also. And something else, a tiny residue of the past, affecting her judgement, because he was *Alex*, the man she had felt all those things for. She couldn't look at him without all that being there, compacted between them. He was her daughter's father. So when she had first realised she was looking at *him* again there had been a little bit of isolated hope, in the middle of all the crushing anxiety; the hope that he was someone who wouldn't hurt her, someone she could trust.

But it hadn't taken long for history and reason to switch that into a fear of him, and then an anger. Because he was in Viktor's house, so she assumed that he must have had *something* to do with taking Rebecca (which he had, if she was to believe even his own account of it all). Later, he had convinced her that he was safe, had brought her nearer to her original intuition. Not with the words – though she had asked him many, many questions, over and over again – but with the look in his eyes. The eyes she remembered all too well. The same eyes. She could not look into his eyes and believe that he would hurt her.

He looked different, much older, no longer a little boy. But when she met his gaze the thing that had lit up inside her whenever he had been near flickered again – weaker, but with that same tenuous reaching out to him. She had to acknowledge that, though that was as far as she could go with it. They had not spoken about it. They had spoken functionally, filling in the gaps – her life in Spain, his in London. But nothing about these feelings, nothing about why she had left him. The constant need to concentrate on the pressing immediate issue – recovering their daughter – blotted out any possibility of innocent catch-up. She could only bring herself to glance flinchingly sideways at the stark reality of this dreadful situation, and when she did the view was utterly dominated by the imminent possibility of incomprehensible horror, by the likelihood that this man's psychotic brother would kill their daughter before they got anywhere near her. That mental backdrop didn't leave much room for light chat. So the whole of it was just sitting there between them, an aching gap and an unanswered question.

And maybe that was the best way. She had left him for good reasons, and the gun he had taken from the bike, and his whole story of being hired to kill his own daughter ... almost everything he had told her, in fact, about the intervening ten years and the world he lived in confirmed that her decision all that time ago had been correct. His brother, his family, he himself – they were all criminals and killers. That was the truth. The man she had picked instead – Juan Martin – her poor dead husband who had died because of her connections to these thugs – *he* had been a good man, a harmless man, despite his distractions with other women. This emergency aside, regardless of any emotions he might provoke in her, did she want Alex anywhere near their daughter?

The car came to a wider, brightly illuminated area, with signs in Russian, Swedish and Finnish. There was a truck in front of them now but it filtered off into another lane and he kept going. Up ahead she could see the squat sheds and buildings of the border post. There were bulky, six-wheeled army vehicles to one side, Finnish flags everywhere. And barriers. Cars stopped at booths, small queues, even at this time of the morning.

'There are two checks,' he said quietly to her. 'The Finnish one will be quick, the Russians might ask more questions, but not too many more, just enough to keep face. You need to be calm and let me talk to them.' She saw he had placed his passport in the tray by the gearstick. There was a tightly coiled roll of crisp banknotes beside it. To try to thank him, or encourage him, or communicate something – she wasn't sure what – she reached a hand across and briefly touched his arm.

50

Rebecca woke suddenly, opening her eyes, but lying still. She was in the bed, in the exact position she could last recall, halfway to the pillows. There was a table by the bed with a glass of water. Her throat was dry. She needed a drink and she needed a pee. She sat up quickly, looked around the room. She was alone. The room was very warm.

She slid over the bed, put her feet on the floor and reached for the water, then remembered what she had thought before she fell asleep – that they had put something in her drink, a sleeping pill or something. If that was possible. She had seen it in movies, so maybe it was.

She took her hand away, stood up and walked to the big window. Her legs were a little shaky. Is that what they would feel like if someone drugged you? She could see light coming in through a crack in the heavy drapes. She parted them carefully, peeked through, squinted. It was daytime, she could see hills, trees, snow, everything covered with snow, but the sky was clear and blue, the sun in her eyes. She moved back. How long had she been asleep?

There was no clock in the room. There were two doors though. One, she thought, was the door they had brought her in through. She stepped over to it and placed her head against it, listening. There was a corridor outside – she could remember that, remember walking up it, hanging onto Viktor's arm because she was so dopy. She couldn't hear anything through the door now though. Everything was very silent.

She went over to the other door and opened it onto an en suite bathroom. The light came on automatically. It looked luxurious – white marble, gleaming chrome, a huge oval bathtub. She stepped in, left the door open, used the toilet, then went to the sinks and splashed cold water onto her face, drank some of the water direct from the tap. She felt better, her head clearer, a hunger pain gnawing at her gut. She started to remember everything that had happened.

Her eyes found a clock on the wall – 10.45: in the morning, she assumed, but again wasn't certain of that. She had lost track of time over the last few days. Her mother had said five hours until she could get there, but when had that been? In the middle of the night – longer than five hours ago. And she wasn't here. She took a breath, feeling the confusion again.

Her mother had told her not to trust Viktor, to hide, but all she'd done was sleep. So she would do it now – look around, find a place to hide, do what her mother had told her to do. Her mum would get here. She always did what she said she would, always kept her promises.

She went back over to the main door and listened again. She put her hand on the handle and carefully eased it down, then pulled gently. The door didn't move – it rattled, but wouldn't open. She yanked on it as hard as she could but someone had locked it. They'd locked her in, trapped her.

51

Carl could feel the tension building – inside his head and inside the car. Nearly ten o'clock. They were almost there, he thought. He slowed the car, watching carefully for roads he recognised. They had been off the satnav for a long time now, in a vast blank space on the map. He was navigating from memory.

He had guessed it would take seven hours to get to Viktor, but it had taken nearer nine. The going from the border had been steady at first but then the snow had started falling again. Up until two hours ago they had been crawling along a road that was barely visible, deep in drifts, expecting to get stuck at any minute. Then the weather had suddenly cleared, the blizzard vanishing and the sky appearing from the night, clean and blue. At the same time the temperature started dropping, freezing the compacted surface of the snow into ice, making driving on the chains a bit easier. He had put the chains on just after the border crossing, with Liz pacing around shivering beside him, worrying about how long it took.

She had started talking after the border crossing, but only desultory sentences about Rebecca, half-expressed thoughts that were meant to try to create an image of her as somehow safe, despite everything. She talked about how sensible Rebecca was, how careful, how she had warned her about many things. She said again and again that she had told her to get away from Viktor, to hide, but that she wasn't sure now if it was the right thing to have said. He could hurt her, she kept saying, *he could hurt her.* She sat there for a long while repeating the words, the tears running down her face.

He couldn't help much with any of it. Her call to Viktor had cut off any last illusions about his brother's sanity. Viktor hadn't even asked about him. And clearly Viktor had known Liz would call, and anyway, it was his phone. Liz had told him she had taken it from a policeman in Spain who had tried to kill her.

Viktor was behind this, behind all of it. Presumably because Carl had betrayed him ten years before, slept with the woman he loved, conceived a child with her. Somehow he had found that out, plotted this revenge – thought this an *appropriate* response – not merely to kill his brother, but to get his brother to kill his own daughter first. If he was capable of that then Carl had no idea where his limits were. And if he still couldn't imagine him killing Rebecca *personally*, he knew Viktor wouldn't find it hard to locate people who would. And every extra hour it took to get to him thrust them deeper into a terrifying void of ignorance – what was happening to Rebecca *right then*, as they were driving, trying to get to her? What was she going through?

There was no use to these thoughts, so he tried to turn his mind from them. He could drive better and quicker if all his concentration was on the road. But Liz was doing less driving and a lot of the time when he looked over to her, or reached his hand over to hold hers, to console her, all he could see in her eyes was a kind of stunned horror, as if she couldn't handle any of it. He wanted to talk to her, bring up what had happened to them ten years ago, ask why she had run away and left him. But there was no chance of that. And anyway, it was obvious why she had left him. He was a man who could kill other men for money. His family were the same. That his brother was truly psychotic might not even seem something distinguishing to her. She might justifiably think they were all like that, himself

294

included. She would have been insane to have stayed with him.

'When did he find out?' he had asked her, at one point. 'When do you think he first found out about us?' But she didn't have an answer to that. He had an answer, but didn't want to believe it. Because if Viktor had arranged the funds for the hit on Rebecca, then it was possible that he had arranged all the other five hits over the last ten years too, it was possible that he *was* the cartel, not Zaikov, not anyone else. Carl might have spent the last ten years unknowingly eliminating his brother's business rivals while his brother quietly searched the world for Liz, biding his time, plotting what he would do when he found her. And that in turn would only make sense if Viktor had known almost from the very start about Liz and him. It was possible. The idea brought a very bitter taste to his mouth. The bitterness of guilt. Because he, Carl, had caused all this – he had started the betrayal, broken the rules.

He stopped the car. 'We're here,' he said. 'I think we should walk it from here, so he doesn't see the car.'

'Where is it?' she asked. She looked terrified. She stared out through the windscreen. 'Where is the house?'

'It's about five hundred metres further on, past where the road bends and goes over the crest of the ridge. We're on the hill to the west of the house, on the other side of it. Maybe you remember?' He pointed. 'We'll be able to see it from there, up ahead, where the road starts to go down.' He twisted in the seat and looked at her. 'You don't have to come, Liz. You can stay here. It will be safer.'

'I want to see the place,' she said, starting already to open her door.

They got out, pulling on the thick winter coats they had taken from Viktor's, the hats and gloves. Carl went to the rear of the car, popped the boot and bent inside. The MP5 was lying on a pile of blankets, already assembled.

Liz watched him with a numb fear. She had been intending to tell him to leave the gun, but she couldn't now. For the last hour all she had been able to think about was the thing she had seen Viktor do. She had known from then what he was capable of. On that day, ten years ago, she had got the hood and noose off Michael Rugojev and for a moment had been too shocked to do anything but stare at him, as he spluttered and gasped for breath. She had not been able to believe it wasn't Alex.

But then it had sunk in, and at the same time she realised the man she had stabbed – Uri Zaikov – was far from dead, and that she still had no idea where Alex was. So she had stood without thinking, leaving Michael there, and run to the doors through which the stabbed man had staggered.

Uri Zaikov had got only halfway across the next room, it seemed, stumbling through his own blood. He was there now, in the centre of the room, flat on the floor, making a kind of high-pitched keening noise. As she came through the doors she saw that Alex was with him, crouching over him, alive, unharmed. He was doing something with his jacket, talking quietly to the man. She knew now he had been trying to save him.

She was about to run over to him, to tell him what had happened, but then Viktor had come through doors at the far end, marching straight across the floor, his heels rapping on the hard, wooden surface. His eyes had crossed hers without a flicker of acknowledgement or recognition.

She hadn't seen the gun in his hand until he was over the stabbed man, pushing Alex away from him. Without a moment's hesitation he had then pointed the gun at the man's face and fired. It had been so sudden she hadn't even had time to anticipate it, to look away. So she had seen it all.

She had collapsed to the floor then. She felt like collapsing into the snow now. Alex had told her repeatedly during the last few hours that his brother wouldn't hurt Rebecca, but she had seen for herself what Viktor could do.

She followed Alex along the road anxiously, keeping close behind, sinking up to her knees in the snow. The clothing they had brought was meant to be winter clothing, but already she was freezing. The boots she was wearing were inadequate and already soaked through. She hoped that Rebecca was inside, not out, that she was warm, not shivering to death. She hoped that she hadn't heeded her advice to such an extent that she had run off into this weather without protection.

Alex turned to her and asked if she was OK. She nodded, peering past him into the trees, looking for the house but seeing nothing. There were pine trees everywhere, very tall with thick black bark, the branches laden and drooping with snow. They lined the road and stretched off into the distance, following a slight slope. Every now and then some snow would slide off a branch and fall with a thumping noise. She stamped her feet and watched her breath billowing out in clouds of condensation. It didn't seem like the place she remembered. Everything was horribly silent now, the snow dampening the sound. She looked at Alex. Was he the same man? She didn't recognise the gloominess in his eyes.

After a few paces he went into a crouch and turned back. 'We will come over this rise and see it, I think,' he said quietly. 'Go slowly. Stay low.'

He brought the gun up from his side, held it with two hands. She could see the land rising ahead. He left the road and started moving at an angle beneath the pines. She kept about three metres behind him, also crouching.

As they got closer to the rise he stopped and went down onto one knee in the snow, told her to wait. He crept forward, then crawled on his belly alongside a fallen trunk and pulled himself up to the edge. She waited for him to signal her, then followed and looked.

It was about half a kilometre away, the view crystal clear through the frozen air. It was at the bottom of a long slope of land, so that it was well below them – towers and minarets, windows everywhere. Hundreds of windows. The sunlight was falling on the panes so that parts of the structure looked like a complicated shard of ice, reflecting and glinting so brightly that she had to shield her eyes.

She could see the old stable block immediately below them – the building looked derelict, the roof fallen in, the inside filled with a snowdrift. Her eyes followed the path leading away from it down through the woods and found the garden wall outside the kitchen area, where ten years before she had seen the guard shot dead. The main building looked the same. She could see no one moving around, no signs of life, many chimneys but no smoke. There might be lights on behind the windows but the sunlight was too strong to see that.

He moved away from the edge, pulling her with him. They walked back to the road and he held her arm. 'I need to know who is down there,' he said. 'You go back to the car and wait. Give me an hour. I'll come down at the back, where the forest is close, try to find out how many people he has with him ...'

'You don't think he's alone?'

'Possibly. He was alone in Helsinki and I realise why now. I'm not sure he has anyone he could trust enough with what he's doing. But I need to know for sure. I'll be an hour, no more. Don't do anything. Just wait. OK?'

She nodded. 'What if you're longer than an hour?'

He considered that. 'I won't be,' he said.

52

Rebecca had to stop herself from banging on the door in a panic. She could scream and shout for them to let her out, but then they would know she was awake. Viktor had promised it wouldn't be locked, but it was.

Now she remembered very clearly her mother's voice on the phone. She had been crying, frightened. And she had told her to hide from him. The only reason she hadn't done that was because she had been unable to move. That wasn't normal. She had been very tired before, after sleepovers, but she had never collapsed.

She was scared now – just thinking about it made her tremble. What was going on? She thought that even the water she had been drinking in the car, before she got here, had tasted off. So had they drugged her? If she had a computer she could look it up on the Internet, find out if it was possible to put something in people's drinks without them knowing. She went to the glass of water by the bed and sniffed it. She couldn't smell anything, but the water didn't look clear. There was a slight sediment at the bottom of the glass.

She started searching the room for somewhere to hide. There were empty wardrobes and cupboards, and the space under the bed, but that was all too obvious. In the bathroom she examined the side of the bathtub. She had seen her dad fix a pipe under their bath once by taking a panel off the side. Then one of their cats had wanted to hide there. There would be a big enough space under this bath for her to squeeze in, but she couldn't see any way to get the sides off – there were no screws or loose edges. And even if she did – how would she get the panel back on?

She wondered where her dad was, and if he had been with her mum when she had spoken to her. Her mum had said nothing about him and she hadn't heard anything in the background.

She was getting nervous now about Viktor coming to check on her. She didn't want to see him again. The more she thought about him, the more sick she felt. He had been speaking very weirdly to her. And he had promised not to lock the door.

All the time she was in the bathroom she kept listening for noises from the door, through in the main room. Once she thought she could hear someone talking and ran through to the bed, jumping onto it to try to pretend she was asleep. But no one came.

Still, she had to do something quick. She parted the curtains and looked out of the big window, to see if anyone was out there. It was the same scene of snow and sunshine. The room was on the first floor, if you came in from the front, as she had, but the ground looked closer at this side, as if the land was higher here. The window had a big sill, more like a ledge – wide enough to sit on. She kneeled on it and took a more careful look.

The drop was straight down to the ground, a bit less than four metres. Not *that* high. Her mum once told her that when people did a parachute jump the last part of it was the same as jumping off a house. You just had to land properly, roll. She didn't know how to do that, but her mum had told her it was possible, if there was ever a fire or anything. *Better than burning to death.* That's what she had said. The ground below was deep in snow which might make the landing softer, or the drop further than it looked, but she couldn't tell how deep it was. What if it was really deep and there was something spiky underneath, like a railing? But that didn't seem likely.

After that where would she run to? There were trees and bushes down there, all bare of leaves, and maybe the outline of some paths. It was probably a garden in the summer. The land sloped away from it gradually, falling towards a line of trees where a really tall pine forest started. She couldn't see any fence there. She could run straight into the trees. That wouldn't take her long – it was sprint distance and she was one of the fastest in the entire Malaga area over that distance. Maybe there was a fence further back, though, deep inside, maybe even an electrified fence. What would she do then? She was less adept at climbing. In the gaps between the trees all she could see was darkness. Would it be colder or warmer there? It looked scary. But her mother had told her to hide.

She thought about that again, about what her mum had sounded like. She had never heard her like that before, so distraught – so it was serious. She didn't have an option to just wait here. She had a sudden image of the house in Spain, the fire there, the dead policeman, the blood running out of his head. That was the kind of thing that could happen to her. She could remember running from him, hearing him shouting at her, then the cracks as he fired at her. She had almost wet herself. She had been really terrified for a moment, more than she was now. Carl had told her they were trying to kill her. She had trusted Carl, but he had vanished.

She had to do something.

She reached up and pulled the window handle. It was an old window, not double-glazed, a big single frame with four panes of glass. At the other side of it was another window in a thick wooden frame, acting like a kind of double-glazing system. The handle was very stiff, so she had to lean on it with both hands. Then it moved. She was sure the thing was going to be locked, but as the handle came down it sprang back. She moved off the sill and swung it open, then unhooked the catches for the second window. This one was in two parts that creaked outwards. She thought she would just be able to squeeze through one of them. As it opened the air was like ice in her face. She started to shiver at once, then went back to the bed where she had taken off the oversize leather jacket and fleece they had given her. She put them on, then leaned through the opening and looked down.

She thought she would be able to crawl through backwards then dangle, so that her feet were only two metres from the snow. Two metres was a safe drop. There was a stone ledge about ten centimetres wide running round the outside of the house. She could get her feet onto that. She looked to the left – craning her head out into the freezing air – and saw that it went along the wall under another widow, not in her room, then joined a lower part of the building with a flat roof. Could she walk along it, hanging onto the window ledges, then get to the flat part?

She heard a noise from behind the door. She wasn't sure what it was. Someone walking out there? Maybe they were coming for her. Maybe when they saw she was awake they would really put her to sleep, force an injection into her, like they did in the hospital. She decided immediately. She was going to try it, she was going to go.

It took Carl fifteen minutes to skirt around the back of the stable block, keeping on the blind side of the hill. He went quickly, holding the MP5 with both hands, cocked, safety on, his thumb resting against the selector switch. He tried to keep his eyes moving, but thought he was going too fast to spot anyone crouching or stationary. The snow deeper into the woods was thinner, so he ended up making a lot of noise stepping through the sticks and mould. His breathing was loud too. But he had told Liz he would be an hour, so the clock was against him. He should have said two hours, then he could have moved more cautiously. But she wouldn't have accepted that.

He had thought about how to handle this all the way since the border, whenever they weren't talking. At first he had been inclined to rely on his instinct that Viktor wouldn't be able to hurt him, if it came to a direct confrontation. Viktor had already had plenty of opportunities to do something himself, had he been capable. Instead, he had hired people. He had felt the same intuition about Rebecca, until a few hours ago – that Viktor wouldn't be able to harm her. It was a particular kind of person who could look a little girl in the face and shoot her. That wasn't Viktor, he'd thought. But Viktor had broken all the rules, so Carl was far from sure about these assumptions now. Maybe Viktor was sick, seriously mentally ill. Could he be otherwise, to have dreamed up a scheme whereby his own brother was contracted to kill his daughter? To have paid so much to pull it off?

And then there was the question of who Viktor might have with him. That seemed the most important thing right now. Whatever he might think about dealing with Viktor, if he had with him a team of trained security guards then Carl was going to have to go back up to Liz and suggest alternatives. The police were out of the question, but she had some lever-age with their uncle – Mikhael Ivanovich, or 'Michael', as she called him – due to the fact that she had undoubtedly saved his life ten years ago. Michael had got her out of Spain, so it might be better to try to persuade her to get his help again. She had expressed some doubts about whether Michael wasn't in on all of this, whether he wasn't a part of the deal Viktor had spoken of, but Carl couldn't see that. Viktor and Michael had been on bad terms for over two years. And what Viktor had done wasn't something Michael would sanction. It was like twenty years ago, bandit country – eventually it was going to attract the kind of official attention people like Mikhael Ivanovich spent most of their time trying to avoid.

He was making a line to get down to where he remembered the perimeter fence might be, when he heard something off to his right, back in the direction he had come from. He stopped and crouched low, letting his breathing settle. The forest floor was almost bare of undergrowth here, so there was no chance of cover. The big padded coat he'd taken from Viktor's cloakroom, however, was predominantly off-white, with a big black stripe running diagonally. So when he was sure he couldn't see anyone near, he dropped down to his belly in the snow and listened. He had thought he was making too much noise to hear anything. Since starting he had seen movement twice, out of the corner of his eye, but both times it had been crows taking off for the treetops, and he had seen them before he heard anything.

He let his eyes focus in the general direction of the sound. What had it been? Someone talking, maybe even laughing. As his breath fell to normal the forest seemed very silent. He got back to his knees, pulled the binoculars from beneath the coat. They were a powerful set he had taken from the house in Gumbacka, not the cheap pair Liz had brought with her.

He scanned carefully, slowly, methodically. Within seconds he saw he was much further forward than he had thought. Through the lenses he could clearly see the perimeter fence, about one hundred and fifty metres to his right through the dense mass of tree trunks. As he watched he picked out movement on the other side of it, and at the same time a voice floated over to him.

Because of the folds of the land he could only see the head and shoulders. He got to his feet, braced the binoculars against a tree trunk and watched. It was a man, walking just the other side of the perimeter fence, perhaps two hundred metres distant, heading up the hill Carl had just descended on the blind side. He had his hand to his ear and was talking either into a mobile or a radio. Carl started to move at a forty-five degree angle from him, closing on the fence. He paused frequently to check he could still get a visual on the man.

Within a few minutes he was at the fence. It ran right through the forest at head height in a dead-straight line, overlapping layers of chain-link suspended on concrete posts. The top strand was electrified, but there was no razor wire and considering its general condition Carl had a feeling the electric circuit wouldn't be working. This fence had been there when he was last here, if he was remembering properly. He followed the line and saw many places where trees grew directly through it, or over it, branches crossing the top strand. He could see no CCTV fixtures.

Mikhael Ivanovich had given this place to Viktor, the story went, a couple of years after Zaikov's son tried to hang him here. After that he hadn't wanted to ever set foot in the place again. The expectation had been that Viktor would sell it. But Viktor had set it up as some kind of hospitality package instead, a place he could fly prospective business partners during the summer months for luxury weekends in the middle of nowhere. Viktor rarely visited himself, and when he did there would usually be the standard security entourage at his side. The function of this fence, then, was just to mark the boundary of the property. Carl put a gloved hand out and gripped the top strand. It was dead.

He forced the chain-link down about midway between two posts and pulled himself over with ease. As he came off it he heard it twang with a metallic vibration that would run the length of it. He got down low and kept still, watching to see if the man walking alongside it in the distance would hear anything. He didn't react. Carl was close enough to see him without the binoculars now, on a path that had been cleared beside the fence. He was about a quarter of a kilometre from the stable building. He had a rifle slung over one shoulder.

He got the binoculars up again and followed the fence round

the back of the stables. He could see no sign of Liz. But if she was waiting in the car then she was only about two hundred metres back from where this man was going to walk, assuming his role was to cover the perimeter. He would be there in about ten minutes. That made Carl nervous. It would have been better to have got her to drive the car back down the road, well out of range.

He got his phone out – a new one taken from Viktor's office – and saw there was a signal. But he had neither of her numbers. He had spent some time much earlier, whilst she had done a spell of driving, trying to extract the numbers from the phones, without any luck. Calling his phone from them hadn't worked either – somehow, the number hadn't been communicated: one of them had come from Viktor, the other from an employee of Mikhael Ivanovich, a man called Drake. Either it was the models or they had set them up like that, as a precaution.

He turned his attention from the man and examined the land ahead. The forest fell into a small valley where he remembered there was a stream in summer. From the other side he would come out into the gardens to the rear of the main building. From there he would have a good clear view of the property. He could get there in a couple of minutes, check out as much as he could, get back to Liz twenty-five minutes after that. It was either that or follow the guy walking the perimeter, make sure he didn't come into contact with her.

He got the binoculars up again. The guy had his head down, and he was still speaking to someone, on a mobile, Carl thought. It was a risk to ignore him. But if Liz did what he had asked her to do then the guy wouldn't see her. He was pretty sure she wouldn't be pacing around in the woods exposing herself to unwanted attention. She was more frightened than he was. And he was frightened. He could feel his heart, the sweat across his forehead. This wasn't something he was good at. It involved getting in close. He liked to keep away from danger, use a long range sight. That was what he was trained to do, not sneaking around on his belly with a gun that he probably wouldn't even be able to shoot straight.

He checked the time on the mobile again. He would take the risk. He stood and started to hurry towards the frozen stream bed.

53

Julia waited fifteen minutes in the car, then had to get out. The anxiety was like a worm in her brain, screaming at her, telling her she had to get to Rebecca. She got out the phone many times. She needed to make the call to Viktor – she had told him she would call when they were near – but there was no signal in the car. She had told Rebecca she would be five hours but it had been a lot longer than that. She needed Rebecca to know she was here, that she was coming. It was absurd that she had arrived, that her daughter was only a few hundred metres away from her, yet she could do nothing but sit here fretting. If she called Viktor then he would bring Rebecca to the phone. She needed to hear her voice, to know for certain that she was still unharmed.

But what if Rebecca had done what she said, what if she had actually managed to get away from him? She cursed the advice she had given. It was reckless, ill thought out. Or not thought out at all. Where could Rebecca possibly hide? If she got out of the building then there was nothing but forest and sub-zero temperatures. If she tried to hide inside the place they would find her, do something to her. The advice had been insane.

But what else could she say? She had no idea if Viktor intended to wait until she arrived. Maybe he had planned to kill Rebecca once he knew she was coming, in which case it was essential that Rebecca not just sit around waiting for her, waiting for Viktor to end her life.

She started crying again, gagging in her throat, but nothing came out of her eyes. They were red and swollen and sore. She had cried so much there were no tears left. She felt utterly stupid and helpless. The despair was like a massive weight inside her, pulling her into the ground.

So she got out and walked towards the house, following the road, phone in her hand, watching for a signal. Alex had left the shotgun on the passenger seat, beside her, loaded and ready, 'safety off', as he said. He had even showed her what to do with it – point it and pull the triggers, one at a time. There were two triggers – that was the only complication. But she had barely listened, and she was cautiously approaching the bend in the road – the point where it crested the slight ridge and started downhill – before she realised she had left the gun on the seat.

Like Alex had done, she cut away from the road, into the forest, then crouched and crept closer to the edge. She needed to see what was going on. If something went wrong and she could see things happening, then maybe she could react, do something about it. She couldn't just keep out of it, sit there blind and helpless.

It was only when the house came into view again that she got a signal on the phone. The house was the same as it had been twenty minutes ago, still and silent. She couldn't see Alex anywhere. She rolled sideways, onto her back, and put in the number Viktor had texted her. She pressed to call and held it to her ear, held her breath. She was already shivering violently.

'Liz,' he said. 'Are you here?' The same calm voice. She bit down on her knuckles to stop herself from sobbing aloud. 'Can you hear me, Liz?' he asked.

'I can hear you,' she said.

'Where are you?'

'I'm near. I need to speak to Rebecca.'

'Are you on the road? How did you get here?'

'Let me speak to her. Please. Let me speak to her.' She had to stop herself screaming it.

'I'll get her. She's sleeping.' There was a pause, then he said, 'I'll call you back.' The line went dead. Had there been a different tone in his voice?

She waited, then turned onto her stomach again and stared at the building. He was in there, moving from one room to another, going for her daughter. But she could see nothing.

Suddenly, she heard something from below her, from down near the old stable block, a crackle and a voice, high-pitched, mechanical, like over a radio set. It came to her very clearly through the still air. She could hear words being spoken, but in Russian, or some other language she didn't understand. She twisted in the snow and looked off to the left, then froze. There was a man standing there, not fifty metres from her. He had a long gun in one hand, a handheld radio in the other, pressed against his mouth. He started to speak into it as she was looking. She squirmed back a little, pressed herself flat. The crackle came again across the snow, then the same voice over the radio, very loud. Was it Viktor? She felt the breath catch in her throat. The man said something curt, then lowered the radio into his pocket. He seemed to be looking straight at her. She kept still, paralysed with indecision. Wait, or get up and run? He had a gun, but as soon as she moved away from the edge she would be out of sight, unless he ran up and over it, after her. Then it would be a race to the car. There were many trees to cover her.

She let a breath out, pressed herself even lower. Maybe he would walk away. At that moment the phone in her hand began to ring.

Rebecca was facing backwards, hanging onto the inside edge of the window sill, one knee still inside the frame, the other leg outside and feeling against the wall with her toes, trying to find the ledge. She got her foot against it and brought the other leg down, still hanging on. She stood as best she could on the ledge, straightened her arms, without looking down, and looked past the open window pane to where the ledge led along to the flat roof. It was about three metres away. But to get there she would have to get past the open window pane. She could take one hand off the sill, she thought, get it around the central window strut, then shuffle nearer to the pane, lean out and close the window so she could get past it. But would she then be able to reach to the next window ledge?

She didn't think so. She started trembling, her knees shaking so much she could feel her feet starting to slip. She bit her lip and a little squeaky noise of fright came out of her throat. There was no way she could move along the ledge without hanging onto something, and past her own window there was a two-metre gap before she could get her hand on the next window. So she couldn't do it. She looked down and gripped the sill even tighter, forcing her knees against the stonework. From her feet to the ground was further than she had thought, but still less than a three-metre drop. She could do it. But she didn't know how deep the snow was, or what was beneath it.

She started to change position, moving her left hand to get a better grip so she could lean out and lower her right leg a little more. Then she heard a noise from within the room, an unmistakable noise – someone turning a key in a lock. She moved her weight quickly back towards the wall, thinking she would try to hide there, on the outside of the window, keeping her head down until they left, but her training shoe slipped and her left leg dropped into mid-air. There was a moment where she thought she could recover the position, get the leg back up. But her balance changed as the leg swung out and she twisted sharply, one hand automatically coming off the sill. She tried to get her fingers into the window hinge to stop her body moving further round, at the same time lifting the left leg to try again with the toe, but before she even properly knew what was happening her other leg had slid off the edge and she was falling.

There was no time to do anything like think about how to land. Her hands were off and the next moment she was striking the ground. She felt the impact, then was rolling in snow. She didn't even have time to shout.

She was breathing fast. Above her she could see the open window. She was on her back, half-buried in a snow drift, her bum smarting a little, her head spinning, but unhurt. She rolled onto her side and got to her knees. She stood carefully, bracing herself against the house wall, just in case something was injured. There was a scraping noise above her and she turned her head up to see the window pane moving, a hand pulling at it. She flattened herself against the house wall as a head looked out – Viktor, she thought, though from the angle it was hard to tell. He shouted something very loud. There was a pause and she thought he would pull his head back, disappear, but instead he looked straight down, straight at her.

He yelled at her immediately, his face red with anger. She pushed off the wall and tripped in the snow, fell face first into the drift. He was shouting her name as she got herself up again, swearing at her in English. She didn't look up but half stepped, half ran towards the part of the building with the flat roof. If she got round it she would be out of his sight. Her head was very clear now. She sucked the icy air into her lungs. She could see the line of trees, the darkness beneath them. She gritted her teeth, put her head down and ran.

A trap, a fucking trap. Viktor had hung up and rung back to give her position away. As Julia scrambled backwards, the phone stopped suddenly. She glanced back, saw the man bringing the gun up, then twisted and dived headfirst down the slope. As

312

she staggered to her knees the phone came out of her hand and spun off, causing her to hesitate just long enough to hear the crack of a gunshot close behind. She heard a splintering noise in the branches above her, ducked her head and yelled out, forgot about the phone. She started running for the car, one hand fumbling in her pocket for the key card.

She was quickly over the ridge and out of sight, weaving through the mass of tree trunks, panting, trying to look behind without crashing into anything. She was almost at the car before he came into view. She tumbled out of the forest onto the road and tried to sprint the last few metres, but her feet slipped treacherously on the compacted, icy surface. She heard him yell something, then a terrifying bang as he fired again. She thought she saw a spray of snow kicked up from near the driver's door. She got to it, skidding, falling, dragging herself up, wrenched the door open and looked back. He was running full out for her, the gun at his side.

She got in and banged the door shut, pressed the ignition and got her feet onto the pedals. It was an automatic, a diesel. It seemed to splutter to life in agonising slow motion. She saw herself engaging the gear stick into drive, yelling incoherently, heard the wheels spinning, then catching on the chains. With a lurch she was moving.

She spun the wheel to keep to the road, flattened the accelerator and felt the whole car slip and skid. It came out of it and started picking up speed. She saw him stop, off to the left, still deep in the trees. There was a flash and the next second the windscreen erupted into a rain of shattered glass. The screen collapsed and the frozen air rushed in at her. Automatically, she floored the brake, twisting the car to a halt, then screamed with frustration. She had stalled it.

She tried desperately to start it again, her fingers fumbling with fright. She was still below the bend in the road, stopped at right angles, across the road. She could see him moving in front of her, no more than ten metres away, moving towards her through the trees. Everything was clear because there was only a broken rim of glass where the windscreen should be. With horror, she saw him pause a second time, raise the gun to his shoulder and fire. She yelled and ducked low, moving sideways across the passenger seat, so that her right arm was pressing on the stock of the shotgun. For the first time since she had seen him she remembered it was there.

She brought it up with two hands and pushed it through the hole where the glass had been, her finger pressed against the first trigger, ready. But now he had vanished. She dropped her left hand off the gun, leaving it lying across the dashboard, resting against the broken glass, pointed straight out, her finger still on the trigger, then found the starter button and pressed it.

The engine came to life just as he jumped into view. He had come from the left, from behind a screen of bushes. He came onto the road right in front of her, not two metres away from the bonnet, the gun held at his shoulder, pointed directly at her. She pulled the trigger.

There was an ear-splitting bang. The shotgun leaped up and struck the top of the windscreen frame, twisting her hand. Behind it she saw him picked from his feet and thrown back. She pressed the accelerator. The car turned sideways and started grinding up the hill, the tyres spinning. She ignored the pain in her wrist and hauled at the wheel. The car righted itself slowly, but she had control. She pressed the accelerator more cautiously, felt the chains get traction, ducked her head low and prayed that he wasn't capable of getting up.

54

Rebecca was running for all she was worth. She heard the shots but they sounded distant, off to the left and behind her, two sharp cracks that echoed multiple times off the slopes in front of her. Ahead, from deep within the tree line, a large flock of big dark birds took off in alarm, squawking loudly. She stopped running and looked frantically behind her, back to the main building.

The front of the house had pillars and arches framing the windows, the back was a messy jumble of smaller buildings and more modern extensions. She could see almost to the front now, but no one was coming from there. She was clear of the flat garden area and almost at the edge of the woods. The distance had been further than she thought. Still, another dash and she would be in the shadows, she could drop down and hide, rest her lungs and legs.

She tried to pick out the window she had jumped from, but the house was maybe a hundred metres back, and there were so many windows. She couldn't see Viktor anywhere. She sucked big breaths of air, felt her face burning. Running was hard because she was sinking knee-deep in snow with each step. She had been giving it all she could but it wasn't the same as running on a race track.

Another shot split the brittle air. She flinched automatically, started off again, then caught movement at the edge of her view, coming from the other direction, from around the back of the house. She hadn't looked there. But when she tried now the sun was full in her eyes, blinding her. She brought her hand up and felt a sudden kick of fright. Someone was very close, running at her, throwing up great flurries of snow as he came – a man in heavy coats, holding something. She heard him shout, was sure it was one of the guys who had been in the car with Viktor. He was going very fast.

She had to try to out-run him. She started to sprint, putting everything into it. In front of her the land rose sharply up a three-metre bank where the forest began. If she got that far maybe she could lose him in the trees. There was a tangle of undergrowth and young trees. If she could get into it and hide, get down low, keep still.

She was thinking she could do it – he was fast, an adult, but she was trained for this – but then suddenly the snow got deeper and she started to stumble. She was determined to get over the top and down into the shadows beyond. He was still shouting as she heaved her knees up the gradient, pulling with her gloved hands at the saplings poking through the snow. She glanced back as she was past the first tree, took a breath, saw him still coming at her.

Carl was near the edge of the woods, about thirty metres to the side of her, when she came over the top, running, stumbling, falling through the thin cover of bare saplings and broken branches. Her eyes were wide with fear, the breath puffing out in front of her.

He had been crouched, past the frozen stream, scanning what he could see of the main building over the top of the little fold of land that ran like a wall along the edges of what would have been the garden. Seconds before there had been three shots from the direction of the hill where he had left Liz. That had panicked him so much he had changed plan immediately, decided to get back up there, but before he could start moving the shouting had started from somewhere near the rear of the house. He thought the voice might be Viktor's. So he had hesitated. Within seconds she was there. Rebecca.

Between them there was an actual wall, or the knee-high remains of one – the old boundary wall – broken stones tumbled in the snow. She was dashing towards it, cutting across to the left of him. She hadn't seen him. He stood to shout to her as another man came over the slope behind her, running very fast, a long rifle in one hand. In seconds they were past his position, into the woods, the man gaining rapidly, chasing her.

There was no shot he could risk. The separation between them was less than ten metres and he had no idea how the MP5 would fire, except that it would definitely be more like a spray than an accurate, tight pattern. He straightened and started to run for them instead, coming from the side and a little behind the man, trying to pick a course through the light undergrowth that would cut him off, but without getting into his field of vision.

The man was focused on Rebecca, shouting at her, head down, concentrating on leaping through the litter of obstacles. She was going very fast, considering the snow, but he was bigger, with a longer stride. He would get to her before Carl could stop him.

Carl kept his eyes on them. He was still fifteen metres away when the man reached her, stretching out and catching her hair, dragging her back with a scream. She twisted round and fell, then rolled towards him and started kicking at his legs while he was still recovering his balance. At that moment, Carl was less than ten metres from them, closing fast, weaving through the branches, the MP5 held to the side of him. He was making so much noise he was sure the guy would turn, but he was too busy yelling at Rebecca, trying to control her hysterical struggles. She was shrieking and shouting, kicking with all her might at his shins. As Carl got to within five metres, the man raised the rifle to bring it down into her face, and at that moment he saw Carl hurtling towards him. His eyes widened with surprise, his arm froze.

Carl leaped with the MP5 swinging towards the guy's face. The man had just enough space to duck, let go of Rebecca and step sideways. He was trying to get two hands onto the rifle, but Carl was coming too fast, with too much weight. His left shoulder smashed into the guy before he could get a good grip on the gun, knocking him flying. They both crashed into the snow, Carl on top.

As they recovered, the man dropped the rifle and started lashing out, with feet and hands. Two blows connected before Carl could get back onto one knee, then he brought the MP5 above the man's arms, just out of reach, intending to jab it down into his face, or club him with it. But he was clumsy with the thick, padded clothing, everything too slow. Before he could strike him the guy got his legs behind and they both went down again, Carl to the side of him, the gun knocked from his hand. He tried to get a hand round the guy's neck as he fell, but the clothing was too thick.

They rolled, locked against each other, snow and sticks in Carl's face. He started to thump at the man, putting all his strength into it, hitting anywhere he could reach. The guy was grunting and swearing at him, still on his back, but pushing himself away, stronger than Carl, determined to open some space between them. He got far enough off to kick straight through Carl's arms, hitting his forehead with a heavy, booted foot. Carl dropped to the snow, the world swimming in front of him. As he pushed himself up, he glimpsed Rebecca off to the left, up on her feet and fleeing.

He got onto his knees then stood, his head clearing rapidly.

The man was five metres away, scrambling on all fours, pulling at his clothing as if trying to loosen his coat. Carl's eyes found the MP5, someway between them. He lurched towards it, stooped, straightened up with his finger over the trigger. The guy was turning towards him, pulling a pistol from beneath the coat. Carl had the MP5 pointed right at him, an easy shot, but behind the guy Rebecca was still in a direct line, running for all she was worth. She was twenty metres off, but it wasn't enough. Anything going past or through the guy would hit her.

Carl knew at once what was going to happen. He changed his plan and tried to dash forwards, to kick the pistol out of the guy's hands before he could fire it, or at least spoil his aim. He screamed as he ran, waved his arms, but it was all useless. The guy fired before he could get even half the distance.

A little gun, he thought, as he heard the bang, saw the flash, felt the whack into his chest. Not powerful enough to pick him off his feet, but it stopped him.

He had never been shot before. He straightened up with difficulty, saw Rebecca still sprinting behind the man, nearly thirty metres away. 'Run, Rebecca!' he yelled. 'Run!' Then felt it, the snapping compression in his chest. Like a heart attack.

Time seemed to unravel and slow. He was still standing. He got both hands onto the MP5 again, braced his legs, waited for the next shot. But the guy was distracted, doing something with the pistol. It was either jammed or empty. Carl saw him throw it aside and bend down to retrieve the big hunting rifle.

His balance was going, he needed to sink down, drop the gun. But he had to stay standing long enough to get a shot in. Even if the guy fired again he couldn't go down, couldn't give in. He saw Rebecca start to turn, curving away from the man, opening up the angle. In a couple of seconds she would be clear enough for him to shoot.

He was surprised by how quick it was – the effect of the bullet.

A tiny .22 calibre, he guessed. He was astonished by how lucidly he could think about it all. He had felt nothing in his back, no tearing of flesh and bone as it exited. So maybe it was still in there, not even enough energy to get right through him, from point-blank range. But it had fucked him. He was done. He was bleeding all down the front of his clothing, bleeding inside. Any moment now he was going to black out and collapse. He kept his eyes on Rebecca, the gun up. His vision started to blur.

He sank into a kneeling position as the guy worked the bolt on the rifle. He could hear himself coughing and gasping, taste the blood welling into his mouth. Rebecca seemed way off now, very distant, the angle safe. The guy was bringing the rifle up to finish him. He summoned all the strength he could muster and pulled the trigger. The gun shook crazily, making a small crackling sound. Almost instantaneously, the burst was over, the magazine empty.

Now he couldn't see the man, couldn't see Rebecca. His eyes were fixed on a small patch of snow-covered ground thirty centimetres in front of his face. His hands wouldn't move. He tried to breathe without choking but it was like he was drowning. He knew there was blood running out of his mouth. He moved his eyes with immense difficulty, trying to lengthen the focus. Where the man had been there was a heap of darkness against the white. He fell forwards, flat onto his face, the gun beneath him.

This was what it was like, then, he thought, to die of a gunshot wound. He had considered what it might feel like so many times. There was no pain, no sensation at all from his body, except a kind of detached awareness of the choking. He had imagined he wouldn't care when this happened. But he did care. He didn't want it, not now. A wave of dizziness washed through him.

He wanted to see his daughter. He wanted to hold her, hug

her, say sorry, tell her he had tried his best. She was running, getting away. There was nothing more he could do. It was down to Liz now. He was going to go in seconds, pass out. And that would be it. He was certain of it. He couldn't get enough air. The blackness was already rising through him like a tide.

55

The road twisted down through the trees, dropping quickly towards the house. Julia drove as fast as she dared, her heart thudding heavily in her chest, her eyes more on the rear and side mirrors than the road right in front of her. She was frightened he would be running at her, cutting the corners where the road curved, trying to get a clear shot in. But she could see nothing in the mirrors, no shape moving through the woods, no one on the road behind. She had seen him falling backwards, hit, but couldn't get herself to believe it.

She drove for seconds like that, not thinking clearly about where she was going. From way ahead, over the other side of the house, she thought she heard the crackle of gunfire, an automatic weapon firing off in a long burst. But she could see no one. She braked through a long bend and then suddenly it was there in front of her, no more than fifty metres away: the house. The trees dropped away, the land levelled out and she could see it. She braked harder and the car skidded to a halt. She was already where the road opened out onto the wide space in front of the place – a car park or turning circle. She could see the long façade, the big entrance, the door open, she could even see lights behind the windows.

She was trapped. She had driven the wrong way. But there had been no space to turn the car round. She needed to turn it now, to get away from here and wait for Alex. She started to pull it round and the engine just cut. She forced herself to think methodically, tried to start it again. A metallic clunking sound issued from somewhere in front of her, a wisp of smoke curled from beneath the bonnet. He had shot at it, twice, she remembered. She tried to start it again. This time there was no response at all.

She couldn't see Alex anywhere. But she had his number. He had given it to her. She fumbled in her pockets, feeling pinned and exposed, in full view of the house, the panic rising in her gut. At any minute they could come out of the house with a gun. They were going to kill her. She would never see Rebecca again.

She needed to call Alex, tell him what had happened, get his help. She started to shake, her vision blurring so that she couldn't see the numbers clearly on the phone. She wiped her hands across her eyes, squinted, opened them, started looking for the number he had given her. But it was the wrong phone. His number was in the one she'd just dropped. A high-pitched scream cut across the land in front of her, coming very clear through the smashed windscreen. Her heart jumped with a different kind of terror.

Rebecca. It could only be her. It had come from directly in front of her, from past the house, not inside it. She grabbed the shotgun, fumbled the car door open, stepped out into the snow. And saw her.

She was about one hundred metres distant, way past the house, at the other side of the shallow valley. She was a tiny shape running through the whiteness, the dark line of the forest behind her. She was coming from behind the house, moving up towards the far side of the hill Julia had just come down.

Julia started running forward at once, shouting her name at the top of her voice, dropping the phone, sprinting across the flat area right in front of the house. She had to get to her.

She got past the front door, her legs picking up speed, her

arms swinging. She shouted again, but either Rebeca didn't hear or couldn't stop, because she just kept going, heading up the hill towards the forest.

Julia got past the flat parking area and vaulted a low wall, into what might have been a meadow. She sank almost up to her thighs in a drift of snow, pushed out of it and yelled Rebecca's name with all the energy she could find. She saw her daughter pause, turn, see her, heard her small voice float over the flat, pure white field of snow – 'Mum,' she shouted. 'Mum.' She changed direction and started tumbling across the meadow towards Julia. And exactly then Viktor Rugojev came into view from the right, from round the side of the house, rushing towards Rebecca, a blur of movement as he closed the distance.

Within seconds he had caught up. Rebecca tried to dodge him, swerving sideways and going under his arm. He lunged in the snow, fell, got up, started chasing her again. She swerved again and Julia was sure she could hear him laughing. Like they were playing a sickening game of catch in the snow. She kept going towards them, running full speed, her lungs heaving at the air, running harder than she had ever run in her life, going towards it because there was nothing else she could do.

He caught Rebecca by her coat and hauled her back against him. Julia could see her struggling and kicking back. She was about ten metres from them, still going fast, when he brought a gun up and placed it against Rebecca's head.

Rebecca stopped squirming, stood still, her eyes bulging like a crazed animal. His free hand was around her upper body, pulling her back into him. He was tall, but her head was against his chest.

Julia slowed, skidded to a dead stop, one arm stretched out towards them, the shotgun dangling limp in the other. She was paralysed with fear. She thought he was going to pull the trigger. 'Viktor,' she shouted. 'Please don't. Please, Viktor.' She couldn't see his face properly because her eyes were blurred from running through the cold air. She forced her limbs to move, started to walk very slowly towards them.

'That's right, Liz,' he shouted. 'You come to me. Keep coming forward. Get closer.'

She got to within five metres. Rebecca was very still now, catching her breath, her face twisted up. Julia could see her terrified, pleading eyes, looking straight at her, her hands hanging onto Viktor's arm, the knuckles white.

'Please leave her,' Julia said. 'I'm begging you, Viktor.' She didn't have to shout. She was close enough to whisper.

'My brother is dead,' Viktor said, almost in a whisper, his eyes darting off to his left. 'There's no point in running any more. There's just us now.'

The words stabbed at her heart but she had no idea if he was telling the truth. She didn't look where he had looked. She kept her eyes right on him. 'You said you wanted to talk,' she stammered. 'I can talk. But *please* leave Rebecca. *Please* let her go.'

His thoughts seemed to pause, some other expression coming into his eyes.

'I'm here now,' she said. 'I'm who you want, not her, not him. It's me, Viktor. It's Liz. We can talk, right now. Please don't hurt anyone else.'

She watched him look at the ground, then up at her again. 'You *are* here,' he said. A strangled noise caught in his throat, then angrily he brushed a sleeve across his face, the one holding Rebecca. He took his arm off her, then stepped back from her. 'We're alone now,' he said. 'We're finally alone.'

Rebecca looked like she couldn't move for fear. She was almost close enough for Julia to touch. Viktor took another step back, further away from her.

'Walk to me, Rebecca,' Julia said. 'Come to me.'

Rebecca took a step. Viktor was standing perfectly still,

shoulders slumped, the gun hanging at his side. He did nothing to stop her, so Julia stepped forwards to meet her, caught her arms, pulled her roughly sideways. Rebecca wanted to get her arms around her, to embrace her, but he still had the gun and Julia had to keep her eyes on him, get Rebecca behind her. She stepped forwards so that she was between Rebecca and him, her body across Rebecca's. 'Stay behind me,' she hissed. 'Stay there, Rebecca.' She could hear Rebecca sobbing violently. 'It's going to be OK,' she said. 'It's OK, Rebecca.' She kept one hand on her arm, behind her, holding her there, the other on the gun.

'Nothing is OK,' Viktor said quietly. 'I wanted to kill you, Liz. I wanted to kill all of you.'

She nodded frantically, her brain racking up the possible moves. What did she do now? What *could* she do?

'I looked for you for years,' he said. 'I was thinking there must be a mistake, that you must have been mistaken to leave me. But I couldn't find you. I couldn't find you anywhere.' He looked up at her. 'I can hardly look at you, Liz.' He started to cry. He was standing like a helpless, grief-stricken little boy, just standing there crying, the tears running down his cheeks. 'I couldn't find you,' he repeated. 'But Mikhael Ivanovich found you. He wouldn't tell me where you were, but I paid a lot of money to find out.' He looked up, wiped his eyes again, using the hand holding the gun. 'You had a daughter. I couldn't believe it. When I first saw photos of her ...' he pointed through Julia, towards Rebecca, cowering behind her, 'I thought she must be ours. I thought she had to be our child.' He gave a short, bitter laugh. 'I paid one of her teachers to get a drop of her blood, had it tested, because I thought she had to be mine. Almost my DNA they told me. Almost. It took me a while to put it together, a few more samples, a few more tests, because I couldn't get myself to believe it. She was my fucking brother's child.' He was silent for a long time, not looking at either of them. Julia could see his jaw working away. He shook his head, as if confused. 'I thought it would work, put things right. I thought it would be a kind of justice if that bastard killed his own kid. Justice for me. But that all went wrong. And here you are in front of me. He's dead and here you both are.'

'You don't have to hurt anyone else,' she said quickly. 'We can talk about all of it. I can tell you why I left, I can explain it all ...'

'I don't think so,' he said.

'If Alex is hurt we should help him,' she tried. 'He's your brother—'

'He's dead,' he said, flatly. 'Forget him.'

'You can tell me what you want, Viktor,' she said, her voice so strained, so high-pitched with stress that it sounded like someone else talking through her. 'We can talk, Viktor. That's what you said you wanted ...'

He shrugged his big shoulders. 'I don't need to,' he said. 'Not now. I've seen you, seen your face again.' He brought the free hand up and rubbed it through his hair. 'You don't know how much my life has depended upon seeing your face again.' He tried to smile, but it didn't work. 'You don't understand,' he said. 'You don't understand any of it. What I feel here ...' He took a huge breath, then smacked his clenched fist against his chest. 'What I feel for you, Liz. What I felt then, what I've always felt. I told you it would never go away and it hasn't. It's *still* there, Liz, still massive inside me.'

She didn't know what to say. She opened her mouth to apologise, to start to try to explain something, to plead with him again, but he held a hand up, stopping her.

'Shut up,' he said. 'You're only going to lie. You're frightened of me, right?'

She nodded, biting her lip, desperately keeping Rebecca pushed behind her. She thought this was it, that he was going to start shooting, right now. She took her hand off Rebecca and held the shotgun with both hands, brought it up and pointed it at him, pulled her finger through the first empty trigger so that it was resting against the second. He shook his head, did something to the pistol in his hands, pulled the slide back so that it clicked, then looked up at her as if he had only noticed for the first time that she was armed. 'What are you going to do?' he asked quietly, staring at the shotgun. 'Shoot me? Do you feel nothing at all for me, Liz? Is *that* what it's like?'

She put the stock into her shoulder, tried to hold it firmly, the little iron sight right over his chest. 'I don't want to shoot you,' she said. 'I want this to stop.'

'But you don't love me, do you?'

'That's not what this is about.'

'Tell me the truth. Last chance. Did you *ever* love me?'

All she could hear was her heart and a scream of fright that couldn't get out of her mouth. She pulled the trigger.

The blast took her off her feet, the recoil forcing her back into Rebecca, sending the gun flying out of her hands. She went over her and down to the ground, then spun round and got her hands over her daughter's head, trying to protect her. They were both on the ground. She thought he would start shooting, thought he would somehow roll through the snow and come up with the gun. There was nothing she could do. The shotgun had only two cartridges – Alex had told her that – and she had fired both.

In the silence that followed, crouched over her daughter, waiting, the sequence ran through her mind several times before it all sank in.

He was not going to just roll, get up and start shooting at them. Because she had seen him take the blast in his chest and head, seen what happened to his chest and head, seen the gun flying off, seen his arms in the air, seen his body driven backwards in a hail of shot discharged at near point-blank range. The mess, the torso slamming off the ground – she had seen it all as she tumbled backwards over her daughter. And now, when she forced herself to open her eyes, move her head and look, she could see the body lying there trembling.

56

They sat for minutes in the snow, hugging each other, rocking back and forwards, crying, Julia stroking Rebecca's head, Rebecca's face buried into her chest.

Then her brain started to work again. She told Rebecca to stay where she was, then walked quickly over to Viktor's body. She didn't want to look, but she forced herself, then turned away, retching. She moved back to Rebecca. 'Where's Alex, Becky?' she asked. 'Do you know where he is?'

But Rebecca just frowned, shook her head.

'The guy you called Carl?' Julia tried.

That worked.

They walked slowly through the field, following Rebecca's footprints in the otherwise pristine snow. They came to the huddled body of another man first. Rebecca said it might be someone who had worked for Viktor, someone who had been in the car with them. But they couldn't see his face. He was dead.

Alex was just past him. He was lying near the start of the trees, at the other side of a broken wall, the ground disturbed all around him. Beside him Julia could see blood, very red against the bright, white snow. His arms were stretched out, the legs together. He was on his side. Rebecca started to sob. Julia stopped about five metres back and put her hand in her mouth, bit down on the gloved knuckles.

'He tried to get them off me,' Rebecca said, her voice faint.

Julia nodded. She couldn't see his face, and didn't want to. She didn't think she could bear it. She had been here once before and thought he was dead. That time she had been wrong. It had been Michael hanging on the rope. But she had still run from him, tried to put it all behind her. That had just delayed it, it seemed. Now it had caught up.

She edged cautiously around him, not wanting to see his eyes, if he had been shot there, if he looked like Viktor. She was still two metres back when she realised his chest was moving. He was breathing.

57

She found Alex's phone and used it.

It took Michael Rugojev almost three hours to get to her, but the military helicopter he arranged to pick up Alex was hovering overhead within forty minutes. Forty desperate minutes trying to keep him alive. She had no idea how to do it, no real medical training aside from a first aid course.

Rugojev connected her to a doctor, in a hospital somewhere, a man who spoke bad English, who had no sympathy. Rebecca held the phone whilst Julia followed his instructions. At one point they had to take a film of the wound and mail it to him. There was only one wound – the 'entry point', he called it – in Alex's chest, to the right of where she guessed his heart was. It was small, gently pulsing blood when she first uncovered it. She had to stop that, by compressing the injury and moving his body to another position. She held her hand there until it ached, then was told to stop – too long was dangerous, because if he was still haemorrhaging internally the pressure would build and collapse his other lung. One lung, the doctor decided, was already punctured and collapsed. But he could live if they could keep his airways clear. It was possible.

She heard the helicopter but didn't see where it landed. Four very young Russian soldiers appeared from the back of the house. They had a stretcher, no guns. They spoke no English. She assumed this was the kind of favour Michael Rugojev could call up.

They took over from her, took him away. She held his hand on the stretcher and hung on to it all the way round the house until they got to a helipad she hadn't seen before. There was a painful, percussive clatter as the helicopter came into view – a huge, military black and green thing.

She held her bloody hands over her ears and watched them load him on board, then ran back as it took off, fleeing the vicious downdraught. She watched it disappear over the trees, then went back to where she had left Rebecca, sitting in the snow, too cold, too shocked, too frightened. They went into the house to wait for Rugojev, to warm themselves. They sat in the kitchen she had once worked in. She could see the place in the floorboards where she had hidden. It was still there.

Alex had said nothing to her. She had spoken to him all the time she was doing what the doctor said. With Rebecca listening she had talked about them, about their past, about what they had felt for each other ten years before, about how that feeling had been with her ever since. She had begged and begged him to just hang in there, to stay with her. She had even promised that if he did then they could start again. At the time she had meant it all. But he had said nothing, hadn't even opened his eyes. She wondered if he heard any of it.

58

In the days that followed, Michael Rugojev took control. It was what he was good at. The man whose life Julia had accidentally saved. He looked just the same as she remembered him. He had the same patronising tone, the same oddly disturbing, myopic eyes. She suffered him because they had few options, but she hated every minute and felt the same contempt for Rugojev that she had experienced ten years before. She knew what he was.

She tried to hide it, to keep her feelings to herself, and he didn't seem to notice. Or maybe most people were like that with him and he either didn't care or thought that it was all just normal. To be disliked, in secret, to be never told the truth. There were plenty of people around him radiating a kind of awestruck respect, of course; all the entourage: the assistants, organisers, managers, hangers-on.

There were things to take care of and they took care of them. Julia rarely had to do anything. They were driven in an armed convoy to St Petersburg – Rebecca and herself. They were put in a luxury apartment with armed guards on the door and down on the street. Michael came to give personal assurances that they would be protected, personal apologies for the actions of his family. They were given a PA called Arisha Vostrikova to cater for their needs. Julia quickly grew to detest her. It was Arisha who told them what was happening outside the apartment.

Alex had been flown to a military hospital, then to another clinic in Moscow. He was lucky, they were told. Julia could believe that. She tried to think that it didn't matter how he was doing – whether he was crippled, brain-damaged, in a wheel-chair, but lucky to be alive, or whether he was exactly as he had been, fully recovered. It didn't matter because she didn't want anything to do with him. She had made that decision – the right one – ten years ago. But she found it difficult to keep her thoughts off him. He had saved Rebecca's life. And Rebecca spoke about him every day. Rebecca wanted to see him.

Julia didn't ask for other details but Arisha gave them any-way. Zaikov was being dealt with. He had been told a version of the truth – that Viktor had shot Zaikov's son Uri ten years ago, that Viktor was dead, that Rugojev would take over where Viktor had left off, that their families were safer together, that it was time to move on. 'Michael will probably put a contract on him,' she had added, poker-faced, then saw Julia's expression and smiled, as if it were – obviously – a joke. Arisha thought Zaikov was nothing to be afraid of. 'The only man to be frightened of,' she remarked, 'is Michael. And he loves you as a daughter.'

'He doesn't even know me,' Julia had replied.

She was wanted in Spain but they had hired lawyers to deal with that. Michael thought money would solve it – Spain was as corrupt as Russia, which made life easy for him. Molina was alive and had said nothing about her stabbing him. So far the investigations in London hadn't identified her, though she was advised to keep out of the UK. She heard almost nothing of how they were dealing with the bodies at The Ice House – though the one she had shot on the road had lived, they said. She learned nothing of Michael's attitude to the death of his once favourite nephew. She didn't ask and aside from his apology, Michael never once mentioned Viktor. He spoke in glowing terms of Alex, however – Aleksi, as he called him.

All this washed over her head. She had her hands full try-ing to keep herself together, trying to take it all in without breaking down. A confusing life filled with alien faces speaking in a foreign language swam around her. She felt drugged, as if she was existing in a subtly altered reality. She stayed close to Rebecca, tried to shut it out. But sooner or later she was going to have to work out what to tell Rebecca. Rebecca had accepted her silences about Juan so far, but that news was going to hit hard when she could face giving her it.

They were in Russia only three days, then a helicopter flew them both to Finland, to Helsinki, to a property Michael had on an island in the south harbour. Alex had been moved to a private clinic in the city, they were informed. He was doing well. The bullet had missed everything it needed to hit. He had lost a lot of blood, but not enough to kill him. The suggestion was that he would be in hospital there for another two months. They were asked if they wanted to visit him.

She should have told Rebecca everything before they went, she realised. But she couldn't do it. Rebecca was distressed enough as it was.

The hospital looked more like an expensive, chic hotel, at least in the public areas. Visitors drove up to the front entrance and handed over their car keys to some uniformed flunkey who went off and parked the car in an underground garage. In the reception area there was a wall that looked more like a huge red cliff on a tropical island. And palm trees, and fountains, and designer label shops. The floors gleamed. Octogenarian women dripping tasteless designer opulence were pushed around in wheelchairs as if they had an appointment in a beauty salon.

Once she was in the room with him the reality was undeniable. He was propped up in bed, in a restricted space that smelled like any other hospital room, the odour of disinfectant mixing with less identifiable traces of sickness and decay. There were tubes and monitors all over, including those coming out of his nostrils. On the floor there was a big glass container attached to a device of some sort with flexible plastic pipes that ran into his side, through blood-stained bandages. It made a mechanical sucking noise and a pink, frothy liquid seemed to be moving slowly down the tubes, gathering in the jar.

But he was awake, eyes open. And he could speak. Julia sat on the edge of the bed with her heart thundering and told him tearfully that she had asked Rebecca to wait outside. She told him she was glad that he was alive.

'I need to see her,' he said. He spoke slowly, breathed slowly. They had told her one lung had a hole in it.

She reached out and found his hand, held it. 'I haven't told her yet,' she said. 'I couldn't do it. I'm sorry.'

'Doesn't matter. I just want to see her.' He squeezed her hand gently. 'Please.'

She nodded. 'She wants to see you too. She has spoken about you a lot.'

When Rebecca came in, Julia sat on a chair to one side and watched them, watched Rebecca's eyes light up as she saw him, watched the smile that flickered across his lips, transforming his appearance, even with the wires and drips. There was something between them – more than what they had experienced together. Or maybe only that – but it was enough.

Rebecca sat on the bed, where she had sat, held his hand and thanked him, over and over again. He looked at her with his eyelids drooping, the daft smile on his face. Then there was silence. What could be said was too heavy, too horrible. No one wanted to deal with it while he was still plugged into drips and drainers, heart monitors and catheters. And within five minutes his eyes were closed.

Julia stood up and touched Rebecca's shoulder, got her to leave the room. When she was out she stood for a long while just looking at him. He was asleep, she thought, or drugged. Each breath he took brought a gurgling rattle, magnified through the tubes running out of him. But they had assured her that he would live and be fine, that his lung would work, his chest heal and his life return to normal. *Normal.* She no longer had any idea what that was.

The things she had felt for him hadn't changed at all. She had run from those emotions ten years ago and it hadn't worked. It definitely hadn't worked. The world had thrust him back at her. He was the father of her daughter. She had made promises to him while they were carrying him to the helicopter, and had thought afterwards that, since he hadn't heard any of them, it would be OK, at some point, to just forget them, to say goodbye, to get her daughter away from him and away from all this. But now she thought that probably wasn't going to be possible.